SPELLBOUND

BY REBECCA L. GARCIA

An Embracing Darkness Novel

SPELLBOUND

Editing by Angie Wade at Novel Nurse Editing
Proofreading by Janna Bethel at Novel Nurse Editing
Cover Design by Dark Wish Designs
Interior formatting by Dark Wish Designs
Character artwork by Laura Richelieu

This book is dedicated to Kelly Kortright,
for loving this world as much as I do,
and for helping make it shine

Rebecca L. L.

And to you, the reader, may you find
adventure and love between these pages

SPELLBOUND

PART ONE: DEAD WITCHES

PROLOGUE

The sky grumbled in warning as the matte-black carriage approached the orphanage. Inkblot clouds shrouded the sun, darkness prevailing in a fog of deep, thick gray. Thick droplets fell from above, beating on the thin glass windows.

Storms weren't unusual this time of year in the kingdom of Salvius, but they were never this strong. "It's an omen," I said in caution. I'd read all about them. "Because they hung that witch." I ran my fingers along the dirty window, waiting for the carriage to open, but it remained shut. Everything was starting to feel like an omen since today began, a dreadful day I wished I'd not woken up for.

Avery, the head of magical enforcement in our small town, leaned against the peeling wallpaper on the back wall. She scribbled something in her notebook, then climbed her gaze back to me. "Our saints will not allow the darkness of witches to bring storms to our land, Elle. It is bad weather, nothing more." The look in her eye and hesitant wobble of her bottom lip told me that was a lie.

"The carriage is here," I said, only because I couldn't hold it off any longer. They'd come for me, to take me away. "I'll only go if I can take Mona."

"You're lucky you're going at all." Avery moved toward the door. "After the stunt you pulled, your director insisted you go to a jailhouse for minors, but the treaty"— she seethed on the word—"between us and Istinia insists you go to them. It's one of the reasons their council of witches continues to keep the magic barrier up between the mountains."

My lips hardened. I had no regrets for what had happened to Miss Thompson, the director of the orphanage, but as the repercussion of my actions marched up the path between the carriage and the wrought iron gates of the orphanage, panic flitted through me. I hadn't thought they'd follow through on their threat. I'd spent the last seven years there, since I was brought to the orphanage at four years old with my younger sister, who was separated into a room somewhere downstairs.

Avery opened the door, glancing back at me. "You've brought demons into our town." Her green eyes narrowed as she referred to both the warlock sitting at the carriage, behind the two stallions, and the one heading through the grounds.

A loud knock sounded at the front door, jolting us both.

"Grab your suitcase," Avery snapped. "Now."

I swallowed thickly, an attempt to remove the thick lump that had formed in my throat since I'd been locked away. It had been an attempt to keep me away from the rest of the children. "I'm not going."

"You're going." Avery tapped her black laced shoe against the creaky floorboard. "That man downstairs will make sure of it. They're already waiting for you."

I crossed my arms over my chest. "I'm not leaving without Mona."

Avery took a step forward but recoiled when she saw my hands uncurl. She tightened her necktie, then pushed her notebook back into her pocket. "Mona is better off without you, and your kind."

I shuddered as her last two words sharped through the air. "Please. I was only protecting her from Miss Thompson." I was pleading my case for the hundredth time, but nothing could change the truth. I was, as unlikely as it was, a witch. It didn't escape my mind that if I'd been born merely twenty years ago in Salvius, I'd have been burned for it, but times had changed. Avery was right. The barrier between our kingdom and their territory brought a new treaty, one where any witches found, unless they'd committed murder or a high crime, was to be sent to their territory, Istinia.

"I'll not leave," I threatened. "I won't. You can't make me."

"If you don't come now, your sister might just be the one who pays the price. The world isn't kind to orphans, and Miss Thompson only has so many spaces here."

I imagined my sister curled up against a building, begging for dramair on the sidewalk. A thunderous roar pulled my attention back to the rain-stricken window.

Lightning flashed the sky purple, and the cold seeped in through the cracks around the glass pane.

Closing my eyes, I grabbed my teddy, the one I felt too old to have on my bed at eleven years old but couldn't bring myself to get rid of. It was all I had left of the parents who'd abandoned me. In my other hand, I picked up my suitcase, then followed Avery out of the door.

A barrel-chested, burly man wearing a long brown trench coat and a cap to match, greeted me at the open door. The overhanging porch shielded him from the rain, but drops still shimmered among the light-brown waves.

I looked over her shoulder at Avery, then up to look at my home for the past seven years. "Please," I begged one last time. "Let me say good-bye."

Avery's mouth pinched into a frown. "It's best you don't. For everyone. You don't want rumors to start about Mona, do you? She's already under scrutiny, considering your lineage."

The warlock stepped inside, and Avery flinched back into the shadow of the staircase. He fumbled, then grabbed my suitcase. "I'll take 'er from 'ere then." He patted my shoulder, making me flinch. "Come on, lass. We need to leave now if we plan to make it ter Istinia before morning."

My stomach ached. My gaze rolled up the dirty stairwell to the chalk drawings made by the other children. "Mona!" I yelled before they could stop me. "Sister!" I screamed louder, swearing I heard someone yell back before I was pulled onto the porch. I tugged my arm from the warlock's grip.

He looked at Avery, then cleared his throat, grabbing my arm again. "Sorry, lass."

"Mona." My voice dried out as I was pulled down the path and through the gates. The world glossed around me. Statues on either side of the building seemed to come to life under the shine of rain coating them. The windows on either side of the front door filled with faces. I strained my neck, trying to see if one of them was Mona's, but I couldn't make any of them out in the slash of rain and dim gray light.

My tears merged with the droplets running through my hair and down my cheeks. The warlock pulled me into the carriage, then slammed the door behind me as I glared up at the building. "Mona." My whispers fell silent as we pulled away.

He sighed, shaking the rain from his jacket as he leaned back in his seat across from her. "Sorry about that, lass. They'd have arrested ya or summit if I didn't get ya out of there with ya shouting like that. Humans don't take kindly to witches. As you 'eard back there." He handed me a flask of warm tea. I took it, then wiped my nose on the back of my sleeve. "They'll welcome yer back in Istinia. You'll find a family there, a coven. They'll take care of ya."

My stomach dipped. I already had a family here, my sister. After a few sips of tea, I found my voice. "How is it my sister is human and I…" I trailed off, looking at my hands again, the very thing that had got me into this mess.

"And you a witch?" he asked, finishing my sentence for me and arching a tangled eyebrow. "Tha great mysteries of our world, but yer are rare. It's been known to 'appen. Human-born witches, that is. What that woman was saying back there, pay it no mind. Yer sister's likely human. Sometimes there's a witch in yah lineage somewhere, and generations down the line, one of ya pops up with powers, but it's rare for more than one."

I fell silent as the carriage growled over the bumpy road toward the mountains and the magical barrier separating Salvius from Istinia, a place filled with witches, demons, and dark gods. I'd been taught to fear them, to be afraid of things that go bump in the night, and to be grateful for the barrier keeping most witches out—except those who desperately wanted to get through. Like the one earlier, the one they'd hung. She was the reason we were in this whole mess. If I hadn't gone out to see it, if I hadn't taken Mona, nothing would have happened. This wouldn't have happened.

"What's your name?" I asked after several minutes of quiet.

"Frederick."

I nodded, then looked at my lap. He wasn't as bad as I'd thought. I'd been told witches were evil, demonic things, but if that were true, then I was of them. Now I had no choice but to join them. I moved back the curtain of the carriage as the mountains came into view across the deep, dark forest.

CHAPTER ONE

Nine years later
Istinia

My fingers trembled as I reached for the old grimoire, its decaying pages barely held in the middle. It, like the three others shelved next to it, was bound with human skin. I pulled it from the dusty shelf, willing the bile in my throat away. However much I wanted to burn the thing, its contents were irreplaceable, its cover a reminder of the witches' grisly past with the humans, a time when they'd hunt humans and humans would burn them in return. It was over—for the most part.

My nose wrinkled when I noticed the rough texture on the front cover under my fingertips, probably hair follicles. The golden-brown, plain cover looked unremarkable when compared to the other books in our library with their fancy lettering or symbols. I turned the book over, my lip curling when I noticed areas where the skin pigmentation had darkened.

"Let's get this over and done with, Edmund" My gaze drifted to my coven's grandkeeper, whose lips unfurled into an amused smirk.

"I thought you said this was 'no big deal,'" he said with an attempt at mimicry. His heightened pitch sounded nothing like me.

"It's not." I clicked my tongue. "Now where's the damned spell?" I didn't want to hold the thing for a moment longer than I needed to.

"That damned spell, Elle"—he gave me a look—"is a ten-page complex ritual, which will require studying. The pages are faded and the text with them."

Looking around the small, dimly lit room, where candlelight cast shadows onto velvet-red walls and flickered light to the tall shelves that reached the flaky ceiling, I spotted a rectangular oak desk covered with papers, scrolls, and stacks of books. "Here." I motioned us toward the desk.

Edmund cleared the space. I placed the book down, relieved to be rid of it. I wanted desperately to go wash my hands, but the lure of the pages scratched with symbols of stars and pentagrams kept me rooted to the spot.

Long-forgotten magic resided on the pages, begging to be practiced. Edmund had been right; the spell was more complicated than anything I had ever seen in my nine years in Istinia. His blue eyes glittered with darkness as we both felt the compulsion from within the pages. Closing my eyes, I blew out a long, shaly exhale and opened them again. I noticed he did the same. Blowing a fluff of hair from my eyes, I sighed. My hair often got in the way but it was no surprise, it did reach down to my waist. I pulled my brown waves into a ponytail and tied it back with a hair tie I'd left around my wrist. Leaning over the book, I dragged my finger along the page.

"Careful," he snapped when my finger pressed along a word scrawled in Lor, the ancient language of Istinia.

"How must it feel for normal witches if even we, who are mostly immune to the dark magic residing inside the dark objects, still feel some compulsion from them?" I mused aloud. Other covens, like the casters or potioneers, would fall immediately to its pulls of power. Our coven, the cursekeepers, managed held curses or dark magic. They lured witches and humans into wanting to touch the magic inside them, as if that brand of magic had a mind of its own, then once they did, the magic could then attach itself to the living, then possess, control, and drain them until there was nothing left.

Edmund glanced at me, then looked back at the book. "You mean other witches?"

I smirked. "Right, other witches."

"This room is our most guarded for good reason." He paused, looking at the pages thoughtfully. "Well, next to the vaults."

It was unlikely I would get to see the vaults anytime soon. Only the keepers or grandkeeper in our coven could go to the vaults in the basement, and I was still an apprentice.

I turned my head, scanning the room. My gaze landed on a globe, the color of parchment with long-lost lands, that stood seemingly powerless on a shelf of its own. I knew all too well it was not. Nothing in the room was.

Edmund snapped his fingers, jerking my attention back to the grimoire, the reason we had ventured into the basement of the fifteenth-century mansion we called home. Because we didn't succumb to the compulsion of dark objects, we were tasked with keeping them safe and, in some instances, deciphering them.

"Do you truly believe this spell is the only way to help?" I asked, noticing some of the etchings pointed toward a sacrifice of some kind.

Worry lines deepened under his eyes, and his thick dark eyebrows pinched down toward his straight nose. "If the elder witch requires it, then I trust her judgment."

I ticked each of the recent deaths off in my head. "Three deaths so far."

"Hmm." He turned the page carefully. "I thought it was two."

"No. Remember the human girl who was found cut open in the woods by the mountains?"

"Ah, yes. The human."

Of course he'd forgotten the only victim who was not a witch. The barrier between the mountains separating us from the human kingdom had kept us apart for so long, humans were often an afterthought. Not to me. Not when my sister was one. Not when I had been one.

The thought of her stole my next breath, and I pushed my pain back into the place so deep and dark, it could almost be forgotten. Almost.

Edmund cleared his throat, looking from the pages to me. "Are you paying attention?"

I nodded.

"It doesn't seem like it," he said. "The call is next month. If you want to put your name forward, you'll need to focus more."

"I'm going to put it off this year," I admitted, finally saying what I'd struggled with for the past month. Putting my name forward to try to get promoted within the coven, meaning I would finally be a keeper, meant the truth would come to light. I wasn't good enough yet, but no one could find that out. "I'll give it a real go next year."

"You said the same thing last year." He shook his head, sighing with disappointment, but I was used to it. "You can at least try."

"If I fail, I'll need to wait three years before I can retake it. I'm gonna wait until I know I can pass."

"You'll never know if you can pass until you give it a go." He pushed his spectacles back up his nose. His blue eyes regarded me through the misty glass. His were several shades darker than my baby blues. "Or is it your goal to remain an apprentice?"

"You know I want to be a keeper." Being one would give me access to the magic and authority I needed to go to my sister in Salvius. I needed to pass more than he knew. "I'll take it next year… Promise."

"You're ready, Elle. You don't need to wait another year. There's only one spot left for a keeper."

I gave him a small smile. "I'm the only apprentice you have. Who else is going to take it? Benji?" I asked, referring to the black cat who roamed our mansion.

"We could use your help."

Guilt tugged my conscience. "I know." I cast my eyes to the ground. With only Maddox and Dora as keepers and

Edmund as grandkeeper, our tiny coven was stretched thin. They were often sent to different locations, to transport or collect a dark object or to translate Lor, as we were the only coven who studied the forgotten language because it could still be found in old text or on runes. "Next year for sure I will take it."

"You're twenty, Elle." His sympathetic tone made me wince. "You became an apprentice five years ago. You've been an apprentice for the longest of any in Fairwik."

I swallowed thickly. "Thanks for the reminder."

"I really think you should put your name forward at the call. You won't fail."

I couldn't tell him the truth, that I'd failed at some of the more complicated spells he'd given me to practice. I'd excelled when I was first brought to Istinia at eleven, but I couldn't master the advanced magic needed to be a keeper. I didn't want to prove them right, all those who looked down on human-born witches for our magic being weak. But the advanced spells weren't the only thing holding me back.

The stack of dusty spell books dating back a century loomed over me in the library.

To become a keeper, I had to get a perfect score. Anything less was a fail, and I couldn't afford to wait three years to take it again. "Please, stop." My tone came out harsher than I expected. "Sorry, but I'm not going to do it this year. As I said, next year I will. I promise."

He shook his head, then turned away. "If your mind is made up, then there's nothing I can say."

"So…" I looked at the page, needing a topic change. "What now?"

I breathed in the stale, musty air and tapped my fingers against the side of my legs. I wanted to help, but the markings on the pages were ones I'd never encountered. I knew I'd only been brought along to learn, not to aid, but Edmund would pretend otherwise. He wanted me to feel like I was needed, but as he was the grandkeeper, I knew that wasn't true. He didn't need me to go down there with him or hold the book.

"For now, nothing. We are the only ones who can read it, and as you know, it cannot be copied."

"It's as if they have a mind of their own."

He looked at the open pages wearily. "Yes, they do."

"What happens again? When you try to copy the spells?"

"You forget. As soon as we close the book, the instructions inside will leave my mind. It's a part of the curse placed on this thing a century ago." He blew out a long exhale as his gaze trailed over the symbols inked onto the parchment.

"I guess it's clever, like it's preserving itself." I shoved my hands into my pockets, then rocked back onto my heels. "A failsafe, preventing anyone from copying the spells we need and just getting rid of the book."

"Yes." He tapped his fingers against the spine when he closed it. "It's going to take a few days to complete the tracing spell. Maddox will bring a caster in and help them translate so they can cast it while the book remains open."

"Oh." It made sense. Maddox, who also happened to be one of my best friends, was almost as skilled as

Edmund. "Then why did we need to come down here now?" I asked, keeping my tone kind. I hated when Edmund and I would have disagreements. He was one of the few people in my life who hadn't left but believed in me, so I made a conscious effort to structure my tone to come across light and breezy with him.

"To ensure I had the correct one, and it was where I thought it was."

He always did have to double-check everything, even though he was almost always right. I watched him place the book back between two others. Edmund glanced at his watch. "It's almost time. Frederick will be arriving back from Salvius shortly."

I thought back to when Frederick, the fetcher who was tasked with traveling between Salvius and Istinia when necessary—had picked me up and taken me to Istinia.

My eyes were beginning to burn. I rubbed them, then rolled my shoulders back. "Let's go. My bed calls to me, and you know how I feel about sleep."

He let out a small chuckle. "We all know how you feel about your bed, Elle. You spend half your mornings complaining about leaving it."

I played with the heart on my necklace as we left the basement. When he opened the front door of the mansion, the cold, crisp air hit my lungs, forcing me to cough. The moon was high in the sky, and time ticked by slowly as we walked to the drive. Edmund looked up at the starry night and cast his bespectacled stare toward me. I glanced at my watch, a gift from him for my twentieth birthday a few months back. It was black and matched my long, painted nails. On them, tiny specks of white shone out. They were meant to be stars, but I wasn't great at doing my own nails.

It was our job to retrieve the Serpent's Ring, a dark object used to deactivate the spelled arches that nestled between the only passable part of the mountains separating Istinia and Salvius. I had almost forgotten about us needing to retrieve it from Frederick. I'd have slept in that morning if I'd remembered I'd have to be up this late.

"It's going to be one soon."

"He shouldn't be much longer," Edmund replied. "He'll be here. I know you're tired, but this is what comes with being a keeper, so think of this as practice for the future."

"Why has he gone?" I asked, drumming my fingers against the side of my leg. My pants were dark blue, contrasting my white top, and four of my fingers were lined with rings. All of them protected my physical body from the magic of the objects I worked with daily. My particular magic protected my mind. "Do you think they found a dark object? I mean, it's been two years since they've brought one in."

"I'm not sure." He gazed up at the moon. "Our job is to retrieve the Serpent's Ring, not to know the latest news. That's Alma's and the other elders' concern."

I bit down on my bottom lip. "I bet one of the humans found a cursed hair comb or something."

Edmund attempted to contain his smirk. "Why a hair comb?"

I shrugged. "It's always something ordinary. They find one in an attic somewhere in an old house or locked away, and because it looks normal, they use it. Then they die, get sick, or end up possessed or something. It's been the case with the last three."

"Want to bet?"

I couldn't help but smile. Although he tried to be serious most of the time, occasionally I brought out a hint of mischief and fun.

"One skal."

He arched a tangled, dark-brown eyebrow. "Only one?"

"Two." I glared. "Two skal."

"On a hair comb?" He shrugged. "It's your coin."

I knew it was unlikely, but I got bored, and I enjoyed a good bet, even on the most improbable of scenarios. It passed the time.

Looking out over the cast-iron fences and tall black gates, I sighed. My feet were aching from standing in the same spot. I placed my hands behind my back and clasped my fingers together, then paced in a circle. The long path stretched down into tall hedges, then blackness. Behind the gates, two gargoyle statues stood on either side of the double, red-glossed doors of the large mansion.

"I bet Dora's having a panic about now." I chuckled, looking up at the top window to Dora's room, where an oil lamp flickered against the darkness. "She'll scold Frederick for being late. I'll bet you on that."

"No need to bet. I know for certain she will." His eyes sparkled, and a glimpse of a smile danced on his lips. "If she comes downstairs."

"Here he is." I stepped forward. "Finally."

The matte-black carriage with frilled deep-purple curtains on the windows, pulled by two stallions with red eyes, rode through the open gates, which magically closed behind him. Shoving my hands into my pockets, I waited for it to ground to a halt.

"Take your time," I said jokingly through the closed curtain. "What happened, Frederick? Hit a bump in the road?"

Stepping out, Frederick shook his jacket, and some dirt rolled off. "Something like that." He glanced behind him, then turned his attention back to me. "It's in 'ere somewhere," he said, fumbling through his pockets. "Aye." He pulled it out. The ring was silver and thick, with a serpent coiled on top of it. On its head, two ruby eyes glistened under the moonlight. "It's been a long night. Ya don't mind if I head off?"

"Go, Frederick. We could use some sleep ourselves," Edmund said as he stepped up behind me.

I peered around Frederick. Shock rooted me to the spot when a second set of eyes found mine from within the darkness. The person's pupils were big in the low light, circled with blue rings and a blackness so deep it shivered my soul. His lips curled into an amused grin.

"Who are you?" I questioned.

"Hello, doll." He looked me up and down. "I'm Viktor."

I glanced at Fredrick, then back at Viktor. "Are you from the north?"

Frederick must have picked the man up on the way back from Salvius, unless he was—

"In a way."

Frederick took a step back, bumping into me. Steadying myself, I moved out of his way.

"He's from Salvius, lass."

My eyes widened. "The human kingdom?" I asked, uncertain if I had heard right. Human-born witches, or in his case warlocks, weren't common. There had been only one since me.

Frederick climbed back inside, and Viktor gave me one last amused look. Everything about him reminded me of the night, from his midnight-colored suit to his thick, dark waves. He fit in perfectly among the shadows of the carriage. "That would be the one." He smirked. "You know, you still haven't told me your name."

"Oh. Great. I mean, that's interesting." My brain faltered for a moment. I wanted to say I was a human-born witch too.

Edmund suppressed a smirk. "Her name's Elle."

"Elle." Viktor rolled my name on his tongue. "I hope I'll be seeing you around."

Frederick gave us both a nod, then closed the door. The carriage growled over the gravel, pulled through the gates, and down into blackness. My eyes bulged, and I turned toward Edmund, placing my hand on my hip. "Her name's Elle?" I repeated, then pushed my fingers along my forehead, smoothing the line that had formed.

"You looked like you were struggling." He half-chuckled, quickly stopping himself.

"I was shocked. That was all."

"Sure."

"He's human-born. I was just surprised to see someone like me."

"All right, fair enough." He curled his lips inward, and I supposed I could appreciate he was at the least trying not to laugh. "Let's get inside. It's getting cold."

He took the ring in his hands, closing his fist around it. I couldn't help but eye it greedily. The item could pass me through the arches and into Salvius, and it was only feet from my grasp. I looked away. Even if I could get my hands on it, I wouldn't risk it. Not when the last time I'd tried to help my sister went so horribly wrong.

CHAPTER TWO

The day started far too brightly for me to want to get out of bed, but Naomi was coming over, and I missed my best friend. Between her coven and her father, she didn't have much time to hang out anymore. I shielded my eyes from the harsh light, the sun catching on the silver band around my wrist.

I gazed out at the sprawling gardens and rolling hills, statues, and fountains. The mansion stood in a semicircle in front of the pale-blue horizon. The blue shutters on the windows creaked in the light breeze. Naomi waved from behind the iron gate. Tight black curls coiled around her heart-shaped face, matching the deep brown of her eyes.

"Nai," I called.

Her full lips pulled up into a wide smile as I pressed the button to let her in. "Good morning, sunshine. I'm happy to see you awake this early!" she exclaimed as she strutted up the drive.

I looked at my watch. She was right. It was seven in the morning, and last night's 1:00 AM trip still burned the back of my eyes. "Only for you."

She grinned. "So where's the pompous ass today?" She'd swapped her red robes, which signaled her position within the magician coven, for a pinstriped black-and-white shirt with ruffles and a black pencil skirt. "Didn't come to greet me?"

I chuckled. "Maddox is inside." I wrapped my arms around her, breathing in the fresh, peachy smell from her shampoo. "You look nice."

She pulled away and tugged at the collar of her shirt, posing. "It's new."

I glanced down at the off-white dress I always wore. It was tattered at the knees, corseted at the bust. To compliment it, I wore the same black leather jacket I'd had since I was eighteen. I needed new clothes but kept spending my skal on weapons for training or supplies for my art closet instead.

"It's pretty. I've made coffee if you want one." I motioned my head, gesturing us into the mansion.

I looked around the cluttered kitchen with wood shelves covering the yellow walls, filled with jars of dried fruits and herbs. Naomi walked to the kitchen table and sat on one of the six wooden chairs. I poured two cups, breathing in the deep, rich scent. There was no smell better than coffee in the morning.

"I have news." Naomi's eyes gleamed as I sat across from her. She hit her hands against the table, leaning forward. "There's a new guy."

My heart skipped a beat. "I know."

Her eyebrows pinched together. "He's just come into town, like last night. There's no way you could know."

"He came by here first."

"Why?"

"We needed to get the ring back from Frederick, who bought him here."

She leaned back. "Oh, yeah. That makes sense. Well, anyway, isn't he hot?"

"Who's hot?" Maddox asked.

I whipped my head around, watching as he walked through the doorway. He was the epitome of elegance. He was always well-groomed, with his hair styled to the side, sleek with whatever product Aaron, his boyfriend and potioneer, had brewed. His black shoes with white tops were shined to death. His black pants were ironed, a crease down the middle, and held up by a leather belt with a silver buckle.

"Who's hot?" he asked again, grinning.

"Did you finish studying the stone already?" I asked. The ancient rock etched with markings in Lor had been brought in a few days ago, when some witches found it near the mountains.

He placed his hands into his pockets, then strode toward the counter. "Yep. It didn't take long to translate. It was an old spell supposedly used to form a bond between this world and other realms, like the underworld. Probably some crazed worshiper trying to make a deal with a god."

"Show off," I smirked, and he chuckled. He'd always been our best keeper. Dora was okay, but she didn't hold a candle to him. "At least it's safe here with us now."

"Yep. Locked away in the vaults. So who's this hot guy you were talking about?"

Naomi raised her eyebrows, a seductive smile on her lips. "His name's Viktor. No one knows much about him, but oh my." Her eyes rolled up. "You should see him. Muscle galore. He's super tall too."

Maddox's eyebrow raised. "Gay or straight?"

She bit down on her lip. "Not sure, but I hope straight."

I interjected. "What about Craig?" He was Naomi's only friend, outside of me and Maddox. She'd liked him since I'd known her, and I was pretty sure he felt the same, but neither would admit it out loud.

"If he liked me, he'd have told me by now. It's time to move on." Hope brightened her eyes, but uncertainty darkened her smile. "Elle's seen Viktor too."

"When?" Maddox joined us at the table, coffee in hand.

I gave Naomi a look. "Last night," I said, turning my head toward Maddox. "He came with Frederick. He's a human-born warlock."

"Ooh, like you." He sipped, then placed his cup on the table. "Maybe you'll finally give someone a chance."

"I do give chances… occasionally," I said. He had a point, but I didn't want to linger there. "Besides, I have all the men I need." I poked his arm, a teasing smile playing on my lips. "Between you and Edmund, I'm already exhausted. I couldn't imagine having a boyfriend as well."

Naomi cleared her throat. "To be fair, Elle does need to focus. The call is coming up soon." She clasped her hands together, her voice rising a whole octave. "My grandmagician said I'm ready to take the test. If I pass, I'll finally be a full magician and will be able to travel, you know, to places that require magicians."

Maddox whistled out a breath. "That'd be great. Speaking of the call… Edmund had a word with me not long ago." His disapproving gaze met mine. *Fuck.* "Why aren't you putting your name forward? We need you. I can't always carry the entire coven on my shoulders." He was joking, but there was some truth there. Between the three of them, he and Edmund did 90 percent of the work.

Naomi looked at me incredulously. "Well? Why aren't you putting your name forward?"

"I want to wait until I'm sure I'm ready."

"Edmund thinks you're ready," Maddox said, but Edmund didn't know how I was failing the advanced spells or that I hadn't memorized all the history and translations. "Come on, Elle. Stop worrying you're not good enough all the time."

Naomi pressed her lips into a thin line, tapping her finger against the dip in her chin. "He has a point. You do do that."

They both nodded, and heat flushed my face. "I'll think about it," I lied. "So are you going to ask him out? Viktor?"

She rolled her eyes at my obvious change of topic but took the bait anyway. "Possibly. Depends on where he's placed."

"He'll probably be a caster," said Maddox.

"Or a protector," Naomi said. "He looks like one."

"Maybe he'll be a magician." I smiled in her direction.

Disappointment guided her tone. "Unlikely. We're the second smallest coven, next to yours. Besides, he has that ambitious look to him."

"We'll find out today," she explained. "The ceremony is this afternoon."

I swallowed thickly. "I have a prior en—"

Maddox tsked. "Attendance is mandatory. Edmund told me to remind you, in case you were going to say you were too busy."

I sighed. The man knew me. "I'll go," I said, relenting as if I had a choice. "Did Edmund also tell you about the spell he had us go check on last night?"

He nodded. "The tracing spell? Yep."

"Do you think the murderer is cloaking themselves? I mean, to use a spell of that magnitude…"

"He believes so, yep. Or, even more unlikely…" He paused, looking at the last of the coffee in his cup. "They're not a witch or warlock."

Naomi's eyebrows pulled together. "A human then, but how? Even if one did manage to get into Istinia, there's no way they could overpower a witch and get away with it."

Maddox shrugged. "It could be a shapeshifter. Normal tracing spells wouldn't be able to locate them."

I shuddered, thinking about the creatures who lived in the depths of Hoai Forest to the east. "But the bodies were found intact. Wouldn't a shifter have, you know, stripped them of their flesh?" I questioned.

"That's true." Maddox nodded.

"It could be a god," Naomi said, earning looks from us both.

Maddox scoffed a laugh. "Are you kidding?"

"I mean, they're the only other option that isn't a shifter, human, or witch."

I shook my head. "The gods are imprisoned, Naomi. We'd have heard if they got out."

"Supposedly imprisoned," Maddox stated. "No one even knows if they exist anymore. There's only mention of them in old texts. Maybe they died in their prison realms."

Naomi bit her bottom lip. "What about Freya, the goddess of the hunt?" she asked, as if we didn't already know from the many religious lessons shoved down our throats from the high council and elders. "She's real and still exists."

"She's the only one," Maddox said, "and hardly anyone has seen her in our lifetime. She sticks to hiding out in the mountains. Who knows if she's even a goddess? There are always imposters."

"She is a goddess, Maddox," Naomi scolded.

He clicked his tongue. "Even if she is, she doesn't do anything for us. I don't even know why we include her in worship."

I tilted my head. "Maddox, come on. We've read about them on ancient runes, in Lor."

He tugged the small black ring, pierced on the side of his ear. "I'm not saying they didn't exist. Only they could have died."

"They're immortal."

"Freya wasn't an original goddess," he argued, and he did have a point. "Originally, Leda was the goddess of the hunt. She obviously died or something."

Naomi interjected. "I mean, yeah, but Freya took her place. Someone had to."

Maddox finished his coffee, then sighed with exasperation. "It doesn't matter how it's done, only that a god is not running around sacrificing people. If they do still exist, then they're locked away. If not, they're dead. We'd know if they were walking among us. Even back in the old ages, they were known to be dramatic."

I rolled my eyes, sarcasm lacing my tone. "Dramatic? Really, the texts said that?"

He gave me a look. "The stories told through them show it. Thalia tried to destroy the underworld because she fell out with her father."

"Supposedly," I said.

"Then there's Raiden, the god of beasts, who set a pack of wolves after his brother because of an argument," he said. "Not to mention how they all started sacrificing people for no good reason." He sat back, folding his arms across his chest, a smug smile on his face. "See. Dramatic."

"Still," Naomi said, leaning over the table, "the murders are getting closer to home. Someone or something has to be causing them."

A grim look shadowed Maddox's soft features. "We don't know who's responsible yet."

Naomi gave him a look. "People are being murdered, and no normal tracing spell can find them. Who else could be doing it?"

"A murderer," he said deadpan, and we both laughed.

"Obviously." I clicked my tongue.

He cleared his throat. "I just mean it's probably a warlock, one who's skilled at cloaking themselves, seeing as my shifter theory can't be." He drummed his fingers on the table. "And about the gods, I don't care to think about them. All I know is they're gone, and good riddance. To think, our ancestors worshipped them, and they sacrificed people."

"Probably appeased them into not ruining the crops or whatever," I said. "Or so I read in one of the texts. That's what Freya said when she wasn't a recluse hiding in the mountains."

"Yes, let's give the creepy immortals human bodies to eat so they won't ruin the land they're supposed to protect."

"Someone's sarcastic today."

"Girl, I'm sarcastic every day." He smirked. "Changing the subject, you should know Aaron and I broke up."

My eyes widened. "Why didn't you tell me?"

He looked at me incredulously. "It wasn't at the top of my priorities. Also, I'd assumed you were sleeping in. You all do most of your work in the evening."

"It's not my fault. Nighttime is full of quiet. I think it's the best time to study dark objects."

Naomi shuddered. "Or play with them."

"Never again," I retorted. The memory of when we were fifteen, after we'd messed around with a hexed candle, floated into my mind. It had been spelled to trap any in the room when it was lit. I could leave, as I wasn't compelled like the others by dark objects, but Naomi couldn't and found herself stuck in the small library until Edmund managed to break her free. It had messed with her senses, and she'd have starved to death if he didn't get her out. The candle never burned out, not without

Edmund's expertise anyway. "Anyway, why did you break up?"

He shrugged. "He was getting paranoid."

"In fairness to him." I put a finger up, then waggled it. "You did enjoy making him jealous… a lot."

"I didn't enjoy it."

"Lies," I teased.

"I might give him another chance. I'll let him stew a little."

I rolled my eyes. "Poor Aaron."

Naomi got up to make another coffee but paused to look out the little window. "I'm excited to see what happens this afternoon. It's been a while since a human-born took the test, or since anyone came from Salvius."

They both looked at me. Maddox broached the building silence. "How are you feeling about it, seeing someone else brought here like you were?"

"Honestly, I hadn't put much thought to it." I tapped a long nail against the side of my cup.

Maddox smirked. "I'm so sure."

"It's not a big deal."

Naomi poured herself another cup, then grabbed a scone and covered it with cream. "It is," she said, dismissing my lie, then mumbled through a mouth of crumbs. "We can meet him. I bet his accent is like yours."

"My accent is normal."

Maddox tilted his head. "It does have a slight Salviun twang."

"His doesn't." I sighed. "I talked to him."

Naomi's eyes widened. "You left that out. I thought you only saw him. What was he like?"

"It's hard to say. It was brief, but I guess he was charming."

"I knew it," Naomi said. "I wonder, though, how he managed to get away with it for so long."

"With being a warlock?" Maddox asked.

"Yeah, like, how do you hide your powers for that long? He must have had people helping him conceal it. They have hunters actively seeking witches in Salvius."

"Maybe his family helped him." Maddox grabbed a slice of toast and covered it with marmalade, which filled the kitchen with the most delightful smell. He pointed the toast at me, his eyebrow arched. I nodded at the silent question.

"It's all a bit iffy to me." I recalled Viktor's dark eyes. Something about them screamed danger. It was ridiculous to assume, but my intuition told me I was right to be afraid. He seemed nice enough, but the bad ones usually did at first.

***

The pastel-blue sky darkened into a dove gray, swept with clouds that warned us rain was coming. It was hardly a surprise. It rained two hundred days out of the year in our province, Fairwik. I didn't mind it. I loved hearing the pitter-patter of drops hitting windows, and I loved breathing in the earthy aroma that lingered long after it stopped.

Maddox snapped his fingers, jolting me back to the present. He'd finished going over a spell, then had slumped into the armchair in front of the crackling fire.

Naomi picked her nails, sitting on the ledge next to the large window. "Pay attention, Elle."

I blinked twice. "Sorry, I was thinking."

"This is why you're afraid of not passing the test. You're not even trying," he said simply. He was always so matter-of-fact, even if it hurt the other person's feelings. I didn't think he realized he was even doing it.

"Maddox," Edmund snapped as he walked in, hot chocolate in hand. "Be nice." He handed me the steaming mug of hot cocoa. "This is for you."

I smiled. "Have I told you how much I love you recently?"

He pushed his glasses up his nose. "Only when you want something." He turned his attention to Maddox, who drummed his fingers against the book. "How're the studies coming along?"

"Someone isn't paying attention."

"Are you teaching her or chastising her?" Edmund asked as he walked to the fireplace and warmed his hands.

Maddox puffed out his cheeks, rolling his eyes. "Both, but she needs it. *I* just don't baby her."

Edmund tsked softly.

The fire's crackling filled the silence. It mixed with the first drizzle of rain against the glass panes of the library, forming a melody and lulling me to sleep. I snuggled against the back of the chair, closing my eyes for a second. A hiss sounded, as Edmund must've moved the logs with the iron poker.

Dora, the other keeper in our coven, walked in holding a bright-yellow umbrella and wearing a pair of knee-high yellow socks and a white skirt and top. "It's raining." Her voice tinkled, bringing me back to life.

Edmund's face lit up, like always when she was around. I didn't know why he didn't just tell her how he felt. It was obvious to everyone else, maybe except her.

Maddox looked her up and down. "How are you wearing that right now? You must be cold."

"A bubble spell on the umbrella."

"Clever," Edmund praised.

Her pleated skirt hugged her wide hips, and her white top was tucked in at her small waist. Her brown skin had a golden hue under the yellow lights, matching the honey color of her wide eyes. "Thanks." She turned from Edmund to me. "How are your studies coming along? Edmund told me this morning you won't be taking the test this year."

Naomi jumped up from the ledge and skipped toward us. "Actually, she said she'll think about it. Isn't that right, Elle?"

"Mm-hmm."

Edmund nodded. "I am glad to hear it."

Benji ran into the room and purred, curling around Dora's ankles. She leaned down and stroked him behind the ears. He loved the attention and got plenty of it from Dora.

"What about you, Naomi?" Dora asked, moving her eyes to look at her. "Will you be putting your name forward in your coven, if there are any openings?"

Naomi nodded. "Yeah. There's a couple of openings. One was taken last year, and all but me and one other are waiting. Quite a few haven't even progressed from student-magicians to apprentices yet."

I recalled how she had moved up from student to apprentice a couple of years ago. Most promoted in the coven within three years. I had been an apprentice for five, and her taking the test only sought as a reminder. For the longest time, I was revered for moving up from a student so fast, until I wasn't good enough. "You'll pass," I said. "You're getting better by the day." It was fascinating how they could make something appear as something else entirely. One time, she'd made me believe I was in a meadow. I could even smell the wildflowers before she pulled back the illusion and we were both standing in the living room.

Dora smiled. "Your father should be proud."

She cast her eyes downward. "You know that next to my precious brother, I'll never be good enough."

"Don't be silly," I told her for the thousandth time since we'd been friends. "You're more than good enough, but I'm sure your dad loves you regardless," I said, not entirely believing my own words. I really did hate that man.

"I'm just glad he isn't on my case. Since my brother started his own spell-sealing business for out-of-town trading, I've all but been forgotten."

"He's lucky to have you." Dora squeezed her shoulder, then pulled Edmund to one side. "I need a word."

40

He nodded and they moved out of earshot. I turned toward Naomi. "When you pass, we can go to one of those new picture theaters you like."

"I'd love that." She flashed her pearly white smile at me and curled her fingers around a book Maddox had been reading. Her nails were painted gold with black stripes dragged across them. "We should get going if we're going to make it to the ceremony," Naomi called to Dora and Edmund. "Edmund, we'll be back later."

Edmund looked back at us, excusing himself from Dora. He looked at me through his black-framed glasses. The wrinkles around his eyes showed his age. They weren't profound yet but still visible. Sometimes, he reminded me of a wise old owl when he stared at me like that. "Be careful. Try not to aggravate any of the casters." He turned toward Maddox as he said it.

Maddox shoved his hands into his pockets. "When they learn to get their heads out their asses, I will."

Naomi giggled softly, and I suppressed a chuckle.

Edmund regarded us. "Dora and I will be there later. We have business to attend first."

Maddox smirked. "I'm sure you do."

Edmund shot him a scowl as I pulled him and Naomi with me toward the door.

CHAPTER THREE

I looked up at the rolling clouds of gray and black as we rode into the town center, which reminded me of the night I was forced out of Salvius. Rain lashed down, soaking the stone statues and coating the trees surrounding the temple, so the leaves appeared like wax. The heavy doors had been left open. Surrounding the frame were contorted faces of creatures made from stone.

Deep drumbeats lured us inside, thumping in unison and controlled with magic. Balconies wrapped around the building, allowing witches and warlocks to look down onto the center stage, where the three large bowls stood.

We didn't go upstairs, where the protectors gathered; I could always tell them apart. They were muscular and usually had a sword or dagger in their belt. Occasionally, I'd see the odd quiver of arrows and bow on their back. They looked out for us, kept us safe, and when I thought about it, it was probably the protectors who'd retrieved the dead bodies from the sacrifices found recently. They stayed out of the other covens' business for the most part. According to the elders, protectors were picked because they showed incredible strength and bravery. They could sense danger and had remarkable reflexes. They had what they called light magic.

There were three kinds of witches, and the elders used three things to represent us. Water represented light magic, which the majority of covens, the casters, potioneers, and protectors had. Blood represented dark magic, as my coven had, and gold represented illusory magic, which the magicians had. As a result, we were called blood witches which was just *great.*

Naomi knotted her hand with mine, then tugged Maddox's arm with her other arm. "Over here." She ushered us to a quiet spot under the balconies, where potted plants had been placed on shelves pressed against the smooth, gray walls. I looked at a pot that held purple adins and white blossoms. They were used quite commonly to heal from viral infections, brewed by the potioneers into consumable remedies.

The smell of smoke from burned sage mixed with crushed herbs lingered in the air. Maddox leaned back against the wall, kicking one leg behind him and pushing the sole of his shoe against the stone. He crossed his arms over his chest, and his cufflinks caught a glimmer of light as he did.

Naomi entwined her fingers together behind her back, then rocked back and forth on her heels. "I still think he'll be a protector." She grinned at Maddox. "Or a caster, but I'm putting my skal on protector."

I placed a hand on my hip. "I'll put a skal on protector too." I rolled my gaze up to the balcony overhead. I could hear them walking around. "He has the right... build."

Maddox scoffed a laugh. "Build?"

"Yeah, well, I didn't get a good look at him last night. It was dark. But he was tall and well built."

He snorted. "Well built?"

"You know what I mean."

He shot me an appreciative look. "Hmm. Well, I'm sticking to caster. I haven't met him yet, but most of them are casters, so I'll play it safe. In fact, I'll take you up on your bet." Maddox pulled four skal from his pocket, then turned them over in his palm. "If I win, I get eight. If he's a protector, you each get two."

"Unless he's something else," I said.

"Unlikely," Maddox answered.

"Always stats and facts with you," I replied.

Maddox pushed the skal back into his pocket. "The servers are here." He motioned toward the group of men and women. Some had come from the kitchens and were still wearing aprons. I spotted a woodchopper among them wearing green overalls. "Of course they'd come to watch," he said as we watched them take their seats. "They'll do anything to be a part of the magic."

They weren't required to be there like the covens but were extended the invitation anyway. Most of the servers had enough magic to be classed as a witch or warlock, but not enough to be placed into one of the sectors. A small number of them had strong magic, but it had been repressed through some kind of traumatic event, and a small minority were prisoners of minor crimes who'd been forced to join the servers as a way to lessen their sentences. They served the community.

While many looked down on them, I saw them for what they were: the backbone of Istinia. Without them, we couldn't survive. Spells and potions could be used for many things, but not everything, and someone needed to keep track of day-to-day living: make the beds, clean the academies, run the stores, send and deliver the mail, and everything else. Our town was up and coming, so businesses were beginning to boom, bringing more servers in than ever before.

Alma included them. Each town, or province in Istinia, had an elder from the council, and she was ours. She had also created the arches spelled to keep the passable area between the mountains from being able to be crossed. I looked at her frail body and graying hair, and it was hard to believe, but she'd been younger then—and as powerful as they came, according to the stories.

My attention diverted as a group of casters arrived. All of them were girls. Some smiled in our direction, others scowled.

I breathed slowly. My heart rate amped up a little when I saw all the covens mix. Like the magicians, we were looked down on, and more so on me because I was human-born. Our magic wasn't seen as important, like the casters or potioneers, and wasn't as exciting, like the protectors'.

"Oh, it's Craig." Naomi smiled at seeing her crush take a seat at the back of the temple. He was followed by two other magicians. He waved, his eyes landing on me for a few seconds, and he glanced at Naomi. Before she could go over there, the sudden drumbeats silenced the room, and Viktor walked inside.

I could see him better in this light. His hair was a dark brown, so deep it could have been black if not for the light hitting it at certain angles. His shirt sleeves were rolled up on his arms. He looked ready to fight at any moment. His strong nose complemented his chiseled jawline and sharp features. He was muscular but trim. He brought his hand up to his short beard when they sat him down. I couldn't see his eyes from where I was standing, but I couldn't forget the darkness in them I'd seen yesterday. The rings of blue had seemed alien against the penetrating black.

Alma lowered the hood of her white robe. She extended her arms in welcome. "Thank you to those of you who came tonight. Daughters, sons," she said, referring to us as family, like always. "I am overjoyed to have you here to welcome our newest resident of Fairwik." Chatter rose until Alma waved her hands down. "Before we begin." She raised her voice over the unintelligible gossip. "Allow me to put some rumors to rest. I may be old, but I'm not dead." A smile played on her thin lips. "I hear the same things you do. I will remind you all that giving life to rumors is never smart. We live by truths, so today, I am here to give them to you. Openness is important to the welfare of our coven."

I chewed the inside of my cheek. Maddox whispered softly. "The truth, for once. Well, only when it suits them."

Naomi shushed him.

Alma's wrinkled eyes trickled their gaze over me, then moved up to the balconies. "Viktor did indeed come from Salvius. While he gets used to Istinia, I hope you will all make him feel welcome."

Maddox scoffed. "Unlikely. They never gave you a chance, Elle."

He had a good point. I was human-born, and the other witches thought me weak, as if my blood were diluted. Although, when I saw the way the girls eyed him, I didn't think that would be a problem for them anymore.

"Now." She took Viktor's hands in hers, then walked him toward the three large stone basins. Inside of them were three different liquids. One shimmered crimson: blood. Another was clear, sparkly: water. The third shined brilliant, bold: liquid gold. "Let us begin."

Silence befell us. Three other elders, also wearing long white robes, explained the rules to him. We couldn't fully make out what they were saying, but I'd gone through it when I was brought here, so I remembered it for the most part.

The liquids in the large bowls reacted against the witch's or warlock's touch. If the person reacted with water, then other tests were performed to see which of the three covens the person belonged to: caster, potioneer, or protector.

He stood over the basins, then turned to face Alma. She looked at him, her gaze transfixed. A shiver snaked down my back, and I wasn't the only one to shudder it off. Several others around me did the same.

"What the hell?" I questioned softly.

Naomi looked from me to Alma. "What's she doing?"

"Or he doing?" Maddox asked.

I stared at them, then after a few seconds, Alma looked away from him. She simply smiled, grabbed his hand, and placed it over the basins.

"That was weird," I stated. "You felt it, right?"

"I felt it get cold," Naomi said quickly, not looking away from Viktor and Alma.

Suspicion crowned Maddox's eyes. I was glad I wasn't the only one who felt something was off.

After a few minutes, the blood in the second basin bubbled to a boil. Alma bowed her head, then looked up at Viktor, who's expression gave nothing away. His lips were set in a hard line, his eyes focused on the scarlet.

My lips parted. "There's no way."

Naomi's eyes widened. "He's in the…"

As Naomi said it, Alma announced his new coven.

My stomach lurched, and beads of sweat dotted my forehead.

"Cursekeepers." Alma looked at me and nodded. "You'll be joining our dear Elle and Maddox over there."

Everyone looked at us. My insides knotted. He glanced over, and I felt my cheeks flush with heat.

"I guess we were all wrong," Maddox said as Viktor walked in our direction. Alma didn't usually address us face-to-face. She was far too important and spoke to us in large groups, but tonight, her eyes were focused on mine. Viktor scanned the three of us. He strode next to her, closing the distance between us.

Alma's green eyes matched mine. She, like me, had soft features. There wasn't anything sharp about her, yet she wielded incredible power. "Elle. Maddox." The authority in her voice made me stand straighter.

"Elder Alma," we said in unison.

"You will take care of Viktor, show him how we operate here, and introduce him to Edmund and Dora."

My gaze flickered to Viktor's. An arrogant smirk unfurled on his lips as he thanked Alma. His voice was deep and smooth, and I detected something ingenuine in his thank-you. He watched her walk away like a predator watches prey.

"I believe we already met." He turned toward me when she was gone. "Elle."

"Yesterday," I said quietly.

Naomi extended her hand toward him. "I'm Naomi."

"I'm Viktor."

"Obviously," Maddox said with a sarcastic smirk, and I loved him for it.

"I'll assume you're the sarcastic one." He didn't appear shaken. "Good. I like a challenge."

Maddox's cheeks pinkened, and by gods, he was actually silent. No quick-whipped response? Viktor looked back at Naomi. "I'm in trouble. Are all the keepers so attractive?"

She giggled, flicking back her tight curls, and Maddox grinned. "I'm not a keeper, but I wish I was now." Her eyes brightened. "Dora and Edmund are old, so probably not your type."

Maddox scoffed a laugh. "I'm sure they'd appreciate hearing that."

Naomi continued. "The only trouble you'll have is Maddox and Elle."

Viktor let out a low chuckle.

I giggled, and his gaze flicked to mine. "Well, I do love trouble."

The stars were bright tonight, shining against their inky canvass. The moon was a putrid yellow, hanging beyond the forest's edge in the distance, reflecting off the lake at the edge of town. The cobbled roads wound toward each of the houses, some bigger than others. The casters had a small village within our town, with many houses, an academy, several training halls, and even their own small stores. The magicians lived in a mansion hidden within the confines of a wood, close to the cemetery. Ours was a mansion too, but up on a hill. It overlooked the town, hidden behind neatly trimmed hedges, wrought-iron gates, and a long winding path leading up to it.

Viktor had spent the rest of the afternoon talking to the other covens, who all loved him. I shouldn't have been so bitter, but I hated it. None of them had given me the same treatment, and Viktor and I were both human-born witches.

"I better be taking off," Naomi said before we could set off in the direction of the mansion. "They'll be worried."

Viktor flashed her a charming smile. "I'll see you soon, doll." He half hugged her. She looked intoxicated when she turned toward me. "Night, Elle." Her tone lightened. "Maddox."

"Be safe," I called as she walked into the darkness. "Send me a magic quill if you need me."

"I will," she called back, leaving us three alone.

Maddox broached the silence. "You'll love the mansion. We have so many artifacts, books, and magical objects."

"If he even likes history."

Viktor arched a dark eyebrow. "History is the only way to prepare for the future. I'm looking forward to learning all about Istinia's."

Maddox grinned. "Hear that, Elle? You could learn something from him. History isn't boring."

I shot him a warning stare. "History doesn't bore me."

"If you say so," Maddox said simply, then shoved his hands into his deep pockets.

Viktor looked at me, his blue eyes meeting mine. "What are you interested in, Elle?"

My heart raced. "Oh, I like to draw and go for walks in the woods near here. It's so beautiful." I sounded dull so searched through the clutter in my mind for anything else. "I do some gardening from time to time."

His smile didn't falter. "The woods are one of the best places to be."

"Right? I love the smell of it." I stopped myself, realizing how weird I sounded.

"Me too. Maybe you can take me there soon."

"Straight," Maddox said out of the blue.

We both looked at him, and I tilted my head.

"Definitely straight."

Sorry, I mouthed, but I wasn't too sorry.

Maddox shrugged. "Aaron will be glad."

"Mm-hmm," I mumbled, then looked up at Viktor. Damn, he was tall. He seemed to be coping so well. I'd spent the first few weeks here crying when I'd been dragged from Salvius. "I'm sorry you had to leave your home."

"Me too. I'm okay." His lips curled from a smirk to a softer smile. "Thank you for asking."

"Did you have family there?"

His expression hardened. "Yes."

"Do you miss them?" I closed my eyes after I said it. What a stupid question. Of course he did.

Maddox turned, staring at me wide-eyed. Viktor didn't answer. I parted my lips to speak but thought better of it.

We didn't say anything else on the way back. When we reached the mansion, Dora opened the gates and walked us up to the mansion. "Welcome home."

CHAPTER FOUR

A melody from a songbird followed Edmund, Viktor, Maddox, and me as we walked around narrow, tall trees and over the muddy ground. Golden-brown leaves, decayed with spots of black, carpeted the well-trodden path leading to a clearing.

Wildflowers of white and royal blue peppered the area, growing against the luscious blades of green in the center. The grass stretched out through the clearing, spreading thin and browning at the edges when it reached the tree line.

It was my preferred place to come and train. Only protectors originally had weapon training as a part of their curriculum, but Edmund had pushed for it to be in ours too, after Dora had asked for it when she became keeper some twenty years ago. He argued with the council that it was needed due to keepers' frequent travel to dangerous places, to retrieve dark objects or translate ancient runes. None of them had ever needed to use it, but I admired his want for us to be able to defend ourselves. It also made me feel powerful, and I liked the break between studying language and history. Next to deciphering dark objects and researching their properties, it was my favorite lesson.

I looked up and smiled. Cotton-candy-shaped clouds set against a pastel-blue sky, and a gentle breeze cooled the warm air. The day would have been perfect if it weren't for the presence of death hanging over Istinia.

Edmund white-knuckled his dagger as we reached the log stumps we sat on between sessions. "How many more will need to die before they take it seriously?" He ran his free hand through his dirty-blond hair, which naturally swept to one side. "We need to bring a caster in today. I requested one to come yesterday but they were 'too busy.'"

Maddox leaned against a tree trunk. He brushed dirt from his white cotton top. He never looked so casual, but it was only during training when he'd replace his suit with anything else. "I'm shocked Alma hasn't bothered coming to the mansion, considering we hold the key to ending this."

"We only hold the spell, not the ability to cast it," Edmund said with an exasperated sigh. "Never mind that now. Let's focus on training." He shifted his gaze to Viktor. I wasn't sure how Edmund felt about him yet. He'd, thus far, been unreadable. "First you're brought to a territory you don't know, right when people are being murdered left and right. You must feel out of sorts."

Viktor shrugged. "There were murders in Salvius too. It's nothing new." He grabbed a couple of throwing knives from his belt. His white top hugged his abs and barrel-shaped chest. My gaze moved down to the front of his black pants, when Maddox cleared his throat. Flushing with heat, I whipped my head to the side to take in Maddox's amused smirk.

Edmund pointed at a tree a fair distance from where Viktor stood. "Hit that tree."

The muscle in Viktor's arm tightened as he pulled it back, holding the knife between his fingers and thumb. The knife left his hand at dizzying speed and sliced through the air with deadly precision. I peered through the arrowed sunlight to the gray-brown trunk of the tree. He threw another three, one quickly after the other, forming a line of knives down the middle—except for one, which landed to the left. I wondered if he'd done it on purpose.

Edmund's forehead wrinkled as his eyebrows shot up. "You've done this before."

Viktor's calculating gaze washed over each of us. "I practiced in Salvius."

Edmund's eyebrows pinched in the middle. "We were told you came from a farm. Why would a farmer's son need to use weapons?"

Viktor arched a dark eyebrow. "I could ask you the same question."

"We're often put in at-risk locations," he recited, as if he were explaining to the council, again, why we needed to keep the training program. "There may be situations where we need to defend ourselves, and there are so few of us, we can't afford to lose someone."

Viktor nodded slowly, an appreciative smile unfurling on his lips. "I like the way you think. It's good to know my mentor is competent."

Edmund stood, unfazed by the half-hearted compliment. "I'll ask you again. Why did a farmer's son need to use weapons?"

I couldn't help but grin. Nothing got past Edmund, and if Viktor thought flattery would work on him, he was in for a surprise. Viktor glanced at me, then looked back at Edmund. "I had to protect the land from beasts in the woods who'd try to slaughter our cattle," he explained, although it didn't make sense as to why he'd be able to use throwing knives of all things. "Over the years, I learned not only to train with a sword but the agility and speed that came from learning the art of attack. I would fight in rings with the locals for dramair."

It had been a long time since I'd heard dramair used in a sentence, the currency used in Salvius. I remembered the large gold coins and the smaller silver and bronze coins. I had mostly used the latter, as we were too poor to have a coin purse filled with gold.

He continued. "Over time, I practiced with more weapons. It became a hobby of sorts."

Edmund paused, tapping his fingers against his knee. After a minute of painful silence, he nodded. "All right. In that case, I will instead focus on honing your skills." He gestured toward me. "Elle, would you like to give it a go?"

"Give what a go? Him?" I looked at Viktor wide-eyed. "I guess I can."

Maddox chuckled, and even Edmund laughed. My cheeks heated again. "That's not what I meant. I meant—"

"We know what you meant, Elle." Edmund cleared his throat, stopping his laugh, but his amused smile didn't waver. "Yes, I want you to fight Viktor. Let's see if he's as good as he says. You're best with a dagger and pistol, but we want Viktor in one piece, so let's stick with the dagger for today."

I felt the first splash of rain. Pillars of black blotted the pale blue on the horizon. As fast as the pretty day had come, it fizzled into gray. I'd gotten used to it. Sunshine and clear skies seldom lasted for more than half a day.

Viktor gazed up, then looked at me. "A storm's coming."

"We don't let rain stop us," Maddox said from under the cover of a tree. "Else we'd never get anything done."

He was right. It rained more in Fairwik than anywhere else in Istinia. With our vast forests, glacier-blue lakes, and gray coastline, we lived in the most beautiful part of Istinia, but the weather kept most away. I was glad. I didn't want crowds of people taking over our pretty towns dotted between areas of forest.

Edmund handed Viktor his dagger, then gave me a curt nod. "Don't hold back."

"I won't." I gripped it tight, my determined stance poised to fight.

Viktor stepped forward. His blue irises were swallowed by the glittering darkness of his pupils. His penetrating stare locked onto mine, menace in his eyes as his fingers gripped the hilt of the dagger. The blade shone in the corner of my vision. "I'll go easy on you."

I scoffed a laugh. "Please don't."

Challenge flashed in his gaze. "Have it your way."

He was bigger than me, so I'd have to use my speed to beat him. Brute force wouldn't go in my favor. My heart raced as Viktor pushed his blade forward. He grabbed my wrist and tugged me closer. I twisted my wrist in his fingers, twirling to his side. I tried to knock the blade from his hand, but he was too fast.

"Nice move."

"I'm usually fast." I looked down. "Not quick enough, apparently."

"Don't beat yourself up. I've had a lot of practice." He let me go. "Try again."

A daring glint crossed my expression. I tried to back away as he stepped to me, but his arm wrapped around my waist, pulling me closer. His blade trembled for a moment. I'd have missed it if not for my adrenaline-fueled state. Everything was sharper as blood pumped through my veins, sending my heartbeat into a frenzy.

A faint smell of pine and leather accompanied him as he pressed it against my chest. I gazed into his eyes, and something in them changed. His lips parted, and his grip on the blade loosened a fraction enough. I tore it from his grasp and pushed the blade against his throat. The smooth edge of the dagger pressed against his windpipe, the sharp edge against his skin.

A trickle of blood trickled down his neck as a smile stretched his lips. "You win."

I didn't mean to actually cut him. I'd gone too far. I stared at the blood, listening to Maddox clap from the sidelines.

"Woo. Go, Elle."

Edmund watched, his eyes fixated on us. "Good girl."

A panicked breath left me as I moved my eyes to meet Viktor's. "I didn't mean to cut you."

He shrugged it off, wiping his blood against the back of his hand. "It's just a scratch."

I lowered the blade, passing it to him, then took a step back. Letting out a shaky exhale, I stared up at the sky as rain pattered into the clearing. The world around us turned glossy as wind-swept rain gushed through the woods. "Maddox is next." I offered him my dagger.

He wasn't as good with it, but he was brilliant with throwing knives and, surprisingly, an axe. Edmund favored pistols. Viktor, to everyone's surprise, excelled with them all.

***

Dora made us tea after we hurried inside.

"You didn't come with us today," I complained as she set the flower-patterned teapot next to the tea caddy. I eyed her sunflower apron.

"Someone has to cook for you all."

Maddox gave her a look. "I still don't know why you don't let the servers do it. It's why they're here."

She rolled her expressive brown eyes. "I won't have anyone coming into my house and messing things up. Also…" She slapped the side of his arm, tut-tutting as she did. "The servers are not here to do whatever we can't be bothered to do. They are a part of our community. We serve them by keeping them safe, using our magic to heal them, and they work the jobs we can't so we can focus on practicing magic."

Maddox rubbed his arm, scowling. "Then why are they called servers?"

Ignoring yet another of their squabbles, I searched for a pack of cookies, rummaging between cluttered boxes on the shelves in the kitchen until I found a box hidden behind a blue tin. Maddox didn't eat sugar. He was healthier than any of us. Dora had an allergy to chocolate of all things so wouldn't touch them, which left Edmund. Like me, he had a sweet tooth. I shook the box at him, and he grinned.

"Ah, you found them," Edmund remarked.

"I always do." I grinned back, then put them on a plate. Dora berated me as crumbs danced out the box and landed all around me. "I'll clean them."

She laughed in disbelief. "That'll be the day."

Maddox looked at Viktor, a knowing glint in his eye. "Welcome to the madhouse."

Viktor leaned back in his chair. Dora swept the crumbs before I had a chance to, then hurried me to sit.

"Nai will be coming up in a bit," I said, spotting a gap in the conversation. I eyed Viktor for his reaction. His dark gaze moved to mine, and my heart hammered. Swallowing thickly, I pulled myself away and looked down at the tea and collection of jams and creams.

"Good. Maybe she can ask her father why they haven't sent a caster yet." Edmund pushed his fingers through his blond strands.

I gave him a look. "You know how she feels about him."

Dora clicked her tongue. "He's too hard on the poor girl. She needs love and encouragement. Acting as if one coven is better than another… He'll learn his lesson one day." She reached up to her neck and feathered a touch along the silver medallion hanging there.

Viktor leaned forward. "Nice necklace."

She smiled, touching it again. "It's a symbol of Estia. Oh, naturally, you wouldn't know about the true gods."

Edmund gave her a look. "Come now, Dora. We can't dismiss the humans' god or their saints."

She inhaled deeply. "Estia," she said, conviction guiding her tone, "is the goddess of love. She rules the otherworld. It's where you want to end up."

"What's the alternative?" Viktor questioned.

I cleared my throat. "The underworld. It's the dark realm, filled with monsters, killers, and everything dark they want to vanquish from the world."

Dora's smile fell into a hard line. "The underworld's ruled by Lucius, the god of justice. You don't want to end up there, but as long as you follow your moral compass north, then you'll need not worry about your fate in the afterlife."

He pulled his arms behind him, entwining his fingers behind his head and stretching back. "What are the rules? If you steal something, do you go to the underworld, or is it only for murderers? Where's the scale?"

"The gods know what is in our hearts," Dora explained. "They measure the weight of good and bad in our souls when we die."

Maddox interjected. "Supposedly."

"Don't mind him," she said. "Maddox has always been cynical."

Maddox shook his head, with pinched eyebrows and an amused smirk. "I prefer the term logical."

Viktor exhaled slowly. "So this Estia is supposedly all good?"

Dora nodded. "That's right."

I didn't agree. No one was perfect. Even a goddess. According to legend, the gods—well, the children of Estia and Lucius—were locked away in prison realms. "That's not entirely true."

All eyes shifted to look at me.

"She didn't try to intervene when her children were locked away. I mean, that's pretty terrible mothering if you ask me."

"Language!" Dora said, berating me, although I was sure some of her anger related to the truth in my statement. Dora was more religious than anyone I'd met.

Viktor suppressed a smile but nodded in my direction.

Maddox finished his tea. "Elle's right. That's not very maternal for the goddess of love."

Dora clenched her jaw. "It's not her fault her children turned out to be monsters. They spent too much time in this world and allowed greed, desire, and anger to corrupt them. She's done a service to humanity by not allowing them out. They're a danger to us."

"Allegedly," Maddox said again, earning a smirk from Edmund, who'd so far managed to keep out of it.

"The tea is getting cold." Dora hurried, grabbing the teapot from between us with more force than needed. "I'll make a new pot."

Viktor stood. "I'm actually going to head out and explore, but I really appreciate the effort, Dora. It was a lovely spread."

Her temper faltered, and a hint of a smile crossed her lips. "Take an umbrella if you're going out, and wear a jacket. You'll catch your death out there."

"He's a grown man," Edmund said.

"He's new here." She placed a hand on her hip. "I'm sure the weather in Salvius wasn't like this." She turned back toward Viktor. "I wouldn't want you to catch a cold."

"Right. Thanks," Viktor replied, tight-lipped.

Salvius took up almost half of the land both of our territories shared, so the weather was just as unpredictable as here, depending on where in Salvius one resided.

"Magic quill us if you need anything," I said.

His gaze climbed back to meet mine. "Should I know what that is?"

"Ah, right. One of us will show you when you get back. It's a spell you can use to send messages to another person. You need to already have established a magical link with whoever can send you them. Like Nai and I, we did a joining spell and can send messages to each other anytime. Same as any of us in the coven."

Maddox interjected. "Except for Alma. She can use it to anyone."

"Interesting." He paused at the door. "I'll be back in a bit."

Dora pointed at the door. "There's my umbrella in the stand. You can use it."

He eyed the yellow polka-dot umbrella, then from her to me. Maddox and I curled our lips back between our teeth, but as soon as we looked at each other, laughter erupted.

Dora rolled her eyes, and Edmund pressed his lips together, trying not to join in. Viktor relented, grabbing the yellow umbrella, and headed out into the storm. I wasn't sure why he'd chosen now to explore, and to go alone, but I figured he probably wanted some time alone. I remembered when I'd first arrived and how disjointed everything felt. He'd done better than I had, sliding into his new life with suspicious ease, but he didn't seem the type to wear his emotions out loud. Besides, he probably felt nervous under his calm exterior. Tomorrow was going to be the first day Viktor would have to use his magic, and if he was anything like I was, it would most likely go disastrously.

CHAPTER FIVE

Maddox leaned in the doorway to my bedroom, wearing a white shirt and black pants. His blazer was tossed over his shoulder. "Morning." His tone lifted at the end. "Are you ready for the day?"

Pulling the covers up to my chest, I jolted up. "What the hell are you doing, Maddox?"

"Viktor's about to start his training. I figured you'd want to help."

I glanced at the alarm and shook my head. "It's seven in the freaking morning!"

He rolled his eyes. "You'll be fine. Edmund wants you there too. You should come. Remember how nervous you were when you first practiced?"

I groaned under my breath. "I won't be able to go back to sleep now."

"Good, well get up. Shower. Try to do something nice with your hair for once."

I let out a long breath. "Get out."

"See you downstairs," he called as he left.

I closed my eyes for a few moments, enjoying the comfort of pillows against my head and fluffy covers shaping around my body. I guessed I should be there. It was scary, especially when we didn't grow up with magic, him especially. He had to be in his early twenties, and I'd at least had my teenage years to come to terms with it, although I was barely out of those.

Opening my eyes, I blew out a tense breath, then tore myself from the bed and plopped my feet against the thick carpet. I pulled on my V-neck black button-down dress, which stopped at my knees—one of the outfits I seldom wore—and attempted to detangle the waves in my hair.

After showering, I applied a clear gloss to my lips and added a caffeine balm I'd bought from the local potion shop, to brighten the lack of sleep from under my eyes.

I stretched my arms out, then ventured to the atrium where we spent most of our time practicing. The walls were reinforced to withstand the wayward curses that occasionally escaped the dark objects. Viktor leaned over the table, his muscles bulging under his navy-blue shirt. His sleeves were rolled up, as always. He must have gone shopping yesterday. I didn't imagine he had much. When I arrived, I was given an allowance of skal, I think forty a month, so I figured he was given the same courtesy. Alma was tasked with ensuring the covens took care of their students and apprentices with boarding, food, and allowance, unlike in Salvius where parents were made to take care of their children. Here, after a child became a student in a coven, that was it. Their responsibility was turned over to Alma and the grand-person of each coven. I looked forward to the day when I'd no longer need an allowance from the council, which had replaced our kings and queens almost seventy years ago, and get paid to be a keeper.

"Open it carefully," Edmund told Viktor, who wore two new rings, as he turned the sides of a puzzle box. I assumed Maddox or Edmund made them for him, to protect his hands from the physical damage these curses and spells could do. As he carefully but gently clicked the box into place, I recalled the first time I'd been tasked to open the box and move the curse inside.

It had taken me only a few weeks, which was great when compared to many others—except Maddox, who'd apparently done it in three days.

Hurrying to the center table where they all stood around, I looked at the polished box. It had a grooved lining where it needed opening. Next to it was the smaller, metal box he would need to transfer the curse to. The curse inside was a weak one, which was why this lesson was used for beginners. He'd need to extract the curse from the puzzle box before trying to move it over. Viktor glanced my way, and I felt heat flush through me. Maddox watched us from the other side of the table.

The atrium had none of the comforts the rest of the mansion had. It was specifically a training space, with only the large, stone table, reinforced walls and floor, which had a slight bounce to it when I walked, and some chairs stacked next to large, long shelves, filled with a variety of lower-class dark objects and spell books.

"Turn it an inch to the right," Edmund said as Viktor refocused on the task at hand.

He clicked it, and it opened.

I held my breath, then grabbed his wrist to stop him from touching the inside. "No." I gasped.

In the center of the five pieces of wood was a swirling darkness, glittering with green. It whispered, begging us to come closer.

"If you touch it, it will be able to go inside you." I shuddered, remembering when I'd made the exact same mistake and ended up spending the day vomiting after Edmund pulled the curse from my body.

"Right. Thanks." He recoiled his hand, and I let go of his wrist.

Dragging my finger against my lip, feeling the touch beneath my fingertips, I slowed my breaths.

Edmund handed him a wand, one we only used to transfer curses or spells. "Using this, I want you to wrap the curse around it and put it in there." He pointed at the small metal box. "You will need to control it before it can control you. You have dark magic running through your veins, so you're naturally attuned to these curses, and you won't give in to their lures easily. You can do this."

Viktor furrowed his brows, and a line of concentration creased his forehead. Gripping the eight-inch, knotted wooden wand, he closed his eyes, placing it against the side of the box. That was where I would have gone too. Most would go into the center, but the side was best. There were small holes in the side the curse could be pulled through, therefore weakening it. Even Edmund was impressed with his placement, nodding with his arms folded over his chest.

Viktor pulled the wand outward, his hand trembling for a short second, and the darkness danced through the holes, entwining itself like a mist around the wand. Now for the hard part. There was no way he or anyone would do it the first time, but so far, he'd done better than anyone else I'd met, including Maddox.

The curse snaked down the wand and to his hand. Edmund braced himself to pull the curse back, but Viktor pushed back, closing his eyes as he moved the wand toward the metal box. My heart raced as the scene unfolded, moving in slow motion. I blinked twice, unable to believe what I was seeing. My mouth fell open when the wand hit the top of the box, and the curse, at Viktor's will, curled inside and allowed itself to be locked away. He closed the box, and I let out a shaky exhale. Edmund's eyebrows shot up his forehead, and Maddox let out a loud "well damn."

Viktor placed the wand onto the table, then turned toward me, of all people. "Thanks for the help. I'd have been possessed if it wasn't for you."

My heart hammered. I looked to Edmund for some clue as to how Viktor had mastered it so quickly, but he looked as perplexed as me.

"How did you do that?" Maddox arched an eyebrow.

Viktor shrugged. "I willed it to do what I wanted it to, as if it were an extension of my hand."

I swallowed thickly. "No one's done that this fast before."

Edmund clapped his hands together. "Beginners luck, perhaps. Let's see what else you can do." He walked to the shelves and grabbed a pocket watch, which had been spelled to act as a compass rather than a watch. "Make it tell time once more."

It was another puzzle given to students, but usually a month or two after training. The box had to be a fluke. There was no way he'd be able to pass this straight away.

He took the pocket watch, which looked small in his big hands, and curled his fingers around the smooth, gold surface. He fell silent for several minutes. I picked at my nails, wondering what Dora was going to make for breakfast. I wasn't usually up this early. We'd be in here for ages while he tried to figure out the watch, and my stomach growled in protest.

"He's done it," Edmund announced, surprise guiding his tone. I looked over, and a lump formed in my throat. The watch ticked away, pointing to several seconds after ten past nine. "This is unprecedented." Edmund smiled. "I must let Alma know. Maddox, take him to see the books on Lor. I wonder how quickly he can learn to translate." His eyes sparkled with excitement, whereas I felt like I'd swallowed a lead balloon.

Maddox walked to my side, his eyebrows raised. "Looks like you will have some competition for keeper. If he keeps going like this, he'll be an apprentice within weeks."

Viktor smiled in my direction. I looked away. As he stood, with Maddox and Edmund praising him, I didn't see him as the hot new guy. He was going to steal everything I had worked for, right from under me. No one had excelled that quickly, and I didn't stand a chance.

"Elle, you coming to help us show Viktor some Lor?"

I ground my teeth. I hated being petty or bitter, but the ugly emotions rampaged beneath the surface. "I'm going to eat. I'm sure Viktor won't need any help."

Maddox rolled his eyes, then turned toward Viktor. "Let's go. I'll show you the archives first."

***

"Don't be jealous." Dora paced the kitchen table in her sunflower-patterned apron. "You should be pleased our coven is growing."

"I need to become a keeper," I explained as I sat in front of a plate of bacon and eggs. I'd explained everything to her, although I was sure Edmund would tell her again once they were done and came for lunch.

"Edmund said you weren't going to take the test, so it's your own fault. Your putting it off means he'll have a chance. If you put your name forward at the call, then you'll fill the position before he has the chance to train for it."

I chewed on the inside of my lip, looking down at the steaming cup of coffee she'd placed in front of me. Sighing, I fumbled my thumbs. "What if I'm not good enough? What if I can't pass?"

"There's no reason you wouldn't." Dora sat across the table from me and sipped tea from a small, bone china teacup. "You've practiced enough. Just get your head down and study those last books, and you'll be good to go."

I curled my lips behind my teeth, closing my eyes as I did. "I don't think that's enough."

"What's the harm in trying?"

"I can't wait years until I can try again. Next year I'll be better equipped, and..."

"So will Viktor."

My jaw clenched. "Right."

She gave me a look. "It's not his fault, Elle."

I blew out a long exhale. "I know." I rolled my eyes. "Maybe he will be terrible at translating Lor."

"Maybe." She half smiled, then grabbed the day's newspaper and scanned the articles. The latest murder was scrawled across the front page. A girl, no older than me, had been found in the woods.

Young Woman, Eighteen, Found Dead in Another Murder Sacrifice.

Dora shook her head, letting out a heavy exhale. "Whoever is it, Estia will see they're caught."

I stared at my breakfast. I didn't have much faith in anything other than us to find the murderer. I hoped what Maddox had said was true, and it was some crazed witch who was great at cloaking spells, but something in my intuition told me it wasn't the case. If they weren't a witch, then they were more dangerous than anyone was anticipating. Bringing in a caster was of utmost importance, although Edmund was certain they would bring one in today.

I skipped lunch and headed for the woods, my sketchbook and charcoal in hand. Maddox was still teaching Viktor Lor, and he apparently was a natural. Go figure. I needed some time away from hearing everyone sing his praises as he inched closer to taking the spot that was supposed to be mine.

If I had any chance of finding Mona, I needed to become a keeper so I could have access to the ring, powers, and the travel I needed to go into Salvius.

The tall trees narrowed as I walked, the sun casting a glow onto the dewy logs and leaves coating the uneven ground. Peering through gaps in the trees to the left, I eyed the babbling brook leading downhill. I always walked to the meadow, but something lured me in the other direction. I'd only ventured this way a few times before, when I'd felt adventurous on my afternoon runs.

Stepping over roots that had broken through the earth, coiling in and out of hard mud and undergrowth, I moved to my left. I crunched leaves beneath my boots as I ambled forward, taking in the world of hues of green, gold, and red melting into each other as time-chiseled trees grew closer together. Through fallen branches on the ground, pink wildflowers had sprouted beneath. A mossy, ripe scent filled the woods.

I walked for hours, until the sun set enough to cast a deep pink and purple blot across the sky. After carefully tiptoeing through a patch of bluebells, I decided to turn back. I hadn't even stopped to draw as planned. It was just nice to be out in nature and clear my head.

I furrowed my brows when I noticed something out of place behind a tree, among a pile of dead leaves. Squinting, I swore it looked like a pair of legs, but they were grayish blue. As I neared the tree, my heart skipped a beat.

It was a body. There were legs poking out from leaves, which had purposely been pushed over the body. I scrunched my nose as I neared. The smell was unlike anything I'd ever smelled before. It was different than the pungent smell of death lingering around rotting animals' corpses I'd come across before on my runs. No, this was unique, a cloying, thick smell with a sweet undertone to the decay. A stench I was certain I'd never forget.

Trembling, I moved the leaves off their face, closing my eyes as I did, not ready to see what was set to greet me. When I opened them, I let out an unexpected scream. Bugs crawled out of the man's mouth, and ants had gathered on his hands and arms. As I shuddered back, my hand shot to my mouth, masking my next scream. His eyes… They were gone. The markings on his body were the same symbols I'd seen in ancient books I'd studied. They were markings of the gods.

Darkness loomed, enveloping the woods in indigo. The sunset pinched the horizon into purple. Oncoming night splashed shock through me, tingling every nerve to flight mode. I needed to get out of there, fast. Who knew if the killer was still in the area, or if they were watching me right now?

CHAPTER SIX

Someone had covered me in a blanket. Another person brought me a water I didn't drink. Night had coated our small town, but everyone was outside as if it were the middle of the day. A crowd of people surrounded the tape cordoning off the entrance to the woods. Edmund clawed through them, to the same bench I often drew sunsets from.

The body from the woods was taken away in a black bag, after the casters had come to check the area for lingering magic or spells and the protectors came to sweep the area.

"Elle!" Edmund rushed to my side, panting. "We just heard. They took their time telling us. I'm so angry, but..." He paused, seeing my expression. "That doesn't matter. How are you feeling?"

Nauseated. Fragile. Confronted with my inevitable attachment to mortality. I wanted to scream because I couldn't get the smell of death out of my nose. "I'm okay," I managed to say. I looked at his frantic gaze and tight lips. I didn't want to worry him more than he already was.

His forehead wrinkled as he wrapped an arm around me. "Let's get you home." He squeezed my shoulder. "Viktor. Maddox." He waved a hand at the crowd.

The group of people were still gathered, whispering to each other. Some were crying. Maddox stood next to Viktor. Pity softened Maddox's features, but Viktor's was different. Rage guided his expression as he glared into the woods. Maddox tapped him on the back, and he snapped back to reality.

"Elle." Maddox took wide strides until he was at my other side. "You okay?"

Viktor followed. His blue eyes met mine, and his expression softened. "I think what Elle needs is a drink."

Edmund scowled. "An alcoholic drink? Now?"

"Come on, doll."

I hesitated as he held his arm out for me to grab. "No, thank you."

Edmund smirked. "You need a hot chocolate, I think."

I nodded slowly.

"Dora's lit the fire in your room and made your bed."

I closed my eyes. She must be worried sick. She panicked at the best of times. "Let's get home." I shuddered as the stench wafted into my nose once again. A hot chocolate was welcome to remove the taste of bile in my throat, and the thought of the fire and my bed pulled me into action. I wanted to get as far away from the woods as possible.

Viktor glanced from me to Edmund. "I'll clear the way."

Edmund nodded. A loud crack sounded from the tree line behind us. I whipped my head around but was greeted with nothing but darkness. Edmund pursed his lips, and I heard an unintelligible mutter from Maddox. Viktor poised to fight, his muscles bulging under his shirt and his fingers flexing. His eyes appeared almost animalistic as he fixated on the rustling trees swaying against the wind.

Maddox and Edmund helped me to my feet. "Viktor." Edmund tilted his head in the direction of the small crowd. "Let's get her back to the house."

Viktor pulled his stare away from trees, and his sharp jawline hardened as he turned slowly. The pale light of the moon showed off his olive complexion and dark hair. The way he moved reminded me of a wolf or a similar beast ready to attack at any moment.

He created a path through the swelling group of witches, and my friends escorted me back. As we walked, I pinched my eyes shut, unable to erase the scene replaying in my mind. Where bugs crawled between blue lips and ants crawled along grey-tinted skin. Where death hung thick in the air and the absence of sound or a heartbeat was deafening.

Dora brought me hot cocoa, which I drank too quickly, making my nausea worse. I sat in front of the crackling fire, watching it wither newspapers to embers between charcoaled logs. The pale-blue walls illuminated from the shadows as the flames flicked taller. The headline of the latest murder turned to ash as I watched the last newspaper feed the fire. Tomorrow's front page would be splashed with yet another warlock found dead. This time, I was part of the story. Edmund had said something about a reporter wanting to talk to me, but he'd told them no. I was grateful. The last thing I wanted was to speak to people about what had happened.

A light rapping at the door jolted me. Glancing up, I sighed. "Viktor."

"Naomi sent Edmund a magic quill thing. She said she will be coming by in the morning. Thought I'd tell you."

"Maddox sent you up, did he?"

He stepped inside. "No. I made the choice myself, believe it or not."

"I don't need a babysitter. I'll be fine."

"I figured you'd need a friend." He sighed. "I once found a body too. More than one."

I arched an eyebrow. I chewed the inside of my lip, then relented. "Come in," I said, although he was already standing a few steps in.

He closed the door behind him and sat on the chair in front of my dresser and mirror. He looked down at where I sat on my shaggy rug on the floor, in front of the large stone fireplace. "You shouldn't have had that." He pointed at my empty mug of cocoa. "I bet it made you feel worse."

I pressed my hand against my stomach. "A little."

"I suggested alcohol because you're full of adrenaline. You're in shock, and a drink would have helped settle your nerves. Take it from an expert." He winked, then pulled out a small bottle of whiskey from his pants pocket. "Take a sip. It'll burn but help."

"I've drunk whiskey before."

"With the way Edmund reacted, I assumed you weren't allowed to drink."

"I make my own choices. I'm an adult. The legal drinking age is nineteen. I'm twenty."

He leaned back in the chair. "You should tell Edmund that. I believe he still sees you as if you are a little girl."

I rolled my eyes and drank back a swig of whiskey. It did burn, but I didn't react. I wouldn't give him the satisfaction. I exhaled what felt like fire, then placed the bottle in front of me. "How old were you when you found a body?"

"It was a long time ago." He glanced down at his hands, which were clasped together. "It was my sister. She had been… decapitated."

A shiver snaked up my spine, forcing me to shudder my shoulders.

"She was my favorite." He half-smiled, then sighed.

"Why? How did that happen?" I assumed she was murdered.

"I placed my trust in the wrong person." His jaw clenched, and his nails dug into the skin on his hand. "It's my fault."

"I'm sure that isn't true."

"It is." His tone sharpened. "Regardless, it was a long time ago."

I pictured Viktor as a little boy, finding the remains of his sister without a head. I wanted to know more, but his expression told me not to ask. "How…" I paused, not sure how to word my next question. "Was the smell bad? Did it linger?"

He nodded, looking back at me. "Yes. Is it still in your nose?"

I breathed relief. "Yes. Was it for you too?"

"Yes. Every so often over the following weeks, I swear I could still smell her. Perhaps it was psychosomatic."

"Maybe." I swallowed thickly. "I'm sorry for snapping at you this morning. I'm glad you're doing well with your spells. I was jealous."

"That's big of you to admit."

"I'm not used to competition; that's all."

Smoke tinted the air. I breathed it in, glad for the strong smell. Rain pattered down against the window, heavying by the minute. "Did the caster come today to do the spell?"

"Yes." His interest piqued. "They've begun it already, but according to Edmund, it could take weeks."

I stared at everything and nothing, lost in numbness. "In the meantime, people will continue dying."

"I believe so," he said matter-of-factly. "Don't worry, doll. Whoever's behind this will get what's coming to them."

"I hope they get sent to the underworld to be tortured for eternity by Lucius."

He chuckled, breaking the foreboding atmosphere. "I doubt the underworld is quite like that. I'm sure Lucius doesn't have the time to individually torture every soul."

"What makes you an expert?"

He shrugged. "Common sense?"

I couldn't help but smile. At least he'd taken my mind off it for a second. "I should go to bed."

"Good night, Elle."

I loved the way my name sounded from his lips but hated how I liked it. He stood, then kneeled next to me. Leaning in, I parted my lips. His cologne reminded me of pine and rain. Closing my eyes, I could feel the heat emitting from his body. I opened them again as he smirked.

"I'll be taking this." He waved the bottle of whiskey in his hand.

"Right." I cleared my throat. "The whiskey. Yes, take it."

Snapping myself out of the daze I'd unwillingly fallen in, I reminded myself that I wasn't about to let some guy have me losing my sense. I wasn't the swooning type, and I definitely wouldn't swoon for him—not my direct competition for keeper. No matter how nice he was, he was still a threat.

CHAPTER SEVEN

I loved skulls and white roses, dried flowers, and candles. My bookshelf, spread across my back wall, was beautiful. The black shelves held my favorite decorations between timeless books and first editions. I ran my fingers along the spines, delighting in the smell of parchment, old pages, and honeycomb coming from the only lit candle on the small table in front of the shelves. Sitting on the ground, I pulled out one book and placed it in my lap, hoping it would take away the nightmare of yesterday. Getting lost in another world right now would be a welcome relief.

Edmund had given me the day off. I should have been studying books on Lor and the history of Istinia and Salvius, not fiction, but I needed it and he knew it.

A curfew had been placed on the town, and the woods were cordoned off. Protectors had been stationed around various places and the different entrances to the woods. All towns in Fairwik province were on high alert. Viktor had left during the early hours of the morning and had yet to return, despite noon being around the corner.

After devouring half the book, I sat upright, rubbing the sleep from my eyes. I needed a drink and some sustenance. Walking from my bedroom to the kitchen, I jumped when a knock sounded against the front door. My nerves were unbearably on edge. Every little noise had me flinching. Peering through the peephole, I sighed. It was only Naomi wearing her red magician robes.

"I see you finished early," I said when I opened the door. "How did it go?" The call was coming up, and I was sure she would be doing everything she could to get ready.

"It was fine." Her usual wide smile was replaced with an uncertain frown and furrowed brows. "Oh, Elle." She wrapped her arms around me, pulling my head next to hers with her hand squishing my loose waves.

Breathing in a waft of peach and soap, I smiled against the skin of her shoulder. I let her hug me for a moment longer before pulling apart. I needed it, and I knew she could tell.

"We were all shocked. A body, found right near here. It's nuts. His family was alerted this morning. Poor guy."

My stomach flipped. "They identified him? So soon."

She hesitated. "Yeah. It was Bryan Normandy."

I closed my eyes as discomfort nestled into my stomach. I hadn't recognized him when I found him. It had been so many years since he and I played as kids. I hadn't been around him since we were thirteen, but placing a person to their corpse made it even more real. Bile bit up my throat, and I made a face. "I haven't checked the newspaper. Is there any news on the killer? A sighting perhaps?" I crossed my fingers.

She shook her head. "My dad wanted to meet me this morning though."

My eyebrows shot up. "How was it?"

"He just told me to be safe, and gave me this." She pulled a dagger from her bag. "Wants me to use it, just in case."

"That was decent of him, I guess."

"He's worried. I could see it. He never worries. They're not close to catching whoever it is. He said they're sending in a second caster to help with the spell. It's all hands on deck now, with it being so close to home. He said if anyone will catch them, it'll be his coven and not to worry."

I placed my hand over my stomach. Waves of nausea crept over me. "I might go lie down."

"Do you want me to come with?"

"No, it's okay. Go. I know you need to study."

"I'm here for you. I can stay."

I really did want to be alone. I just didn't want to be rude. My brain needed nothingness for a few hours. "Please. I'll magic quill you later."

After a few seconds, she let out a breathy exhale. "Fine. You let me know if you need anything." She spread out the last word, then squeezed my shoulder. "Anything."

I nodded. "Mm-hmm, I will. Promise."

***

After I woke from my nap and wolfed down a slice of toast with jam, I got a magic quill from Maddox. Ink formed words on the back of my hand, like a tattoo. With it came the tingling, like a notification. The note sizzled into nothing after a minute. It was the easiest way to communicate. There were phones, these big clunky things, but hardly anyone had one, and if they did, there was only one per coven or household.

Big meeting in study. Miss at your own detriment. Maddox.

I rolled my eyes. Everything was so dramatic when it came to him. I hurried to the study, brushing breadcrumbs from my shirt. Some made their way down my cleavage. I gave up on them as lost forever.

Edmund stood in front of the dwindling fire in the study, his hands clasped behind his back. His gaze was lost to a smoke screen of amber and yellow. Maddox sat on the ledge by the window overlooking the garden, and Dora sat, legs-crossed, on a stool next to Maddox. Benji, our sleek black cat with olive-green eyes, napped on a chair in the corner of the room, against an orange pillow.

"What's happening?"

"Good, you're here," Edmund said, turning.

Viktor walked in behind me. He must've just gotten out of the shower because his hair was still wet, curled against the side of his forehead as it dried. I took a seat on the four-legged standing sofa next to a desk, which was stacked high with papers surrounded by various stationary. Viktor dropped down next to me, draping his arm over the arm of the sofa. I breathed in his scent, cedarwood with an earthy undertone, as if he'd emerged from a rainforest.

Edmund looked at each of us in turn. He looked more stoic today than normal, if it were at all possible. His blue eyes mirrored the navy-blue of his sweatshirt. He ran his fingers along his light, groomed beard which he'd cut since last night.

"I will cut to the chase. A barrier has been placed around Fairwik and all the towns inside. The elders acted fast, but there was still a chance the perpetrator may have made their way out of Deadwood and into the forests or another town. It made more sense to cut the entire province off."

Maddox stood from the ledge, hands in his pockets. "How will goods come in and out?"

"It's only temporary," Edmund replied. "As soon as the person or persons responsible are caught, the barrier will be lifted."

"I think it's a good idea," Dora said. "We need to catch them, and now they can't escape. Like a rat, now they have their cage."

Viktor's low voice startled me as he cleared his throat. "Caged rats bite the hardest."

"Then we shall bite first." Dora said, balling her fists.

I straightened myself, then cleared my throat. "What can we do to help?"

"We can reinforce the barrier. No one can take the Serpent's Ring from its safety box. It's the only way out, the same as the barrier at the mountains. We must be on high guard. If whoever is murdering people knows the covens well, then they'll know we hold the key to being released, not to mention the dark objects we keep safe that could be used to fight back and harm. We also have spell books with ancient spells that can help trace, as you well know."

"We can strengthen our spells at the gates," I said. "I can call in Nai and the rest of her coven to create an illusion to anyone trying to come in. They won't even see our mansion is here."

A smile broke through Edmund's expressionless face. "A great idea, Elle."

"I'll send her a magic quill."

Edmund nodded. "Viktor, you've been doing well these past few days, better than anyone we've had before."

I inhaled sharply, crossing my arms over my chest. Dora shot me an empathetic frown.

Edmund continued, unaware of my discomfort. "We need everyone together as a team more than ever. We have much to guard, so I asked Alma for her permission, and we're promoting you to apprentice. You'll be able to practice more spells and will have access to more dark objects. Elle will take over with training you."

My stomach flipped. An apprentice? That meant he could put his name in at the call. He was at my level. This was unheard of. Edmund was giving him the opportunity he needed to surpass me, to take my job as keeper. Tears forced through the corners of my eyes, but I didn't let them fall. If they found out I couldn't perform the advanced spells, then they'd want Viktor to try. As much as they were my family, they needed a keeper. They were short-staffed. It was all they talked about.

"Thanks for your trust, Grandkeeper," Viktor said as he pulled a mint from his pocket.

The corner of my mouth twitched. *Suck-up.*

"How about it, Elle? Will you get Viktor up to speed while we increase security and help the casters with the tracing spell?"

No, no, no, no! "Of course I will."

"Great." Edmund turned back and explained the new security measures to the room, but I couldn't think straight.

I needed this. If I became keeper, then I could find a way back to my sister. I'd have standing in the community. I could persuade them to let my sister live here—as a server, maybe. I'd also finally belong here. Other covens had told me for as long as I could remember that human-born witches' magic was weak. Clearly that wasn't true, not when it came to Viktor.

He leaned across and I hated how good he smelled. "Looks like you and I will be spending lots of time together, doll." He winked and sat back.

My heart raced. I prayed to the gods that he wouldn't learn too fast, at least to keep a few steps behind me so I could become keeper first.

I tuned back into Edmund's speech, most of which didn't concern Viktor or me, as apprentices. We couldn't access the high-level objects needed to guard the mansion and fuel the barrier, which apparently they needed to do too.

"Dora and I will be going with Alma to the barrier. We need to ensure the magic at the barrier stays strong."

"Why would it—"

Maddox gave me a look, and I remembered what Edmund had once told me. Magic like that, to create a barrier, required so much life force, it could take down a normal person. Fortunately, Alma was an elder and could withstand it, but it took its toll. With her as the only elder in our province and the others unable to now get in, the barrier would have almost drained her. It made sense she'd need additional help from dark objects. Some were filled with so much energy, they had literally crumbled temples and towns before.

"Maddox, you will remain here and keep the spells around the mansion up."

Maddox nodded. "You got it."

Edmund looked at me. "Get that note to Naomi. Tell her to come tonight, if possible, before we leave. If she can bring her grandmagician, even better."

I nodded. I went to stand, but Viktor grabbed my hand, stopping me. Maddox walked behind Edmund and Dora. Once they were out the door, I pulled my hand back from his. "What in the underworld are you doing?"

"I needed to talk to you. Alone."

My heart raced. "What is it?"

He glanced at the door, then ensured we were in fact completely alone, save for Benji who was still cat-napping in the corner. "I need your help with something." Uncertainty laced his voice, a vulnerability I was not accustomed to since he arrived. "I need to get out of here and into the woods, tonight, but with the extra security…"

"You need a way out of here no one else knows about."

"Yes."

"You figured I'd know?"

He shrugged. "Yes."

"Why do you need to go into the woods?"

His gaze searched mine, and I felt oddly vulnerable. "To train."

"We have gardens."

"I prefer the woods. Like you."

"You're asking the girl who found a dead body to tell you a way to the same place where said dead body was found, at night, when there's a murderer on the loose?"

He scratched the back of his head. "When you put it like that…"

"It's a dumb idea, and I'm not helping you. Live a little longer and just stay inside. Maybe study, not that you need to."

He tilted his head. "Are you upset I'm an apprentice?"

I swallowed thickly. "No."

He squinted. "You are."

My cheeks flushed with heat. "I'm not. Anyway, I have things to do. Edmund gave me the day off, and I have a date with a piece of cake and a book."

He smirked. "Lucky cake… and book."

I shook my head, heat creeping over me again. My stupid body was betraying me. "Good day, Viktor."

He chuckled. "Good day?"

"I mean, well, have a good day." I shook my head and stood to leave.

"If you change your mind," he called after me, "and do want to get me out of your space and into those woods, I'll be in my room, to which you're welcome anytime."

CHAPTER EIGHT

Looking through my closet, I ran my hand along each vintage white, black, or green dress. I really needed to open up my color palette. I pulled out a pair of black pants and a flowy white top, finished the look with a black waist belt, and tied my hair back. Today would tell how good he really was.

I leaned down to stroke Benji's head. He'd curled up on my bed, taking over my pillow. He purred appreciatively, turning his head to look at me as I left my room to meet Viktor in the atrium.

Maddox locked himself in the study with every ancient book written in Lor and a high-level grimoire, trying to help as much as possible from the mansion. I, on the other hand, was stuck training Viktor until Naomi came that evening. Naomi would have come last night, but their grandmagician had been called off to do something for the caster coven, and they came first in the hierarchy.

I'd awoken with a new attitude after mulling things over last night. I decided I wouldn't hate Viktor for becoming an apprentice. It was silly for me to assume he'd become keeper any time soon. We still had years of work to go through, and no matter how good he was, he couldn't beat the volume. Learning Lor, an entire new language, would take at least three years for anyone. I'd let anxiety and doubt get the better of me. Like Dora had said, I should be glad the coven has expanded, something she'd reminded me of again when they left late last night.

"Good morning," I said.

"You're in a good mood. Considering."

Considering I found a body or considering our chat last night? My sunnier self decided he meant the former. "There is no point dwelling on the past. We have work to do."

"Dismissing the past doesn't make problems go away."

"Okay, Ensmich." I chuckled. "Oh, he's a well-known philosopher," I said, realizing he probably had no clue whom I was talking about. "Was always on about peace and understanding one's self, etcetera."

"All I'm saying is you can't run away from what happened. I know how it feels to find someone dead."

"He wasn't my sibling though. No offense."

"It doesn't matter. It leaves a mark. You're telling me you've not had one nightmare since?"

I chewed the inside of my cheek. My sleep had since been dreamless. Usually I dreamed vividly, in a sea of colors, but since the incident, everything had been gray and numb. "No."

He arched an eyebrow, disbelief in his stare. "Right."

"Are you ready to train, or are we going to stand around and chat all day?"

He gestured toward the large stone table, where a ruby ring sat. It was the piece I'd had the most trouble with since I'd arrived. "This is the blood ring. The curse inside of it causes temporary insanity. Its effects are watered down on those of us with dark magic, but it still will make you question your sanity. Your job is to, well, not go insane."

"I thought we were transferring curses to other objects."

"Nope, we have to tame some before we can keep it contained in an object, pushing the curse to see us as its master, in a way."

"Do I just put it on?"

"Yes, but please be careful." I flexed my fingers instinctively to touch him but decided against it. The ring brought back my darkest memories, and from what Viktor had told me, the curse would have a field day with him. "It will make you face your worst fears."

He eyed the glossy red. "Ah."

"Don't worry, it can't get out of here." I gestured at the reinforced walls and closed steel door. "Nor can you, should you go mad."

He smirked. "I'm sure you won't hesitate in putting me down if I get out of line."

"Not for a second."

A glint of challenge crossed his gaze. "Let's do this." When he placed the ring on his finger, his eyes changed. His pupils took on the night as their blue dissolved into blackness. His expression turned blank, and his hands trembled.

"You must remember, it isn't real. Fight through it. It's an illusion," I explained. The curse had been created by a rogue magician gone dark some hundred years ago, to especially torture gods and shapeshifters, although it also had a detrimental effect on witches. "Viktor?"

His bottom lip shook as he attempted to open his mouth, but no words left. After his doing so well at the previous tasks and ones he did alone with Edmund and Maddox, I assumed he'd pass this one with flying colors.

A scream erupted from his mouth. I leaped toward him and grabbed his wrist. The ring burned on contact, and something hot sizzled under his skin. I groaned, trying to pull the ring from his finger, but it was stuck.

He screamed again.

"Maddox!" I shouted, but it was doubtful he'd hear me from the study. He'd know what to do. "I'm trying," I told Viktor, hoping he could hear me as I pulled at the ring. "Fight through it. Don't let it win." My eyes watered as tears fell down his cheeks. He begged against something I couldn't see, and I pulled harder, letting it burn my fingers.

Finally, after what felt like an eternity, the ring slid from his finger and into my palm. The curse felt stronger than ever. It wanted more, coiling itself around me.

The memory of the night I was taken from my sister flitted into my mind. It engulfed me, and when usually I'd have the power to fight the curse, this illusion, the memory, pulled me in and kept me there, helpless. I was eleven again, and the clock chimed eight.

The woman was the first witch to be hung in over twenty years in the kingdom of Salvius, and she wouldn't be the last.

The bitter cold winter swept through the town. Orange hues illuminated the windows of thatched cottages as fires were lit in an effort to stay warm against the iciness. The comforting woodsmoke smell lingered as me and my sister were swept through the streets in a growing crowd. Together, we hurried toward the town square where conversations buzzed, alight with words of "execution" and "hanging." Many of the townsfolk white-knuckled charms that were said to repel magic, which was useless considering the witch would have already been rendered magicless, but fear often lorded over logic.

I tightened my grip on my sister's hand as we became lost somewhere in the center of the jeering townsfolk. The last of the sun's rays faded from the buildings by the time we reached the freshly erected gallows. Oil lamps flickered on as they were lit by lighters, men who were paid to light and maintain the oil lamps on the wide roads. Gray buildings surrounded them, including the town hall, the lord's mansion, and the apothecary.

"Will they hang her from her neck?" Fear sparkled in Mona's blue eyes. "Like Miss Thompson said they used to do?"

"Shush, Mona, you'll get us caught," I whispered as the crowd dispersed, scattering through the benches and statues in the large, concrete area. All of them stared at the wooden structure with long boards and four steps leading up to it. Hanging between the large beams at the top was a single noose, made from thick rope. Beneath it, a lonely stool.

I pulled Mona behind a statue of a man with a horse. My breath fogged when I spoke. "Don't do anything to draw attention to us. If we're caught here, Miss Thompson will not allow us dinner for the next week." My stomach ached at the memory of the last time I'd been forced into a short starvation, when I'd been caught in town without permission.

Mona nodded. "Okay." She was two years younger than me and the only family I had left. Freckles dotted her petite nose and rosy cheeks. Her hair reminded me of autumn, when the leaves turned from red to brown, shining a beautiful auburn. My medium-brown hair, unlike Mona's, remained frizzy no matter what I did.

"They're bringing her." Mona's eyes widened.

I moved us around the statue slowly to get a better look. I was careful to not get the attention of any of the adults, which was easy as the townsfolk were far too transfixed on the willowy woman, with jet-black long hair, to notice.

The witch wore a floor-length white dress. In the center of the flowing fabric, crimson veined out along her torso, the blood of her last victim. The newspapers had reported the capture and short trial, which had found the woman guilty, delivering the news to every doorstep in the kingdom.

Skeletal leaves floated from the bare branches overhanging the gallows. Frost covered them like body bags. Rain drizzled from the indigo sky, causing me to shiver and wish I'd brought our jackets. I'd been in a rush, sneaking out before we could be caught.

I pointed at the gallows. "Look at her." Excitement sizzled through me, racing my heart. I'd never seen one before, a witch. I'd heard so many stories of the powerful and dangerous witches and warlocks from the Istinia, and their deadly gods. I'd always secretly longed to see a witch up close.

The witch's eyes glistened with cunning as she looked out upon the crowd. Her eyes were black, her thin lips pulled tight into a grimace. For a moment, I could have sworn the woman was looking directly at me, as if she recognized me or something in me.

My stomach dipped. Pulling my gaze away, I wrapped an arm around a shaking Mona. "Do you want to go back?"

Mona shook her head. Excitement had pulled us into the night, the lure to see a witch in the flesh, but it was curiosity that kept us there.

Mona nestled into my side, her eyebrows fixed downward. "Why doesn't she use her magic to get free?"

"I told you before, Mona. They have the shackles. Every big town has a set. It stops her from being able to cast spells."

I eyed the shackles on the woman's bony hands. They were the only thing preventing her from killing them all and turning the noose into ash. They were given to Salvius from Istinia when the peace was made.

Mona pouted. "But how did they get them on her if she's so powerful?"

"I think when she was sleeping." The thought of the rotting bodies of the ladies she'd killed for their youth, their years of life, made me want to vomit. When the witch had come to our town, leaving the young wife of a farmer sliced open and drained of blood, she'd been caught quickly. The guards in our town, unlike those who lived in the small villages, were highly skilled and trained.

"I don't understand why they don't kill all the witches who are found in Salvius," Mona said, placing her thumb against her lips.

"Because they don't all commit murder and sacrifice rituals. If a witch is found in our kingdom, then they send them to Istinia. It's a part of the agreement, which protects us with the elder council. Besides." I gave Mona a watery smile. "Hardly any witches or warlocks are born of humans. It's really rare. Don't worry."

Mona puffed out her cheeks. "I wasn't worried."

The crowd jeered as the woman stepped up onto the stool. I tugged at the collar of my white blouse. No emotion crossed the witch's features as the rope was placed around her scrawny neck. The crowd grew louder until I couldn't hear myself think. I couldn't see the woman's feet, as my view was blocked by the tops of the adult's heads, but I could see her neck.

Watching as she stumbled, then the stool kicked, I gasped. Her death wasn't as fast as I'd expected. The woman's eyes bulged as she slowly suffocated from her own weight. Her body convulsed. Seconds ticked into minutes, until the witch stopped moving.

The crowd quietened.

"She is dead," the doctor announced loudly after checking her pulse.

That was awful. My next breath caught in my throat. My knees almost buckled under my weight, and I grabbed the statue to steady myself. I covered my mouth with my hand as my stomach flipped, pushing vomit into my throat. I turned to Mona, who paled at the sight of the dead witch.

"Oh, no." I looked to my left.

A man marched to us and grabbed Mona's arms, a whiff of liquor on his breath. "What're ya both doing down here? Orphans." He shook his head. "Yer coming with me. I'm taking ya back."

I grabbed the man's jacket, ready to beg him to let us go. Mona would be punished too, and I couldn't allow it, not without a fight. "Please, sir, let us go. We will go straight back." My fingers gripped into the crinkly fabric. "Sir, please!" I shouted, but he ignored me. "Let. Us. Go."

"Miss Thompson. These yours?"

My heart skipped a beat. Turning slowly, the director of our orphanage stood tight-lipped, staring down at us with thunderous pale-green eyes and her hands crossed over her chest.

Miss Thompson held her cane, bending Mona over a desk once we were back at the orphanage. My tears fell thick and fast, but no matter how much I begged, she wouldn't punish me instead. She knew this was the way to get to me. Mona had three lashings, and the skin on her back was bleeding. I couldn't breathe through my nose through the snot. I wiped it on the back of my sleeve. "Please, stop."

"This'll teach you snotty-nosed brats to sneak off again. I spent an hour looking for ya. I could've caught my death out there."

"I wished you would've," I mumbled under my breath.

Her eyes widened. She'd heard me. I immediately regretted the quip. "We'll see how your damned mouth likes this."

She lifted the cane and came down hard again and again, until Mona was screaming and I couldn't take any more. I ran at Miss Thompson and grabbed her wrist. "Mona, run."

Miss Thompson snarled, then smiled sinisterly. "Come to help ya sister, have ya? How sweet. For it, I might just cut open her pretty face with his." She laughed and held the cane up, where a piece of Mona's flesh dangled.

"No!" I screamed. A spark left my hands as a power unlike anything I'd felt coursed through my veins. My insides burned, like flames licking through my veins to the point I wanted to tear off my skin.

"Elle." Mona's voice flooded me.

Miss Thompson screamed when I felt the power leave me, momentarily bringing her to her knees. Mona stood at the other end of the room, hugging her arms around her torso and crying.

Miss Thompson shrieked once more, then stiffened. My grip, which had left half-crescent marks on her arms, loosened once she fell to the floor.

"What did you do?" Mona whispered.

The pain was gone. "I-I don't know."

"Elle, wake up." Viktor's voice pounded into my ears.

The ring tumbled from my grip. I looked up at Viktor, my chest heaving as I attempted to catch my breath.

"You okay, doll?"

A lump formed in my throat. I swallowed thickly, but it didn't move. My heart fluttered, as if there were a pair of wings in its place, and my legs felt as if they'd turned to gelatin. "Caught me off guard." I said, breathless, and took his hand to help me to my feet. I steadied myself against him. Grabbing his shoulder, surprised at how hard it was, I looked down at the ring. "I was remembering when I first felt my powers. It was…" I searched for the right words. "Eventful. It usually takes some kind of traumatic or emotionally heightened thing to happen for a witch's magic to present itself."

"What big event was it?"

I leaned my hands against my knees, closing my eyes. "Nothing crazy," I said slowly, then breathed deeply. "I need a minute." I looked him up and down. "You were worse. You were screaming and crying—"

"It was powerful. You did warn me."

"I didn't realize it was *that* powerful." I glared at the ring. "How awful was it?"

"Like reliving hundreds of suppressed dark memories."

"Ah."

We both stood in silence. I wanted to ask more, but his pained gaze told me not to.

"I'll tell Edmund we passed this one," I said after a minute.

"I want to master it."

I gave him an incredulous stare. "Are you serious? It almost killed you. I've never seen someone affected like that." I paused. "You must have so much anguish for the curse to hurt you like that. I can't expect you to go through it again."

Sadness softened his gaze. He looked at me, then at the shelves behind me, shaking the emotion off. "Let's try something else then."

"You don't want to rest?"

"I don't have time."

I parted my lips. "What do you mean?"

He glanced at me. "I mean we don't have time. We need to be a help to the coven, with this threat."

"Right," I said slowly, but something felt off. I didn't want to interrogate him over something so small, especially after what had happened, but I was surprised he was still standing and wanted to do more. The curse had even caught me off guard, and I was used to handling it. I'd been shown that memory of my sister countless times until I mastered it. It never got easier, remembering her face when it dawned on her I was a witch. I could still hear her screams as Miss Thompson hit her. The thought made my blood boil.

"What about that?" He pointed at the book of Midas. "What will you have me do?"

"Ah, that one." I smirked. At least it wouldn't hurt like the last one did. "It belonged to a king who was cursed to turn everything he touched to gold."

"Midas."

I eyed him, one eyebrow raised. "How would you know about that?"

The corner of his eye wrinkled. "I read it."

"In the last few days?"

"Maddox gave me some materials to go through."

"Oh, right." I was getting way too paranoid. "Sorry, um, well then you know. This book, while holding it, will give the same curse, until you put it down at least. The challenge is to be able to hold the book without turning anything to gold. Do not let the curse leave your fingers. You'll become the bridge that stops it from touching another object."

"I'll give it a go."

"Mmhmm. I'm going to get the box and put this ring back." My heart still hadn't slowed from the racing I'd awoken to. "You go ahead." I gestured toward the book, which was relatively harmless—to us anyway. "Don't touch any of the dark objects though. Only the stack of cards next to the herbs and the glass bottles. They can be touched to practice."

Leaning down, I hovered my hand over the ring. If I couldn't fight it anymore, then I had grown weaker than I comprehended. Magic pulsated as I cautiously touched it. Unlike before, it didn't snake into me or try to latch with might. Instead, as it had done when I'd mastered it years ago, it bent to my will. I placed it back in the box and closed the lid. I'd tell Edmund we passed the test. I couldn't put Viktor through the pain again, even if it meant he wouldn't progress faster. I knew Edmund. He'd force Viktor to keep going no matter the pain, like he had me, but I couldn't do it.

I turned after putting the ring back in one of the safes on the wall, which locked the grade two dark objects, whereas the shelves held the grade ones. The grades evaluated their danger levels, and I shuddered, thinking about the grade ten objects locked away in the vaults below the basement. I hoped I had the courage and strength to handle them once I became keeper. If I became keeper.

I turned and looked at Viktor. He held the book in one hand. Several of the cards had turned to gold, as expected, but that was it. He touched everything around him without anything else changing. He'd done it, again. I forced a smile, but the truth slid like lead into my stomach. Maybe he really did stand a chance. If I didn't put my name forward this year anyway, he really would. "How's the studying of Lor coming along?" I asked.

"Great, Maddox has been teaching me. I've learned the grammar and basic phonics."

I chewed my bottom lip. *Fuck.* I really couldn't wait another year. I had to put my name forward at the call, which meant potentially failing—probably failing.

"You've done good today. Take the rest of the day off." I needed to study if I stood half a chance. The stack of books finally beckoned me.

"I want to continue, but I guess I can take a break. I just wish I could leave here." His eyes narrowed. "Get out of these grounds for a while."

I pressed my lips into a tight line. I really needed to get ahead. Sighing, I relented. "I won't tell you how to get into the woods, because it's dangerous, but if you want to go into town or find another place to train, then I can help you sneak out." Maddox wasn't letting anyone leave until the threat had been eliminated. "Just please don't go into the woods."

"I won't. I swear."

CHAPTER NINE

I couldn't make it through one of the oversized books on our history before I fell asleep at the desk in the smaller study. It was at the back of the house, in a room big enough to fit a desk, chair, bookshelf, and houseplant. How was anyone expected to focus when the writing was so dry? I could feel my brain cells slowly dying as I forced myself to internalize fact after fact, date after date. Rubbing my temples, I sighed. Benji had jumped onto the window ledge after squeezing through the gap between the door and wall. I looked at him, tilting my head.

"What am I going to do, Benji? How am I supposed to read through twenty of these and remember everything?"

He looked at me, tilting his head, then after a few seconds looked back out the window, as if to say I was on my own with this one.

I really should have started studying sooner, but I kept putting it off because I needed to master the advanced spells and grade four dark objects. I couldn't even do that. I was close to banging my head against the table when an idea popped into my mind. It wasn't the first time, nor would it be the last. It was a terrible, terrible idea but was awfully tempting considering the circumstances. A little over a year ago, I'd come across something I shouldn't have in Edmund's office. They called it the Joker's Ball. Found by witches, retrieved by Frederick from the south of Istinia, it was a rare object made by the same dark magician who'd made the blood ring that had hurt Viktor. According to Edmund and Maddox, it could force powerful illusions onto whomever the user desired. It would be difficult to master, but if I did, I could use it to pass the exams. It would only be me, Edmund, Dora, and Maddox overseeing my passing the tests. If I could master that one object, I could delude them into believing I'd passed with flying colors. Once a keeper, I'd be able to work on the stacks of books and tricky spells without so much pressure, and there would be no way Viktor would be able to rise high enough to become a keeper before me.

I knew where Edmund kept the key. I also knew he wouldn't miss the Ball, not really. He probably wouldn't even notice it had gone. They'd stopped working on it months ago. He and Maddox had both mastered it, naturally, but they didn't use it for their own gain. Neither would cross that line, and normally I wouldn't—

"Have you seen Viktor?"

I jumped in my seat, placing my hand against my chest, where my heart raced a mile a minute. "You could have knocked!"

Maddox rolled his eyes. "I'm glad to see you're studying. For once."

"Yes, it's riveting," I snarked. "No, I haven't seen Viktor."

"I've looked everywhere." His forehead wrinkled, and he chewed on one of his nails. "Can you help me? I'm about to reinforce the spells outside but need to make sure everyone is within the limits. If not, things could get ugly."

My stomach dipped. I'd be in so much trouble if he found out I'd told Viktor how to get out of the mansion. "I think he went out onto the grounds, to practice with his throwing daggers or something. I can go look for him if you want."

"I don't know if you should go alone."

"We're nowhere near the woods, and the spells are up," I said assuredly. "I'll be okay."

After a few seconds, he relented. "I'll search the front and the attic, also the basement and vault. I doubt he'd be able to get down there. It's heavily guarded, but you never know."

"Meet back here in an hour?"

He nodded.

I grabbed my black umbrella patterned with purple skulls when I noticed the clouds forming overhead, and I walked out the back door and down the three steps to the path leading down the garden. Running between flowerbeds of whites and blues, I headed out, then between two hedges and a small garden, which was fenced off from the rest, where the pond remained stagnant. Viktor had probably gone into the woods. It was precisely where I'd said not to go, and he didn't seem the type to keep promises. He'd been far too insistent on going the other day, but nonetheless, I hoped he hadn't.

Moving through the overgrowth, past stinging nettles and through a hole in the fence, I emerged into a small collection of trees that made a U shape around the secluded garden area. The grounds were so big, Maddox and Edmund often forgot about the small area, so the magic surrounding the mansion, like a large dome guarding it from sight, was weaker here. Touching it, I absorbed some of the power and broke through. I'd told Viktor to do the same. It was the only way in and out whenever the mansion was on high alert. We had more intruders than any other coven, which was expected with the treasures we held.

My hand tingled. Wide-eyed, I brought it into my line of sight. "Not now, Naomi." A magic quill appeared, letting me know she would be leaving in a short while with her coven. It would take her at least thirty minutes to get here and maybe thirty minutes until she left, which left me an hour to find him before it was too late.

I hurried out of the collection of trees and down the bank, treading mud against my boots as I slid onto the gravel path. I was on the edge of town, and darkness was beginning to fall. I shouldn't have told him how to get out, but he was an adult who could make his own choices. *No. I am justifying my recklessness.* He was new here, therefore vulnerable as he didn't know the area, but I'd had to get him out of my hair so I could practice. If he wasn't trying to climb the ranks so quickly, I wouldn't be forced to enter my name at the call.

Ambling down the road, I rolled my eyes. Playing tug-of-war between my head and conscience was exhausting.

I bit my bottom lip as I stared at the little lights of our town. Now what? How could I possibly know where to find him? Even if he had made it into the woods, which was stupid, there was no way I was going back in there after the other day. I prayed he'd come to his senses and gone into town instead.

Hovering my finger over my hand, I whispered the incantation: *Bind the words to become one, send to Viktor...* I paused. I'd forgotten his last name, or had he even told me it? How could I send him a magic quill if I didn't know his full name? I was sure Maddox had already tried, and he, unlike me, would make sure to remember his last name. Either way, Viktor had clearly ignored any messages he'd gotten. He hadn't come back, and I was going to pay the price for it. Edmund would kill me if he found out I told Viktor how to get out. I would send him a magic quill, but we hadn't performed the joining spell yet, allowing us to exchange messages that way.

Red-bricked houses lined the road I hurried down. Banners of white hung from windows, signaling one of the many holidays we celebrated in Istinia for some historical event or another. I didn't participate in most, except for the call festival, because it was fun, and Yuletide, because I could drink as much hot cocoa as I wanted without excuse and eat all the cookies. It was my favorite time of year, and I loved winter, so it was a win-win.

Frostbitten air reached my lungs, paining them as I strode uphill, pausing every now and then to catch my breath. I licked my lips, then flicked my waves over my shoulders and out of the way. Hugging my jacket around me, I watched the sky pinken, then blot to purple as the sun's rays left the town. Fires flickering from inside the houses illuminated their windows orange.

Finally, I emerged onto a main road, where shops lined either side. Displays from different shops sparkled in the darkening night. I made a face when I took in one packed with brightly colored clothing on mannequins, and I grinned when I saw gorgeous dresses for the call festival in a shop called Mystique. My stomach rumbled when I paused in front of a local bakery, where jams and honeys lined the display. Behind it, glass cases filled with freshly baked breads, donuts, cakes, and cookies, beckoned me. I had several skal on me, enough to buy some dinner—not that cake was dinner, as I'd been lectured on before. Still, the smell of cinnamon, flour, and gingerbread wafted from the shop.

A couple of caster girls looked at me as they passed. Fortunately, I hadn't seen them before, so they ignored me and made their way to the Mystique shop.

Fairy lights illuminated, over the shops' striped awnings and all the way down the town's center. The sky turned black, shining out dots of silver and white around the quarter moon. I peered around, frowning as I left the smell of the bakery behind me. I needed to find Viktor. He was my priority.

After a half hour of searching, I turned back. There was nothing more I could do, and I didn't want to be trapped out when Maddox and the magician coven put up new barriers. My little get-out spot at the back of the gardens probably wouldn't work after the magician's magic was placed over the mansion.

I pulled my jacket tighter around me, gripping my umbrella, and hurried back up the path leading to home. I had to pass near the entrance to the woods again, on the way back. My stomach churned as the tree line became visible. Evergreen dotted into the distance as the vast forest and woods before it stretched into oblivion. The hairs on the back of my neck stood erect. The bench where I'd sat after finding the body still had the blanket discarded on it that had been wrapped around me.

"Viktor!" I gasped, my eyes bulging as his six-foot-two figure emerged from the blackness between the trees. He was covered in mud; his hair was wet and curled around his ears. He looked over at me, his eyebrows pointing downward.

"You shouldn't be out here," he barked, and I took a step back. He strode toward me and grabbed my wrist. "It's dangerous."

My brain faltered. How was I the bad guy here? "You went into the woods when you swore you wouldn't. I had to come find you, Maddox is doing another spell to guard the coven, and the magicians are on their way over. In fact"—I looked at my watch—"they're probably already on their way. You would have been trapped outside."

"Thanks for the concern, but I can take care of myself, but whoever the murderer is, you are their target. All the victims were young women, actually, except for the last, who was—"

"A boy, I know. I remember." I scowled.

"My point is you need to be careful. If I knew you'd come after me, I wouldn't have gone."

"You shouldn't have anyway, you crazy person." I looked him up and down. "What happened to you?"

He looked at his mud-soaked shirt. "I slipped. Let's head back. It's getting late." He looked over his shoulder as he led me away.

*****

Maddox was about to have a fit when we arrived back. I heard him in the kitchen as we snuck through the hallway. I'd kept us out of sight, sneaking Viktor back to my room before anyone could see the state he was in. Hovering my fingers over my hand and whispering the incantation, I sent a quill to Maddox, telling him I'd be back soon and found Viktor in the garden.

I closed the door behind us, panting. "I need to start running more again. I'm so unfit."

"You're fine." He slicked off his white shirt, which was now mostly brown, revealing his abs and tanned torso. My heartbeat crept faster as he tossed the shirt over my dresser. "I should have gone to my room."

"Which is next to Maddox's."

He arched an eyebrow. "Who's in the kitchen."

I closed my eyes. I was such a dumbass. "You're right."

He grinned. "I figured you were looking for a reason to get me into your room. You could have just asked."

I blushed, mentally kicking myself for allowing it to happen. Turning away so he couldn't see my red cheeks,

I cleared my throat. "That's not what happened. Anyway, I'll, uh, go get you clothes."

"I could just go by myself."

I shook my head. "Of course. My brain clearly isn't working."

He chuckled. "See ya in a bit." He grabbed his shirt from the dresser, then paused in the doorway. "Unless you want me to stay, Elle."

I hate-loved the way he said my name. "No. I'll meet you downstairs."

Once he left, I ran my hands down my face, pulling the skin under my eyes. "Get it together, Elle. What in the underworld." I shrugged off my jacket and tied back my hair.

I heard Maddox and Naomi talking as I walked toward the front door. They'd all gathered out front, on the gravel where the shiny automobile stood. Everyone wanted one, but few could afford such luxuries. This one belonged to the grandmagician of the magician coven, Felix Astotle. His eyes were bigger than those of anyone I'd ever met, reminding me more of a cat than a human. His bright-orange hair made him difficult to forget.

"Eleanor. How are you this evening?"

"Grandmagician Felix, it's wonderful to see you again. Thank you for coming."

"The pleasure is ours." He kissed my hand, and I smiled awkwardly. I never knew what to do when he did that. He was the definition of odd though. I was glad his greetings never caught on.

"Where would you all like us to begin? I would like to first place the Felician spell of Lure."

"I haven't heard of it," I said.

Maddox walked up beside me. "It's a Felix original. Isn't that right, old friend?"

"Yes, it is." Felix's cheeks balled.

Maddox pointed at the gargoyle statues. "Start there and go all the way back to the tree line at the back of the grounds and between those hedges. In fact, I'll walk you." Maddox glanced at me before leaving to escort Felix. "I thought you messaged saying Viktor was back."

"He is." I gulped. "He's coming. He went to his room."

"You took over an hour to search the gardens." He didn't look convinced.

My stomach swirled. "He found some hidden corner and was reading."

"Reading?"

"Yes. One of the history books you showed him."

A smile crept on his face. "Good, well, I will be back then."

"See you."

I waved Naomi over once Maddox and Felix were gone. "Thanks for coming."

She beamed. "Always."

"You look so professional in your robes."

She twirled them around herself. The red complemented her honey-brown eyes and black curls. "They're new. The coven kind of rebranded. Felix's idea."

I laughed. "I bet."

She giggled. "Where's Viktor?"

"Getting dressed."

She raised her eyebrows, and I rolled my eyes. "Not like that. He got dirty in the garden."

She held her spell book to her chest, looking up as if lost in a dream. "I'm sure he did."

I hit her arm lightly. "Stop."

"How's the spell coming along with the caster?"

I shrugged. "It's not. They stopped it once Edmund and Dora left, due to security measures."

"So no one can come in?"

"Nope. Once you're done here, I won't be able to see you for however long."

"No."

"Yes. It sucks."

Her frown tugged at the corners until she grinned.

I shook my head. "What?"

She bit her lip. "I mean, at least you'll get to spend all that alone time with Viktor. How long are Edmund and Dora gone for?"

"I'm not interested in spending time alone with him."

"Liar." She winked, then looked behind me. "Viktor, hi."

He walked up beside me, leaned down, and hugged her. "What are you two talking about?"

"You."

I flushed red. "She's joking."

She gasped. "Am not."

"She is." I gave her a *shut it* stare, then turned toward Viktor. "Maddox has gone to help Felix with—oh, wait." I noticed Craig walking up the path. "Look who's turned up finally. It's Nai's crush." I smirked. "They both like each other, but they won't admit it to the other, so we've all been stuck watching the same season for the last four years."

Naomi whipped her head around, then turned back to face me, her cheeks darker. "Don't, Elle. Please," she whispered. "He doesn't like me in that way, and—" She looked behind her. "He's coming. Shush, don't say a word."

Viktor and I exchanged amused looks as Craig approached us. His black hair was tied back into a knot at the back of his head, and his bright-amber eyes matched his robes. His thin lips stretched into a smile when he saw me. "Elle, it's been ages."

"It's been a month." I laughed and hugged him. "You're late."

"Nah, you're all just early."

I rolled my eyes. "It's funny, we were just talking about you."

Naomi glared at me. If looks could kill, I'd be dead. It served her right for doing it to me when Viktor came outside.

Craig scratched the back of his neck. "All good things, I hope."

"Always good things when Nai and I talk about you."

Naomi cleared her throat. "We should join Felix."

"Right, uh, I'll find you later, Elle." He looked at me hopefully before being dragged away by Naomi.

Once they were gone, Viktor leaned toward my ear, sending a tingle through my skull. "Careful, doll. He likes you."

My heart skipped a beat. Had I heard right? "What, Craig? No. No, no."

"He does. I can tell. I'm a guy, trust me."

"He likes Nai."

He shook his head. "Not like that. It's all in the body language. Don't worry, I can see you don't like him. You were standing far too close to me to notice him."

"You're so full of yourself."

"I guess a little."

I placed a hand on my hip. "Well, I'm not amused."

He held his index finger and thumb close together. "You are a tiny bit."

I crossed my arms over my chest. "You're wrong about Craig."

"I'm never wrong, but you're welcome to stay in denial. Your friend can do better than him anyway. She's beautiful."

My stomach dipped. Did Viktor like her? I should be happy. She clearly crushed on him, but my heart still ached a little. Stupid heart. "She is. Maybe you should ask her out."

He chuckled. "I'm good; plus, I'm not the girlfriend kind of guy. I don't imagine you'd want me to have a fling with your best friend."

My stomach settled. "No, not a fling." *Not anything.* The thought flashed into my mind, unwelcome. "I'm going inside. I'm hungry."

"I'll join you."

Maddox appeared from around the gate with Felix. "Elle, Viktor. I'm letting everyone stay tonight. It's late, so I figured we'd make a night of it, and they can leave tomorrow."

I looked Felix up and down. I'm sure he had one more reason for this spur-of-the-moment sleepover. After what Viktor had said about Craig, the last thing I wanted was for them to spend the night. Not that I fully believed it but he had always been eager to hang out with me, and the more I thought about it, the more the truth seeped in.

"Oh, Nai." I sighed when I saw her round the same corner, with Craig, both laughing. He stopped and waved when he saw me.

I didn't wave back.

CHAPTER TEN

Viktor went to his room. I wished I could go to mine too, but Naomi was here, and I wanted to spend time with her, even if it meant staying with Craig and the two other male magicians we were stuck with. Felix and Maddox had gone to the study to read. They'd tried to hide their flirting, but it was obvious. I'd have thought it cute if it wasn't for Maddox's ex, Aaron, who we all liked. I'd hoped they'd get back together, but it didn't seem like they would now.

I leaned forward, rolling my aching shoulders as we all sat in a circle on the floor in the living room. The red ornate rug warmed the chill of the wood floor, and the fire, set under the oval stone-framed mirror, hissed and crackled as embers floated out from the grate.

"Let's drink." Craig shook a bottle of whiskey in his hand, grinning. "Swiped it from the cabinet upstairs."

"Maddox is going to kill you," I said with a clenched smile.

He shrugged. "Worth it."

Naomi leaned in his direction. "Oh it's fine, Elle. He won't even notice it's gone."

My eyebrows knitted together. She knew he would, but of course it was for Craig, so anything went. Viktor's little revelation had put me on edge. I could see the truths, but a part of me hoped he was wrong.

"Let's play cards," one of the men said. I couldn't remember their names. I think one was called Eric. They looked around eighteen years old, or not far off. "Poker?"

Naomi shot me doe eyes. I sighed. "Fine, I'll play."

Craig poured shots for himself and Naomi as cards were dealt. He tried to give me one, but I refused.

She downed one, then coughed. "Ohhh. This is fun."

"I'll bet one more skal," one of the magicians said.

I had a bad hand so I folded. The one who bet a skal won, and Craig poured more shots.

"Slow down." I clicked my tongue. "You don't want to vomit."

"I'll slow it down if you actually drink *one*." He grinned at me, urging one in my direction.

Naomi gave me a look. "Come on, Elle."

I let out a long exhale. "One." I took the shot glass. "Then I'm done."

The corner of his mouth lifted. "Sure."

An hour later, I was ten skal up and three shots in. I pushed the coins into my pockets. "I'm heading to bed."

Naomi rolled her eyes. "It's ten. You never go bed this early."

"I'm tired," I lied. I wanted to get away from Craig stealing glances at me when Naomi was talking to one of the other guys.

Naomi drummed her fingers against the floor. "I bet if I persuaded Viktor to come down, you'd have a change of heart."

"Not true." I placed a finger in the air.

Craig was six shots in and sloppy. His hair had come loose from the tie and hung around his shoulders, and the collar beneath his robes was half up, half down. "One more drink, Ellie."

I grimaced. Only one other person called me Ellie in my life. "Don't call me that."

Naomi laughed, grabbing my arm as she did. "Please." She elongated the word, pulling me back toward the floor.

"I…" I paused. What could I say? "I need to study tomorrow."

She let go of my arm, then crossed hers over her chest. "Since when do you suddenly care about studying?"

"I'm going to put my name forward at the call," I announced.

Viktor rounded the corner. "What's going on here then?" He leaned in the doorway, grinning with amusement.

"Yay." She clapped her hands together, hurrying to Viktor. She grabbed his arm and pulled him into the room. "Come play with us."

Craig's smile faltered. Viktor's appearance wasn't entirely unwelcome. "Come in," he said, deflated.

He looked at me. "Do you want me to stay, doll?"

"Elle was talking about going to bed." Naomi rolled her eyes. "She needs to study tomorrow. Oh." She squeaked. "The call. My brain." She rolled a finger next to her temple. "I think I'm a little drunk."

"You think?" I mumbled quietly, and Viktor laughed.

She beamed. "I'm so happy you're putting your name forward. See, it wasn't that hard."

Viktor's eyebrows raised. "Name forward for what?"

I glared at her, shaking my head.

"The call," she announced, clearly not getting my non-verbal warning. I didn't want him to know. Honestly, I didn't want to give him any ideas to go ahead with it himself.

"What's the call?"

Craig stood, almost stumbling, and caught himself by grabbing the mantel above the fire. "It means you can put your name forward to promote within the coven and become a proper member."

"Only apprentices can do it," Naomi said.

"Which Viktor now is."

She mouthed a *wow* in my direction.

"Impressive, man," Craig said. "You've not been here long. How did—*ope.*" He stumbled, then caught himself again. "Ah, yes, sorry. How did you manage it?"

"I'm just lucky I guess."

That was unexpectedly modest. He was brilliant, but I wasn't about to stroke his ego.

"Lucky?" Naomi scoffed. "You must be like, really good if Edmund promoted you so fast. You're only a short jump away from keeper."

Craig cleared his throat. "Man, you should put your name in that call too."

I glared at Craig. "He's drunk too much." My voice dripped with anger. "It's a terrible idea. You need to learn like, a lot to pass, so it wouldn't be a good idea this year. Maybe next year. There's no way you could digest all the knowledge that fast."

Naomi laughed. The high-pitched shriek hurt my ears. She downed another shot, then looked at the window. "We should go out."

"We can't." I pointed at the magic bubble guarding the house, outside the window. "We're stuck in here. Well, you guys can leave tomorrow, but that's it."

Naomi poked my side. "Then you'll be here all alone with…" She brought her whiskey-pinched breath to my cheek and whispered loud enough for everyone to hear. "Viktor. Maybe you two can—"

"Okay." I stepped away, letting her topple a little. "I think I've had enough for one night. See you all tomorrow."

I left the room, my cheeks burning as I marched down the hallway and into a side room. Stopping to catch my breath against a side table, I pressed my hands against my knees. I hated being around drunk people.

Breathless pants greeted me, in the form of Craig. He stumbled through the doorway and into the small, dimly lit room. "Ellie."

"What is it, Craig?"

"I need, wait, needed to tell you something." His voice cracked. He placed the bottle, which he'd brought with him, on the table and closed in on me. I stepped back until there was no more space between me and the wall. "Is important." His words slurred.

"Now is not the time." I ushered him back, but he didn't move.

Craig pressed me against the wall, pushing his body against mine. The stench of whiskey lingered around his mouth as he brought his lips to mine.

"Craig, stop."

"I like you." He closed his lips before a burp could come out.

I scrunched my nose. "No, you don't."

His eyebrows knitted together. "I do. I've wanted to tell you for years, but I couldn't." His eyes glazed as he looked at me. "All I needed was some liquid courage."

"Craig, I know you're drunk and not yourself, which is why I haven't beat your ass, but if you don't get away from me in the next three seconds, I will hurt you."

"Don't be like that. I know you want me too. I could see it when you looked at me. You flirted."

I clicked my tongue. "I was friendly. Because of Nai."

"If that's why you're scared to do this, know I don't like her like that. Not like you." He moved his lips toward me again, and I moved to push him back when a gasp stopped me in my tracks.

"What is this?"

I whipped my head around and saw Naomi in the doorway. Tears glossed her big brown eyes. "Are you... kissing?" Fury guided her tone.

Pain shot through my chest. "Gods no. I'm not interested in him in the slightest."

She looked us up and down. "Certainly looks like it."

I rolled my eyes back toward Craig, grinding my teeth. I pushed him off me, with more force than I expected, and he toppled back and landed on his ass. I was grateful for

Edmund's training now. It did come in handy. "He came on to me," I explained. "I'm sorry. I told him no."

"You wanted it too," Craig said from the floor. "Tell her. Sorry, Naomi, but we like each other."

My eyes widened. "You fucking liar. I never wanted it, and I don't like you." I shook my head. "Delusional," I mumbled under my breath.

Naomi's bottom lip trembled. She clasped her shaking fingers as her tears fell thick but slowly down her cheeks, dragging her makeup with them. "Some best friend and—" She looked at Craig. "Forget it."

She turned on her heel and ran. I went to go after her but Craig vomited all over Edmund's expensive rug. I pinched my nose as the stench of regurgitated alcohol and lunch hit my nostrils.

"What's wrong?" A voice sounded from the hallway as Naomi hightailed it down the corridor. Footsteps sounded toward the door, then Viktor appeared. He looked from me to Craig to the vomit. "I missed something. Why was she crying?"

I pressed my lips into a hard line. "You did, and asshat in there ruined everything!"

"Did he hurt you? Are you okay?"

"I am now." I stared at Craig as he threw up again. "He can't handle his drink."

"Should we help him?"

I gritted my teeth. "No. I took care of him anyway."

I stormed past Viktor and into the hallway. Naomi probably hated me. The look in her eyes made me feel nauseated. I could see it, the look of absolute betrayal.

Years of imagining her and Craig shattered in an instant. For it to be with me too... I rubbed my temples.

Viktor cleared his throat. "I think you need to find your friend."

I nodded slowly. "I think you're right."

After twenty minutes of looking, I found Naomi curled up on my bed, crying into a pillow. She pulled my blue comforter around her and rubbed mascara onto my fresh sheets. My room was the last place I thought she'd go. I tapped on my open door. "Nai." I lulled my voice, softening my tone. "Can I come in?"

"No."

It was my room, but she was delicate. "I never came onto him, I promise. I don't like him. I don't want him."

She punched my pillow and sat up. "It didn't look like that. He likes you and wants to be with you."

"I know you're hurt."

"Hurt doesn't begin to cover it. You looked like you were going to kiss him."

"I really, really wasn't. He cornered me, and I should've pushed him away first, but I felt bad. He was drunk and not himself, but still."

"This is all your fault. You always want what you can't have, and you had to have my Craig." Venom dripped from her words. Her posture stiffened, and her fingers curled around the corner of my comforter. "You can't stand me having something of my own."

"That's not true. I don't want what I can't have."

She scoffed. "Edmund says the coven can't have something, but you always push for it, and he gives you whatever you want. That's just the start of it. You're a…"

"Go on," I dared.

She was scathing. "A bitch."

Tears pushed through the corners of my eyes. "I know you're hurt right now, so I'll forgive you tomorrow when you come to your damned senses. I didn't come onto Craig, who doesn't deserve you anyway." I turned on my heel. "You can have my room tonight. Try not to throw up on anything." I slammed the door behind me and let my tears fall. *She didn't mean it*, I told myself over and over as I ambled the hallways. When I reached Edmund's room, I cursed under my breath. He'd locked it, and I knew Dora always locked hers. I eyed the spare room and found the two magicians, one asleep on the bed and the other on the sofa. Sighing, I walked to the other spare room and found Craig. I didn't dare wake him.

The rest of the rooms were filled with dark objects or locked. It was nearing midnight. I found the bottle of whiskey and took a few swigs. Everything had gone to crap, and I needed something to take the edge off things. I made my way to the study. Perhaps Maddox was still up. Maybe he'd let me steal his room. Unlikely. He loved his bed as much as I loved mine.

"There's another spell!" Maddox exclaimed as I all but fell into the study.

Felix leaned over his shoulder, reading the book in front of them. He looked up from his book. "Elle. You're just in time." He waved me over. "I found this. They're doing sacrifices to access darker magic. That's how the killer is cloaking themselves."

The alcohol hazed my vision. I did my best to internalize his words, but everything was a little fuzzy. "Great, I'll tell Edmund."

The corners of his eyes wrinkled. "By magic quill?"

"Oh, right, Edmund's not here. Yeah. Magic quill."

"You've been drinking," he stated.

Felix shook his head. "Probably Eric. He's always getting into my liquor."

"It was Craig," I said, tattling unapologetically. "He also threw up all over Edmund's rug—oh, and tried to make out with me and Nai found us. Now she thinks I came onto him, which I did not and would not."

He blew out a whistle, leaning back in the wood chair. "Seems I missed all the good drama."

Felix flexed his fingers. "I will see to it Craig is punished."

I glanced at the book. "That's amazing, what you found."

"I will let Edmund know. Go sleep it off, Elle."

I pressed my lips together. "Right."

I moved to the door and heard Maddox whispering to Felix. "There will be more murders yet. If I'm right, then the intricate tracing spell we were doing wouldn't have helped. The amount of blood needed to keep the strength of this type of cloaking spell up is astronomical. It only makes you wonder what the person is so desperate to hide they'd kill this many people."

"Or," Felix said, "they enjoy killing, and the spell only helps them continue."

His last sentence sent a shiver down my spine. "I'm going to bed," I said, although I had no idea where bed was. I clicked the door shut behind me and walked up the hall. The sofa it was.

I was surprised to see Viktor still awake, sitting in the living room where discarded cards covered the rug.

"Did you find her?"

"Hmm? Oh, Nai. She's in my room, ruining my sheets and hating me."

He arched a dark eyebrow. "What *did* happen?"

"Craig made a move on me. I pushed him off. Naomi thought I wanted him. She's hurt because she's had a crush on him since forever, and now I'm the bad guy." I slumped down next to him.

"Want a drink? I can tell you all about being the bad guy." He smirked.

My stomach swirled. "I've had enough for one night."

"Coffee? Tea? Wait, hot cocoa. Isn't that your favorite?"

"Very observant of you."

He leaned back against the sofa cushions. "We can move to the kitchen."

"I'm actually kinda tired."

"Good idea. It's been a night."

I pursed my lips. "Actually, you're sitting on my bed."

He glanced down. "Ah, right. Naomi is in your bed."

"Yep, and all the spare rooms are taken. Edmund's is locked."

"I have a bed."

My heart raced. "I don't imagine you've been sleeping on the floor."

"You can have it. I'll crash on the sofa."

"I can't do that."

"You can and you will. Come on." He helped me up. The whiskey was hitting me hard. "Let's get you to bed."

"Wait." I paused, the alcohol making me way braver than I normally was. Buzzing ran under my skin. "Please don't put your name in at the call, if you were thinking about it."

"I told you before, doll, I have to do what's best for me."

"I need this." I let tears gloss my eyes. I didn't care how I looked anymore. "The sister I left behind in Salvius, she needs me. I'm the only family she has left, and being keeper means I might be able to get to her, maybe even bring her here. Also, everyone likes and accepts you here. I've never been accepted by the other covens, except for the magicians. My magic's always been looked at as weak because I'm human-born, like you."

He wrapped his arm around my waist as I stumbled forward.

"Please don't. I need this. Promise me."

"Look…"

"Don't make excuses. You can wait. Another slot will open in time. Oh, no. I feel a little sick."

"Okay, doll. Let's get you to bed. If you're going to throw up, let me know."

That okay was all I needed. I relaxed and walked with him to his room.

CHAPTER ELEVEN

I awoke in one of his white shirts. Panicked, I felt the sheets next to me, but he wasn't there. Last night's events rushed back to me. Naomi. My heart pattered to the sound of the rain hammering down outside. What time was it? The sky had barely blued from behind the curtains.

Viktor rolled his shoulders back, stretching his arms out. I remembered now; he'd fallen asleep on the sofa in here. I'd forgotten he had one in his room. I flattened my hair, which had gone frizzy from tossing and turning against his sheets. I sniffed the collar of his shirt after getting a whiff of cedarwood. I even smelled like him.

"You are truly devastating in my shirt."

"Oh, uh." I flustered, attempting to push my hair back and detangle it with my fingers. I recalled him giving me a shirt to wear when we noticed some of Craig's vomit had made its way onto my clothes last night. I buried my head in my hands. "Last night was awful."

"I've seen worse. Naomi will come around. Don't worry."

I swallowed thickly. "I should go find her, but gah." I tugged at his shirt. "If anyone sees me in this, they'll think we slept together."

He moved toward the bed. His white top hugged his muscles. I breathed through parted lips, then scrunched my nose. My breath smelled like whiskey. I didn't want to talk near him. He sat on the edge, dipping the mattress. "I've been thinking about what you said about your sister. You don't need to be a keeper to go to her. You can find a way into Salvius. The barrier can be disabled with the very object you're tasked with guarding."

"I won't steal the Serpent's Ring." I didn't ask how he knew about it but guessed Frederick had told him when he used it.

"No one would blame you. Edmund and Dora are gone and won't return yet, and Maddox is busy with his new lover."

"Ah, Felix. Oh." I perked up. "Maddox actually found out something about the murderer last night. About the cloaking spell."

His shoulders tensed. "What was it?"

"They are killing people to cloak themselves. Blood can be used to fuel powerful spells, or so I've read, and Maddox said he thinks that's what they're doing and there will be more killings yet. So the tracing ritual Edmund was attempting to do wouldn't have worked anyway."

"Did he say if he found a way to break the spell?"

"No. Only that he would let Edmund know."

"Elle." He hesitated. "I've been meaning to ask you something. What do you know about the vaults down below the—"

Both our hands tingled. It was a magic quill from Maddox.

Downstairs. Now.

Viktor sighed. "I'm going to regret doing that joining spell with him, aren't I?"

I couldn't help but smile. "He's not too much of a pain with sending quills."

"Good."

I eyed a green glass chess set over by his closet. "You like to play."

He looked over his shoulder, his eyebrows raising. "Yes, I do. Do you play?"

"I have." I shrugged. "I prefer to read or draw."

"We should have a game sometime."

My eyes narrowed. "Maybe, but for now, we should go downstairs before Maddox has a panic attack."

It felt good to brush my teeth and be back in my own clothes, a black top with frills and a high-waisted dark-green skirt that stopped just below my thighs. I brushed my hair back, but it was too wild.

When I reached the kitchen, I breathed in the smell of fresh coffee.

Maddox and Felix stood side-by-side, weary-eyed. Naomi's hair stuck out at different angles, her curls crooked in places. Craig looked like he'd been dragged from a lake.

"Good, you're all here." Maddox's hardened stare landed on me. "Finally. What took you so long?"

Viktor's gaze found mine, then trailed along my body as he undressed me with his bedroom eyes. I glanced down, realizing my outfit might not have been the best choice, considering what had happened last night. I could practically feel Naomi's stare burning into me.

He continued. "Magicians, you will be leaving this morning with Felix. We thank you for your help."

I heard a meow behind us and saw Benji run in, looking for the bowl of food I'd forgotten to put out.

"Due to the new security measures, the call festival has been canceled."

Relief flooded me. I wasn't ready anyway.

Maddox continued. "Anyone willing to put their name forward can today, with me." He gave me a look. "The same goes to you four, with Felix." He nodded toward Naomi and the others. I couldn't help but notice she was standing with her back toward Craig. "Before we all depart, who will be putting their names forward in my coven?" He looked at me, smiling. "Elle?"

I was about to decline. Without Viktor in the running, I didn't need to.

"I will." Viktor's voice splashed shock through me.

"Are you sure?" Maddox hesitated. "You need to pass completely, and you haven't touched on the grade two curses."

"I'm sure."

"You will need to wait three years when you fail," he explained.

"If I fail," Viktor said, correcting him. "I'll be formally putting my name forward."

My mouth parted. That liar. He'd told me he wouldn't. He was trying to steal my spot, and he knew how much I had riding on it.

A lump formed in my throat as Maddox wrote Viktor's name on the official parchment. He looked at me. "I assume you will be too."

"Yes." I managed to say, my voice croaking at the end. I cleared my throat. Naomi wouldn't even look at me, and Craig looked sheepishly at the ground.

Naomi and Craig put their names forward, and the two others were told they'd become apprentices from students if Naomi and Craig passed.

"We'll be off then." Felix hovered around Maddox for an extra moment.

Maddox gave him a smile, then turned and left. He was known for being cold the morning after. Why did I think Felix would be any different?

"See you," Maddox said.

"Nai," I called as she reached the back door.

She looked back over her shoulder, tears in her eyes. "Don't speak to me again."

I watched after her, slack-jawed. It was a good thing Craig left when he had because I wanted to punch him for doing this. How could she seriously think I had anything to do with Craig's move on me? I'd never shown interest in him, although he seemed to think different.

Once they were out of the magic barrier, I closed the back door.

Maddox chewed on his bottom lip. "You both have four days to prepare for the test."

"Four days?" I gasped, wide-eyed. "Edmund isn't even back and—"

"Edmund has given me permission to hold the test. Alma trusts me, and we need another keeper with everything going on. I wouldn't worry, Elle." His gaze wandered to Viktor. "You don't have any competition. Viktor is too inexperienced. Sorry, I'm just being real with you. Elle's got this."

"I disagree," Viktor drawled. "Under your guidance, Maddox, I think I can achieve anything."

Maddox couldn't help but smile, and I hated Viktor for it.

I picked the lock to Edmund's office, breathing relief when it clicked open. I'd found a handy trick in one of the normal books in this place. With the door clicked shut behind me, I breathed in the musky air. I needed the Joker's Ball.

It was wrong to cheat, but I'd been left with no choice. As much as I wanted to believe Maddox, that Viktor was too inexperienced, his ability to learn quickly and soak in information, plus his ability with curses, left me questioning if he would beat me. I already struggled with the advanced curses, and I had barely touched the history books. My Lor was a little rusty. I hadn't kept on top of it like I should've.

This was all Viktor's fault. I'd told him something I hadn't told anyone, about my sister and why I wanted to be a keeper so badly. He took my vulnerability and discarded it like it were nothing. This, and Naomi hating me, was too much. My tears threatened to break through again, but I kept myself in check. I had a way out of this. The Joker's Ball. If I could just find it. Please, please, please tell me he didn't lock it away. Then, once Naomi had time to calm down, I'd force Craig to tell her what had really happened and I'd have my best friend back. Until then, no one could get in or out of the mansion, so I needed to focus on the test. Four days was nothing. It went against my favor, as it was too short a time for me to master everything, let alone Viktor.

I searched through the clutter in the drawers of Edmund's fancy mahogany dresser, then moved to the cabinets. Nothing there either. I bet he'd locked it in one of the rooms with wall safes. Speaking of, I believed he had a safe in here if I remembered rightly. Ah. Behind the painting of the river and ducks was the code-locked safe. I'd bet my skal it was in there.

Footsteps sounded outside, and I held my breath. Once the footsteps faded into the distance, I left the room. I'd come back when it was night.

***

Benji curled up next to me as I read through a history book. I had taken it into the living room and lit the fire into dancing flames, then had plopped myself onto the sofa.

Just in case the Joker's Ball failed, it wouldn't hurt to study. I dragged my gaze along the thin pages. I swear whoever wrote this was tasked with fitting as many words on a page in tiny text as possible. At least they'd modernized the wording. Still, I was going to be there forever.

Benji meowed.

"Sorry I forgot to feed you this morning."

He gave me an accusatory look.

"Hey, I put extra in your bowl for dinner."

He purred up against my thigh, calming me as I gruelled over the forgotten ages. It wasn't until I reached the chapter about the gods when I perked up. Something interesting.

A millennium before our nineteenth century, Lucius and Estia ruled the only realm where souls of the dead were welcomed to spend their eternities exploring a realm so vastly bigger than ours, where disease, death, and hatred did not wander or threaten; the otherworld.

I skimmed several paragraphs about blissful afterlife until I got to the good stuff.

Vengeful spirits of the dead created demons who lurked our world, preying on weak souls to haunt and possess, wreaking havoc on families, and unleashing more plagues and despair. Some practitioners of magic grew darker as gambling, lustfulness, and deadly sins plagued our world, feeding the demons. The gods, the children of Estia and Lucius, were sent to cleanse it. They were Leda, the Goddess of the Hunt, Thalia, the Goddess of the Afterlife and Protector of the Dead, Aziel, the God of Thunder, and Raiden, the God of Creatures. Unlike their parents, their children were given physical forms and therefore could mate with mortals and enjoy the pleasures of the flesh. They were granted with eternal youth and a lifespan that could stretch over millennia.

Benji jumped up, his ears perking as he did. Something rustled the bushes outside. "It's just the wind, silly cat." I stroked him down as he fixated on the window, until he calmed, settling again. "Hush, it's getting good." I ran my finger down to where I had left off and devoured the words. *Who knew history could be so fascinating?* This part of it anyway.

The gods lavished in their new lives with mortals, partaking in sins and having children with humans, mostly Thalia, who created four demigod children. Estia and Lucius's children cut themselves off from their parents, refusing to return to the otherworld.

The number of demons grew, more witches and warlocks turned to darker magics, and the once-pure world turned to one of sin. Lucius, God of Justice and father to Leda, Thalia, Aziel and Raiden, created the underworld, a place separated from the otherworld where demons could be trapped and those with sinful souls would be sent, once the darkness in their hearts was weighed upon death.

The gods, who spoke in their native tongue, Lor, taught the language to Istinia. Eventually, they were individually locked in their own prison realms, after Leda was killed and another took her place.

"What are you reading?"

I looked over the top of my book. Viktor held my stare. "You."

He smirked. "There's a book about me?"

"Hilarious." I gritted my teeth. "Go be funny somewhere else because I don't want to even see you right now."

"I knew you'd be mad." He leaned against the doorway. "I came to explain."

I put my hand up to stop him. "No explanation needed. You owe me nothing. I know your type. You're out for yourself and don't care who you hurt to get there. Trust me, it's noted. You can go now."

"Despite what you think, I do care that I hurt you."

Huffing, I closed the book, dropping it on my lap. "That's worse, considering you did it anyway."

"It's not like that." He sighed. "It's a long story."

I clasped my hands atop the cover. "I have all night."

Benji meowed, looking around, jumped off the sofa, and hightailed it out of there. I couldn't blame him. Things were about to get ugly.

"You don't need to be a keeper to get your sister back. I've thought about it, and—"

"No." I was seething. "Don't you dare go there. I trusted you telling you that, and you promised you wouldn't put your name in at the call."

"I didn't promise anything." He crossed his arms over his barrel chest. "I said, 'Okay, doll. Let's get you to bed.' I knew I couldn't promise you anything, so I didn't. You said you felt sick."

Apology swam in his eyes, but I didn't care. My blood boiled just from looking at him. "You're a liar."

He winced, only for a flash of a second. "I'm sorry it had to be this way."

I shook my head. "No you're not. Stay out of my way, and don't talk to me."

"It's going to be hard, since Maddox wants us to train together for this."

"He must be mad." I pushed the book next to me and stood. "I won't train with you. Why would I? So you can see my weaknesses?"

His blue eyes glittered with amusement. "It's not a competition where we fight against each other, doll. It's a test."

"Don't call me doll!" I balled my fists at my side. "You won't win this. You don't have a clue what you're doing. You can't even speak Lor."

"Look, I know you're upset, but—"

"Get out of here." My jaw clenched. "I felt something off about you since day one. You're bad news. I could sense darkness in your eyes. I hate you more than anyone I've ever met. I bet it's you killing those people." I didn't mean to say it. Or did I? I was so angry. I didn't actually think he was, but then he'd insisted on going into the woods, and the murders did begin not long before he arrived… or around that time.

The corner of his eye twitched. "You don't know what you're talking about."

I closed the distance between us, my eyes narrow with rage as I glared into his. "I see right through you. I don't know what your plan is here, but I see you." I didn't know why I was saying what I was. It was a horrible accusation, but I was so angry, my brain was no longer connected to my mouth.

"*Elisivanes, himniulo, efgeloi, Lor. Meso via jafiloir, ao.*"

My heart skipped a beat as he spoke in perfect Lor: *I can speak Lor. Good luck trying to win.* He'd even used the right syntax. Shock rooted me to the spot. Adrenaline coursed through my body. I clenched my fists so tight, my nails dug into my palms. "Who are you? No one comes from Salvius and is that good this fast. No one. Not even witch-born witches." I took a step back. "I'm right, aren't I? You're not who you say you are. You're the murderer."

His intrusive gaze latched onto mine. "I'm not a murderer."

"Why not? We've already established you're a liar."

Warning laced his features. "Careful."

As much as I wanted to scream at him, I didn't. Something in his expression told me not to push it. "I need to go to bed anyway."

"I think it's best." He stepped aside from the doorway to let me pass.

I edged toward him, then quickly passed him, uneasiness consuming me. I felt him watching me as I ran down the long hallway toward the staircase up to the bedrooms.

Chapter Twelve

The next day after training, I pulled Maddox aside. "I need to talk to you about…" I lowered my voice to a whisper. "Viktor."

"What about him?" He took a bite from his toast, then brushed the crumbs from the front of his blazer.

"There's something off about him," I whispered. "Last night, he spoke to me in Lor."

"Good. I've been teaching him. I'm glad he's practicing."

"No, Maddox. It was perfect Lor. He shouldn't be learning it this quickly."

"I doubt it was perfect. Yours is a little out of practice too. It's not that difficult to pick up on once you get the hang of the grammar and the way the sentences are structured. I'm sure he just remembered a phrase or two to worry you. You *are* his competition."

"No." I wanted to shake some sense into him. Viktor had even said it wasn't a competition. It was a test. He was wrong, but then maybe he really didn't see me as competition because he thought I wasn't good enough. "Don't you find it off how fast he's learned everything? It's not normal."

He shrugged. "Don't get jealous. You have years on him. Get your head down and study, and you'll be fine. If you both pass and it's a tie, I'll pick you due to your experience. Feel better?"

I looked down. No. Because I wasn't going to pass. "Explain to me how he's so good."

"He spends all his spare time reading. When he's not reading, he's training in the atrium. He spends his evenings in the study while you take a nap. When you're sleeping in, he's up, working on the next cursed object. Sorry, Elle, he's just hungrier for it. If you want to win, you need to be too. You have experience on your side, like I said."

"He's too quick, Maddox. You're smart; why can't you get it through your head? You're blind to him."

"Enough," he snapped. "We may be friends, but I am also your superior. You'll mind how you talk to me." He glanced at his watch. "I have more important matters to attend to than your petty jealousies."

My face flooded with heat. "I'm not jealous."

He waved his hand dismissively. "Stop, Elle. I need to go. Alma agrees with my theory about the cloaking spell and sacrifices. They're heading east to bring back someone they think can help with uncovering it. There's been two more murders, as suspected, and they're all within a twenty-mile radius. We need to find a way to catch them in the act. The cloaking spell they are using, it's old magic, dark magic, and it can only be broken using old magic."

"Who are they bringing back?"

He paused. "I can't believe I'm saying this, but the goddess. Freya."

"I thought you weren't sure if she was one."

"Of course she is. I just don't like the idea of worshipping her. We need her, and if they can track her down, then we can stop this murderer. I've been tasked with breaking one of the top-level objects from the vaults and to carry out the test so we can have another keeper. I'm under a lot of pressure. I don't need you adding to them. We good?"

"I get you're under pressure, but you're not thinking straight. I won't let this go."

He shook his head, pushing his hands into his pockets. "Jeez, girl."

I watched him march away. Worry lines were aging his young twenty-five years. If Maddox wouldn't listen to me, then I'd have to prove it myself. Although, it'd have to wait until after I'd stolen the Joker's Ball. I hadn't got a chance to last night because Maddox had spent the evening reading in the room across from Edmund's office, but tonight I would.

***

Weapons training took my mind off things. I desperately wanted to hit something… or someone. Viktor had offered to be my sparring partner, as Maddox was busy, and as much as I didn't want to be in the same room as him, I couldn't resist having him be the one I laid hits on. He deserved it.

He stood across from me, dressed all in black. "I'm glad to see you're trying harder."

I balled my fist around the hilt of my dagger. "Shut it."

"That's not nice."

I wanted to wipe the smirk off his face.

"You've had quite the week. You put your name forward at the call, you're fighting me, telling Maddox off, falling out with your best friend…"

How did he know about Maddox? "Don't antagonize me. You know nothing about my life, and you're nothing to this coven."

"I wouldn't agree." He leaped forward with his dagger and almost grazed me.

I jumped out of the way, then twirled to the floor and toward his waist.

"The others seem to like me a lot. Compared to you, I'd say I'm two friends up."

He moved just as I pressed the dagger against his chest. I wouldn't actually cut him, but the allure was strong. "I hate you."

"That's a strong word."

I stopped for a moment to catch my breath. "What can I say? You provoke such strong emotions."

He grabbed me around my neck with his arm, and I couldn't move. "I really hoped for other emotions than hate." His whisper danced in my ear, sending tingling through my lobe.

I pushed my elbow back, hitting him between his legs. He let me go. I stumbled back and watched him as he glared at me red-faced.

"What the fuck, Elle." He closed his eyes and inhaled slowly.

"Was that a threat?"

He stepped back, gulping, red faced, and bent over. After a minute, he slowly stood upright. "You're lucky I have a high pain threshold."

I scoffed. "High pain threshold? You're telling me. That didn't hurt long." I glanced at his pants. "There must not be much there."

An amused smile lingered on his full lips. "I can assure you that isn't the case."

"Sure." I rolled my eyes.

He took a step closer. "I'd be happy to prove it if you want."

"I'd rather be set on fire."

"I'm sure you would. You think so low of me. I'm pure darkness, right? A murderer."

I felt a little bad about saying that, without proof, but I wasn't about to tell him that. "You did lie to me."

"That's not a good reason to accuse someone of murder." His jaw clenched. "Anyway, I didn't lie to you," he said nonchalantly. "You heard what you wanted. I'd never make a promise I couldn't keep."

"Why do you need to do this now?" I asked angrily. "You've only just got here. Why can't you let me have this? I need it more than you."

He rested the end of the blade against his chin. "Excuses. You know you could reach your sister now if you really wanted. You're afraid."

I swallowed thickly. "You don't know anything about me."

He closed the distance between us. I white-knuckled the hilt of my dagger. "You and I aren't all that different. We both have been made to feel powerless."

My heart raced. "I'm not powerless."

"You're not, but you feel like you are. Don't deny it." The blue rings in his eyes were swallowed by darkness. Something moved in his eyes, swirling like storm clouds when I stared close enough. He blinked, then looked away. "You feel it now. I think you know you can't beat me. You were brought here against your will and torn from your sister. Don't feel bad. I know how it feels." He looked back at me, pausing. "I know you've painted me as the villain here, but I've been forced away from the people I love too. I'm doing what I can to get them back."

Goose bumps prickled along my arms. "Are you doing this so you can go back to Salvius too?"

"Not quite." He didn't elaborate. "If you're going to hate me, that's fine, but you should know I'm not hurting you on purpose."

My breath hitched. Questions flashed through my mind, but only the result was important. "I'm going to win."

He lowered his gaze. "No, you're not." The conviction in his tone boiled my blood.

"You're so sure of yourself."

"I don't want you to get your hopes up." He leaned back, shaking his head. I wanted to hit him.

"We're done here."

"We've only just got started."

I balled my fist. "Why even help me with weapons training? Shouldn't you be studying some more?"

"We both needed to let off some steam, especially after yesterday, and this was one of two ways we could let some off together."

I closed my eyes. I hated, hated, hated him. "You know, I could just have Maddox make the ring a part of the test." I smiled devilishly. "The blood ring that tortured you. You couldn't manage that one, and I know the truth."

His eyes glistened with challenge. "Go ahead. I'll persuade him otherwise."

"You think he'll listen to you?"

He scoffed. "I have more of a chance than you right now."

I couldn't help it. I threw the dagger at his hand. A part of me wanted it to miss, but another darker part of me wanted it to land.

He swept it out of the air with startling speed, then swirled the handle around in his hand, whistling out a breath. "Who knew you had it in you?"

Reasonability washed through me. What the fuck was I doing? "I wanted to miss."

"I don't believe that's true."

I chewed the inside of my lip. "No really. I didn't want to spend the afternoon cleaning up blood."

He laughed, an actual joyous laugh. "You do pass the time, doll."

"Don't call me doll!" I exclaimed, and a revelation popped into my head. "Besides, all of this might be for nothing. They might just stop the test."

He tilted his head. "Why would they do that?"

I smiled. Maddox must not have told him everything after all. "They're bringing the goddess Freya here to help find the murderer. Something to do with using old magic to break old magic. The coven is going to be too busy, and the elders will have a field day with an actual goddess visiting."

His expression darkened. His pained stare latched onto me as his fingers curled around the blade of the dagger, which cut into his skin.

I watched, eyes bulging. "It's not that big of a deal if they postpone the test." I couldn't look away from the bloody dagger in his grip. "Viktor!"

He shook his head, uncurling his fingers. "I need to go."

It was as if he were looking through me. Eyes unfocused, he stepped around me.

CHAPTER THIRTEEN

I took a walk around the grounds, then sat down with my paints and painted the sunset in blotches of orange, reds and pinks, trying to distract myself from yesterday. Viktor hadn't been around since our session, which was insane seeing as we were locked away from the rest of the world, trapped in the mansion on grounds.

It's not like I was trying to find him though. The psychopath underneath had shown itself when he grabbed that dagger as if it hadn't even hurt him. The thought sent a shudder through my body. I sat on a rock, sighing as I looked out at the rustling underbrush between the trees at the bottom of the garden.

I sent another ignored magic quill to Naomi, then sat back and opened a book, letting the words pull me away.

A siren sounded. The shrieking sound faltered my brain. For a moment, I forgot all my training. When that siren was alerted, it meant danger, but it had never been set off before, so I had forgotten about the magical warning alarm. The bubble of magic that had been surrounding the mansion lowered. The shimmering, almost-see-through magic dissolved, unveiling a clearer, unprotected world beyond the mansion.

Someone or something had disabled it.

My brain caught up with my body and I stood, knocking the painting onto the grass, then took off toward the mansion. Maddox was there. Where was my dagger? My pistol? *Think.* In the atrium or the armory? Or did I take it to my room? It was times like this when I hated myself for being an unorganized mess.

I reached the back door, frantically whipping my head left to right in the kitchen, looking for anything out of the ordinary. The same cluttered shelves and sink filled with plates and cups awaited me. The alarm shrieked in my ears, defending me as I rushed into the living room.

Come on, Maddox. Where are you?

Atrium. The image snapped into my mind. My pistol was in there. I'd left it on the shelf after weapons training.

I took off, knocking over a plant as I raced around a corner. Sweat beaded on my forehead. My breaths quickened as I reached the heavy door to the atrium and threw it open.

I spotted my pistol on the second shelf. "There you are!"

I ran at it, when someone grabbed me from behind. A scream climbed up my throat, but a hand closed over my lips before it could alert anyone. Kicking my legs, I tried to look up.

Viktor's whisper danced into my ear. "Don't scream. Be very quiet, understand?" Viktor slowly removed his hand from my mouth, then closed the atrium door.

I pushed him away from me. "What the fuck are you doing?" Tears coated the skin below my eyes.

He placed a finger against his mouth. I wanted to argue back, but a loud thud sounded outside the heavy door. The alarm continued blaring. Adrenaline coursed through my veins. I grabbed my pistol, glaring at Viktor as I did.

I stepped back when the pounding shook the closed door. Viktor stood in front of me. I stepped to the side, pistol in hand. I had one shot, and I couldn't miss. My hands were shaking and teeth chattering. I tried to compose myself, but my arms weakened. Why did my body have to shut down when I needed it most?

The door slowly opened. My eyebrows furrowed when a woman walked inside. She was tall, with long dark wavy hair and maroon-red-painted lips. Her icy-blue eyes roamed over me, but her gaze landed on Viktor.

She smiled her pearly whites at him, placing her hand on her hip. "Well, well." Her red silk dress matched her lips, covering every curve and leaving little to the imagination. I pointed my pistol at her, moving it slowly to follow as she paced Viktor. It was like I wasn't even there.

"Freya," he said, his tone contemptuous.

I blinked three times. Freya? As in the goddess?

"I've been wondering where you were." She grazed her finger along his chin, sweeping it up to his ear.

"Darlin', why hide then?" he asked, taunting her through gritted teeth.

"Not pleased to see me?" She tilted her head. Hesitance played on her lips. Appearing dewy, the tanned golden undertones of her skin contrasted the darkness in her waves and thick eyebrows. She was beautiful but intimidating.

How did she know Viktor and he know her? The pistol trembled in my fingers. If she was in fact the goddess of the hunt, I didn't stand a chance. Still, I couldn't bring myself to put down the only weapon I had to protect myself with.

He grabbed her wrist when she went to touch him again, and he crushed the bones under his tight grip. The cracking barely made her wince.

Shaking him off her, she sighed. "Now, now. Let's not be hasty. You know I can heal in less than a minute." She took a step back. "I wonder why you've not yet burned this place to the ground and killed the coven. Without them, you could take what you've clearly come here for."

"I will kill you," he warned. "Why have you been cloaking yourself only to show up now?"

She sighed, as if this entire thing was such a hindrance. "They've been looking for me." She clicked her tongue. An unnerving smile unfurled on her lips. "Someone's been killing people apparently. Such a horror."

"Give it up, Freya," he spat. "Did you get what you came for?"

"No." She looked over his shoulder, noticing me for the second time. "Alexander has the boy. I came for her. Once they're dead, we can access the vaults. I tried, but it set off this awful noise."

I assumed she meant Maddox, but who was Alexander?

"Mmm, hello, pretty little thing."

I didn't like the way she looked at me, like she were a snake and I was dinner.

He growled. "She's not yours to take."

She tilted her head at me. "You were going to kill her anyway. Now, you won't need to carry the burden on your conscience, my love."

I gasped, and the pistol almost tumbled from my fingers. He was going to kill me?

He scoffed. "You lost the right to call me that a long time ago."

She looked up, sighing with exasperation. "You see, Raiden, I can't have you letting the others out. It's bad enough you escaped. I can't have three of you. That's just not playing fair."

My eyebrows shot up. Who in the underworld was Raiden?

He stepped toward her, grabbing her wrist again. "I don't need the others to kill you."

"I didn't come here without protection, you fool." She stepped back, pulling her arm from him. She pulled a ring from her pocket, as if it should mean something. "Remember this?"

"My greatest mistake."

She winced, stretching her lips thin. "Ouch. Anyway," she said with a smile. "It still works. Whoever you got to spell this for me was strong."

"It won't work for long."

She put it on her ring finger. "No, it doesn't have a lot of magic left, but there is enough for me to use now and get out of here before you come after me." She brought her finger to her mouth, and I noticed there was dry blood on her nail. "I also have this to sustain me." She showed off the blood on her hands. "They give me strength, the young ones I kill. Now I'm able to fight you one-on-one."

The alarm stopped. "Oh, thank—well, me." She laughed. "Alexander must have made the boy turn off the alarm. They will be coming soon. I'm sure the townspeople will have heard it."

I finally found my voice. Clearing my throat, I gripped the pistol with both hands, pointing it at them both. "You're the goddess."

"Good detective skills, sweetie." She laughed. "That isn't going to get you far."

Would a bullet even hurt a goddess? "I'll still shoot."

"Go ahead."

"Elle," Viktor warned. "I need you to get out of here."

Freya arched a perfectly groomed eyebrow. "I see what's happening. You're still trying to prove you're a good person. My love, you can be many things, as we both know, but you'll never be that. Now, stand aside so I can put this poor girl out of her misery."

"Run!" he shouted as he lunged at her.

I didn't need to be told twice. I lowered the pistol as I stumbled through the doorway. I headed for the front door but stopped. She'd said someone had Maddox. Alexander, I think.

Dammit.

I turned and ran down to the vaults. She'd said she wanted to get into them by killing us. I remember Edmund saying the coven was the life force of the magic that protected the objects. Without us, the barriers would fall. With Edmund and Dora out of town, I assumed the protection was left to us.

Normally, I'd never be allowed down there. Massive locked doors were my first barrier to them. "No, no, no." I pounded on the door.

"Elle, don't." Maddox's voice came from the other side. "I am being held captive in here. If you open the door, he will kill me."

I wracked my brain for anything. "Freya sent me to tell you that… uh, he's dead." I didn't know what I was saying, but I hoped it meant something. She clearly hated Viktor, whom I couldn't even think about right now. She knew him. He was able to fight her. How? "She wants Alexander to bring you and me to the front." I tried to overcome the shake in my tone. "Now that he's dead."

My body was shaking when the door finally pushed open. I breathed relief, but panic swallowed it. Now what?

A man with shoulder-length ash-blond curly hair with soft features and thick lips walked Maddox out, holding a dagger to his throat. Maddox's pained look broke me. I forced tears back, not letting them break out. "This way," I croaked.

He seemed unsure as he stepped past me. "You first. No funny business or I will kill him." His accent was unique, from the far west of Istinia. It was bold with sharp Rs.

Before I knew what I was doing, I pointed the pistol at his shoulder, connected to the dagger-holding arm, and pulled the trigger. The shot reverberated through the room. He stumbled backward, dropping the dagger.

"Oh my gods, Elle." Maddox looked from me to Alexander. "You-you shot him."

I stared at the smoking pistol. Even I couldn't quite believe it.

"We should go." Maddox grabbed my hand, tightening his fingers around mine. As he pulled me forward, I dropped the now-useless pistol. It had only had one shot in it, as I'd stupidly not reloaded it the last time I'd used it.

"Where's Viktor?" he asked as we fled for the front door. I couldn't even get into *that* whole mess right now.

"Atrium. I—" A loud boom silenced me.

Maddox speared through air, flung from me, and landed against a wall. His head crunched when it hit the baseboard. My hand muffled my scream as my eyes widened, and a sob climbed up my throat from my sinking heart.

"Maddox!" I cried when Freya grabbed me by the throat and lifted me from the ground. Was he dead?

"Say good-bye."

Viktor came from behind and pulled her from me. With a hand around her neck, he slammed her into the ground, cracking the floorboards to splinters.

I shimmied my way to Maddox's side, holding his limp hand. Freya pulled herself from the dip in the floorboards at dizzying speed.

She picked shreds of wood out of her bloodied skin, then tilted her head. "That was mean."

She whipped her head around to look at the front door, wide-eyed. Viktor hurried to Maddox's side, despite the bits of brick embedded in his arm from where he'd hit the wall. Freya ran out the door, and I let out a sob.

"Get away from us," I croaked as Viktor placed his hand over the bruise forming on Maddox's head.

"He'll be fine. He's breathing, Elle. It looks worse than it is. He's just unconscious."

"You're a monster. You're like her… a—"

"Freya ran because she heard them coming. The council. Elle, they're about to enter. Do not tell them what happened."

I didn't even want to imagine what he would do if I did say anything. "I shot Alexander, her boyfriend or whatever, in the shoulder."

"He's gone. I heard him go out the back. She would have gone to him."

"How?" My eyebrows furrowed.

The front door creaked open, and three members of the council stood, slack-jawed. "What happened here?" asked the first.

Viktor spoke first. "Intruders trying to steal things from the vaults."

It was half true.

"The floor," said a man in his seventies as he stood in front of the massive dip in the ground.

"They used dark magic. A curse hit the floor. Our friend here needs to go to the infirmary."

The man looked at me. "Are you okay, miss?"

I looked at Viktor, who's glare sent a shiver down my spine, then I gulped. "Yes. Fine."

***

Thunder rumbled through the gray-purple sky. Thin dark clouds stretched to the horizon, where the sun hid behind the storm. Rain splashed mud around my ankles, releasing a rich, earthy scent. Tall trees dizzied up, their bare branches holding no shelter from the thick droplets hammering down. I appreciated the rain more than ever, as it shielded the tears that trickled down my face. Breathless, I closed my eyes, finding steadiness.

The first chance I got, I'd hightailed it out of there and down to the woods. The murderer was Freya all along, and she was gone now—probably far away, as the council had come to Deadwood. It was nice being back between the trees, even if the flashbacks of finding Bryan's body forced their way into my mind.

How could I have been so blind? The Lor. His incredible skills with weapons. The knowledge. The way he seamlessly blended into our society after supposedly coming from Salvius. He was a god. A ruthless, vengeful god who sacrificed people and had planned on killing me.

Edmund was on his way home with Dora and Alma after getting a magic quill about what had happened. Fortunately, whatever was in those vaults she or they were after was still there. Maddox was staying overnight in the infirmary but would be okay. He only knew about Alexander. He didn't know anything about Freya or Viktor and had been unconscious during the fight.

"Elle."

I jumped. He'd followed me. I stepped back, almost tripping on a log. "I didn't tell them." I swallowed thickly. "Please, don't."

"I'm not going to hurt you." His tone softened. "Is that what you think?"

I opened my eyes, flexing my fingers at my side. What could I possibly say? I felt as if someone had reached their fingers into my chest and twisted them around my heart. "You're a god. You lied about everything. You planned on killing me."

Wind-swept rain hit me from the side, soaking me through. I looked him up and down. His black hair curled on his forehead, leaking rain down the side of his face. His white shirt clung to his muscles, showing his skin and tattoos beneath, tattoos marking his life, a history spanning centuries. "I was never going to kill you."

I hesitated. She'd said he was going to kill me, but then he could have killed me any time and hadn't. He'd stopped Freya from hurting me, too. But he was dangerous.

"You must have a lot of questions."

I held my breath.

He tilted his head. "Please talk to me."

"Which one are you?"

"Raiden."

Right. She'd said his name. I inhaled deeply. "The god of beasts." I remembered from the conversation with Maddox and Naomi.

"God of creatures," he said, correcting me.

"Right." It said as much in the book I'd read the other night. "Why are you here? In Deadwood, I mean."

"For my family. That's why I need to be a keeper, so I can access the vaults."

My heart pounded; I could feel my pulse in my closed fist. "What's in them?"

"I can't tell you."

"Why not?" I blew out a tense breath. "I *already* know too much."

"You're not going to leave until I tell you, are you?"

I shook my head.

He blew out a tense breath, his eyes darting up as he took a moment to consider. "I'm searching for two keys belonging to my sister and brother's prison realms. They're in the vaults and that's why I've been trying to gain access."

"Oh great." I glanced down then climbed my gaze back to him. "You want to free more gods. That doesn't sound dangerous at all."

"It could be, but they're my family." He closed the distance between us. "Let me get you out of this rain."

I crossed my arms over my chest. Cold seeped through my skin and into my core, but I didn't care. "I'm not going anywhere with you. You ruined my life. Maddox almost died because of you."

"I didn't expect Freya to turn up like that. She had been hiding from me."

"Still your fault." Tears trickled down my nose and cheeks.

"Anything else?"

"Yes. I have no chance of being keeper. You're a god. An actual god. You can pass any test, so I'm never going to be able to see my sister now."

He brushed his fingers against my cheek. I batted his hand away. He stretched his rain-soaked lips into a smile. "You can find her, still. You're the only one standing in your way."

"I can't go." I looked at him incredulously, blinking droplets from my eyelashes. "She might…"

"She might not want to see you?" he asked, and my stomach knotted. No one had ever said it out loud before, not even me. "She will."

"You can't know that."

"Don't let your fear hold you back."

I scoffed, shaking my head. "You're one to talk. I'm not the only one standing in my own way." I gritted my teeth. "That's why you were in the woods, right? Looking for Freya? She's the one who's been killing the people. I put two and two together, and for whatever reason, you hate her. You could have found another way into the vaults, but you were busy looking for her. Why is vengeance more important than your own blood?"

Darkness flashed in his eyes. His stare was impenetrable, and no matter how hard I tried, I couldn't bring myself to look away. "Careful, Elle. I've been doing everything I can to get those keys."

I hugged myself, shuffling my weight from one foot to the other. "You like calling me out. Well, I'm doing it back for once. If you can't take it, don't dish it, Raiden." Hearing his name on my lips silenced us both.

The rain picked up, turning stretches of mud into streams of brown, dragging dead leaves and twigs deeper into the woods. Hearing him talk about my sister had hit a nerve. I was braver than I should have been. He could kill me as easily as snapping a twig.

"We're getting out of here." He grabbed my arm, but I pushed back.

"I'm not going anywhere with you."

He clenched his jaw. "I'm not asking."

I stepped back, almost toppling over an out-of-place rock. He reached his arm around my back and pulled me up before I could hit the ground. His unworldly speed jolted me as the air whooshed from my lungs.

A low growl left his lips as he pulled me back against him. "You never listen. I'm taking you home."

As much as I loved rainy days, I preferred watching them from behind a window, snuggled in the warmth of a blanket. The cold made me shiver, dancing my spine into a full-body shudder. "I'm going because I want to."

He picked me up into his arms, as if I weighed nothing, then sped us through the woods. My heart raced as the world around us blurred into browns and greens. Before I could catch my breath, we were at the closed iron gates of the mansion. He pressed the button and waited.

"I could tell them," I said flatly.

"You could." He ran his hand through his rain-soaked hair and looked down at me. "But you won't."

"Does your arrogance have no bounds?"

He smirked. "Not really."

I gritted my teeth and flexed my fingers. The gates opened, and before I could say another word, Dora opened the front doors, beckoning us inside. She was home. Thank the gods. No, wait, thanks to something else. Not gods. I hated gods… and goddesses.

He walked ahead of me, shooting her a charming smile, and I watched her melt. I hated him for it. Who did he think he was? The goddamned puppet master? He couldn't get away with manipulating everyone, but… He was a god, and his powers were, well, godly. Goose bumps raised along my skin. He could kill us all in a heartbeat if he wanted to. We were no match for him, and if I told everyone the truth, he'd be forced to show his hand.

He wasn't leaving without the keys to free his family, and I was pretty sure if I tried to stop him, he'd only end up hurting me or the others. It was why he wasn't concerned about my telling the others or getting in his way. He didn't see me as a threat. He glanced back, his bottomless dark eyes focused on mine, as an arrogant smile danced on his lips.

Part Two:
Vengeful Gods

CHAPTER FOURTEEN

Three More Dead, the headlines read. I glanced over the newspaper, glaring at Viktor—or should I say Raiden—as he drank his morning coffee like nothing had happened.

Edmund dragged a chair out, placing his breakfast on the kitchen table. "Maddox should be released today. The potioneers did excellent work healing him. I believe Aaron was one of the ones healing him."

I smiled. "Of course he was. Not that it matters because Maddox doesn't see a good thing when he has it."

Dora finished making her eggs and grabbed a bread roll from the middle of the table, leaning over Edmund's shoulder. "I'm just happy he's okay. My poor Maddox. He must have been so afraid. Those intruders," she said, balling her fists, "they could have killed him. I'm furious. Alma has been looking for the ones you both described, but they haven't found them yet."

My gaze caught Raiden's. They would never find the "intruders" because we'd made them up. I wasn't going to set them on the trail of a goddess who could tear them apart, and I didn't want to face what Raiden would do to me if I did tell anyone. I imagined it would start with my death and end with my coven's. Their intelligible words floated around as I lost myself in dark daydreams.

"You okay, Elle, honey?" Dora asked.

"Sorry." I snapped back to the conversation. "Yesterday was a lot. That's all."

She reached across the table and grabbed my hand, gently squeezing my fingers. "You've been through so much as of late."

I inhaled deeply. "What were you saying before?"

"We couldn't track down the goddess either," Edmund explained.

Yep, because she had been here, locked in a divine fight with the liar over there. "Perhaps it's best to let sleeping goddesses lie."

Edmund gave me a look. "I suppose. She always has been elusive. Supposedly." He drank the last of his vanilla bean coffee. "How many did you say broke in here yesterday again? That floor is costing a bucket of skal to fix."

Raiden grinned. "Five," he lied. "Elle almost shot one of them."

"What?" Dora's eyes widened.

"Almost." I scowled. He knew I did.

"That's my girl," Edmund said and turned his attention to Raiden. "Viktor." Edmund pushed his glasses back up his nose. "Why did you decide to put your name in the mix for the position of keeper? You have no experience and couldn't have had time to learn everything."

"I've been studying a lot."

I scoffed. Edmund looked at me, and I masked it as a cough.

Raiden continued. "I know how important it is to the coven to have the keeper slot filled. I put my name in on the off chance our Elle here wouldn't pass the test."

I balled my fist under the table. He knew I wouldn't pass. "How lucky we all are to have you," I said snarkily.

"Eleanor," Dora chastised.

"I'm glad you're back," I said, standing. "But I'm tired. I'm going to my room. Tell me when Maddox arrives. I want to see him."

***

"Still sulking?" Raiden arched an eyebrow as he entered my room.

"You're not welcome in here." I scowled at him over my drawing. "*Raiden*," I whispered.

He peered at my artwork, then raised his eyebrows. "Is that for me?"

"No," I said and glanced at the dagger I'd sketched. "I'm sure it couldn't kill a god."

The corner of his lip tugged up. "I wouldn't tell you if it could."

"Why are you in here?" I moved my papers from the bed to the nightstand, sighing with exasperation. "Unless you've come to torment me some more."

He chuckled. "It's my new hobby."

Was he... flirting? "You're shameless." I clicked my tongue, then pushed myself back against my pillows. "Unless you've decided to kill me because I know the truth." I eyed him, evaluating his expression. Only amusement trickled through.

"I already told you, I'm not concerned with your telling them. I know you won't."

"Because you'll hurt everyone if I do and they try to stop you."

"There is that, but it's not why I'm not worried."

"Then why?"

His expression darkened. "You won't tell them because you don't want me to go."

My eyes widened, and a laugh escaped my lips. "Your leaving is literally all I want."

"If I leave, then you'll have to go back to your life." He sat on the edge of my bed, dipping the space next to me. "Unsatisfying and unremarkable, where fear ruled."

I leaned toward him, watching him for a flinch or a flicker in his expression. "Perhaps, but it begs the question as to why you're really here." My gaze fixated on his. "You're a god, and yet you're climbing the ranks of a small coven when you could just—" I paused.

"Kill everyone and take them without putting myself through all this hassle?" he asked. "I could. I'll admit, I've thought about it more than once."

My stomach churned.

"But I won't. I'm not the monster you've been told I am, Elle. I won't kill innocents to get what I want, no matter how alluring."

I'm sorry, what? My eyes widened as I rolled his words in my mind. "You sacrificed people all the time back in your time." I looked at him incredulously. "Why the sudden change of heart?"

He shook his head. "That's not true. When Freya locked us away—"

"Yes. Because you were killing people."

"No." His jaw clenched. "Because *she* was killing people. She framed us."

I ran cold. Was he just saying that? What would be his motivation to lie? He didn't care what I thought about him, and he knew I didn't have the power to stop him. "Why would she frame you?"

He winced. "She killed my sister."

"Leda, the original goddess of the hunt," I said slowly, remembering the books I had read on the gods, and my conversation with Maddox and Naomi when Raiden had first arrived. She had been killed and replaced by Freya.

He rubbed the back of his neck. "Leda was my favorite." A small smile flashed in his expression as he looked up, lost in a memory of someone who no longer existed. "Freya found out how to kill her, then did it while she was sleeping, like the coward she is."

"I'm sorry." My lips parted. She'd not only taken away his freedom but she'd also stolen his sister, tearing apart his family. At least when he'd told me about finding his sister's body, he was telling the truth, except I had believed him to be a little boy when it happened, not a man, a deity.

He shot me a pained stare, and my heart cracked. "Don't pity me too much. I'll have her head soon enough."

I reached out instinctively but thought better of it. I was still angry, but seeing his tortured expression, I wanted to take it away. I knew that kind of pain, of losing someone I loved. "If I'd known yesterday, I'd have shot her while I had the chance."

"It wouldn't have hurt her, but the sentiment isn't lost on me." He inched closer. "We don't have to be enemies, Elle."

"I need us to be," I admitted.

"Why?"

My heart skipped a beat. Because if we weren't, then I'd have to admit the truth.

He inched closer again, my gaze settling on his full mouth. His breath tingled my lips, as the small distance between us seemed heavier somehow. "I don't want us to be."

I didn't think about it. I cupped the side of his neck, running my hand into the line of his hair where Freya had played yesterday. He must have hated to have her so close, taunting him like that. My heart ached when I thought about it—him, locked away, grieving his sister while separated from the rest of his family.

Something in my gaze widened his. My other hand touched his, and electricity buzzed through us. My lips parted. "Raiden," I whispered.

His hand ran up my back and into my hair, knotting my curls through his fingers. "Fuck," he cursed before pressing his lips against mine.

His fingers grazed the inside of my leg, trailing a path to the top of my thigh. I closed my eyes as he deepened the kiss, instinctively rocking against the whisper touch of his fingers.

His body pushed against mine, his hard length pressing against the crease of my thigh. Wetness gathered between my legs as throbbing coursed from within, begging for him to take me on my bed. I rolled my hips against his, and a low growl escaped him.

I should have stopped. I knew this wasn't right, but my body moved of its own accord. He moved his hand down, pulling away from my lips. He pulled my pajama top up, breathing heavily against my chest as his lips grazed my cleavage. "Beautiful," he whispered against my skin, moving his touches to my hard nipple.

His hot tongue ran over one, jolting my hips upward. I moaned as he flicked his tongue again, making my back arch. His hot breath trickled from my breast to my stomach, over my navel, and to the top of my bottoms. After unraveling the tie on my shorts, he grabbed the sides, ripped them down my thighs, and met his lips against my wetness. I grasped the sheets, and my eyes rolled back as his tongue flicked my clitoris. He swirled it around, then pushed his tongue inside me, tipping me over the edge. A wave of pleasure rippled through my body and down my legs into my toes. I moaned, thrusting myself harder against his lips as my orgasm sent my eyes toward the back of my head.

Left panting, I wanted more. I wanted him, every inch of his godly body. Wild-eyed, I grabbed him and pulled him over me. I unbuttoned his pants, my breath hitching as his erection sprung free. Wrapping my fingers around it, I moved gently first, then faster as his breaths quickened.

"Tell me you want this," he demanded. "Like I want you."

"I want this," I admitted.

His gaze burned into mine, his eyes moving down to my breasts. He thrusted in my hand as I moved faster. Feeling his want for me caused my clitoris to throb. "I want you, Raiden."

"Fuck, Elle." He moaned, his dick pulsating under my fingertips as he released onto me.

"I'm back," Maddox said.

Shock coursed through me as I scrambled back, pushing Raiden away.

Raiden pulled the blanket over me. "We're in the middle of something."

I pulled my shorts up under the covers. Maddox had turned away, and my face flooded with heat. "It's not what it looks like."

Maddox tsked. "Are you decent now? I need at least four martinis to erase what I just witnessed."

Raiden tsked too, then pulled his pants up and buttoned them. I brought my hands up to my face, cupping them around my nose and mouth. "I'm sorry." I breathed slower, trying to calm my racing heart. I could still feel the pulsating from the wetness that had gathered between my legs.

"I was wondering when you two would hate-fuck."

My stomach knotted. "It wasn't like that."

Raiden stood. "If you don't mind, we're not finished."

"I'll leave." Maddox grinned at us, then walked back out the open door. "Oh, you should consider not leaving your door open if you're going to be partaking in salacious activities."

Raiden closed the door. By gods, I was mortified. He sauntered over, his eyes darkening when they met mine.

"No." Reason splashed through my brain. "I don't know why I let you do that."

"Let me? You wanted me to."

My face reddened. "A lapse in judgment," I said. "I don't do this sort of thing."

"Sex?" he smirked, with an arched eyebrow. "Well, we haven't done that yet, but I *want* to keep going."

"I have, I mean, before, but I'm not like you. I don't sleep with just anyone."

"I don't like to think I'm just anyone."

I rolled my eyes. "You know what I mean."

His gaze rolled over my figure, making me feel naked.

I bit down on my bottom lip. I still wanted him, and I didn't know why.

"Not just anyone can make me come like you just did, not with only their hand. You moaned so hard for me, Elle. I want to make you scream again. I want to feel your tight pussy around my cock."

Holy… "Stop."

He splayed his fingers against my chest, smirking. "Your heart is racing."

I pushed him away. "This… This is never happening again. I was vulnerable… Then you told me about your sister, and it reminded me of mine, and I felt…" I paused. "Something for you. Pity probably."

"I don't think that's what you felt at all, but I'll let you wallow in your denial, love."

"I'm not in denial." I clenched my jaw. "I don't want anything to do with you. You're a liar and dangerous and…"

"Let me know if you change your mind. I'm always down for hate-fucking, as Maddox so poetically put it."

He turned to leave the room, and I threw my pillow at his back. He didn't flinch when it hit him, but he clicked the door closed behind him.

Maddox would think we were… something, when we weren't, and Raiden has the upper hand. I'd never felt so powerless.

CHAPTER FIFTEEN

Today was the day. I slumped my shoulders as I ambled toward the test room to take the pointless exam I didn't stand a chance of passing, especially when pitted against a god. One I'd done things with yesterday. I closed my eyes. The embarrassment of being caught was still fresh.

I sent a magic quill to Naomi before going inside. *Good luck today. I know you can do it. I know you're still mad but please come to the realization Craig is an ass faster. I miss and love you. Elle.*

I needed to see her. I wished I could talk to someone about everything that had happened, but Maddox was a no-go for obvious reasons, the same reasons I couldn't tell Edmund or Dora. Naomi was a possible option, but I was also afraid that if I said anything to her and Raiden found out, he'd hurt her for it.

Maddox stood in front of the doors to the study where the test was being held. I hadn't seen him since he caught us. I'd tried to find him, but Edmund said he needed his rest. "I'm glad you're home and okay," I said when I reached him. I wrapped my arms around him, and he held me tight.

"I'm worried I wouldn't be here if it wasn't for you shooting that guy."

"I wouldn't tell Edmund that part," I said. "He thinks I *almost* shot someone."

"Where is the guy you shot?"

"Got away." I glanced at my feet. "I'm sorry you saw what you did yesterday."

He chuckled. "Girl, I am not one to talk. Pot, kettle, black. You do you. He's hot and you're beautiful. It's a good match."

It was my turn to laugh. "It's a terrible, terrible match and will never happen again."

"Sure," he said rather unconvincingly. "Now focus. I want you to pass." He touched the side of my cheek, and I wanted to cry.

My eyes glossed, watering the image of Maddox. I wasn't going to pass. There was no way. Raiden would and then he would become the next keeper, steal the keys, and then what? Would he leave? Would the keeper spot open up again? I hadn't thought that far ahead.

"Also, Elle." Maddox arched an eyebrow. "Don't try to cheat again. There's a charm placed on the room to alert any magical interference."

"What do you mean?" I feigned innocence. I hadn't actually stolen the Joker's Ball, and how would he know I'd wanted to?

"I heard you searching through Edmund's office. I know what's in there."

That was why he'd taken to reading in the room across from Edmund's office the nights after. It made sense now. "I was never going to take it."

"Good." He didn't say anything more. "Go on in. You've got this."

He opened the door. Edmund waited for me behind a desk. The room had been mostly cleared out, save for one bookshelf. In the middle of the room was a polished stone on the ground, marked with various symbols.

Edmund pulled at the sleeves of his tweed suit, then looked at his gold watch. "Just in time. Now, step into the middle." He pointed at the large round stone lying flat, engraved with ancient symbols. It covered half the room. "It's a magic enhancer. Today you'll be given two top-level objects to manage, and an ancient text stone to translate."

"This is it?" I looked around for exam papers. "Why did I need to study so much?"

"Knowledge is important to become a keeper, and I wanted to make sure you took it seriously. If I told you this would be the test, it's all you would have worked on."

My heart raced when I saw the first object. Pandora's Box. I'd heard of it. Who hadn't? It was filled with forbidden magic and had killed the seven humans who found it. Filled with deadly sins in curse form, it was one of the most powerful objects in the mansion. My lips parted. I couldn't control them.

"Is this used for everyone's test?"

"If you're asking if we all passed it, then yes, we did." He placed the chest on the stone. "The stone will contain all magic and enhance your own. We use it when accessing the objects from the vaults. I need you to concentrate. They are only curses. It's not unlike any you've managed before. Remember, you have dark magic running through your veins. Any fears or self-doubt the sins will try to use to make you submit. The stone will now be cloaked, and the barrier will go up for our safety and for you to concentrate. We won't be able to see or hear you now. You're on your own for this test." He moved his black-framed glasses back up his nose. "Good luck. I know you can do this. You just need to focus." He snapped his fingers, and darkness covered me. A small orb of light floated overhead, illuminating the black barrier surrounding the circular stone.

I reached down, hovering my hand over the black lock on the chest, when I noticed a key. I pushed it into the old lock and cracked open the lid.

The first sin hit me with force, throwing me back. I crumpled against the edge of the stone circle, hitting the barrier.

Green smoke, flowing upward in an illusory dance, told me it was envy. It snaked toward me, then dissolved into my chest. I squeezed my eyelids shut as the curse rippled through me, bubbling a rage of feelings I didn't even know I had to the surface, magnifying how I felt about Naomi and Maddox being accepted for their magic and not me. Suddenly, a part of me despised them. But my feelings toward them weren't half as bad as what I was feeling for Raiden. He was respected and loved despite everyone thinking he was human-born like me.

I inhaled sharply, focusing on an image of Mona in my mind. My auburn-haired sister would dance in the meadow near the orphanage, despite the rain, and would laugh at the most random things. She was still there, in that dreadful kingdom, and I was the lucky one for getting out when I did.

The jealousy bubbling under my skin moved like it was its own entity, curling my thoughts of Mona into warped, dreamlike images where everyone else got everything and I didn't.

"No." I exhaled shakily. "This is just a curse. This isn't real."

It weakened, but the curse continued to fight resiliently. I loved Naomi and Maddox, and Raiden... Well, he was something else. I may not be loved by the other covens, but I was loved by mine, and that was what mattered.

Perhaps there was a small chance I could pass. If Raiden and I both passed, then Maddox and Edmund would pick me.

The thought strengthened my resolve. The curse weakened and dissolved. I'd barely caught my breath when the next one crept out in pink-and-purple smoke. It danced toward me, glittering, captivating in its essence, and curled into my body through my parted lips.

It moved silkily through my veins, lulling me into a false sense of security. My fingers tingled, reminding me of yesterday. I rolled back my aching shoulders, letting my neck and head droop back. Heat and wetness gathered between my legs. Every nerve ending was on fire, and all

I could think about was Raiden. His tongue between my legs, sliding over me until I came in his mouth…

I wanted him now, to ride his big cock and feel him release inside me. My nipples hardened at the thought. I didn't care where I was anymore. All I could feel was a need to release myself. The heaviness down there begged to be touched. Nothing else mattered.

Moving my fingers down my stomach, over my navel, and under my pants, I moaned. Everything else could wait. I wanted to leave this barrier, go find Raiden, and spend the rest of eternity under the sheets. It didn't matter if I found my sister or not.

Wait.

What was I doing?

Realization splashed through me. My sister. She was who I was doing it for, for her and for me to belong.

I stood, forcing Raiden from my mind. The idea of him amplified every desire pulsing throughout my body right now. Instead, I focused on Mona and the rest of my family: Edmund, Maddox, Dora, and Naomi. I imagined their smiling faces, our early morning breakfasts, and how it would feel to be able to go with them to translate ancient texts and bring back dark objects—to finally belong. The magic of lust faded slowly, dissolving into nothing.

It, like envy, returned to the chest. My heart hammered. Next was pride, a royal-blue smoke, thicker than the others, and it entered me with a choking gasp. I closed my eyes, keeping my focus on my family, on my friends, and on my goals, enough that it never did get its claws in. After several minutes trapped in a mental tug-of-war, I came to a realization. I didn't need to be the best or the brightest. I was good enough, and I had people who loved me.

Pride left me, stealing my next breath with it as it poured itself back into the chest to join the others. I gasped for air, pressing my fingers against my knees when gluttony climbed across the ground and found me in a cloud of orange. I swallowed thickly as overwhelming hunger dipped my stomach, but like pride, it didn't take much to push out.

Greed shot into me at an alarming speed, glittering gold, and a trail of silver smoke stayed behind. I gasped, my eyes snapped shut as they seeped into my thoughts, distorting them, changing them. My heart raced at the idea, at the image it created: revered, loved, with my sister here, and me as grandkeeper. No one would look down on me again. I was even better than Maddox and Edmund at managing curses.

Greed painted a picture in my mind, stoking my deepest desires, amplifying them. I saw myself not only as grandkeeper but an artist, an author, and everything I could imagine. I owned businesses and had more skal than I knew what to do with.

The thought was exhausting. I smiled. That was it. I didn't want fame or a grand fortune. I'd love to be grandkeeper one day, but I was perfectly content with waiting decades for it.

Greed left me, stinging like a scorpion as fled my mouth, choking me. I sucked in a deep breath when sloth came in a thick brown. It dissolved into me, lulling me into a want to sleep. My eyelids growing heavier, until I could barely keep them open.

I wasn't sure how long had passed… minutes, half an hour, maybe more? I lay on my back with my eyes closed, unable to find the energy or motivation to get up. I knew sloth would get me. I always did like slacking off when I could.

I could take a short nap. Maddox and Edmund could wait. Just as a light snore escaped my lips, my eyes flung open. Like my mornings when it was an effort to get out of bed, I still did it, even if it was sometimes nearing noon. All because I had to take the day, to work and become something.

The desire to become a keeper outweighed my desire to do nothing. With a heave, I sat upright, moving in what felt like slow motion to my feet. Sloth slugged out of me, crawled across the ground, and slumped back into the chest.

I felt a thousand times lighter.

Was that all of them? I was counting my fingers when wrath erupted in a cloud of red smoke. No. This was the last, and the one I feared the most. I braced myself when it darted toward me and hit through my chest. A burning behind my eyes forced them shut. Kneeling, I grasped at the ground as wrath took over my body. Flames of heat licked through my veins, my body convulsing on the ground until pain turned to seething hatred of everything and everyone. He was more than a sin. Wrath was alive, an entity, and everything I believed was brought into question.

They all deserve to die, a voice tinkered in my mind. Wrath tugged at every painful memory. My sister being torn away from me. My past mixed with scenes that hadn't happened. Images were shown to hurt me, to provoke rage. He fed off it, delighting and ravishing in the anger as it spilled through me.

Mona would hate me when she saw me. She wouldn't want to see me again because I'd left her. She hated me for being a witch. She had to. I tried to help her, to protect her from the awful Miss Thompson, who'd enjoyed hitting us, but what had I got for my troubles? Demonized, called evil, and sent away to a territory that didn't accept me either.

My heart hammered as I curled my fingers, digging my nails into my palms. He tugged at every insecurity. Every time I tried to bring in some light—a memory of Naomi and me—wrath reminded me of how she believed Craig over me, her best friend. I thought about Maddox, but wrath showed me how he didn't believe me when I had tried to warn him about Raiden.

Finally, when the darkness was too much, I found something I'd buried deep long ago. It was a faded memory of the mother who'd abandoned Mona and me long ago, leaving us with a father who drank himself to death, leaving us to the mercy of the orphanage. Salvius wasn't as forward-thinking as Istinia and didn't look after their weak or old. No one cared for us. My mother had moved away, built a life for herself with a wealthy merchant. I didn't care if she ever thought of us after. She had abandoned me, I'd been taken from Mona, my dad left me by choosing alcohol over his daughters, and Naomi had decided she'd had enough of me.

I opened my eyes, staring at the large stone beneath me through red-tinted eyes. I blinked twice. "No." I sucked in a deep breath as I fought wrath. I wouldn't let it beat me. I couldn't. It didn't matter how hurt I was, or the pain I felt. It would be nothing compared to failing this test. I'd lost hope, but I was at the end, and maybe, just maybe, I actually stood a chance.

I thought of Dora, Edmund, and Maddox. He wanted me to win. He'd told me so. Edmund was rooting for me too. Dora took care of me as a mother would. I had family here, and I was worth something to them.

It recoiled slowly, then left my body, slipping back into the box with the others. The lid closed with a slam, the key shooting out of the keyhole on its own accord. I curled into a ball as the magical barrier fizzled away. Bright pale light hit my eyes. I rubbed them, then looked bleary-eyed at Edmund and Maddox. Dora wrapped her arm around me, helping me to my feet.

Edmund clasped his hands together. "You did it."

Dora smiled as she steadied me. My legs were weak, and my knees felt like they'd buckle at any moment. "Pandora's Box is the most difficult part of the test. You can finish this." She handed me a bar of chocolate. "Eat this, honey. It will help you regain some strength."

Maddox patted my shoulder. "Good going."

Edmund held a black cane, with skulls and roses made from metal as the handle. I looked at the old crow's cane, the second object. "You know how this works. This one, like the others you've done, you need to contain the curse without allowing it to pass to another object."

I wolfed down the chocolate, closing my eyes as the bitter, smooth cocoa coated my tongue. It was like Midas's book, where the curse of turning everything one touched to gold must be held within the person so it didn't transfer. I still couldn't believe it when Viktor—no wait, Raiden— had mastered it so quickly. Sometimes I still got them confused.

I couldn't think about him right now. I had more important things to think of. My sister, my place in the coven, getting everything I'd worked for over the years… I placed my hand over my stomach, where nausea still lingered from being hit by the seven sins. "Give me the cane."

He handed it to me. I closed my eyes, wondering what curse lurked inside. It was a grade ten object, strong enough to hold in a vault.

Maddox cleared his throat, stepping into the circle. "Touch me." He extended his hand.

With the cane in one hand, I touched Maddox and he aged thirty years. The skin around his eyes sagged into wrinkles, his laugh lines deepened, and his dark hair grayed.

"Oh, gods no." I let him go, and his youthfulness returned. No matter how much I tried to contain the curse before it left my fingertips, the stronger it grew.

Minutes fell into hours, and I was exhausted when I finally found the strength to touch Edmund without him aging twenty years. I gasped when the curse neared my wrist but didn't reach my hand. The blocks I'd formed in my mind, the resilience of my own magic syncing with my body, and pure will stopped the aging curse before it could leave me.

I touched Maddox's, then Dora's hands in turn. They both, gratefully, looked exactly the same. "I did it." Tears seeped from the corners of my eyes. I held the cane longer, delighting in the power beating through my veins as the curse tried but failed to move through me. I'd beaten it.

With my peripheral vision, I noticed the headstone carved in Lor on the desk. Newfound confidence pushed me forward.

"Let's get this over with." My voice charged with hope as I approached the text.

Could I really be a keeper by the end of the day? Could I beat an actual god?

***

I paced my room. I couldn't stay still as we waited. He hadn't told me if I'd passed the Lor translations, but apart from two words I'd stumbled on, I thought I got it all correct.

Tingling pulled my gaze down to my hand. A magic quill appeared. *Come to the garden. A decision has been made.*

My heart skipped a beat. The moment of truth. Goose bumps ran along my skin as I walked downstairs. I stopped halfway, placing a hand against my stomach. Bile climbed my throat. Scrunching my nose, I willed it away, closing my eyes and finding peace in the temporary darkness.

"No hard feelings, Elle."

I spun around, peeling my eyelids back to take him in. Pine with spicy undertones wafted into my nose as he passed. "Same goes to you."

"I know you've been having trouble handling some of the more advanced magic."

I tried to keep my expression as apathetic as possible. "What makes you say that?"

"I've been watching you. I had to ensure I wouldn't have any real competition."

"Wow." I shook my head and placed my hand on my hip. "Are all the gods assholes, or is it just you?"

He chuckled. "None of this is personal. I hope you know that."

"You could have just asked one of us for the keys, you know," I said, having realized the thought had probably never even entered his mind. "We're not without compassion."

His eyebrows knitted together, creasing above the bridge of his nose. "I'm not going to trust your people with something so important. Also, Edmund, Dora, nor Maddox would have just handed over such heavily guarded objects without permission from the elders."

I clicked my tongue. "I get it. You don't trust people, right? Freya betrayed you and killed your sister."

"It was more than that." His expression darkened. "Her death was my fault. I won't place my trust in the wrong people again. I can't."

"How was it your fault?"

He hesitated. "As I said, I was too trusting."

"Not everyone is bad, you know."

"I don't have time for this." He stepped in front of me and walked the rest of the way to the garden in silence.

Stepping out into the brisk air, feeling the satisfying crunch of red and golden leaves beneath my boots, I hurried to where Edmund, Dora, Alma, and Maddox stood. Edmund held a parchment rolled up in one hand. Why was Alma there? My stomach dipped as I walked over cracked mud and the occasional white baby's breath flower. Raiden must have won. Why else would she be here? A student going to apprentice, then keeper so fast was unheard of. She would be here to witness the greatness of Raiden.

I wanted to turn back, not wanting to embarrass myself further. I thought I might have messed up some of the translation. Perhaps I got the last part of the text wrong.

Maddox pinched the front of his bowler hat, tipping it down, when we reached them. Mud and stretches of grass turned to concrete as we moved onto the patio. Everyone was standing in front of a weathered fountain filled with murky waters and forgotten skal turned to wishes by those who'd lived there before.

"Eleanor Moore. Viktor Raiden."

I scoffed loudly when I heard his supposed last name for the first time. He really was far too cocky for his own good. His eyes twinkled with mischief, and I curled my lips behind my teeth.

"Something amusing?" Alma asked, and I shook my head. Her gray, thin hair was pulled into a tight knot at the back of her head. Her eyes, duller now, watched me carefully. "Good, then we shall proceed. I have been called here, as we find ourselves in an unusual situation."

Raiden smirked. I wanted to throw another dagger at him.

Edmund cleared his throat. "It appears there was a tie."

My lips parted, and I held my breath as Maddox gave me a wide smile.

Edmund continued. "As Elle has more experience, we have decided she will be the next keeper in the coven."

Every hair on my arms and at the back of my neck stood erect. A lump formed in my throat as a single tear crept down my cheek. "I'm the keeper?" I asked, double-checking I'd heard right.

"Congratulations, Eleanor," Alma said, then turned her attention to Raiden. "You are a clever, studious young man with unprecedented talent. Because of the close tie, the council and I have decided to offer you the option to immediately fill a keeper slot once another opens up."

"If it does," I mumbled under my breath, then realization shocked me still. Raiden would do anything to get his family back. Would he go as far as to use brute force to get the keys? Would he want to kill one of us to take the spot? He said he didn't before because he'd wanted to avoid killing innocents, but he'd lost hope.

Suddenly, my win felt more like a loss. He eyed me as they gave me the keys to the vaults and read the oath of being a keeper. Shaking, I took the oath, and before I could process it, I was a keeper.

CHAPTER SIXTEEN

The next afternoon, a magic quill tingled my skin. My heart leaped when I saw her message. *I'm ready to talk. Our old meeting spot? Naomi.*

I quickly sent one back. *On my way.*

I grabbed my black leather jacket from the back of my chair, then put on the makeup Naomi had made and gifted me. She was so talented at creating things. I picked up the black paste with an applicator she used to create a line over the eyelids. It really made my eyes pop. Some others in town had caught onto the trend, but none of their makeup made a dent in what Naomi created.

After spending a few minutes to do my eyes and paint my lips in crimson red, then a coat of gloss, I smiled. I pulled on my emerald-green pleated skirt, buttoned it at my waist, and tucked my long-sleeved black top into it. The colors matched the four rings on my fingers.

I hadn't been in town since I went looking for Raiden that night, and I hadn't had a chance to enjoy it.
I headed to the front door, successfully avoiding Raiden in the kitchen as I grabbed my umbrella in case it rained.

I walked through the iris, a part of town where artists painted on the streets, musicians played on the corners, and palm readers sat at small, erected tables covered with purple cloths. I tapped my fingers to the sound of the saxophone. I threw a skal inside the sax case, then shot the man dressed in a red suit a smile.

People sat outside tearooms and coffee shops, enjoying the late-afternoon sun. I paused at the fence, where local artists hung their paintings, then past the red tent where the paintings were sold. I moved through the open gateway between the black wrought iron fences and made my way into the park. I spotted Naomi sitting on our bench in front of Mr. Star's Potions Store.

I could hear the frown in her voice as she stood. "Elle. You're here."

"Nai." I smiled, reaching out to hug her, but she stepped back. I took a seat next to her. I had assumed by her message that we were okay and she'd finally come to her senses about the whole Craig ordeal.

"I didn't get it."

Before I could say anything, her tears fell thick and fast.

"Craig passed, but I missed one spell and—" Her voice broke.

I put an arm around her and squeezed her to my side. "Oh, Nai." I rubbed the top of her neck. "I'm sorry."

"I have to wait three years, Elle. My dad sent me a quill, letting me know I was an embarrassment to the family, so I haven't seen him since."

"Ignore him." The muscles in my jaw tightened. "You're not the first person it's happened to."

"Most who don't pass just drop out of the coven and look for some other career," she said between sobs, sniffing against her blocked nose. "It's so embarrassing being an apprentice for that long." She gave me a look. "Sorry."

"Don't be." I didn't want to tell her I passed. Not yet.

"You were right about Craig. He told me you didn't come on to him. Eventually."

"I hate that you didn't believe me," I admitted. "It hurt, Nai. I'm your best friend. Or was."

"Was?" She blinked tears onto her thick lashes.

"We are if you still want to be. I wasn't sure."

She looked at her feet. Bright yellow boots. "I'm the dick here."

I couldn't help but laugh. "A little bit," I said teasingly. "But you get a free pass this time." I thumbed away a wayward tear, then rested my forehead against hers. In so many ways, she'd become a sister to me, filling the hole of a loss I couldn't cope with at eleven years old. Having her close to me again made everything feel right.

"How was the test for you?"

I swallowed thickly. "It's not important right now."

"I heard Viktor was taking the test."

"Yes, he did."

"Yikes. How did that go?"

I hesitated. I didn't want to make her feel worse. "He didn't become a keeper."

She scoffed. "No doubt. He's not been here long enough. What was he thinking?"

I sighed. I mean, he did technically pass the test, but I won through experience. I wished I could tell her the truth, that he was thinking he could probably get his family back, but I was afraid of what would happen if he found out she knew. Freya had said he was trying to be good, with emphasis on trying. He hadn't killed us to get what he wanted, but he was a god, and if history was anything to go by, they had their tempers.

"He was trying to do the right thing," I said, wishing I hadn't.

"What do you mean?"

"By him, anyway." My heart hurt. He was a man trying to get back his family, and now he'd lost it all. He could be dangerous right now, and I was sitting here, a mile from the coven that needed protecting.

"Nai, I need to go. Will you come by tomorrow?"

She nodded. "Thanks, Elle."

"We'll go shopping," I said.

She gave me a watery smile. "I'd like that. We can talk about what I'm going to do next over lunch after."

"We will. So many people are starting their own businesses and stuff. You're talented. Together, we'll come up with something." I wanted to spew some crap about how this might be the opportunity she needed to spread her wings, but I know if it were me, I wouldn't want to hear that right now. "Tomorrow."

"Tomorrow."

I headed off. I needed to face Raiden. I couldn't keep avoiding him, especially when he was a loose cannon.

***

I found him in his room. His queen-size bed was made with navy sheets. Fresh white shirts were folded on the chair of his dresser, ready to be put away. Above his bed was a small painting, a landscape of the main city in Istinia, a place of art, culture, music, and gangsters, from what I'd heard. I bet he got it from the iris in town. I hadn't noticed it the last time I was in here.

He glanced at the painting. "Yes," he answered, his tone clipped. "I saw it in the iris and liked it."

"I've always wanted to go to Navarin." I exhaled slowly, fumbling my fingers with my necklace as I searched for the words to say.

He broke the silence. "Before, when we spoke, you said to ask, so I'm asking. Can you get me the keys? You have access to the vaults now."

I bit my bottom lip. "It's not as straightforward as that. I'm a brand-new keeper. They'll know it was me if something goes missing. Maybe we can ask Edmund. I can't lose my position."

"He'll say no. Trust me. He knows what those keys are for. If anyone finds out I'm a god, the entirety of Istinia will come after me."

"You're a god. Why are you afraid of witches?"

He arched an eyebrow. "Even I can't fight thousands of witches with magic on their side. Now, a large group of you on the other hand wouldn't be difficult."

"Is that what happened?" I pursed my lips. "When they imprisoned you? Was it hundreds, maybe thousands of us?"

He nodded. "It was your coven actually. Well, back then, keepers were simply witches with dark magic, and there were a lot more of you. It was they who created the realms with Freya's help, and the keys which kept us in there. Your coven was created to guard those keys, then it turned into something else over time, I see. To guard all dangerous objects."

I blinked in disbelief. "I had no idea."

"I doubt many do. You'll find some things are eradicated from the history books when it doesn't suit their needs. Your council was formed after the kings and queens of Istinia fell. The monarchy nor the council after wanted the grizzly details of the once-revered gods remembered, but they couldn't stop the stories."

I arched an eyebrow.

He continued. "Stories passed down through generations, of the deadly gods who sacrificed people. The tales twisted as they did, into all sorts of fables. All the while, we remained rotting away in prisons, helpless to stop the lies from spreading." His fingers flexed. "My brother and sister still are."

I swallowed thickly. "I'm sorry."

His jaw clenched. "Why would you be sorry? You already think I'm awful, remember? Pure darkness, wasn't it?"

"You could have killed us, and you didn't. You protected us from Freya. I'm not an idiot. I can see you're trying."

He slammed his fist on the dresser, sending a crack through the wood top to the standing mirror. "And where did that get me?"

"Calm down." I inhaled sharply, sitting down on the edge of his bed.

He closed his eyes. "I forget my strength. I don't mean to scare you."

"It's okay."

"I can't lose my family, Elle."

"I know, but I can't steal the keys. I need to talk to Edmund first."

He shook his head and stood. "If you won't help me, then you leave me no choice."

"What are you going to do? Kill us?"

He paused.

My shoulders tightened. "Freya said you're trying to be good. Killing us would just prove her right when she said you couldn't be good."

"Trying got me nowhere."

"Not true."

"Hasn't it? Even you hate me. I tried to do this the right way." He walked to the door.

"Don't." I hurried to him and grabbed his hand before he could open the door. "Let me just think, at least."

"I'm not going to hurt your coven," he growled, pulling his hand from mine. "If that's what you're worried about."

"Wait. Raiden, please." I tried instead to hook my finger around his belt. He turned to face me.

"What, Elle?" His tortured gaze never left mine.

I relented. "I'll try to help you."

"You'll steal the keys?"

I parted my lips. "Well, not exactly. Look, you're wrong about him. I think I can get him to listen."

"No." He turned his back toward me. "You'll make things worse. Don't tell him anything."

"Where are you going?" I asked when he opened the door.

"Hunting."

"What or… who?"

"Freya." He growled something under his breath. "I've wasted too much time on this foolishness. I should have been working on killing her first."

He left. I called after him, but he never turned back. By the time I ran out of the house, he'd already gone, left for the forest. A part of me knew he wasn't coming back. What reason did he have?

***

I must have been mad to consider it. If I was caught, I'd lose my position as a keeper. I'd finally proven I was good enough; people would have to respect me. I'd gotten everything I wanted. I could go to find my sister, maybe even find a way to bring her here, but worry weighed heavy in my chest. Concern for him. I hated I felt it, but I knew firsthand how it felt to lose family.

Pacing in front of the vaults, swinging my keys around my finger, I closed my eyes. Edmund was going to kill me. I would definitely lose my position if they found out it was me. I'd have to lie, and Edmund would never condemn me without proof.

Was this worth lying to my family over?

I walked back and forth again. The vaults were a couple of feet taller than me and reached up to the ceiling, with large, heavy bolted doors made from reinforced steel. Around them, a bubble of magic buzzed so clear, a person wouldn't see it unless they were looking for a sheen in the air.

I licked my dry lips. Maddox said the gods were dramatic and bad-tempered. I was putting everything on the line over his word. He could well be manipulating me. Freya was obviously the bad guy, but Raiden's brother and sister might not be as innocent as he makes them out to be. Didn't Maddox say Thalia had almost destroyed the underworld in an argument with her father? Then, Raiden had said tales had been twisted over time. Not all the stories were true, but what I did know for certain was every single one about Freya was a lie.

I sighed. She'd surely come back at some point. Raiden was tracking her, and I hoped he could kill her, but she was goddess of the hunt. She wouldn't be easy to put down... or find. How could a goddess even be killed?

Three gods after her, however, would mean imminent death. She was killing witches and warlocks my age, one who I'd once known. Who would be next? Naomi? Maddox? I shuddered. This wasn't just about Raiden anymore.

Blowing out a tense breath, I stopped twirling my keys and took a step forward. I'd been afraid of taking risks since I'd lost Mona, and this was the biggest since. Everything I had worked for could be taken from me. The chance to see Mona again would dissolve with if I were caught, but I couldn't risk not protecting the coven from Freya. She needed to die, and it would reunite Raiden with his family. Even if he was an ass, he at least deserved that.

A thud sounded from above. Edmund, Maddox, or Dora might come down here. My heart tugged me one way, whereas my head tugged me another, and I knew what I had to do.

Chapter Seventeen

I ran through the forest, the keys to the realms containing two gods pressed against my leg. They were snug tight in the pocket of my black pants. Red leaves crunched under the soles of my boots. The laces had come undone at the top, but I didn't care. I did, however, wish I'd left my brown leather jacket at home.

Sweat beaded my forehead as I pushed on. Stopping for a moment, I pulled the jacket off and flung it over one arm. Pressing my hands against my knees, I tried to catch my breath.

Where in the underworld are you, Raiden?

Taking off once more, I raced past time-chiseled trees. Raiden was angry, impulsive, and in no state of mind to face off against his sworn enemy.

By the time the sun set the sky into indigo, lighting the feathery moss hanging from low branches with the moon and starlight, I was utterly lost. The memory of finding Bryan's body swam unwantedly into my mind, stilling me.

Would Freya have stayed so close, knowing Raiden would come after her? She had to have cloaked herself again, and I wondered when the next body would be found—or if there was already a body but no one had come across it yet.

My stomach churned. I peered through the darkness, ignoring the hissing of a nearby snake. My ankle twisted when I stepped on a stray root. The air whooshed from my lungs as I fell onto the mossy mattress below. Rustling sounded as a squirrel scurried from where I'd fallen, disappearing into the underbrush. The smell of damp earth mixed with decaying leaves lingered as I sat up, coughing out a small leaf. Picking a twig from my hair, I looked around. There was no way I was going to find him in this darkness. I rolled my foot around, readying myself for the pain that didn't come. I sighed relief. It wasn't broken.

A sound came from within the trees. I tried to slow my raspy breaths, pressing my hand against my mouth. Every nerve in my body screamed danger as I stood. My breaths quickened, and I begged my racing heart to calm as cracking sounded from the branches above. After a few seconds, a thud came from behind me.

I froze, fear rooting me to the spot. My fingers tingled as I turned slowly, listening to the slow, steady breaths coming from the blackness over my shoulder. A shiver snaked down my spine when I felt hot breath against my neck. A finger grazed against my cheek, pulling a lock of hair behind my ear and jolting me back.

"I don't know what he sees in you." Freya stepped in front of me, her unnerving smile and venomous stare both meant for me.

I looked around us.

"Raiden's gone," she said through a grin. "I sent him after a false trace, left my scent on trees leading up north. He was so upset, he didn't even stop to wonder why I'd leave such an obvious trail.. He just smelled me headed for that." She showed me her hands, waggling her fingers. Dried blood coated her nails. "The heart of the last man I ate," she said, explaining my unasked question. "At first I went after girls, but I found I enjoyed killing men so much more."

I swallowed thickly. "Why?"

"To cloak myself. I thought you'd all figured that out."

"Why cloak yourself just to antagonize him in person when you came?"

She cackled, lost in a joke I didn't understand. I flinched when her nail gripped into my shoulder. "I wasn't trying to antagonize him. I was trying to lure him away from your coven. He was always so easy to anger, and it worked. He came after me, and here we are." She brushed a finger against her bottom lip, then pressed her teeth against it. She laughed again, and I saw the glimpse of insanity behind her gaze.

My stomach dipped. If I'd said yes to the keys straight away, this wouldn't be happening. "He'll come back."

"Eventually, but without those keys, he won't be a match for me. You see..." She stepped back, and I breathed relief. "When Raiden escaped, I was concerned the others may have to. I had to cloak myself. I'm not a match for three gods." She paced, circling me slowly. "Raiden's the strongest. It's what initially attracted me to him, but he does have his weaknesses. He wants to be good, to be revered and appreciated. Because of those ridiculous wants, he won't kill innocents, although he didn't always have that problem."

"It's not a weakness," I spat from behind gritted teeth.

She waved her hand dismissively. "While Raiden is strong, I can still evade him. Being goddess of the hunt has its perks. I'm fast, great at tracking and hiding... I can blend in with nature, and I have better hearing and eyesight than him. I just need to stop him from letting those siblings of his out." Her mouth twisted. "They'll come for me, and I can't have that. So you see my dilemma."

Suddenly the keys felt heavier in my pocket. "You want me to retrieve the keys."

She stopped in front of me and booped my nose with the tip of her finger. I wanted so badly to punch her. "Good, you're not completely clueless then, for a mortal."

"Weren't you once mortal?"

"A painful lifetime ago, yes." She shook her head, as if to scatter the memory. "Now, I am going to kill you, *obviously.*"

My heart skipped a beat. She pressed her hand against my chest, as if she could sense it.

"Don't panic." Her tone sweetened. For it, she appeared even more deranged. "I'm not a complete monster. You see, you know too much, but the rest of your little coven doesn't, so they're safe, for now."

"Don't you dare hurt them."

She squeezed my arm. "Sweet Elle, you can relax. Their fates rest on your shoulders. If you get me those keys to the prison realms, I'll let your friends walk away unharmed. You'll be a hero." She laughed again, and it tinkled around us in a high-pitched shriek. "Not that anyone will know, but I will. Raiden will be harder to evade with you dead, but hopefully he will be too lost in his grief like the last time."

"I'll get you the keys, but you should know you're wrong. I don't even care about him, and I can assure you he doesn't care about me, especially not enough to mourn for me."

"Then why are you out looking for him?"

"I wasn't looking for him," I lied. "I was going for a run. I used to go more, but then I found the body of one of your victims."

"Ah." She walked next to me. I wondered why she didn't run us back like Raiden had with me once, but when I saw her scratched yet quickly healing arms, and heavy breaths, I realized. She was weak. I didn't know why, but it was an advantage I didn't plan to let on I knew. I'd have to find a way to stop her before we got to the coven, but nothing was coming to me, yet. In the silence, she sped up, and I matched her pace.

"Why did you kill Leda?" I asked, stopping.

She halted, turning on her heel. "Hasn't Raiden told you the whole story?" She rubbed her hands together. "You might not think so highly of him once you hear this."

"Like I said before, I don't care about him."

Another lie.

She placed a bony hand on her hip. Dried blood crumbled from her knuckles as she curled them. "I'm not the villain as you believed. I've done what I needed to, to survive. Over time, of course, the lure of the dark side certainly has had its perks." She tilted her head, taking me in. "Kindness is weakness. You'll learn this in your life. Well..." She laughed, then shrugged. "Perhaps not. Anyway," she said, dismissing the thought. "Raiden, the so-called brilliant god of creatures, was feared by my village. I grew up in a poor area of Regedam Province, to the east. His beasts would come and tear the people apart. He let them roam. He had certain controls over them, but he allowed them to embrace their savage nature. We called them demon hounds. They belonged in the underworld. He stole them from Lucius." She moved her gaze to the ground. "The times were different a century ago. Girls like me were married to the best suitor for the family, but my father drank and didn't make enough dowry for me to find a decent husband. Instead, he would hit my mother, blaming her for our situation. One day, he beat her too hard, and she didn't make it."

"I'm sorry," I said, although it was hard to sympathize with someone as awful as her.

Her eyes glittered with insanity as she gazed at me, the moon swallowed by her pupils. "Don't pity me. I ended up more powerful than any of them in the end."

I stumbled, not wanting us to move again. The more time I could keep her in the forest, the better. "I know, sorry, so your mother died. What does that have to do with Raiden?"

"It has nothing to do with him, but it did start me on a path I wouldn't be able to return from. You see, my father's friends would come, and they would, well…" She paused, briefly lost in a thought of another time. "Regardless, I ended up pregnant."

I could fill in the blanks. If she wasn't running around killing people, I might have felt bad for her.

She continued. "The baby was born, and I couldn't cope." Her expression turned blank, numbness guiding her tone. "I gave him to another family to look after, but Raiden's beasts came in the night and they—" Pain filled her tone. "They killed that family and my son."

My eyes glossed with tears. To lose a child. Even an unwanted one. A small part of me began to understand her insanity, to pity the woman she felt she'd had to become to survive.

"My father blamed me for his grandson dying and beat me. I couldn't take it, so I hit him over the head with a rock, but I hit too hard, and so he was my first. Raiden found me. He didn't know what his beasts had done. I wanted to hurt him for it, to destroy every man who had stolen parts of me I couldn't get back, but I saw opportunity in him. Immortality. A way to get everything I wanted. So I let him fall in love with me. I shared his bed and gained his trust."

I gasped, covering my mouth with my hand. They had been lovers? He loved her? My stomach swirled. He had certainly left out that nugget of information.

"He kept his beasts," she explained after clearing her throat. "Said he needed them to protect himself because

Lucius, his own father, was hunting them. Their family was more messed up than mine ever was, and that says a lot. Then there was his horrid sister, Leda. She clung to Raiden for everything, never letting me get too close... always saying spiteful things to me when he wasn't around. She was selfish, manipulative, but he couldn't see it."

I suppressed a scoff. How could Freya, of all people, have the nerve to call someone else selfish?

She continued. "One night Raiden told me the truth, that Lucius planned on replacing his children. He said they'd become too dangerous, too sinful, and were leading Istinia into darkness and not into light as he'd intended. He said Lucius had sent knights to cut off his head, and the heads of his siblings, as to do so would kill them and replace them with whoever killed them. That or Lucius could do it, take the essence of that god or goddess and choose who to replace them with, but he liked watching men fight for the chance, to prove themselves worthy of such a position."

The temperature dropped, and I hugged my jacket around my arms. Everything made sense now. Raiden had said it was his fault his sister had died. It was because he'd brought Freya into their lives and told her how to kill them. "Why didn't you tell him what his beasts did?" I questioned. "You said he loved you. He would have killed them if you told him."

She balled her fists, clenching her jaw. "Killing them would have done nothing to bring my son back. No. I saw a way to protect myself from letting anything happen to me again, and I would have lost my opportunity if I let myself fall for him."

"So you cut his sister's head off, then trapped them all in prison realms to stop them from hunting you," I said, feeling sick to my stomach.

"Yes. I see he told you something then. Naturally it would be the part where I'm the villain. Trapping them wasn't easy," she explained. "I had to get you mortals on my side, which was easy. Once I was a goddess, I went after the men who hurt me, and I tore out their hearts, then after, the women who'd belittled me, and anyone who'd made me feel inferior, and I took their hearts for myself."

I had to stop myself from speaking my little quip about how she had called them dramatic but she was worse. "You made them look like sacrifices."

"A few ancient markings and people were ready to believe the deaths were the work of the gods. They wanted a reason to hate them. The king of that time despised them. It was easy to rally support because people are willing to believe a lie when it suits their needs. So the witches and warlocks who used dark magic banded together and created three realms, with three keys, and together, we banished them. I was safe. Until now."

I already knew this part. Those with dark magic in their veins had helped Freya. Begrudgingly, I was going to have to do the same. "You didn't need to kill everyone who hurt you. You didn't have to kill Leda."

She shrugged. "You still think I'm the villain after that? Fine. You mortals will never understand." She grabbed my hand and tugged me along. "Storytime's over. I need those keys."

***

My heart cracked as we neared the house and my family. A foolish part of me hoped Raiden would have come back, having realized he'd been led on a false trail and would have heard us talking among the trees, but it was a fool's dream, and I was out of time.

Maddox stood behind the window to the kitchen, and Dora stood behind him, probably arguing with him on some topic, their favorite pastime. She poured the teapot, then stirred her cup. I could almost taste the chamomile tea from memory.

Freya dragged me by my arm around the side of the house and away from the kitchen, over to the door. "You have twenty minutes to get those keys and bring them to me, or I'll go in, happily kill everyone in there, and get them myself. Understand?"

I nodded, not wanting the tears in my eyes to fall. This was more convenient for her, as I assumed she didn't want the council or the entire town after her, and by killing us all, they surely would. Even Raiden had said he couldn't take on that many witches, but there was no way I could get anyone here within twenty minutes or make them believe me.

She walked away toward the garden, speeding to the edge and out of sight. With a deep breath, I turned the handle.

Dora came running down the corridor from the kitchen, her floral nightdress snagging on the coat holder. "Stupid thing," she said, tugging the fabric, then looked at me. "Where have you been? It's late. We've been worried sick. You look freezing. Let me make you some hot cocoa."

I stared at her, taking in her worried frown and kind eyes, uncertain if I was ever going to see her again. "I'm okay." I gulped. I was really coming to say good-bye. I already had the keys and would have no choice but to hand them over. None of us were a match for a goddess, and I couldn't let them die alongside me.

"Good." She hugged me. "I'm so proud of you for becoming keeper. I knew you could do it. I told everyone we had nothing to worry about."

Maddox called from the kitchen. "Tell Elle to go see Viktor. He's been moping in his room," he said over a clatter of dishes dropping.

"You better not have broken my new pots. I swear you do it on purpose," Dora said, hurrying back into the kitchen. I followed and put on the radio, which buzzed with jazz music. I couldn't risk her overhearing, and I hoped the dishes dropping covered what he'd said. She did say, after all, that she had better hearing than anyone else.

"Viktor's here?" I questioned once the music started playing.

Dora glanced at the staircase. "He's in his room. Where else would he be?"

"You've seen him?" I asked, wanting to make sure.

"He came about an hour ago. Shortly after you left."

I took off running for the stairs, following the hallway to his room. When I opened the door, I saw him. His hair had been curled from the drizzle, and his top clung to his muscles as he stood looking out the window. "You're here." I ran to him and wrapped my arms around him.

His muscles tensed, then relaxed as he hugged me back. "This is... unexpected."

I placed a finger against his lips. "Shh. Whisper, okay?"

"Any reason for this unexpected show of affection?"

I held him tighter. I wasn't going to die. None of us were. "I went looking for you," I whispered.

He pulled me to arm's length, concern etched onto his features. "Why would you do that?"

I pulled the keys from my pocket and placed them in his palms. The skin around his eyes creased as he moved them up toward mine. "Are these..."

"There's more. Freya's outside. She sent me in to get the keys, and well, she's going to kill me," I whispered. "I didn't give them to her."

He cupped my cheek. "She won't get anywhere near you. I promise."

I paused for half a breath. "She told me everything. You should know something. She blames you for her son's death. He was killed by your beasts. I think they were from the underworld. I guess I wanted you to have some context," I said. "I know you loved her, and she broke your trust, but I'm not going to hurt you like she did. None of us are."

214

"The demon hounds killed her son? I didn't know she had one."

"She was raped." I looked away. "She fell pregnant and gave her baby to another family, but the hounds tore them apart."

"They didn't act on my orders." His eyes darkened. "Had I known, I would have…" He trailed off. "She should have told me. There was no reason to kill Leda, to lock us all away."

I reached out to squeeze his hand before he could head toward the door. "She didn't do it for revenge. She wanted to be strong, and well, I believe her, but you're right, it doesn't give her a pass for all the terrible things she's done. She's going to kill us all, so please, don't hesitate."

He squeezed my hand back. "I won't."

After a half hour of me pacing nervously in front of the window, Raiden returned.

"Is she dead?" My voice charged with hope.

"She took off when she saw me. I chased her through the east of the forest but lost her scent."

"What do we do? She's going to come back. She wants those keys."

"She won't come here again. She knows I'm here, with you all."

I closed my eyes on an inhale. "She tried to lure you away with her last visit. She wanted the coven unprotected."

"I realized that halfway to Navarin. Look, Elle, about these keys." He let out a long exhale, his gaze climbing to meet mine. "I'm grateful you did this for me. For my siblings too. What changed your mind?

"A few different things, but mostly, it felt like the right thing to do."

His lips parted, and something changed in his eyes. It was weird being in a closed space without wanting to hit him for once.

After a few seconds, he shook his head as if to scatter thoughts, then cleared his throat. "I'm glad you came to your senses."

"Ah, there's the asshole in you." I couldn't help but smile. "I wondered where he went."

He entwined his fingers with mine. "I think you should come with me."

My heart raced as my fingers flinched, then knotted with his. "Where?"

"To release my sister and brother."

"Oh." I gulped. "Thanks, but no thanks."

"I want to repay you for this. I'm going to help you get your sister back, but I need mine back first. Once they're out, and we've killed Freya together, I'll take you to Salvius, and together we'll find your sister."

"You don't need me to come right now then. You can come back and get me."

His grip tightened. "The coven will be safe here, especially if she believes me here, but just in case, Elle, I need to know you're okay. She's gone after you twice now."

I tugged at my collar. It suddenly felt warmer in here. "I suppose it would be interesting to see the others."

He smirked. "Also, your company isn't *terrible*. It wouldn't be the worst thing to have you come along."

I opened my mouth but closed it again. Before I could say anything, a small earthquake trembled the mansion. I grabbed ahold of the window ledge, but Raiden wrapped his arms around me. Thunder pounded in the sky, followed by flashes of lightning. I held onto him until it stopped. "What the…"

Maddox appeared in the doorway a minute later. "Oh, good. You're okay." He whistled out a breath. "We never get earthquakes."

CHAPTER EIGHTEEN

I was never going to get used to being whisked through a forest in the arms of a god, but it wasn't a bad place to be. We got to the first prison realm in under fifteen minutes and had traveled to the edge of the province. We'd encountered another two earthquakes on the way there, but they were minor, and Raiden could withstand them.

He placed me down carefully. Holding onto his arm for support, I stumbled as my senses reoriented. I didn't want to admit I'd almost thrown up a few times on the journey. He thumbed my chin and tilted my head upward, examining me. "You're hurt."

I reached my fingers to the stinging on my temple. Something had whacked me as he'd run us through the trees. A twig, I thought. I touched the blood, then rubbed it between my fingers as if it were silk. "Oh, yeah."

He touched the scratch tenderly, the callused tips of his fingers feathering the cut, and the stinging went away. I touched it again, but there was no pain. Nothing. "You can heal?"

His smile dimpled his cheek. "I can heal minor cuts, like those. It's my sister who possesses true healing powers. She could have had Maddox fixed up in a second that day." He paused, his gaze drifting up to the moon. "I wanted to, but his injuries were too severe."

"You did what you could," I said. He was different out here, among the trees. "You said when you first came that you liked the woods."

"I did." He played with one of the keys, passing it from hand to hand. "It's where I found the most solace when I was sent here from the otherworld."

"What's it like?"

He chuckled. "Nothing like here. It's vibrant and beautiful, filled with never-ending beauty, no pain, no suffering."

"Sounds divine."

The muscle in his jaw twitched. "It is until it isn't. There's no growth there. No humanity. People learn through pain, and without it, existence is boring and without purpose. When I was given a body and sent here, I vowed to never go back."

"You want to stay here?"

He leaned down, bringing his fingers up my bottom lip and running his thumb across. "You feel that?" "It's being alive, Elle. There is no touch in the otherworld. It's just spiritual. They say everything is sins of the flesh, but I call it living." He looked around us. "The feel of the breeze against your skin and a touch of rain as the skies fill with clouds… every single thing you love, whether it's laughter or just feeling the grass beneath your feet, it doesn't exist in the otherworld. It's a place of passivity and peace masquerading as eternal joy."

My heart was hammering hard in my chest, to the point where I wondered if it would stop. "Dora will be heartbroken."

He nodded slowly. "It's not awful. Most might find it serene, but not me. It's no match to being here."

My eyebrows shot up. It probably wasn't enough for someone like him, with a fiery heart and an electric soul. "Is it really that bad? It's where I'll go one day—well, I hope."

His gaze searched mine. "It's worth living to your fullest here first. Trust me."

I turned my attention to the stone arch ahead of us, which stood on three stone steps. "Is this it? Is there a keyhole? It's hard to see much in the dark."

"Oh, right. You have mortal eyes."

I smirked. "Damn these mortal eyes."

He summoned a ball of light, floating it over the arch. "Here."

"Thanks," I murmured. The arch was out of place compared to everything else. The forest hadn't claimed it for herself. Not a speck of ivy climbed the stone, nor any leaves carpeting the steps. It was pristine. Otherworldly. Etched in the stone were words in Lor. Below them was a key-shaped hole.

"I assume this is it?" I shifted my weight from one foot to the other. "Your sister's or brother's prison realm."

"It's my sister's. Thalia's wonderful. Don't be nervous." He hesitantly put the key in the hole. "Although, I hope she's well. She's been locked away for a century. It... does things to your mind."

"Speaking of being locked away, how did you escape without a key?"

"That is a story for another time."

A portal to the prison realm opened in a swirling mist of black and blue. My fingers touched Raiden's as my arm dangled next to his. His fingers flexed, and I moved away.

"Don't," he reached back. A muscle quivered in his jaw. I held his hand, and he squeezed mine back. Exhaling deeply, I focused on the portal. I wondered what she was like, the elusive Thalia, goddess of the dead.

A woman stepped out. Her pale skin shone silver under the pale light from the moon. Her gray-and-white eyes fixated on her brother. Strands of silver fell like silk over her shoulders, curling down to her hips. She tucked a lock of it behind her ear. Her thick, glossy lips stretched into a smile. "Brother." She glanced down at our knotted hands, and I pulled away.

He rushed to her, sweeping her into a stronghold. His well-defined muscles curved visibly under his tight shirt.

She kissed his cheek. "If you're here, then I'll assume Freya is dead."

He pulled her to arm's length. "No. But she will be soon."

"How did you get out?"

He glanced from her to me. "It's a long story."

"One you will tell me later." She turned her otherworldly gaze to meet mine. "Who is this?"

"This is Elle." His smile widened. "She helped to get you out of here."

"Elle. Short for Eleanor, no doubt." She tilted her head, the corner of her lip tugging up, the expression sweeping similarity to Raiden. She curled her arms around me. She was an entire foot taller than me, so my head landed at her shoulder.

I shuffled uncomfortably as the steel frame around her bust dug into me. The metal dipped downward between her cleavage. It reminded me of the armor the old king's knights used to wear, before the monarchy fell. I'd seen them in museums, but hers was far more striking and sexier.

She pulled away and moved the see-through voile cape buttoned at her neck to around her shoulders, as if it could somehow keep her warm against the chill in the air. "Thank you, dear Eleanor." She squeezed my hands in hers before moving back to face Raiden. "Where is Aziel?"

"We're getting him out next."

Cold seeped through the leather of my jacket. My fingers curled as the temperature dropped a few degrees. Raiden glanced down at me, then gave her a "come on" look.

She grinned, then swept her fingers through the air in a graceful, swirling motion. The chill in the air dissolved. "The dead follow me, brother. What do you want me to do?"

"Keep them at bay for now. Elle doesn't like the cold."

She nodded, her eyes narrowing in my direction. "Are you Raiden's lover?"

The directness of her question stumbled my reply. "No, I mean, not really. Uh, like friends but not friends."

She arched a thin eyebrow. I noticed a scar thinned the middle. "Friends but not friends?"

I looked from her to an amused Raiden. "You know what I mean." I rubbed the back of my neck, awkwardly laughing. "It's been, uh…"

"We're friends, Thalia."

I blew out a tense breath. "Yes. Exactly. Right. Good."

He tried to contain his smirk. "Running out of words there?"

Thalia chuckled a beautiful, echoed laugh that reverberated through the forest around us. "Don't tease the poor girl. Now, let us reunite with our brother before he tears down the world trying to escape. I've felt his rumbles."

My eyes widened. The thunder we'd been experiencing, the unexplained mini-earthquakes, they were him?

"It's been getting worse." Raiden grinned as if the whole thing were humorous. I, for one, was nervous to meet the thunder and earthquake bringer.

***

Stars poked like pinpricks through the black canvas above as we made our way to the mountains. Being in Raiden's arms as we ran next to Thalia made me acutely aware of my mortality. The many of what I thought were near misses but were in fact carefully timed dodges from large stones, trees, or people's houses had my adrenaline pumping. By the time we reached the snowy-peaked mountains, I was ready to collapse.

I took a minute to steady myself against a ragged stone, then sucked in a deep breath. "You could have gone a little slower." I looked around the groove between the mountains where we stood. It was lighter here, as the snow deceivingly lit the night sky with a gray glow. The jagged edges of the stark-white mountains towered through the clouds, which misted their tips from view. "Are we—"

Thalia extended her arms outward. "In the depths of the mountains? Yes." She breathed in flakes of snow as they drifted toward the white blanket around our feet. "There are not many dead here. Only the occasional traveler who had died and got lost on their way to the afterlife." She peered between two slices of rock, big enough for a person, and I shuddered, wondering who was there that I couldn't see. "It is peaceful."

A shiver danced through my body, making my teeth chatter. I licked my icy lips, which were numb under the heat of my tongue. "I'm mortal," I announced, unsure if they'd forgotten. "I don't do well with the cold."

Raiden removed his heavy jacket and placed it around my shoulders. It was far too big, but that only went in its favor against the snow. "Better?"

I buried my chin and mouth in the black fabric, breathing in the fresh cedarwood, forest scent. "Better. Thanks."

"Brother." Thalia walked barefoot in the snow. Her silver cape fluttered behind her as it caught in the gusts of wind sweeping through the mountains, icing her armor. "It is here." She swept her arms up toward an area of the mountain where rocks pointed upward in warning to any who wished to climb above them. "Our brother."

The mountains trembled as a thunderous roar sounded through the mountains. I grabbed Raiden to keep myself up, but he swept me into his arms, catching my next breath in his throat.

"Aziel's upset," he said.

"He's getting stronger."

"He wants out. It's what I had to do."

Finally. "Had to do what?"

He held me tighter as the ground shook. "Let's get him out," he said, ignoring my question. "Before he blows a hole in the mountain."

He handed Thalia the other key and took a step back. The trembling stopped, and he placed me down. "Stand behind me. There's no saying what my brother will be like after all this time."

I gulped and hid behind Raiden's tall form. I wasn't usually so afraid, but I was literally standing with two, about to be three, gods and one was responsible for the ground trembling throughout our province.

The portal opened into a mist of red and blazing orange. My heart skipped a beat as I peered around Raiden. Aziel stepped out and as he did, my hand tingled a magic quill.

Elle, get back here. A woman has us. She says you have something she wants and she's going to kill us if she doesn't get it back. Please. Naomi.

My eyes widened. The message dissolved and another tingled.

You need to get back here. Some crazed bitch has Naomi, Dora, and Edmund and she's going to kill them. She kept asking for you and for someone called Raiden. I escaped. I'm hiding in the vaults.

I tapped Raiden's arm. "We need to go back." Tears swam in my eyes. "Now." Shock erased my awareness. It was only when he spoke that I brought my attention to Aziel. He bore a striking resemblance to his brother, but his dark hair was longer, tied back into sections with bands, and his eyes were green. Tattoos covered his muscular arms, which were bare from the thick black armor he wore over his chest and shoulders. He looked as if he belonged on a battlefield and had a large scar running across an eyebrow and over one eye. I wondered how he'd got such marks when they could heal so quickly.

"Where is she?" Aziel boomed. "Where the fuck is that whore of yours?"

Raiden placed his hands on his brother's shoulders. "It's been a century, brother. She's not mine anymore."

"I'm going to tear her flesh from her bones."

Thalia stepped in front of Aziel, moving Raiden out of the way. Her presence seemed to calm him. His balled fists uncurled, and his muscles relaxed. She spoke, her voice melodic. "Calm, brother." She gazed into his eyes, and he stared back, transfixed. The entire thing made me uncomfortable.

"Don't compel him," Raiden chastised, pushing his hands into his pockets. "You swore you wouldn't use it on us anymore."

She clicked her tongue. "I'm just trying to calm him down." She looked away. "Fine, let him tear down the mountain." She pulled out a glowing dagger. "Unless you want me to use this on you again?" She teased.

Aziel growled. "What the fuck, Thalia?"

Ah. That was how he'd got the marks. I assumed, from the way it looked and glowed, it was enchanted or could hurt immortals. She sheathed it and smiled at Aziel. "Don't be so mad. Raiden got us out. We're back together again."

"I don't give a fuck."

She placed her hand on her hip. "I see your time locked away has worsened your temper."

Aziel's chiseled jaw clenched. "It will serve us well when I tear Freya apart. Where is she?"

Raiden answered. "We will find her. She's been using an old cloaking spell, one our dear sister here can break." He paused and smiled widely. "I've missed you, brother."

Aziel's frown slowly curled into a grin, and all the ferocity and anger that made him terrifying melted away. "Don't tell me being locked away turned you soft, Raiden."

"Don't test me, brother. I can still beat you in a fight." He laughed, and Aziel joined in. Thalia rolled her eyes as if she'd seen this a thousand times.

Aziel slammed his hand on Raiden's shoulder, smirking. "Never mind, it's not turned you soft. It's clearly made you delusional."

My heart hammered. I cleared my throat, and all three of them turned to look at me. "Not to break up this family reunion or anything, but my coven's in danger." I looked at Raiden. "Freya has Naomi, Edmund, and Dora and is going to kill them. She must know I took the keys."

"How?"

I glanced at my hand. "Magic quill from Naomi and Maddox." My eyes clamped shut. We were in the mountains and were one short run with Raiden from my sister, but I had to turn back. "We need to save them."

Aziel's eyebrows pinched into a frown. "Who's the mortal?"

Thalia smiled. "Eleanor."

Raiden stepped in front of me. "She helped get you out of here. We can trust her."

Aziel gritted his teeth. "Fine." He paused. "Let us go. If Freya is where you say she is, then that's where I'm needed."

CHAPTER NINETEEN

By the time we arrived back, it was early morning. Indigo had turned blue, lightening the sky enough to see the silhouettes of the buildings in Deadwood. The largest, the temple, where spikes pointed up against the fading stars, loomed over the smaller buildings. I moved my long waves over my shoulders, brushing flyaway hairs from my forehead and eyes as the wind picked up. I couldn't believe I'd ever worshipped Freya as a teenager, or Estia or Lucius. Now that I knew the truth, the memory of it made me wince.

"We can go from here." Raiden walked me away from his siblings, who talked near the edge of the woods. I stood on the edge of some rocks, overlooking our town from the east of the forest, which was known for having grizzly bears and wolves. "I can take you somewhere else. Anywhere. Until this is done."

"No." I looked at him incredulously. "I'm going with you."

His forehead creased. "You'll get yourself killed."

Aziel called from the tree line. "Or slow us down."

My eyebrows furrowed. "Super hearing?"

"We all do to an extent, but Leda's was the best. Well, now it's Freya's."

My stomach knotted. "She'll be dead by morning."

"Yes, she will." We looked at each other for far too long before he finally looked away. "Still, Aziel is faster than the rest of us, so he will chase Freya should she run."

I heard a low chuckle from where Aziel stood. "Finally, he admits it."

"I'm still stronger than you." Raiden glared, but the slight curve to his lips gave him away.

"Naomi. Edmund. Dora." I snapped my fingers. "We need to go. Now."

"Thalia needs to perform her rituals first, to break the cloaking spell. She's the only one with magic powerful enough to do it," he explained. "If Freya runs, even with Aziel, she might have a chance at somehow getting away. I can't take that risk, Elle. Not this time."

I understood, but I couldn't let the people I loved get hurt because of it. "How long will it take?"

His lips parted, and a sigh escaped. "Five, maybe six hours."

"Six hours?" My eyebrows shot up. "I'm not waiting that long. No way. I'm going now."

"You don't have the keys. She'll kill you all once she realizes you don't have them."

I kicked a small stone lying at my feet. The damn things had dissolved once they'd been used. Stupid spelled keys. "I have to do something."

"You can wait. She won't kill them. They're her bargaining chips."

"They're my family." I swallowed thickly.

"I know." He leaned down, touching my cheek. "You're still cold."

"Being whisked through the night at god speed didn't help." I tried to smile, but the fear for my family wouldn't let me.

"While Thalia does what she does, I'll get us inside somewhere." He looked down at the town. "A hotel? Maybe you can get some sleep until we can go."

I crossed my arms over my chest. "I'm going back. I have to do something."

"We both know all you'll do is put them in more danger by showing up empty-handed."

I hated when he was right. "I-I don't know."

"You can send a magic quill. Maybe they can tell Freya you're on your way. An excuse... maybe that you were looking for me but couldn't find me."

I relented. "Fine. Let's go then. I want a coffee first. I know the shop is open really early."

"We'll get one first."

As we walked away, I heard Aziel talking to Thalia. As soon as the cloaking spell on Freya was broken, he planned on running straight in there. He ignored the fact she would kill them if he did, because he didn't care. If I waited for them, then the only family I had would be dead. I couldn't let that happen. I couldn't sit around and do nothing. As soon as Raiden was out of my sight, I would run back.

Nestled on the four-post bed in the hotel room, Raiden lay back against two pillows, closing his eyes. "I'm surprised you were so amenable," he admitted.

I rocked on the rocking chair next to the large, lead-crossed window, drinking my coffee. The sun was beginning to come up, burning my eyes with it. "Stranger things have happened."

He chuckled. "I guess."

While we were passing time, what had happened earlier that night floated into my mind. I needed something to distract myself. I'd sent a magic quill to Naomi, telling her I would be coming. Then I sent one to Maddox, telling him to stay hidden and that I was on my way. Until Raiden fell asleep or left the room, there wasn't much more I could do.

"How did you get out of your prison realm? You said it was a story for later, and there's no better time than now."

The muscle in his finger twitched. "Perhaps not now."

"Why? Was it so bad?"

He sat up, his dark eyes focusing on me. "It's not something I want to talk about."

"Why not? Just tell me."

"No."

"Just tell me!"

"I can't," he snapped, the dark undertone to his voice shuddering through me.

"Why not?"

"Because I don't want you to think less of me."

My stomach swirled. I thought he didn't care what I thought of him. "I'm not going to judge you. I didn't when Freya told me everything. Not even for a second. She said you didn't always care about not killing innocents. I know it's different for you. You're immortal. You're a god."

He sighed. "Please, Elle. I don't want you to see me as a monster."

I looked over at the red bedspread and bit my bottom lip. I wished he wouldn't look at me like that, with those bedroom eyes. "I won't. Raiden. I don't. You're not a monster." I fumbled with my necklace. "Even if you once were, you're not now. Help me understand what happened."

He inhaled slowly. "You need to understand what it was like in there. To be locked away from your family, trapped in a realm with only a castle for one, no company, in a wasteland world. There was only enough food to sustain me for the first three months. After that, I starved but couldn't die. I wasted away for almost a century, losing my mind slowly until something came to me in the night."

My eyes widened. "What was it?"

"A wolf. I don't know how it found me or how it got in, but it must have slipped through the portal somehow. They always found me. Animals," he explained. "So I did what I hated, and I killed it and ate its flesh and consumed its soul." He tore his gaze from me to the window, his face paling. "It's not something we like to do, but we can do it. Souls make us stronger; eating them does anyway. It's barbaric and not a practice we've done in a long time, but it is one Freya is doing." His voice dripped with anger. "It gave me the strength to force myself through the portal door, shattering the realm. When I got out, I realized what I'd done. The forest around the portal had died after I'd shattered it, and every animal and person in a five-mile radius, they…" He trailed off. I didn't need him to finish. They'd died. My heart sank.

"It's not your fault." I went to him and held his hand in mine. "You didn't know that would happen. It's Freya's fault. She did this. You killed the wolf because it was your only choice. I'd have done the same, especially if my family were out there, needing me."

He moved his gaze to meet mine. "I'm going to end this tonight. I promise. Once she's dead, I'll help you find your sister before I move on to my father."

I jolted. "Your father? Lucius?"

"Yes."

"Why?"

"Don't you remember what I told you? He hunted us, tried to kill us and our children."

"Y-your what now?" I spluttered.

"Not mine, but Thalia's and Lena's. They had children. Demigods."

"Right." I rubbed my temples. This was all so weird. I had read about demigods somewhere. "Half mortal, half god."

"Yes."

"You never had any?"

He shook his head. "I never met anyone I wanted to do that with, well, until…"

"Freya."

"Right." He rubbed the side of his neck. "Then I was locked away, so."

"Yeah, that makes sense, I guess."

He rolled his shoulders back, propping two pillows behind his back. "I never really wanted children anyway, but Thalia did. She loved being a mother. Unfortunately, demigods' life spans are only a little longer than a mortal's. They would all be dead by now."

My heart ached for her. "I'm sorry."

"She'll find them."

Of course. She was goddess of the dead. She wasn't bound by the normal barriers between life and death. "How is it that only she can break the cloaking spell?" I wondered aloud.

"We all have different strengths. While we all possess magic and have heightened senses, each of us has extra abilities, making us unique. Aziel can create storms, shapeshift, and control the waters. Thalia can speak to the dead, is gifted with the power of divination, although she tries not to see into the future when possible as it takes a great toll on her, and has healing powers, compulsion, and strong magic."

I arched an eyebrow. "What about you?"

The corner of his lip curved up. "Aside from being the most handsome?"

I rolled my eyes.

He continued. "I'm the strongest of my siblings. I can communicate with animals, even control them to an extent, and—" He smirked. Ugh. I knew that look. "I'm also incredibly charming."

I couldn't help but laugh. "You might be overestimating that one."

He grinned, a teasing smile on his lips. "I don't know. It seemed to work on you."

Raiden had never fallen asleep. I'd asked him twice if he could go get more coffee or if I could go, but he annoyingly wasn't letting me out of his sight. After finally crashing for a couple of hours, I awoke to the sound of them talking.

"So it didn't work?"

"She's consumed too many souls." Thalia's tone broke. "It's old magic, painful to break. It would require me going out and doing the same."

Aziel's harsh tone interrupted them. "Then do it. Go and eat souls. Whatever it takes to break that spell."

Raiden growled softly. "Then we're no better than her. No one is eating any souls."

"She's awake." Thalia's soft tone swept toward me. How did she know?

I blinked twice and sat upright.

Raiden's worry lines softened. "We need to go after her now, while we know where she is."

"I heard. Her cloaking spell can't be broken." My stomach twisted. "We have no choice then. I can pretend to have the keys. Maybe lure her away from the others?"

The three looked at each other, then back at me. "Sure," Thalia said a little too sweetly. "We'll do that."

I stared at the mansion from the edge of the forest and swallowed thickly. If Freya knew the gods were out, she'd kill Naomi and my coven. I only hoped Maddox managed to stay in the vaults and out of her way.

Aziel rubbed his hands together. "We should go headfirst."

Thalia rolled her eyes. "That's always your response, and everyone always ends up dead." She reached her hand out, touching something I couldn't see. "There are many dead here. I see some in the windows." She gazed up. The mansion was tiny from where we were standing, but Raiden did say they all had better eyesight than me. "Their pale faces are watching out."

I knew the place was old, but damn. I wouldn't be able to shake that mental image for a while. I imagined the windows and shuddered. "Let's not add to them," I said softly. "If Freya knows you're out of your prison realms, she'll kill them, then flee. It will be pointless."

Aziel shook his head. "I vote we charge in before she can get away."

My stomach lurched. "No."

Raiden grabbed my hand and unexpectedly squeezed it. "No one is dying today." He paused. "No mortals anyway."

Aziel growled lowly. "Are we repeating the same story, brother? Putting a mortal before your family?"

Raiden shot him a hardened look. "Don't go there."

Thalia stepped in between them. "I agree with Raiden. We will abstain from as many tragedies as possible. I do not wish to send more souls to Mother or Father if we can refrain from it. We are not beasts, Aziel."

Raiden nodded. "We need a plan. I will go in there. She already knows I'm out. She'll hesitate, but she's strong right now. While I distract her, Thalia, you can come through the back entrance. Hopefully, she won't hear you. You're the quietest of us. You can slip between shadows."

Thalia ran a long finger along her smiling lips. "You know I can, brother."

"Once Thalia is in." He gave his brother a look. "Once the witches are safe, then I will call for you and we will kill her. It will take all of us, with her having consumed souls. I could have had her the other night. She was weak. She'd just fed, and she's always weak right after killing and eating, but then she got away and I couldn't trace her." He balled a fist. "She's had time to digest. She would have taken more souls before this. She'll be stronger than ever now."

Aziel did not look pleased.

I cleared my throat. "Where do I come in?"

Raiden sighed. "You don't, doll. I need you out here. Safe."

Aziel shrugged. "You're a liability, sorry. You'll just slow us down." He lowered his voice. "You already are."

Raiden's jaw clenched. "What was that?"

"You heard."

Oh, gods.

Raiden turned to face him. "She helped get you out of that prison realm."

"If she wasn't here, you would go in there without a single thought for those witches."

Raiden let out a low growl. "It has nothing to do with her."

"That's what you said about the last mortal, then she cut our sister's head off and became one of us."

"Elle isn't like Freya."

"You always did let your heart rule your head. Should another of your siblings pay the price for it?"

"This isn't like that. Freya and I were in love. I'm not now, and even if I were, I wouldn't do that again."

I snapped. "Enough!" I closed my eyes for a second, feeling rage bubble below the surface. "I helped you get out!" I shouted at Aziel, whose eyebrows shot up his forehead. "I am not Raiden's lover or anything like Freya, so you can stop thinking I somehow have any influence over him. All I care about is getting my family out of there, alive. You can have Freya and take her head for all I care, but I will not stand here and be compared to the same woman who's holding the people I love captive. Now, I am going in there with you, whether you like it or not. I will not slow you down. In fact, seeing me just might be enough to make her hesitate if she thinks I have her stupid keys."

Raiden's expression darkened. "Aziel, keep her here."

I gritted my teeth. "What? No. You can't just keep me here."

"Don't let her out of your sight."

Aziel shook his head. "Fine, but when you call for me, she's on her own."

***

Aziel paced as we waited for Raiden or Thalia to send a signal or call for him. It had been minutes.

"What if something's happened?" I asked for the third time. "I should go check."

"I'm not letting you go in there."

I placed a hand on my hip. "You can't just hold me here like a prisoner. Besides, why do you care what happens to me? Just because Raiden told you to keep me here…"

His expression changed. "Raiden doesn't just protect anyone. I don't want to deal with his temper if I let you go in and something happens to you."

"He doesn't care."

He laughed. "You mortals are so blind."

"Hey."

"Look, mortal."

"It's Elle."

He shrugged. "He kept you warm, swore to help you find your sister, took you to a hotel room, and is now protecting your life. You both may not see it, but I do, and I don't care for it, but he's my brother, so."

"You're wrong. He did all of that for his own gain."

"Think what you want." He resumed his pacing. "I need silence now."

"I need it too," I grumbled, then leaned back against one of the gargoyle statues. He was more difficult than his brother, which was an accomplishment.

Finally, after another minute, he relented. "I'm going in. Something's not right. Stay here." With lightning speed, he rushed through the gates and into the front door, knocking it off its hinges.

I was about to run in behind him when something caught me around my waist. I turned, and a hand clapped over my mouth, muffling my next scream. It was Alexander, sporting a scar where I'd shot him, and a scornful look to go with it.

"You're coming with me."

I kicked and punched, but he was stronger. I wished I had my dagger. I finally managed to get my foot high enough to aim for the balls. When I muscled a kick, he staggered back, clutching his prized jewels. I sucked in a deep breath, then turned on my heel and ran right into Freya.

"Well, well." She laughed. "I was wondering when he'd leave you. Naturally, Raiden would keep his new mortal pet under protection."

My eyes teared. "Where's Naomi? Edmund? Dora?"

"Not dead." She cocked her head, then looked at Alexander. "Stop complaining." She glanced at his pants. "Let's get her out of here before they realize."

"What. No—" Something blunt hit the back of my head. Stars filled my vision as everything faded to black.

CHAPTER TWENTY

I peeled my eyelids back and saw a star-stricken ceiling, painted to look like the night sky. For a second, I remained still, mesmerized. Silk hugged my curves, and I snuggled deeper into the bed, forgetting where I was until a searing pain in my head shot me upright. Leaning forward, I pressed my hands against the sides of my head and screamed.

"I said heal her," a voice snapped. "If not just to shut her up."

I whipped my head to my left, and through blurred vision, I could make out Freya's tall figure wrapped in a tight blue dress. Her dark hair was a mass against her back. She stared out of a window that ran the length of the side of the room.

Alexander rushed to my side. Focusing on his long, dirty-blond curls, I let his fingers graze my temples. Heat tingled below his fingertips. As quick as the pain had come, it dissolved. Rolling my head back, stretching my neck, I inhaled deeply.

"Who the fuck do you think you are?" I scowled once I reoriented myself.

"A goddess." She ran her fingers through her silky black strands. "While you are merely a mortal."

Alexander joined her side, placing his hand around her waist and brushing a kiss against her shoulder.

I cleared my throat. "So is your... boyfriend." I guessed.

He smiled. "Not for long."

Freya gave him a look, and he fell silent. "Just stay quiet until I figure this out."

Puzzle pieces connected in my mind. "You're planning on turning him immortal, which can only mean..." I shook my head at the thought. "You're going to kill another of them to turn him into a god."

"Alexander deserves it." She ran her hand down his cheek, and his besotted gaze latched onto hers as if no one else in the universe existed but her. I wished someone would look at me like that. "He's been loyal to me for the last decade."

He only looked to be in his mid-thirties. She must have met him young—probably manipulated him into feeling bad for her. Why else would someone stick around someone so awful?

"You know, for someone who's gone through such terrible things, you really don't mind inflicting the same pain onto others." I expected her to lunge at me, but she remained quite still.

"I'm doing what I have to, to survive. Raiden, Thalia, and Aziel will never forgive me for what I did. They will forever hunt me, and a life spent hiding is not a life lived at all."

"People have died for you to live," I said with a scowl. "Not just Leda. I mean all the witches and warlocks you've eaten."

She turned to look at me. Her left eye twitched slightly. "They were not who you think they were. They had dark thoughts. Dark intentions."

My eyebrows pinched downward. "What do you mean?"

"I can feel a person's heart," she explained, sauntering toward the bed where I lay. "All I need to do is place my hand upon them, like this." She touched my hand. Her touch was too soft, too gentle for someone with her disposition. "I can sense the essence of a person. It's a power I did not expect when I became immortal, but one which has allowed me to dispose of only the worst people."

I thought about Bryan. The quiet, sweet boy I'd hung out with when I first came to Istinia. "No. Bryan, one of your victims, was my friend. A long time ago," I said, although ten years was nothing to a goddess. "He was a good person."

One of her dark eyebrows arched. "Ah, yes, the boy close to your coven. He was not an innocent." She gazed up as if lost in the memory of how he'd tasted.

I shuddered at the thought.

"He wanted to inflict pain. He hurt animals. That's how I found him. He was torturing a deer in the woods, so I tortured him."

SPELLBOUND

"Well." I huffed, my cheeks heating. "You can't just decide who gets to live and die. You're not…"

"A goddess?"

I gripped the silk sheets tight. "I mean, you are, but you can't just kill people."

"Who says I can't?"

I paused. "It's wrong."

"No."

My eyes widened. "No?"

"I needed souls, and I chose to feast upon dark ones. How does that make me bad?"

"Everyone is allowed a fair trial. You can't just feel someone as being bad, then condemn them."

She shrugged, sitting at the edge of the bed all too casually. Peering around her, I noticed the large window overlooked the snowy peaked mountains and an evergreen forest that continued to the horizon. I looked around the wood cabin, which must have been situated on the side of a mountain—or at least built up high.

I moved as far away from her as I could, without falling off the bed. "You kidnapped me. You're not making a strong case for not being the bad guy. I mean, it's like you've taken a page right of the villain handbook."

Freya shifted her weight, then tucked her hair behind her ears, showing off her diamond-shaped face and strong features. I supposed I could see the beauty that had captivated Raiden. Her cupid-bow lips were painted dark red, complementing the dark brown of her hair and her olive-toned skin. "I'm doing what I must to survive. You see, they will not allow me to live, but Thalia and Aziel listen to Raiden, and Raiden cares for you. As long as I have you, he won't come for me, not when your life is in danger."

Panic struck through me, forcing my heart to skip its next beat. "You've got this all wrong. We're barely friends. We hated each other before that. If your life is riding on whether or not he cares for me, then you've made a fatal mistake."

She rolled her expressive eyes and stood, sweeping the creases from the silk at her waist. "I know what I felt when I touched Raiden, and he was protecting you that day I broke in. I am not wrong in this. I never am in matters of the heart."

"Don't you care?" I pulled myself off the bed and stood. "He loved you! Doesn't that mean anything to you?"

She looked at the window, her gaze far off. "No."

"You're so cold."

"I've had to be." She walked toward me, even as I shuffled against the headboard, and took my hand in hers. She closed her eyes for a few seconds, and a hint of a smile curled her lips. "You have felt great loss too. It never goes away, the emptiness after losing someone you love, and you have so much emptiness." She released my hand, gently placing it on the covers. "You feel almost hollow. I can see why Raiden showed an interest in you. He, like you, are both broken."

I scoffed. "You're not?"

"Why do you think he loved me?"

I scowled. "How can that mean nothing? You speak so coldly of him when all he did was love you."

"You know what he did. He is responsible for my son's death."

"He didn't know." My voice cracked at the ends. "This is all one big mistake."

"My son's death is not a mistake." She balled her fists, tensing the lean muscles in her arms.

"You didn't even want him," I snapped but wished I hadn't. "Sorry, that wasn't fair."

She lifted her hand as if to push me but stopped herself. "This is my room." She blew out a tense breath. "You should leave it before I decide to throw you through the window."

I gulped. "Thought you needed me."

"Only alive." Steady, cold rage guided her tone. "Alexander can heal you should you step out of line."

I glanced from her to the window, not wanting to be told twice. I hightailed it out of the room and found myself standing behind the now-closed door to her bedroom. I ran straight for the front door, pushed it open, and found a hundred steps leading down to the meadow, among the forest crowned by mountains. Glancing behind me, I decided to brave it and pushed a foot outside, but I was forced right back in again.

"What the—" I tried again but was forced back inside as if an invisible barrier surrounded the house. I closed my eyes. Of course, that was exactly what it was. Alexander must've been one powerful warlock to be able to cast a barrier spell and heal my head earlier. It was probably why she kept him around. Although, it did show her threat of throwing me out of the window was empty, considering I couldn't even step outside.

After closing the door, I stormed back inside. I kicked the corner of a rug that covered the polished floorboards of the living room. Skulls from various animals were hung decoratively on the wood-paneled walls. Dusty, yellow lamps emitted an orange glow from the two corner tables next to a four-seat cream sofa. A painting of Freya, shrouded in silk upon a horse, hung above the unlit fireplace. Her eyes seemed to follow me around the room as I paced.

I left the living area and ambled through a barely used kitchen with what appeared to be oak countertops and an old stove with an empty teapot on it. I continued out, moving through another door and down a narrow hallway until I reached a well-lit, windowed room, like Freya's. In it, an easel stood in the center over a blue rug, and paintings of all different colors cluttered the walls. At the back, a twin, unmade bed sat under an erotic painting of Alexander and Freya.

I almost knocked into a box of open paints as I walked past a mahogany cabinet. Alexander was looking out the window but turned his dreamy gaze toward me. "The sun will set soon."

My eyebrows knitted together. "Okay."

"You should see it. It's the best time to capture the beauty of the transition of day to night."

"You know what else is beautiful?"

He turned on his heel, tilting his head. "What?"

"Freedom."

"Ah." He nodded in understanding. "I cannot let you out of here, I am afraid. It is up to Freya when you leave."

"You're just okay with her doing this?"

"I love her," he said simply, as if it were the answer to everything.

I admired his many paintings of sunsets and mountains, of skulls, roses, gunshot wounds somehow painted to appear pretty, and a variety of poses of Freya. Some captured parts of her face under different lightings. "The wound." I pointed at the painting of the hole in a shoulder, where blood-spattered paint dripped down into a rose. "Was that what I did?"

He nodded. "I paint all parts of my life. Even the ugly," he explained. "Then I make it look beautiful."

I stepped in front of his current piece on the easel. The paint was barely dry. "Is that me?" I could feel the blood drain from my face as I stared at an oil painting of myself lying on the ground outside the mansion, blood pooling from under my head. A shattered vase lay around me, its shards pointing inward. "Wait, you were the one who hit me."

"Yes." He hid nothing in his expression. Pain tore through his forced smile.

"Why?" I sighed. "Let me guess, love? Or revenge for shooting you?"

"Because Freya asked me to, but let's call us even now."

My anger bubbled under the surface. "I shot you because you were threatening my friend. You knocked me out to kidnap me. Those are two totally different scenarios," I growled, then grabbed the painting he'd done of me. I ran my hand along the paint until the colors ran into each other. I waited for him to react, but he just stood, watching.

"You're insane."

I could have laughed if it wasn't so damn ironic. "Me? You do realize you're in love with a psycho who eats people."

He placed a finger in the air as if to stop me. "She eats souls. Not them. Although, sometimes she will eat their hearts, but rarely."

"You do hear yourself, right?" I laughed sardonically. "Am I trapped in an alternate reality where this is normal?"

He shook his head, shoving his hands into his deep pockets, and walked to the painting I ruined. "I can still fix it."

"You." I pointed at him with bulging eyes. "You are the insane one, for the record."

***

I watched Freya hunt from the window. It was quite mesmerizing, watching her catch deer and rabbits with her bare hands as she hid among shadows, slipping between them with ease. It was a beautiful place. The house was built high up in the trees, on tall trunks of cut-down trees. It looked like it belonged to the forest.

It had been days since I'd arrived, and no one had come to save me. Freya and Alexander had spent the evenings discussing what they were going to do. I tried to do a magic quill, but nothing sent. My magic didn't work here. Alexander must have been blocking it. If I were a little colder hearted, I'd have killed him while Freya was out, and I'd left the house, but I wasn't like her, and as much as Alexander was a part of this, there was something about him that stopped me, a madness deep in his eyes, but soft, not dangerous. Like he didn't understand everything happening. It was as if the lines of reality and fantasy had blurred somewhere between paintings.

"She's hunting your dinner," he explained when he entered the room I had been assigned. My window was much smaller than theirs, but at least I could look out to freedom.

I scrunched my nose. "I'm not eating rabbit or deer."

"There's no menu," he explained gently as if I truly believed there were. "It's that or starve, I am afraid."

"What's the plan then?" I asked, changing the subject. "How exactly do you plan on killing Raiden?"

He tilted his head. "Raiden?"

"I assume you'll be wanting to take his place?"

"No. Freya has chosen Aziel's body for mine. Lucius will take care of the other two."

"Lucius." My eyebrows flicked up in surprise. "Their father, the god of the underworld?"

"God of justice," he said, correcting. "But yes, he does have domain over the underworld."

"You're working with their father to hunt them?"

He shuffled uncomfortably, pushing his blond curls over his shoulder. "We have heard Lucius wants replacements. His children have plagued this world with more sin, and he wants to set things right."

I scoffed. "Says the man who helped kidnap me, and hit me over the head, and is in love with the woman who eats hearts!" Gods, these people were mad. "I thought gods were meant to help mortals. Hmm?"

His eyebrows furrowed. "I suppose."

"Do you really think Freya cares about helping mortals, like us?" I pointed at him so he understood he was still a mortal, because he seemed to be under the illusion he was more.

"You don't understand her. No one does but me. She's been through more pain than either of us can imagine."

"I know what she went through, but it's no excuse. She decided to make the wrong choices time and time again." I inhaled sharply. "Can you really blame Raiden and the others for hunting her? She killed their sister, Alexander. Do you have siblings? A family?"

"I did."

"What happened to them?"

"They left me." He looked down, and guilt stabbed through me. I knew that look all too well.

"So did mine." Silence fell over us both for a moment. "I'd still kill for them though—for my sister anyway. She's all I have left."

"I did not know you had a sister."

I opened my mouth to speak but thought better of it.

He looked back out the window, turning his back toward me. "Where is she?"

I swallowed thickly. "She's… away from here."

"In Istinia?"

I shook my head. "No, uh. She's not a witch."

"Ah," he said slowly. "Interesting."

"Hardly." I scoffed. "Besides, enough about my family. What about yours?"

"Freya is my family. My everything."

"She can't be the only person you care about."

"She is."

"Fine." I huffed. "Then what would you do if someone with a tortured past came along and killed her for her immortality?"

His expression darkened. "I'd kill them."

"Exactly."

"Look, I can't stop Lucius from hunting his children. It's the best thing for you mortals."

"Us mortals," I said. "Us."

"For now." He rhythmically tapped his fingers against his thigh. "He's already come for them from the underworld. There's nothing I can do."

I gulped. "Lucius is in a body?"

"He has come in flesh, with hounds, and he is here already. I am sorry, but there is no plan."

"I heard you all talking in the evenings…"

"Yes." He shrugged. "Not about what to do with you. You are simply here to pause the gods in coming for her, just in case they find a way to trace us here and give Lucius enough time to kill them before they reach her."

I ran cold. "I'm just being used to stall?"

"Yes, but once they're dead, she will let you go."

"Or kill me."

He hesitated. "She will most likely let you go. She will have no further use for you once they're dead."

"When will I supposedly be released?" I asked.

"By this evening. Lucius has already found their trail. They will be dead soon, and you will be released."

He ambled away as if lost in a daydream, and I lost it. I wasn't staying in this house for a moment longer, not when Raiden was being hunted and he didn't even know it. I had to get out to help them, to help him. If not, we could all be dead by sundown.

CHAPTER TWENTY-

ONE

Howling erupted through the night, shattering the silence in the forest around the house.

Freya glanced from me to the door, her eyes widening. She could sense them, I was sure. The gods must have been close, as must Lucius.

I scratched the back of my hand with my nails, their polish chipping, and cursed under my breath. I stared at the oak dining table. I don't know why I'd tried to send another magic quill. It was utterly pointless. I couldn't leave the house, and my magic didn't work—both because of Alexander, whom I'd tried and failed to talk into dropping the barrier.

There was only one other option, and the thought curdled my last meal of rabbit that Freya had put on the table. Alexander joined us, sweeping down and landing a kiss on Freya's cheek. "My love," he whispered against her skin as he pulled away. "They are near."

"Yes." Her red lips pulled into a small smile as the sky darkened, shadowing the trees through the window behind Freya. "Lucius will stop them before they reach us. They must have found her trail." Her gaze danced to mine. "Once they pass through the barrier Lucius placed around the forest, they will be trapped."

My eyes snapped toward hers. "You used me to lure them here. To trap them."

"Yes," she said nonchalantly. "Fear not. Once the night is over, you will be taken back to your coven. Alexander convinced me to let you go."

My chest grew hollow as I looked up at him. It made what I needed to do even harder. "This is not right."

"Do not pity them." She looked me down. "They have had centuries to live."

"Where do they go when they die? To Estia?"

She shook her head. "When a god is replaced, they go to the underworld."

The thought sent a shudder through me. "Lucius's domain."

"They can't inhabit another body again."

"Leda's soul is there."

She nodded. "I am certain it is."

My eyes widened. "Lucius is their father. How can he torture his own children? To wish them dead?"

"Bless your mortal heart." She sighed, looking at me as if I were a ten-year-old. "The realms are not like this world, nor are those who inhabit them. Lucius and Estia created them but did not share the same bond a mortal would share with their child," she explained, pausing for a few seconds. "They were born to help rule this world but instead destroyed it."

I swallowed thickly. "I don't believe that."

She shrugged. "Believe what you wish, but it's the truth. Demons exist because the gods did not help vanquish them. They allowed sin to flourish."

"Nothing is that black and white." I clenched my jaw, remembering back to everything Raiden had told me. "Besides, if they allowed sin to flourish, as you said, then what are you doing? Murder is the biggest sin of them all."

She leaned back in her chair. "Lucius and Estia do not see it that way."

"Have you asked him?"

She hesitated, glancing at Alexander, then back at me. "I haven't spoken to him exactly, but—"

"Then how do you know?" I asked, interrupting. "He might come after you once he's taken care of the others. What's to stop your soul from being trapped in the underworld just like the others? You're not mortal." I gripped my nails into the wood table, feeling splinters press against my fingertips. "By morning, you might find yourself just as dead as them."

"No. I spoke to demons through the portal to the underworld who told me Lucius wished to replace his children. After that, I left the portal open."

I arched an eyebrow. "Did they say you would be spared?"

Alexander entwined his fingers with hers. "She's right, my love. Are you certain Lucius will spare us? That he will use me to replace them?"

She pulled her fingers from his, her face paling under the dim light of the oil lamp. "Lucius will not forsake us. I let him out. He owes me."

Alexander's eyes creased at the corners. "We should, perhaps, go to our home in the mountains outside of the barrier until this is over. Just in case."

Her eyes reflected the flickering of the lamps as fear flashed in them. "He will not hurt us; I am certain. But I had planned to go to the mountains regardless. A fight between gods will cause untold damage, and I choose to be out of the way, at least until they are dead."

I couldn't believe it. She was running scared. With her and Alexander leaving off their own backs, I wouldn't have to hurt Alexander, which was something I'd been considering. Once Freya was gone, which I'd hoped would be to aid Lucius, although that didn't seem to be her plan at all, I was going to knock Alexander out, then bleed him out enough to weaken him so his barrier spell weakened and I could get out.

I was glad I didn't have to do it.

Alexander cleared his throat. "What about Eleanor?"

Freya blew out a tense breath. "We let her go."

"Now?" His eyes bulged.

"Yes." She looked out the large window overlooking the forest and mountains. "Leave her to the mercy of the gods and the wilderness. There is little she can do now, and the gods are already through the barrier. It is made from his blood, therefore only trapping them. So we can leave." She closed her eyes. "I can sense them."

"I will collect my paints."

"There's no time," she snapped, standing. "We will leave now."

Alexander relented far too quickly. I wondered why they were together, but then I saw it. He would do anything for her, and she needed that. She'd been hurt by men her whole life, and Alexander was different. He was softer, gentler than them, and he would die to protect her.

For him, she was his rock in an ocean of madness. I saw it when he'd slip into a dreamy, far-off look and mutter to himself. She grounded him. Together, they were each other's lifeboats. I was curious as to what would happen when inevitably one would have to leave the other.

He looked back and nodded as he lifted the spell. The buzz of magic, which I hadn't even noticed until it was gone, fizzled out. The heaviness in the air dissolved with it.

Freya fled into the night. The white silks of her dress flickered behind her as she took off. Alexander was at her side as she carried him toward the mountains.

I ran to the door, breathing in gulps of fresh air. Howls from demon hounds erupted again. The cool night air prickled my skin as I climbed down the steps toward the ground. Jumping off the bottom one and onto the grass, I closed my eyes.

I sent a magic quill to Naomi first. *Tell me you're all okay - Elle*

Within twenty seconds, a message back tingled onto the back of my hand. *Where are you?*

The forest by the mountains. Freya kidnapped me. She let me go.

I ran into the tree line, which was coated in darkness. Carefully I treaded the underbrush, plants, crunched leaves, and roots as I felt my way through. I felt a message come back, then another, but I couldn't make the words out in the blackness.

The howling grew closer, and suddenly everything felt colder, like the leaves grazing against my hands and the twigs brushing up against my neck and cheeks as I fumbled through the forest. It was as if the ice was pricking at me. The temperature dropped until fog left my mouth with each breath. Slithering accompanied hissing from the underbrush as something slid around my boot. I suppressed a scream as I jolted back. Snakes.

A hiss of a whisper circled the air, trapped in an icy breeze as it danced along the wisps of moss stuck between branches. *What do you desire?* It repeated over and over until I pressed my hands against my ears to block it. My heart hammered as I continued forward, trembling.

Everything fell into dead silence. A forest absent sound was as eerie as a world without people. There was no scurrying of animals through leaves, no scratching against trunks, or even a hoot of an owl. Fog crept through the trees, freezing the tips of my fingers and frosting my lips until my teeth were chattering.

The disjointed voice returned, caught in the wind as it picked up. *We're here. We can taste death.*

I pinched my nose when a waft of rotten eggs and decay hit me. Faltering forward, I did my best to block out the sound. Who did the voice belong to? Why was it dropping into winter in the middle of fall? Where was Raiden?

My scream was muffled against a palm when a hand flapped against my mouth, causing a shock of pain to ripple through me. My heart almost stopped as her voice fluttered into my ear. *"It's Thalia. Don't make a sound. I am going to move my hand now."*

I nodded yes. I was on the verdge of having a heart attack. I swear my nerves would never be the same after this—if I got out of it alive.

Thalia pulled me back into the shadows behind a tree. Her voice softened to where I could barely hear it. "Lucius is here."

"I know." I felt sick from the adrenaline. "Where's Raiden?"

"Close. He's with Aziel, tracking Lucius. We must attack our father before he finds us. The element of surprise is the only tool we have." Her silver gaze found mine. "Where is Freya?"

"In the mountains," I whispered. "There's a barrier around the forest so none of you can leave. It's made from your bloodline. This was all a trap. I'm so sorry."

She pinched her eyes shut, her expression pained as she gripped onto the tree. After a few seconds, she let out a gasp.

My eyebrows knitted together. "What happened?"

"It's the demons." Her deathly pale skin was illuminated by the moonlight hitting her armor. "They have come with him. They are everywhere. Their presence brings death. Everything is dying." She plucked a rotting leaf from a low-hanging branch. "Lucius was a fool to bring them to find us. They now have access to the world. Although I am certain Father believes he can control them, one or two always slip through."

I gulped. "That's why it's so cold?"

"Yes." She lowered her voice again. "You must leave this place. You do not want to be here for the fight."

"But Raiden—"

"Will be fine," she said, interrupting. "Your being here will only see to distract Raiden from focusing on Lucius. He'll be worried about you. You must run east. There are fewer demons there. I will run north, and they will chase me there."

"I can't just leave. Freya said he wants you all dead. He means to replace you."

Her expression hardened, from what I could tell under the slight white light. "We will send him back to the underworld. There are three of us," she said but didn't look convinced. "I will tell my brother you were concerned about him. He will appreciate it."

I shook her words off. "Is everyone okay back home? Freya didn't hurt them, did she?" The tingles from the magic quills told me they were all okay, but I had to make sure. "Naomi is with Aziel."

My brain faltered. "I'm sorry. Did you say Naomi is with Aziel? Like, the god Aziel?"

"She agreed to come with us to help find you."

My eyes widened. "Next time, lead with that." I ran my fingers down my face, dragging the skin under my eyes. "I need to find her."

Thalia's expression softened. "Her illusory magic will be useful in stopping Lucius."

I would have laughed at the ridiculousness of it all if I thought it were a joke, but her face told me it wasn't. "Naomi will die," I stated.

"She understood the price when she insisted on coming with us."

"She knows you're gods then?"

"Yes, as do the rest of your coven, who also wanted to come to find you. Raiden, unfortunately, stopped them before they could aid us."

I breathed relief. "At least he had some sense."

"They could have helped us with Lucius."

I shook my head. "Why did he let Naomi come?"

A hint of a smile played on her lips. "She used her magic to dupe him, then asked me and Aziel to take her. He was upset."

My heart softened. "I didn't know he cared for the coven so much."

She smiled knowingly. "I don't believe he cares for them *that* much."

"Then why would he—"

Thalia placed her finger against my lips, stopping my next question. A twig snapped nearby.

"They're here," she whispered and stepped in front of me. I wondered why she was protecting me. If she cared so much for mortals, then why was she disappointed the coven couldn't come to help? Or stop Naomi from going with them? How did they even find out about Lucius?

Shock rooted me to the spot. As I peered around Thalia, my scream caught in my throat, my next breath stopping behind my lips. Deep crimson eyes found us in the night. With fur so black, the hounds managed to appear as moving shadows. Their long, yellow canines dripped saliva as they pawed the ground, growling toward us slowly. Thalia poised to attack. There were two of them, twice the size of any normal dog, and I didn't stand a chance. Around their necks were thick chains, broken off at the bottom. The stench of singed fur and ash accompanied them as they grew closer.

Thalia backed away slowly, as they were in lunging distance. I moved backward with her. I hated how helpless I was. My magic was next to useless in this scenario. If only I had my dagger or pistol... although I didn't think they'd be much help against the hounds.

"Eleanor," she whispered over her shoulder. "When I move in a moment, I want you to climb this tree." She placed her hand against a trunk we shuffled past. "Do not hesitate, no matter what you see."

I didn't argue. "Okay."

Once the hounds were dead, I'd persuade her to take me to Naomi. There was no way I was leaving the forest without her. I blew out a tense breath, then blinked.

Within a flutter of my eyelashes, she was gone. The hounds growled into the night. Cold swept past me, and something howled in my ears. They barked, and I grabbed a low branch and pulled my weight up, feeling around for a stump with my foot. Finding a groove to stick my foot into, I pulled myself up just as a hound reached me.

My heart skipped a beat, but the creature was thrown aside by Thalia, who emerged from shadows at inhuman speed.

"Climb!" she shouted.

I scrambled to reach for the next branch and pulled up again, wishing I'd spent more time strength training. My arms trembled as I huffed my way up the side of the tree. I didn't look down when a whimper sounded below.

I reached a high, thick branch and felt out for it. I curled around it until I was sitting at its base, overlooking the scene. One of the hounds sank its teeth into her thigh, letting out a demonic growl as it did. Crimson splashed the dirt mixed with leaves. A whelp left her mouth.

She placed her hands in its mouth and forced its jaw open until it stopped with a loud crack. A shiver snaked down my spine. She unsheathed her dagger, the hilt made from precious gems, which glinted in the light. It glowed white as it had before. She sank it into the hound with the broken jaw, and it yelped, then went silent. The second hound snarled, then turned and fled between two trees.

Quickly, I clambered down the tree and over to Thalia. "Will you heal?"

"A hound bite will not heal as fast," she explained. "Their venom is meant to weaken anything and anyone, even immortals." She hissed when she placed her fingers against the pumping blood dripping down around her thigh. I removed my jacket and pulled off my T-shirt, then tore the bottom of it around until I had a thick piece of fabric. I tightened it around her thigh, pushing hard against the bite.

"Thank you." She smiled, but her eyebrows flicked upward as she looked behind me. "Eleanor."

I turned in what felt like slow motion as the second hound returned, lunging across the earth toward us.

I reached out for the only light, the dagger with its moonlight hue, and crouched. Fuck, it was huge. I held my breath as it snapped its canines against the air. I twirled out of the way of its bite when it reached us, then I spun, kicking my leg out like I would in practice with Edmund, but everything was sharper now. Adrenaline fueled, I grabbed a handful of thick, warm fur and felt claws against my arm. Inhaling sharply, I brought the dagger into its head. I lifted it and pushed it down again until I heard a bone crunch under the blade.

I closed my eyes and removed my shaking hands from the stone-encrusted hilt. My arm was soaked, and iron tanged my taste buds. Blood coated my tongue from where I'd bitten my cheek mid-attack.

"You killed it." Disbelief guided her tone.

"I killed it." The same disbelief coursed through me. I scrambled away from the lifeless beast. As soon as my adrenaline began to settle, the cold around us sank through my skin and into my bones. I pulled my leather jacket back on and zipped it over my shirtless torso.

Raiden's voice boomed. "What the fuck happened here?"

Aziel joined us. Naomi's eyes found mine.

"Nai." My voice croaked into a cry as she ran to me and flung her arms around my blood-coated body.

Naomi buried her head in my tangled hair. "I was so worried she'd killed you. Elle, can you believe it? They're gods!"

Blood trickled down my arm to my hand. The adrenaline had numbed the sting from my wound, but the pain seared when it returned, confusing my body onto the ground. I could hardly breathe. "Get her out of here!" Raiden shouted, and someone dragged me to the tree. "Heal her," he said, but Thalia's voice broke.

"Lucius is here."

Chapter Twenty- Two

Lucius was everything I had expected the father of the gods to be: unyielding and deadly fast, with deep intelligence behind his dark eyes. I fell between consciousness and fading blackness, peeling my eyes back to see glimpses of a worried Naomi and flashes of the full blue moon.

"Children," he boomed with contempt stinging his tone. "I am so lucky to have found you all in one place, ready for death."

I forced myself to sit up, pressing my back against the tree trunk.

"Careful," Naomi whispered. She pressed her fingers against the fang marks in my skin. I blew out a long shaky exhale and tried to focus on the man who'd stopped three gods in their tracks.

Wielding a sword in skilled hands, he struck it through the air, slicing far too close to where Raiden stood. I yelped and covered my mouth. Lucius looked at us as if he could make us out perfectly despite the thick cover of night.

"You brought mortals to a fight between gods." He spat in front of his feet. "Weak."

Naomi's eyes glossed with tears. "What an asshole," she whispered, although I was sure he could hear us. Fortunately, we weren't important enough for him to do anything about it.

Aziel's deep voice was the first to shout a *fuck you*, right as a storm swirled out of nowhere. Inkblots of black covered the moon. Thunder shook the ground, and Aziel's lightning gaze matched the green flash in the sky.

Snakes, spiders, and every other nightmarish bug crawled from the underbrush and toward Raiden, where he welcomed them with outstretched arms. He was communicating with them. It was incredible to watch. They rattled the trees and ground with a chorus of clacking, buzzing, and trilling.

Thalia disappeared into thin air, then emerged close to Lucius, sliding between shadows. Her eyes widened, and the same dream-like expression fell over her features as when she'd attempted to compel Aziel earlier, but it didn't work on Lucius. He snapped his gaze away from Thalia, then pushed her back into a tree.

Blackness stole the next minutes of the fight, although I could hear the battle cries and screaming over the storm. Rain landed thick, heavy drops onto the mud, splashing brown onto our shoes and pants.

The hound's venom coursed through my veins like lava. I screamed a breath through clenched teeth as the venom reached my heart.

I opened my eyes and watched the scene unfold. Lucius had his demons, shadow creatures that curled with hollow eyes, surround the gods.

Every move they threw his way, even with Thalia sliding between shadows, he blocked with unnerving ease. Aziel and Raiden ran at him, and I gasped when they shook the ground on impact. Demons rushed toward Aziel, tying him into the mossy mattress while Raiden fought against his father.

Thalia stepped out from behind the tree I was leaning against. She placed her finger against her lips to shush us, then placed her hands onto my arm. I felt the venom dissipate and wondered why she couldn't do it to herself. The bite didn't seem to be bothering her too much, but every so often, when she contorted to a certain position, I could see a pinch of pain flicker through her expression. The marks on my arm healed over, my sticky blood the only reminder of what had happened.

"Now you can run," she said, as if the bite was the only thing holding me back.

Thalia ran back to the fight with her brothers, throwing the glowing dagger at one, which exploded on impact.

I looked at Naomi, who attempted to tuck her tight black curls behind her ears. She looked at me. "I can help."

She twisted her fingers as if she were painting in thin air. My eyes widened as the forest morphed into an island of ice, where shards of blue icebergs broke off, threatening to pull Lucius into a freezing ocean that didn't exist here. He stumbled back as he tried to steady himself.

I stood, using a stump of a tree trunk to pull myself to my feet. "You're amazing." I gasped as I watched Naomi contort reality with her magic. The scene dissolved, but Lucius continued to dodge invisible obstacles.

"Only he can see it," she explained, her eyes concentrated into slits. Gold lit up her irises as the magic in her blood took over.

The gods took advantage, landing several blows to him while he was distracted by Naomi's illusion.

My heart skipped a beat as Lucius turned toward us and charged in our direction, rage spilling into his frighteningly sharp features and bottomless black eyes.

Raiden grabbed me and pushed me to safety, before turning and meeting his father's fist. Raiden slammed into the ground as Lucius gripped his neck, sending a thunderous roar through the mud and roots, cracking the ground. Lucius turned back to us. Raiden's piercing blue eyes found mine in the blackness. "Get out of here. Now!"

Aziel pushed Naomi from Lucius's grasp, flinging her into a tree. "Nai." I screamed as Lucius flung Aziel into the darkness of the forest and ran at Raiden from behind.

He moved from where I lay in time, but he took a hit in moving the attack away from me. Lucius's fist impacted Raiden's chest, knocking him to the ground and burying him several feet deep. Raiden's bones cracked under the pressure, sending crackling through the easing thunder.

I ran toward Naomi. Her chest heaved up and down, each breath a mercy to what could have been. I ran my hand along the poppy bruise on her forehead, brushing off the speckles of bark.

"Wake up," I croaked, but she didn't stir. I sat at her side, holding her unmoving hand in mine.

I looked back at Lucius as he swung his sword too close to Thalia's neck, and I held my breath. She slipped between shadows to escape the fatal slice, moving to the side of Lucius. Her silver cape of silk reflected the pale light of the moon as she curled her fingers around his neck.

Aziel emerged from nowhere, fixing his dislocated shoulder by popping it back as if the injury were a minor inconvenience. He rushed Lucius in an attempt to save his sister, but Lucius flipped himself, and Thalia vomited blood when his elbow met her stomach.

Raiden climbed out of his god-shaped hole in the ground and moved to help Aziel and Thalia. He glanced in my direction before sighting Lucius. "I told you to run!" he growled.

My lips parted. I shuffled back deeper into the shadows of the trees, burying myself and Naomi as much as I could, while each delivered what should be fatal blows to Lucius, who returned them instead. He was overpowering them, and if there weren't three of them against him, I had no doubt he'd be able to kill them one-on-one.

I wished I were a caster. I wished Naomi were awake. Gods, I wished I had the mansion packed with dark objects with me.

Raiden was flung through the air and crunched against a tree that shuddered under the blow. I winced and tightened my grip on Naomi's hand. I'd never felt so helpless.

After a few minutes, Naomi's eyes fluttered open, a yelp sounding as she tried to sit up.

"Don't." I held her arm down. "You hit the tree pretty hard. You were unconscious."

She brought her fingers to her head and brushed them along her forehead and hairline. "That asshole."

"Naomi, you have to help them. I—"

The world seemed to shatter under Raiden's scream. Naomi gasped, slapping her hand against her mouth as her eyes glossed. My heart hammered, and I ran cold.

Thalia's head rolled from the sharp end of the sword to where we sat. Raiden ran at Lucius, who appeared nothing but stoic as he held the bloodied sword. Thalia's body fell limp to the ground a few seconds after.

Raiden hit Lucius with a ground-breaking hit. I'd never seen him so deadly, whisking through the air as if he belonged to it.

Naomi used the last of her strength to create another illusion, forcing Lucius into an alternate reality, buying the brothers moments. My mortal eyes couldn't follow their speed until everything went almost still. Raiden held the sword, and Aziel had Lucius in a chokehold. Aziel kicked the back of his father's kneecaps, forcing him to kneel. He stepped back, and Raiden swung the sword into Lucius's neck, cleanly removing it from his broad shoulders.

Lucius's head rolled in a different direction than Thalia's. Naomi fell back against the trunk, breathing heavily. "I helped."

I nodded slowly but couldn't peel my eyes away from a broken Raiden. He fell to his knees, pressing the sword into the ground, leaned his head against the hilt, and wept for his fallen sister.

***

The mansion looked smaller somehow when we returned. Aziel had carried us back within half an hour. It would have been a three-day journey by foot.

"Thank you for bringing us back," I said to Aziel, who said nothing while he placed us down at the gates. Raiden had disappeared. Neither we nor Aziel had been able to find him. He'd fled shortly after Thalia died, and we left promptly after, not wanting to linger in the clearing of the dead. Aziel would go back later to bury his sister, but it was her soul that mattered, and that had gone to the underworld.

Naomi looked up at Aziel. "I'm sorry about your sister." She touched his hand, and he flinched. "I truly am."

My heart ached for him and for Raiden. "If there's anything we can do…"

Aziel moved his cold gaze to meet mine. "You can stay away from Raiden. He asked Thalia to protect you. It was because she protected you that she was weakened by the hounds, why she had to step out of battle." His accusing stare never left mine. "None of us would have walked into that trap had he not wanted to find you."

Naomi pulled us both to a stop, crossing her arms over her chest. "You're hurt." She looked at Aziel. "I know right now you're angry, and you want someone to be mad at. Nothing in the world can take away your pain, but blaming Elle isn't going to make it any better. She tried protecting you."

He growled quietly. "You helped us. You protected us. Not her."

I pulled away from his venomous stare.

Naomi shot me an apologetic look. "Perhaps you should go inside."

I gulped, parting my lips to speak, but she shook her head. "I, uh." I scratched the back of my neck. "I'll see you inside."

I walked through the open iron gates, looking over my shoulder. Naomi's hands were on his, compassion in her stance and face. His hardened look softened. I felt like I'd missed something.

I hesitated at the front door, but Dora opened it before I had a chance to. Edmund rushed out from behind her, and Maddox wasn't far behind.

Edmund pulled me into a tight embrace, pressing a gentle kiss on the top of my head. "I was worried sick. Is Naomi with you?"

"Yes." I jerked my head in her direction.

"I wanted to go to find you," Edmund said from inside our hug. "Viktor stopped us. He made the woman—ah, what's her name again?"

"Thalia," I said hollowly.

"Her. She placed a spell on the house so we couldn't leave it."

I swallowed thickly. "I know." My shoulders slumped when he released me. "She's dead."

His eyebrows flicked up. "Oh?"

Maddox looked me up and down. "You look dreadful."

Dora pressed her hands against my cheeks, tilting my face up. "You're ever so pale. You need food. Quick, get inside. You can tell us all that happened there."

Maddox patted my back as we walked inside, then smiled. "Good to have you back."

I wanted to smile back, but I couldn't bring myself to force it. "Thanks."

Edmund grabbed a box of cookies in the kitchen as I walked to the table. He shook them in my direction, but I still felt nauseated. "Where's Viktor?" he asked, and my stomach knotted.

"I don't know." I sighed, deflated. "He could be anywhere." I didn't want to tell them what I'd seen in those moments after he killed Lucius. How through his grief-stricken tears, he'd looked at me with a hatred I'd never seen on his face. I wouldn't tell a single soul how he'd never seemed as dangerous as right before he fled, and now I had no idea what he would do. This was Leda all over again, and Aziel was right. She was dead because of me. I had become his new Freya.

PART THREE:

BROKEN GODS

CHAPTER TWENTY-THREE

I hadn't left my bed since what had happened, but life went on. I stared at the rain-stricken window in my room, my mind reeling over every detail of the days with Freya, filling more with vile as I replayed Thalia's death. As it weighed so heavily on my conscience, I couldn't move.

Aziel's words continued to float back, even in my layers of dreams, which grew darker with each passing day. Maddox knocked on the door, bringing me tea and cookies on a tray for breakfast, a new tradition since I'd come back looking like death and covered in blood.

He placed the tray on the nightstand. "Still feeling sorry for yourself?"

"Go away, Maddox."

He glimmered a smile. "I still can't believe you didn't tell me he was a god. Do you know what this means?"

"I don't care." I pulled the covers over my head. They'd forgiven me for stealing the keys, especially after finding out Freya had lied about it all and that we had been guarding the freedoms of three innocent gods.

"You should." He sat, pulling my covers back again. He and Edmund had spent every evening researching since we got back a week ago. Looking for what? I didn't know, but something I'd said had struck a chord with them.

"There's a way for them to kill Lucius for good."

I sat upright. "He's already dead."

"No, he would have simply been sent back to the underworld."

My heart palpated. "What?"

"They need to kill him *in* the underworld. Not in this realm."

"Are you certain?"

He shook his hand. "Seventy-thirty."

I slumped again. "It doesn't really help anything, seeing as Raiden is gone."

"It's still weird to call him that."

I shrugged. "Maddox, no offense, but I really just want to be alone."

He scoffed. "So you can wallow in your pity party for one about how this is all your fault? Hell no. You're a keeper now, and those gods are much older than us and can make their own decisions. You didn't force anyone to do anything. This isn't on you." He squeezed my hand.

I wished I could believe him, but I didn't. "Freya's still out there." My blood boiled at the mention of her name. "I'm pretty sure he's hunting her, but I can't know for sure. Has Naomi said anything?"

Maddox shook his head. "You know, you could just ask her yourself."

I sighed. I didn't want to talk to anyone. "Maybe later."

He rolled his eyes, whistling out a breath. "Enough of this. You're getting out of this house today, whether it kills me. We need you, Elle. You're a keeper now. You've had your time to wallow, so if finding Raiden is what it takes to absolve you of all this bullshit guilt so you can live your life again, then we'll find him." He clicked his tongue, standing. "Anyway, we still need to stop Freya. She's the one who was killing our own, and Edmund plans on going to the council today to tell them."

My breath hitched. "If they know about Freya, they will hunt all of the gods."

"That's why Edmund didn't say anything at first, but we have little choice. We need to kill Freya, and we can't do it on our own."

"No. He can't go to them. Let me try first. Surely Aziel can at least be contacted."

He shrugged. "Naomi said he left shortly after you got back."

"I know, but he didn't say where he was going to?"

"She didn't say so."

I bit my lip. "We have to fix this. Raiden's just lost his sister; I can't have him lose his brother..." I paused, feeling nauseated at the thought. "To lose his own life."

"Ah, there's the spirit. Now go shower because no offense, girl, but." He pinched his nose, and I slapped his arm. He chuckled, then shoved his hands in his pockets. "I'll call Edmund off, but you better have a good plan."

I gulped. "I should go alone."

He laughed again. "Right. Because having your more powerful coven mates with you would only what, slow you down?"

I shot him a glare. "Don't be sarcastic. I just don't want anyone else getting hurt."

"You'll get killed, and look, this isn't just about you or Raiden. We're stopping a murderer. It's our choice. Together, Elle, we might stand a chance. Not alone."

"I... I don't know."

"Either you come up with a plan that involves us or we go to the elders. Don't get me wrong; it'd be a shame to have Raiden killed. We all like him—well, me and Dora do. Edmund is so-so." He shook his hand, smirking. "Only because he could see the way he looked at you. You know Edmund sees you as a daughter, and Raiden is, well, reckless, arrogant, extremely handsome..."

"Enough." I rolled my eyes. "Fine, we will all go."

"I'm bringing Naomi. After the magic you said she pulled off, she's an asset. Get dressed. We're going on a god hunt."

"Oh gods."

"Oh gods, indeed."

I rushed down to the kitchen after having a quick shower and getting dressed. I wore my leather jacket, black pants, a tight white top, and boots suitable for hiking. I wasn't going to be caught out in the wilderness in a dress. In my bag, I shoved gloves, a hat, scarf, extra top, and my pistol with extra bullets. Around my thigh, I sheathed my dagger into the scabbard, then shoved a second, smaller dagger inside my boot.

Maddox grinned when he saw me. "Evening, bounty hunter."

I dropped the bag on the table. "Is it too much?"

He patted his own bag. "I'm bringing ten dark objects, so no."

"That is smarter."

"Of course it is." He smirked. "But then, I am smarter."

I rolled my eyes. "Where are the others? Did Edmund agree?"

"Yes, and don't worry about a plan. Edmund already has one. Dora's staying here to protect the mansion."

A meow sounded from behind me, followed by a nose nudging me.

"Hey, Benji." I leaned down. "Look after Dora for us while we're gone." I scratched his head and stood. "At least she'll remember to feed you." It was my job, but I forgot half the time. In my defense, I tried, but I had told Dora and Edmund when they put me on lunch duty for Benji, to teach me responsibility, that I struggled to keep a plant alive, let alone an animal.

"I'm sure he's grateful," Maddox joked. "What's taking them so long?"

"Edmund's probably trying to pack the entire library. You know how he is."

Heavy footsteps trudged down the hall. Edmund walked in, dressed all in black.

Dora followed, her hands clasped together in worry. "Elle." She walked to me first and wrapped her arms around me. "Be careful. Personally, I do not think it is wise for you to go." She shot Edmund, then Maddox, hardened stares. "After all you've been through."

Edmund cleared his throat. "She'll be safe with us, and she is a keeper now. You can't coddle her forever."

She clicked her tongue. "Says you."

I couldn't help but smile.

Maddox gasped a little too dramatically. "An actual, real smile. Well, I never. You must be feeling better." He walked to me and draped an arm over my shoulders. "You smell better too." He gave Dora his brightest smile. "Edmund's right, Dora. She's a keeper. She'll be sent on missions."

"Not to hunt a goddess!" she snapped. "We should be going to the council."

"No!" I shouted a little too quickly, and everyone whipped their heads around to look at me. "We can't. They'll kill Raiden."

She waved her hand in the air. "They won't. We'll explain."

Maddox interrupted. "When have you ever known the council to listen? Elle's right. They'll see him as a threat. We all thought the gods were monsters until recently. We can't trust them."

She hesitated, tapping her foot against the kitchen floor. "Fine." She walked to the fridge, then pulled out butter and slices of meat and cheese. "You're not going anywhere until I make you some food to leave with."

"We can find food on the way." Maddox tapped his pocket filled with skal.

One look from her and he fell silent. My stomach knotted when the doorbell rang. "Who's that?"

Maddox smiled. "Good, Naomi must have got my magic quill."

***

Naomi was a vision dressed in her white frilled blouse and tight blue pants. Her usually tight curls were straightened and sleek. She only used that hair potion, which cost twenty skal, on special occasions.

Maddox teased. "Jeez, Naomi. We're not going dancing."

"There's nothing wrong with dressing up," she countered.

"You know we're going hunting, right?"

I rolled my eyes. "Let's just get in the motor." I eyed the gorgeous, black shiny automobile Edmund had recently purchased.

It growled to a start, and I climbed in, followed by Maddox, Naomi, and Edmund holding his bags of dark objects. Dora waved from the door, tearfully, and we pulled away, grueling over gravel as the gates opened and starting the long journey toward the mountains: the last place I knew Freya had gone. Wherever Freya was, I was sure Raiden was close.

CHAPTER TWENTY-FOUR

We stopped for the night at a rundown hotel after driving for ten hours. My butt had gone numb, and I'd already taken an hour's nap. We weren't too far from the mountain and forest area where Thalia had died. The motor wasn't as fast as being in Raiden's arms, but it did get us there faster than the three-day journey it would have taken on foot, or a day by carriage.

The roads glossed as rain drizzled, swept by the winds, frizzing my hair and ruining Naomi's. The red-and-white cracked exterior of the three-story building desperately needed some love. The porch was enclosed with white pillars, with doors made from solid, stained wood.

"You owe me." Maddox walked with us inside. "I'll pay for this, but now you'll be getting a keepers' salary and no longer an allowance from the council for being an apprentice, so you can afford to pay me back."

"I forgot about the pay."

His eyebrows furrowed. "Never take your eye off the skal, Elle. Why do you think we do this?"

I fumbled my fingers. I guessed coin was never my reason for wanting to be a keeper. It always had been to belong, to be in a position where I could reunite with my sister, but that dream felt further away than ever before. Raiden said he'd help me, but there was a part of me that didn't want him to, afraid of what she'd say—more so that she wouldn't want to see me. Even worse, a thought had unwantedly climbed into my mind on more than one occasion of if she was even alive. I had no idea what had happened to her, and a selfish, fearful part of me didn't want to find out. How could I live with myself if she wasn't happy? If somehow my actions had caused her to—

"Elle, through here." Naomi grabbed my arm, disrupting my thoughts. "You're bunking with me tonight."

Edmund cleared his throat as he went to the front desk with Maddox to get the keys to our rooms. I looked from them to Naomi. "Great."

"Your eyes are sad." Her shoulders slumped. "I'm sorry. Aziel had no right saying what he did."

"He was right."

"No." She tapped my hand. "Don't you dwell on it for a minute. He was in pain, grieving, and everything he said was because he wanted someone to blame, but we all know who's responsible."

"Freya."

286

She nodded. "She and Lucius."

"He's dead."

"Not really. He went to the underworld, but it's hardly a punishment, considering he rules it."

I bit my lip. "Maddox did say there was a way to get rid of him permanently."

Her eyes widened. "How?"

"To kill him *in* the underworld."

She nodded slowly. "Gah, who thought we'd even be talking about killing a god or going to the underworld?"

I almost smiled. "It is a little crazy."

She pushed her fingers together, then parted them an inch. "Oh right, only a small amount."

Edmund rejoined us. "Your key." He dropped it in my palm. "Both of you are to be up and dressed by six."

"AM?" I clarified.

Maddox snorted. "No, Elle. In the evening. We wanted to make sure you would have a nice lie-in, then we could trek the dangerous forest at night."

"Thanks, Maddox." I glared. "I got it. Six AM."

"We'll be down here, waiting," Edmund said, then squeezed my and Naomi's shoulders. "I'm proud of you both." He looked at me softly. "You took down a demon hound, became a keeper, and are fighting for what you want. You've changed so much."

I shouldn't have told him about that hound. He looked far too impressed, and I was worried I was going to let him down.

"Naomi." He smiled at her. "Your magic helped take down a god. You helped them that night, and Elle said they wouldn't have won without you. When all this is over, I'll be certain to let the council know and see if that three-year ban on retaking the test can't be lifted."

She shrugged. "Actually, after all this, I'm not sure it's what I want anymore."

"No?"

"I love the magic," she explained, "but I think I can put it to better use on my own."

Edmund nodded. "Good for you. Your dad should be proud of you."

She flustered. "Right. Yeah. I mean…"

Maddox chimed in. "Take the compliment. Right, off to bed." He scratched his arm. "I'm already getting hives, thinking about those bedsheets. I want to get this over and done with."

Cold air circled the room, drifting through the open shutters. I sat upright in my bed. Naomi was lightly snoring, hugging her pillow. I didn't know what awakened me but had a gnawing in my stomach and a sense that something wasn't quite right. It was almost as if someone were watching me.

"Murder!" someone screamed from downstairs, almost making me scream myself, followed by a blood-curdling scream.

I grabbed an oil lamp, then hit the floor and ran toward the screams.

The clerk was pale. Edmund and Maddox came running, and so did a few other guests. A maid working for the hotel stood at the open front doors. I pushed past her but halted two steps down. The motor had been destroyed, torn to pieces. Nothing but immortal strength could have done that. Was it Freya? Or worse, Raiden?

In front of the motor was a slain man, his throat cut open. I faltered forward, noticing the familiar blond nest of curls around his face. When I got closer, my hand shot to my mouth, silencing my gasp.

Alexander.

My gaze darted around us. The maid ran out ahead of the now-small crowd gathered near me and the body. She spluttered over her words.

"'E wasn't a warlock or 'uman." She gasped. "I saw 'im. 'E ran too fast and were stronger than a bear. 'E was a god, one of those forgotten ones."

My stomach dipped. Edmund casually moved to my side, leaning down to my ear. "It must have been Aziel," he whispered.

I hugged my arms around myself, as my nightdress did little to block out the cold. "Or Raiden."

"He wouldn't have done this."

I looked at Alexander's empty gaze reflecting the stars. I wondered if he had seen their beauty in the final moments, like he tried to paint. "I'm not so sure. The victim is Alexander." I lowered my voice. "Freya's partner."

"She could be here."

"Maybe, but if he's dead, then she would have fled," I explained. "Question is how did she get close? Was she following us? Was he?"

"Raiden?"

I pressed my lips together. "Yes."

"I don't think he'd do this."

My bottom lip trembled. Edmund hadn't seen the look on Raiden's face before he ran that night. He was dangerous, a loose cannon, and I was pretty certain he hated me. "Maybe not," I lied. "It was probably Aziel, but this still makes no sense."

Edmund stroked his short beard. "We will need to go on foot tomorrow."

I gazed at the inkblots of black and dark green, a sea of trees under the night sky, and I felt sickly. I wasn't looking forward to going back in there.

***

I couldn't sleep. An image of Alexander's corpse floated through my thoughts, strangling them. He was the fourth dead body I'd seen in my life, and three of them had been since Raiden stepped into my life. I couldn't stop thinking about him no matter how hard I tried to squeeze out the memory of the last time I'd seen him. His face… specifically the hatred on it.

"Elle, let's not wait for the sun to set," Maddox joked when I trudged into the lobby. Protectors had gathered in swarms, searching the area for signs of who could have caused the damage. I looked at Maddox, then at Naomi. It was the work of a god, but to say which one was hard. It was unlikely to be Freya, but she would have had to be near for Alexander to be there, and why was he so close? Had they come for us?

If it was Raiden, why had he wrecked our motor? The most plausible was Aziel.

"This way." Maddox jerked his head in the direction of an empty room. I followed him and Naomi inside. "Where's Edmund?"

"Left an hour ago," Maddox said nonchalantly. "He's gone to find an alternative mode of transport. He wants us to wait here until he returns."

I scratched the back of my neck. "I thought we were going by foot?"

"He decided against it, with everything that's happened. He wants us to wait here until he comes back. He's also furious about the motor, but he pretends like he's not thinking about that with everything happening that's more important, but I can tell he's pissed."

"How long is he going to be?"

He shrugged. "No idea. He could be hours. A day."

"A day?" Naomi's eyes widened. "We need to find them now."

"She's right." I looked at Maddox. "We should go on foot. Maybe I should just go in alone."

He laughed. "Are you insane? You barely survived the last two times you went into a forest. Third time's the charm, right?"

"Shut up." I clicked my tongue, then looked at Naomi. "What the…"

Maddox rubbed his forehead, smoothing the creases forming. "Oh, gods. She's only gone and found religion."

Naomi whispered into her closed hands, eyes closed.

My eyebrows pinched downward. "Are you… praying?"

She opened her eyes. "I have to do something. Maybe they can hear us or something."

Maddox suppressed a smirk, but I caught it and burst out laughing.

She glared at us in turn. "It's not funny. I'm just trying something."

"Oh, Naomi." Maddox shook his head, smirking. "You don't pray to these gods. We were taught to pray to Estia only, to show gratitude or whatever, not to ask for them to come." He looked at me, then laughed. "She's trying to summon a god." He paused, trying not to laugh. "Through prayer."

She waved her hand dismissively. "Whatever. At least I'm doing something."

He leaned against the wall, picking a piece of fluff off the sleeve of his shirt. Even after a night like last night, he always managed to look immaculate. "I never said I wasn't doing anything. I actually agree with you and Elle."

My eyes widened. "I'm sorry. You *agree* with us?"

"Don't look so shocked. Sometimes you actually have good ideas."

I placed my hand on my hip. "Sometimes?"

"On occasion," he teased. "Look, Edmund is overly cautious and is too worried about you girls to really go headfirst into this thing. He thinks we need to stay on the road between the forest to stay safe, but we'll just be moving targets to anyone watching. I think we should go in, but"—he put a finger in the air—"not alone, because I'm starting to think you have a death wish. We are all going together."

"When do we leave?" I asked, glancing at a small window. Sunlight arrowed in, illuminating the dust in the air. "We can't be in there at night."

He looked at me incredulously. "The forest is huge, and the way to the mountains is at least a day's trek. We're going to be in there overnight, but fear not. I'm always prepared." He patted his backpack without elaborating. "Get your stuff. We leave now."

"Edmund's going to kill you," Naomi warned, a mischievous glint in her eye.

"No," he said. "He'll kill Elle. I'll tell him this was her idea."

I clicked my tongue. "Can't you take one day off from being an asshole?"

He scoffed. "Where's the fun in that?"

Naomi shouldered me, grabbing my hand. "Who thought it? *Us.*" Her eyes bulged. "Actually saving the world."

"It's hardly saving the world, Nai," Maddox answered from ahead of us.

"Don't listen to him. It kind of is," I said, though it was a bit of an exaggeration. I admired her positivity. If it weren't for her and Maddox, I would still be stuck in a vicious circle of depression and self-doubt. At least I could laugh again, even if it felt a little morbid to do so after finding Alexander's body last night and knowing what was ahead of us. Somewhere in the depths of that forest or high in those mountains were vengeful gods with the ability to rip Istinia to shreds.

Chapter Twenty-Five

We checked out of the hotel and hurried through the small town with quaint shops and market stalls, where whispers of local slaughters were circling like the plague. Maddox rushed to one of the stalls on the dirt road and bargained for some apples.

I leaned into a conversation between a group of three women.

"Oh, yes," one said to the others, her eyes wide. "The entire family, gone. Killed in the night by some monster."

The second, shorter woman said, "No monster. I heard it was a man."

"Serves 'em right," the third snapped back in a whisper. "No-gooders anyway. Good riddance, if ya ask me."

Naomi pulled me away. "I'm sure it's a coincidence."

I knew she was trying to make me feel better, but they'd said it was a man. "Maybe it was Aziel."

She fumbled her fingers. "Maybe, but people do get murdered."

"Alexander," I said to remind her. "Freya's lover is killed right outside our hotel, then in the same night, an entire family is killed. It *has* to be them."

"I doubt Raiden would have done it." She squeezed my arm.

Maddox walked back to us. "Fruit." He offered a collection of apples, bananas, and some plums. "Eat up. I just spoke to one of the locals." He gestured in the direction of the stall. "He confirmed a family was killed last night, some rich folk with more power and money than sense."

I looked around. "Why do they live here then—I mean, did?"

"Probably for the quiet," Naomi said. "My dad's friends who are super rich live outside the city and have houses in the city for work and such."

"Makes sense." I tapped my fingers against my lips. My stomach was in knots. It had to be Aziel. I didn't for a second want to believe this was the work of Raiden. "Should we go see the house?"

Maddox shot me an are-you-mad look. "To an open crime scene? We're trying to avoid attention. Besides, he would have left by now."

"He?"

"Viktor. I mean Raiden."

Naomi glared at him. "We don't know it's him."

He looked at us both in turn. "Who else could it be? They said it was a man, and with everything that's happened, there's no chance it's all a coincidence. Clearly Raiden had lost his mind after losing his sister and has gone on a killing rampage while trying to kill Freya, who I assume is close because her boy toy was right outside our hotel."

My heart sank. I went to speak, but Naomi got there first. "It could be Aziel."

"It could be, but my skal is on Raiden. Aziel seemed far calmer before he fled. Raiden didn't even tag along to bring you both home." He gave me an apologetic stare. "Sorry, Elle, sometimes grief can just make people snap. I know you two had a thing."

I swallowed thickly. "We-we became friends."

A small smirk curved his lips. "More than that, if I remember correctly."

Naomi shook her head. "Really, Maddox? We're going to do this now? She's clearly heartbroken."

I shoved my hands in my pockets. "Enough. I am not heartbroken. Just... surprised. We should get moving anyway. We're close to the forest."

"Fine." Maddox whistled out a breath and crunched into an apple, strutting ahead of us. "But first, I'm stopping to get some hot food and use the restroom."

Naomi pointed at a small café with gray cracked walls and three circle tables with chairs outside. I followed them inside, and a bell tinkled over the door. As I eyed the pastries and sandwiches, my stomach rumbled. I can't remember the last time I'd eaten. Yesterday morning maybe?

"Three of the cheese-and-pickle sandwiches," I ordered and pulled out a couple of skal from the small amount I'd brought. "A hot chocolate too."

A conversation a couple of tables back caught my attention. A balding man sat with a woman, dressed in a pretty summer dress. Over their teas and half-eaten scone, he lowered his voice. "Not just here," he said, answering a question I was too late for. "A couple was killed a town over yesterday, slaughtered in the night. They ran the elite clubs in the south. You know the ones," he whispered. "Invitation only."

"Oh." Her blue eyes glittered with excitement. "Who do you think killed them?"

"I heard a man was spotted both times. Handsome, they said, not dressed like someone you'd expect to be a killer, but you never know these days. A demon in disguise probably. That's what they're saying. That or a god."

My heart skipped a beat.

She laughed. "Don't be silly, Ronald."

"Why not?" He leaned forward. "It makes sense. They killed many before they were locked away. We've heard the stories."

"Maybe you have."

He raised his eyebrows. "My mom told me they sacrificed people before they were locked away. No doubt one could have escaped. They say he's mad. Everyone's saying it."

"Yes, but—" She looked at me over the two tables between us. "Can we help you?" she asked with a pinched frown.

"Oh, no. Sorry." I averted my gaze. I took a seat at the table, looking at the sandwiches placed in front of me, but I no longer felt hungry. I forced myself to eat, if only for the energy to keep going, but I couldn't stop thinking about what that man had said. They had guessed a god. Fortunately, they were only rumors, but those could be dangerous. We were trying to avoid the gods being hunted, but whether it was Aziel or Raiden killing families, they were going to get themselves killed—or at least imprisoned again.

We'd been walking for three hours by the time we reached a house in the middle of nowhere. It stood decadent with a sprawling garden, shiny gates, and a long, winding driveaway. It couldn't have looked more out of place to the forest if it tried. We were close to the main road, so it explained why it was here, but whoever lived there had made an effort to be out of the way.

"We will make camp soon." Maddox walked ahead of us, using a handkerchief to dab at the sweat on his forehead.

Naomi ran her hand through her hair, heaving as she climbed over thick roots and the slight hill winding around the house and its grounds.

"We need to go farther in." Maddox pulled his map and compass out again. He turned on the spot and nodded. "This way."

***

The shadowed canopy above us was dotted with stars. Maddox had brought a dark object and had manipulated it to create a line of protection around us, which temporary but effective. Naomi used her magic to create an illusion around us to any who might approach this area, so they would only see trees, making us invisible. I should have felt safe in our bubble, but something didn't feel right.

A scream sounded in the distance. It was faint, and if it wasn't for the dead silence of the night, I would have missed it. I sat upright, then heard another scream.

Maddox turned onto his side, snorted, and continued to snore. Naomi slept peacefully on her stomach. I looked around, my fingers gripped into the mud around the blanket I slept on.

The next sound set every fiber of my being on fire: a loud growl, one I recognized. I'd heard it when Freya had broken into the mansion and Raiden had fought her, the same one I'd heard when Thalia died and he took off Lucius's head.

I closed my eyes. If it was him, Maddox and Naomi would without a doubt report him, and they'd be right to. They were doing all this so the gods wouldn't be hunted, but if Raiden was killing, they wouldn't care. If he was murdering people, then he was a monster, but I couldn't bring myself to wake them.

Maddox was right. I must've had a death wish. I was definitely an idiot.

I stepped outside of the protection of our small camp and into the night, then took off in the direction of the house we'd seen earlier, the only source of people anywhere close. It had to be where the screams had come from.

Branches whipped my arms and hands, grappling through the dark like fingers. In the distance, a wolf howled from somewhere in the mountains. Glancing up at the crescent, bright moon, I paused to catch my breath. "Please don't be Raiden," I whispered to the sky as another scream sounded. I unsheathed my dagger and grabbed my pistol from my belt before taking off again.

I tiptoed around the side of the building, keeping my back against the wall. The door had been ripped off. As I walked, glass crunched under my boots. To my right was a broken window. Carefully, holding my breath, I edged my way through the door. Splattered blood dotted the beige walls and grand staircase. A man, whose heart was no longer in his chest, was propped against a doorway. Hesitantly, I stepped forward through the doorway and into a large ballroom. My mouth dropped.

Bodies were everywhere. Some were intact, many in shreds. A party must have gone horribly wrong. At least they were all adults. I placed my hand against my chest, feeling my racing heart, when I found him. Raiden's tortured gaze found mine from across the bloodied room.

"Don't come closer."

"What did you do?" I looked over the dead bodies and the blood. Gods, there was so much blood. I blinked twice. This couldn't be. Aziel. I'd sworn it was him. Not Raiden. "Why?"

Fury spilled into his chiseled features. "I said leave." His anger guided each venom-laced word. "Why don't you ever listen? I said get out."

A tear threatened to break through my façade. His glossed eyes averted mine. My lips parted slightly. Everything screamed at me to run. Between us, a pool of blood glistened under the reflected diamonds on the chandelier above, a reminder of what he was capable of: how he could easily tear my heart from my chest and I wouldn't stand a chance. But he hadn't. He never had laid a finger on me. I'd always enjoyed gambling, but now I was betting my life by not leaving. In my darkest hour, he'd come for me. He was in this mess because he'd come to save me from Freya and instead fallen into a trap. I couldn't leave him after that.

"Raiden." I closed the distance between us. Tears filled my eyes. Had he really broken, snapped because of Thalia? "This isn't you." I reached out to touch him, but he flinched back.

"I said don't."

Tears hazed my vision. "They're going to hunt you for this." I swallowed thickly. "You should hear what people have been saying. That you're mad." I couldn't look at the bodies for a second longer. "The local people. They've seen you. One said he thinks these killings are the work of a god." Bile bit up my throat. "I know there's a reason for this. I get why Alexander died. He was with Freya, protecting her, but what about the others?"

He turned his back toward me. "Because I'm a monster."

"Bullshit." I shook my head. "You didn't hurt us when you could have. You protected me against Freya. You said yourself you wouldn't hurt innocents to get what you want." My stomach twisted as I shook away the image of the dead in my peripheral vision. "You came for me when I needed you. So I'm not leaving you."

He punched the wall, and I jumped back. "I said get out." He turned to face me. "Like the rumors said, I'm mad." His eyes widened. "Insane. Dangerous. Heed the warning, and get the fuck out of here."

I crossed my arms over my chest. "From where I'm standing, you look like only your normal crazy to me."

He clenched his fists against the wall, his knuckles whitening under specks of blood. Under his breath, an unmistakable sob escaped. His breath hitched, but he caught himself before he broke.

I touched his back, and his shoulders tensed. "Raiden," I said tentatively. "Help me help you. I know you're not a monster."

"They were the Vordel family." he said after a minute of painful silence. "They owned black magic clubs."

I remembered that man talking about invite-only clubs. "What are they?"

"This family worshipped Freya." His mouth twisted in disgust. "They were in her inner circle. She showed them how to stay young, to get more power, and gain more money through sacrifices using rituals taken from the underworld. Half the bodies you see were already here by the time I arrived. They were having their monthly blood party using people they'd kidnapped from the lower classes, people you wouldn't miss if they went missing. They thought they could do what they wanted."

"And the other half?"

He gritted his teeth. "I lost my temper."

SPELLBOUND

The house was almost falling apart. "If they were sacrificing people, then..." *They deserved it*, I wanted to say.

"I never wanted this." He turned and slammed his fist into the same hole he'd made before, cursing loudly. "Freya's hiding behind people. She knows I'm hunting her and then I found out you are, which was fucking stupid." He picked a piece of stone from his knuckle. "She had her people watching your coven. She's got hundreds of people protecting her. Powerful people. She's got eyes everywhere. Fuck, if I didn't kill Alexander when they came for you, she'd have killed you all in your beds."

"Oh."

"I chased her here. I wrecked your motor, hoping it would prevent you from coming after us, but it didn't stop you. What are you doing out in the forest anyway? You saw what happened to my sister, and she was a goddess. Lucius will come back. Aziel is convinced he won't return, that he can't, but he's capable. I know it. He's going to keep coming back, and I can't protect you from him."

I lightly touched his arm; he didn't flinch. "Raiden." I ran my fingers down to his and pulled him closer. "I'm not going to abandon you. We can fight Lucius. Maddox and Naomi are here."

"Two keepers and an apprentice aren't going to help me take down two of the most powerful forces known to this world."

"You'll have more of a chance with us than without us."

"I can handle Freya."

"You just said she's too well protected."

He pulled his hand from mine. "Stop trying to help. You've already done enough."

There it was: the real reason he was angry at me. "You blame me for Thalia."

"No." He looked down, shaking his head. "I blame myself. I told her to protect you, and because of me, she was weakened by the bite when helping you, and she couldn't fight Lucius off when he came for her in the final blow."

"I'm sorry." A tear trickled out. I wiped it with the back of my sleeve. "I'm sorry she's gone, but this is Lucius's and Freya's fault, not yours."

He looked down. "I don't regret it, Elle. Protecting you. Despite everything. If she didn't, you'd be dead too."

My lips parted. I didn't know what to say. "Why did you?"

He hesitated, then turned, pulled a handkerchief from his pocket, and wiped the blood from his hands. "We're done here. If you have any sense at all, you'll get out of here and go home."

"No!" I shouted after him as he crossed the room. "Please don't run from me."

"Do yourself a favor and forget you met me. You'll live longer."

"I can't." I exhaled shakily. "I don't want to."

He paused mid-walk and turned to say something but instead turned back and fled the room.

Nothing shook the fragility of mortality like being surrounded by the dead. The absence of beating hearts and chatter in a room filled with people was too eerie. Altars of sacrifice, symbols like those found on Freya's victims, were indeed stained upon many of the dead. Most had had their throats slit. The ones Raiden had killed were easily identifiable, mostly because there wasn't much left of them.

He tore people apart as easily as I would paper. I shuddered as a shiver snaked down my spine, a reminder of the sheer damage he could cause in a moment of temper. At his fingertips, he had more power than I could wish for in a lifetime, and now he was gone, out there hunting vengeance. I was afraid of what would happen if he didn't find it, but I was even more terrified to see what would happen when he did. Without Freya, without a focus, someone to hate, he would fall apart, and I had no idea how to help a broken god.

Chapter Twenty-Six

Birds tweeted as the sun rose over the forest, illuminating the golden-brown trunks that narrowed upward into a scrawl of branches. The slow sunrise, a warm glow of oranges and reds behind rolling clouds, reminded me of the mornings in Salvius before I thought much about witches and gods.

Her face was as clear in my mind as a painting, a memory captured and burned forever into my thoughts. She had a nose smattered with freckles, flaming red hair, and glacier-blue eyes, which sparkled when she smiled. She would grab my hand, her smaller fingers curling with mine, and lead me into the woods by where we'd lived. She would go on and on about how oil lamps worked by burning lard and that many were using a new kind of oil and it was better. I mostly zoned out when she rambled on about the newest discoveries she'd learned, mostly by reading the newspapers I'd steal for her but also from books that had been donated to the orphanage from rich families feeling bad around Yuletide. We'd walk around stagnant ponds, cross babbling streams, and venture into woods so striking, silent, and beautiful, we would have stayed in there forever if we knew how to survive it.

I'd always feel lost without Mona. When I wanted to joke about Miss Thompson or rant about one of the other girls being mean and Mona was in her classes at school, I'd feel so low. She was an extension of me in many ways. She was the only one who really knew me. She had gone through the same pain I had, and when someone really understood the same torture as another, it was as if their spirit linked with the other in some way. We had gone through our healing together, and the cynical lens through which I now viewed the world wasn't as lonely.

I shook my head as if to scatter my thoughts. I couldn't be distracted, not when drowning in memories of the past would only destroy my future. I'd waited all these years to see Mona again. I could wait a little longer. Raiden needed me first, and he was the one truly in danger. If he didn't stop, word of his killings, whispers of a god returning, would spread like wildfire. Out of the flames, a sea of fearful witches and warlocks would rise, pitchforks at the ready to rid Istinia of gods they believed were murderers and evil. It didn't matter if we screamed from the rooftops that they weren't monsters. Who would take the word of a tiny coven in Fairwik? Edmund had respect, but not enough to stop that kind of panic. Nothing would.

I reached the trees close to the spot where I'd left Maddox and Naomi, and the illusion they used to make themselves invisible lowered, revealing a disheveled Naomi with twigs in her hair, arms crossed over her chest.

"At least we know she's not dead," she snapped, and Maddox gave me a wide-eyed uh-oh look. "Now I can kill her myself. Where were you? We've been worried sick."

"Please don't shout, Nai." I closed the distance between us and hugged her. I didn't know if it was seeing Raiden so broken or seeing so many dead people at once or even the memory of Mona, but I needed to be held. She sighed, then tightened her arms around me.

"What happened?" Her tone softened.

"I saw Raiden."

She pulled me to arm's length. "What?"

"He was in that house we passed. He, uh, well he may have killed all of them."

Maddox grimaced. "I'm sorry, say what?"

"Well," I said. "They were sacrificing people. They ran these black magic, invite-only clubs and worshipped Freya. They had killed half the party before he showed up so they could get more youth, money, and power, and Raiden stopped them."

"Are any alive?"

I shook my head. "I did a sweep of the house before I left."

Maddox shook his head. "I truly do believe you have a death wish. You want to talk?"

"I'm fine. I heard screaming last night. That's why I went. Well, screaming and growling."

Naomi shrugged her shoulders at Maddox, then looked back at me. "Now everything makes sense. Why

SPELLBOUND

wouldn't you run toward the screaming in the middle of a dark forest…"

Maddox joined in. "Seems perfectly logical."

"Funny." I stared them down. "We need to help him. He's utterly broken. He thinks Lucius is going to return from the underworld to finish what he started. He's running on nothing but anger and paranoia, and honestly, I don't know what he's capable of, but he doesn't deserve to die or be imprisoned again. He needs our help. I think if we can help him capture and kill Freya, then maybe…" I paused. I hadn't actually thought beyond that point.

Maddox lifted his bag from the ground and threw it over his shoulder. "We can tell him how to kill Lucius."

"Right." I pointed at him. "Exactly. With them gone, maybe he can begin healing."

Naomi's lips straightened into a line. "If he can, Elle. Just being realistic here… If he's as far gone as you say he is, there may be no bringing him back."

"You can't just give up on him. He's our friend."

Maddox nodded. "He is."

"Well." Naomi shook her hand. "I don't know him too well. You all spent way more time with him, but yeah, I know what you mean."

I looked at Maddox. "Where do we go?"

"If he's hunting black magic clubs, then I know exactly where he'll be heading to next, and if Freya is hiding behind her worshipers, then they might know where she is—or know someone who knows."

Naomi chimed in. "You don't think she's in the mountains anymore?"

"No," I said quickly. "It would be the first place Raiden would have looked, but undoubtedly, she hasn't left the province. It's all forest here, and she's comfortable among the trees," I explained, recalling how easily she had hunted in the trees when I'd watched her from her window. "She's goddess of the hunt. Here, she's deadly. She knows the territory. Before she emerged again, everyone always said she was suspected to be living in the mountains."

Maddox lightly shook his head, smiling. "If only you could've used that logical thinking for your studies, we would have been one keeper up years ago."

"Always ruining everything," I said, berating him, but I smirked regardless. "So where is the nearest club or house?"

"It's a black magic club, but it's said to be in the forest to the east. I'm not sure where; no one is, but if we're going to find it, we need to head in this direction." He pointed toward a space between narrow trees. "I brought something that could help us." He rummaged through his bag and pulled out a black device resembling something between a compass and pocket watch with green numbers and letters. "It points at the closest dark entities or demons."

"How does that help?" Naomi asked.

"In black magic clubs, they are known to summon demons when doing their sacrifices. Besides, with all the murder and blood they have in them, there's bound to be one or two demons walking among the witches, pretending to be one of them. They're attracted to darkness."

It was brilliant. "Let's go." Tingling dragged my gaze to my hand, and letters inked onto my skin. **Where are you? – Edmund.**

Maddox looked at his magic quill too. It appeared we'd all gotten the same message. My shoulders slumped. "We should say something back. He'll worry."

Maddox shoved his hands in his pockets. "We can't tell him where we are."

Naomi agreed. "Yes, but we can tell him we're safe."

Maddox arched an eyebrow. "Are we though?"

I thumbed the side of my neck. "For now."

Maddox closed his eyes, muttering the incantation, and sent a magic quill. He finished an smirked. "I told him we're sort of safe, for now anyway, and we're out kicking ass and will be back when we're done saving Istinia."

I closed my eyes. Oh gods. "That's not helpful."

He chuckled. "I'm kidding. I told him we're safe and are following a lead in a town nearby, and we'll let him know when we leave our hotel."

Naomi scoffed, looking at our crumpled blankets on the hard ground. "Some hotel."

I whipped my head around when a loud crack sounded nearby. My heart flickered and skipped a beat. Naomi froze, and Maddox stood in front of us. Freya jumped down from high branches, looking very un-Freya-like in tight, brown pants, a thin top, and with her dark waves tied back into a messy ponytail. There wasn't a hint of lipstick on her cupid-bow lips, but her eyes looked different: slightly deranged and a hundred times deadlier.

"Oh, goodie." She cocked her head to the side. "You're here." She latched her stare onto me as if I were prey. "You really fucked my plan, Elle." She sauntered toward us, and I noticed dirt embedded in her nails. "Both of you." She snapped her stare to Naomi. "I heard of how you both helped with Lucius's demise."

I glanced down at my feet. She was wrong. I had been no help at all. Naomi had.

She continued. "Alexander is dead because of you."

My eyebrows raised. "Because of us? You were going to kill us. Raiden killed him to save us."

Naomi shot me a look. I guess I left that part out. By accident.

She balled her fists. "You're going to regret the day you ever met Raiden."

Maddox stepped toward her. I unsheathed my dagger, not that it would have helped. He grabbed what looked like a potion bottle from his bag and unstoppered it. "Try me."

She cackled. "I'm not afraid of some potion. I'm immortal."

"It's an immobilizer. Sure, you can kill me, but I'll still be able to throw this on you as you do, and you, even an immortal," he mimicked, "won't be able to move for the next six hours, giving Raiden, Aziel, and whoever else is after your vile ass enough time to come and end your miserable existence."

She hesitated, wavering for just a second, enough to let us know she was afraid. Maddox was right. She would be able to kill him in the time it took him to throw the potion on her, but he'd still be able to slow her down, and there was nothing worse than being a sitting duck out in the forest.

Naomi closed her eyes and raised her hands, forming a cloud of smoke around Freya. "Run!" She shouted.

Freya fought through Naomi's illusion. Maddox went to throw the potion at her, but she almost escaped the smoke cloud.

"No." I pulled his hand. "We have seconds before—" Hands wrapped around my throat, grappling my skin until I couldn't breathe. I tightened my grip on the dagger before plunging it into her thigh. She didn't even flinch.

Maddox threw the potion, but it missed. Naomi shot an illusion our way, but I was trapped inside with her. I pulled out the dagger, and with the little strength I had, I pushed it into her stomach. She twisted to avoid the blade, and something in her leg snapped, cracking loudly during our scramble—her ankle, I hoped. Not that it would do any good. It would heal within a minute. Her grip loosened, but only for a moment.

The world spun as I flew backward through the air. Raiden's voice boomed, a scream tearing through the sky. Raiden grabbed me, holding me tight in his arms. Freya stopped in front of us for a moment, smiled knowingly, and sped through the trees faster than my mortal eyes could follow.

"You're just in time, killer," Maddox said between heavy breaths.

Raiden turned me around. "Are you hurt?" His gaze moved to my throat. "I heard something snap, and I thought she had—" He gulped. "Elle." He shook me.

I blinked twice, snapping out of the mini trance fear had swept me in. "I'm okay," I whispered. "You should go after her before she gets far enough you lose her trail."

He shook his head. "I'm taking you home first."

The sun lowered in the sky by the time we all arrived back at the mansion. Naomi and Maddox looked at each other, then at me as we stood by the front door.

Maddox cleared his throat. "We'll, uh, give you a moment. We can reconvene inside."

"Sure." I shuffled, moving from foot to foot. They left, and I passed my attention back to Raiden. "What now?"

"I thought she killed you." He exhaled slowly. I'd never seen such pain behind someone's eyes before. It was as if his soul were screaming, but there was only silence on the outside. "Aziel joined me. He was tracking her north, but out of nowhere, the trail changed, and she headed right back to the Vordel house, and I knew then she was going for you. She didn't even try to hide it. Her scent was on everything. It was like she wanted me to find her."

"Where's Aziel now?"

"Probably on his way here," he said. "Or still tracking Freya."

Don't ask. Don't ask. Don't ask. "Why would she come back for me?"

"For the same reason she kidnapped you."

"Which was?" I closed my eyes. I knew why, but I needed to hear it.

"She thinks I... care for you." He scratched the back of his neck.

I chewed the inside of my cheek. A breeze passed between us, and a bird sang from somewhere in the distance. The smell of coffee wafted from the cracked-open window.

"Do you?" My heart almost stopped.

He held his next breath. "I can't, but—"

I didn't get a chance to catch my breath before he placed his lips on mine. Sparks erupted in me as he deepened our kiss. I splayed my fingers against his chest, where his heart raced under my touch. His fingers curled into my hair as he stroked his tongue against mine.

"Fuck, Elle." He pulled away but rested his forehead against mine.

I blinked twice, innocence curving my expression. "What?"

His gaze burned into mine, intensifying the inches between us. "You know exactly what you're doing, looking up at me with those *fuck me* eyes."

Before I could say anything back, he swept me into his arms and up into the house.

Laying me on his bed, he moved on top of me, his breath tingling against my cheek. "I can't be that man for you."

"What man?"

"A hero. The guy who always does the right thing."

I smirked. "Good. I don't want that man. I want you."

He let out a heavy breath and tilted my chin upward, pressing his lips against mine with urgency. There was nothing gentle about him. Each rugged thrust gathered wetness between my legs as his hard length pressed through his pants and against my thigh. I ran my fingers along the muscles in his arms, then over his chest and closed my eyes.

He ripped off his shirt and looked down, his gaze exploring mine. "You're breathtaking, Elle." He pulled my top over my breasts, eased his fingers around my back, and unhooked my bra.

The curve of his chin dipped against my chest as he pressed his swollen lips to my hard nipple. His cock pulsated through his pants, and I moaned. His warm tongue swirled against me, sending shockwaves down my stomach and into my thighs.

I traced my fingers along the curves of his abs as he unbuckled his pants and pulled them down.

I jumped when someone knocked on the door.

"Uh, Raiden?" Edmund asked.

He pressed his fingers against his mouth, a smirk playing on those perfect lips. Slowly, he peeled my pants and underwear down. Edmund knocked again.

"I locked the door," Raiden whispered, grinning.

Edmund's footsteps creaked away and down the hall. I let out a tense breath. "That was close. We could have been caught."

"I don't care," he said, running his thumb along my bottom lip. "It's just me and you right now. The world could be on fire, and I'd still have you."

My breath hitched. He pushed his cock between my thighs, teasing me with just the tip. I spread myself, rocking my hips forward, and pushed him deep.

Something jolted beneath us, then cracked, but I didn't care. I moaned loudly as he groaned. I wrapped my legs around him, my eyes rolling back as want coursed through me. He kissed his way up to my neck.

He whispered my name against my skin. "Elle."

I closed my eyes as I tipped over the edge. My thighs quivered as he came inside me. Gripping my nails into his back, I pressed my lips against his shoulder, groaning loudly. He rested on top of me, rocking his hips as beads of sweat collected on his forehead. He pressed it against mine.

I expected him to move from me, but instead, he ran his finger down my cheek and brushed his lips against mine, closing his eyes. The gentle kiss lingered as he pulled away. For a moment, he looked different, like he had before: carefree.

It was morning when I awoke, tangled in sheets and nestled in his arms. He looked so peaceful in his sleep. I didn't want to wake him. When I moved, the bed creaked, and I realized what the crack had been last night. We'd broken the bed. Edmund was going to kill me. They all must have heard it. It wasn't in Raiden's nature to be quiet. My old self would have worried, got up, and tried to explain, but I didn't care as much anymore. Raiden moved in his sleep, and I settled back, closing my eyes. I found peace in the silence because I knew it wouldn't last long. He didn't need to tell me; I already knew. Between the vengeance with Freya, the grief from his sister, and the fear of Lucius hurting me, this couldn't happen again.

CHAPTER TWENTY-SEVEN

Maddox was grinning far too widely for first thing in the morning. "Morning, sunshine."

I side-eyed him as I went to grab coffee for me and Raiden. "Morning," I said carefully. I didn't know how much he'd heard.

"I would ask how your night went, but it sounded like it was pretty good."

I sighed, closing my eyes. "Did Edmund—"

"Oh, yes," Maddox said, leaning back in his chair at the oak dining table. "We were all here for the show. You were hardly quiet. It was super awkward." He laughed. "Anyway, you missed a bunch while you were off having wild god sex. How was it, by the way?"

I couldn't help but grin. "Unbelievable."

He clasped his fingers together at the back of his head. "Oh, I bet."

"So what did I miss?"

"Well." He drummed his fingers against the wood. "Aziel came back, all brooding and angry. Naomi talked him down from interrupting you and Raiden, so you can thank her."

My eyebrow arched. "She did?"

He smirked. "I think he likes her, which is totally unfair because you might both end up being able to have gods."

I laughed. "Did Aziel say anything?"

"About who, Freya?" Our conversation darkened. "Only that he thinks she wanted them to find her, and you. It was like she set a trap."

"It makes no sense."

"It does." He looked at me incredulously. "God, girl, you are blind. "She needed to make sure. It's why she kidnapped you, and why she tried to hurt you. She wanted to see what he would do, to see how valuable you are."

I trembled while pouring my coffee. "I'm not valuable."

"She can use you against Raiden."

"Not while he's here. Besides, I'm sure he's had sex with tons of women."

"Probably," he said. "But it's more than that with you." He rolled his eyes. "Neither of you even realize it, do you?"

"Maddox," I warned.

"He loves you." He smiled widely, showing off his pearly whites.

"No, he doesn't." I placed my coffee cup on the countertop. "It's... lust."

He chuckled. "Sure. Sure. Denial, but sure."

"We're friends."

"Right."

"Maddox. He's a god. He said before, he isn't a boyfriend kind of guy. He certainly doesn't fall in love. Trust me, it's not like that. It's just a little complicated," I said. "If it really comes down to it, he won't choose me over killing Freya, if that's what she thinks. She's deluded and will be wasting her time."

"Honey..." His expression softened. "He already did. Last night. He got you to safety. He could have gone after her. She was close. He and Aziel could have killed her last night, but instead, he took you here, and well..."

"Stop." I inhaled deeply as footsteps approached.

Edmund walked in, cleaning his glasses against his top. He placed them on, then looked from me to Maddox, rubbing the back of his neck. "Um. Good morning, Eleanor."

My eyes widened, as did Maddox's. Since when was I Eleanor? I rubbed my forehead. "Morning."

"Has, uh, Maddox filled you in?"

Maddox chuckled. "I didn't fill her in yet, but I know someone who did." He rolled his eyes again. I almost threw my coffee at him.

Edmund cleared his throat, ignoring Maddox's last statement. "We know how to kill Lucius and how to kill Freya, but you're not going to like it."

I glanced at Maddox, who gave nothing away in his expression. "What is it?"

"Raiden will need to take his place—Lucius's place that is. With his new powers, he can easily kill Freya."

"What do you mean his place?"

"Lucius is the high god. There has to be a ruler of the underworld, and while Raiden will still be Raiden, he will need to take ownership and rule the underworld."

Maddox peered around Edmund, who stood in front of the table. "It means he'll need to live in the underworld, which is a different realm."

"I know what it means," I snapped.

"I know you like him, but—"

"It's fine," I said. "He'll take it if it means getting rid of his father and killing Freya. Good." I swallowed thickly. "A good find. Well done." I whistled out a breath. "Great."

Maddox blew out a tense breath, puffing his cheeks out. "Aziel offered to do it," he said before I could ask. "But he said it is Raiden's birthright as the oldest and it was up to him."

I chewed my bottom lip. Of course Raiden would do it. He would never agree to offer his brother to such a horrible existence. He wasn't that kind of man, that kind of god. "I should take this to him." I held up a second coffee cup.

Edmund squeezed my shoulder as he passed. "I am sorry."

"Don't be. It's no big deal," I said, then walked away feeling a thousand times heavier.

"You're awake." I smiled, handing Raiden his coffee. He looked too damn delicious with white sheets wrapped around his waist, his abs and muscles on display.

"I am." His arrogant smirk I missed so much returned. "Back for round two?"

I arched my eyebrow. "I could," I said, climbing onto the bed. I paused. "Wait, no." I sighed. Damned brain. "I need to tell you something."

"What?" He leaned forward, holding my hand in his. I wanted him to hold me, and I wanted to beg him not to do it and to stay here with me, but he wouldn't, and I wasn't going to embarrass myself like that. He needed them dead. It was right by Thalia and Leda, and—

A thought popped into my head. If he ruled the underworld, Thalia and Leda would be there. He could be with them, and they wouldn't be in pain. There was no way he would refuse it, and I could never ask him to.

"Elle?" He brushed a lock of hair from my face and smiled a silly grin. "What's up, baby girl?"

Holy. "There's a way for you to kill Lucius." I blew out a long breath. "Edmund found it."

"What is it?" His expression darkened.

"You need to go into the underworld to kill him. I don't know all the details, but Edmund and Maddox seem to think you can, you know, take his place, and with your new powers, you can kill Freya. Aziel said he'd do it."

"No." He leaned away from me. "It needs to be me. This started with me; it'll end with me."

My stomach dipped. My lips parted. There were so many things I wanted to say, but I couldn't. The pain in his expression returned, the sparkle in his gaze tortured.

My heart sank. I placed my cup on the nightstand, then moved to his side and pressed my lips against his shoulder. He leaned back against the headboard and rested his head on me. I ran my fingers through his hair as we sat in silence, our touches saying everything and nothing.

Chapter Twenty-Eight

Naomi slumped in the armchair of the study. "Where's everyone?" She dropped her bag on the floor, looking a little worse for wear.

"Raiden's with Maddox, and Edmund is going over ancient scrolls and stuff so he can take over the underworld."

"Oh, right. Yeah, Az mentioned."

My eyebrows pinched. "Az?"

"Aziel." She cleared her throat. "Anyway, I'm sorry. I know you liked him."

"Forget it." I played it off, but my stomach was in knots. "Since when is Aziel Az?"

She let out a small, sad smile. "He's, well, you know, he's hard to read, but once you get under the surface…"

"How far have you got under the surface?"

"Not like that. He's gone through a lot, and I've been trying to help him. Everyone else just steers clear because he's a little—"

"Standoffish? Assholeish?"

"Yeah."

"You always were too kind."

She bit her bottom lip. "I know he said some things, and he's sorry."

"He is? I haven't heard this apology." I paused when her expression dropped. The closer I looked at her, the more I noticed her fading bloodshot eyes and empty gaze. "Nai, what happened?"

She slapped her hands against her face, letting out a loud sob. "It's my dad." She gasped again, sobbing.

My eyes widened. Was he sick? Dead?

I rushed to her side and held her hand in mine. "Nai."

"He cut me out of the family."

My nostrils flared. "He did what?"

She cried through her fingers. "He was already disappointed when I didn't pass the test and then he found out I've been going out of town, and someone told him they saw me with Aziel, who looks like, well, he looks like trouble, Elle. He thinks I've gone off the rails and I'm whoring myself out, and he said I'm an embarrassment to the family name." She hiccupped through her sobs. "Something about having seven generations of casters, grandcasters, and revolutionary business owners for me to besmirch the name. It was bad enough I was a magician, but to have failed that too and to be 'whoring' around… That's what he thinks."

"That bastard."

"My mom just went along with him. Like always."

I shook my head. "Don't listen to him."

"My brother said I need to try to fix things. Family is family after all."

"Fuck that. Family isn't a reason to put up with his toxic ass." I balled my fists. "Don't worry though. You'll show him. Once you start your own business, he'll regret saying anything, and he can watch from the sideline."

Her breath hitched, and her shoulders slumped. "I can't. You know the influence he has. No one will want to have anything to do with me after this."

I stood slowly. "I'll ask Dora to make you some cocoa, and you can even have some of my cookies." I put a finger up, earning a small smile. "This once. Because you're sad. I'll be back soon."

She leaned forward. "Where are you going?"

"I need to check on Raiden and a couple of other things."

"Of course. Sorry. I know this is the last day you can spend with him."

I swallowed thickly. "I'll see you soon."

I rapped on Naomi's dad's front door five times before I leaned back against the wall of their porch. I wished I hadn't needed to lie, but I knew she'd have had a panic attack if she found out where I was really going.

Naomi's mom answered, her golden hair wrapped among rollers. She wore a white robe and a face mask. "Eleanor, what a surprise. Naomi isn't here."

"I know." I softened my tone, surprised at how sharp it came out. It had been years since Naomi left home to be with her coven and I'd called on this door for her to come out and play. "I'm here to see—ah." I paused, seeing her dad poke his head around the corner.

"Eleanor." He said my name like it left a bad taste in his mouth. He'd barely aged. His dark hair had a few scattered grays in them, and wrinkles barely pinched the corners of his honey-brown eyes. "If this is about Naomi, I don't want to hear any more news. I've had enough for the day."

Her mother nodded along. "Her behavior almost gave him a heart attack."

I placed my hand on my hip. "Oh, shut the fuck up."

Their eyebrows shot upward on their foreheads. "What did you just say?"

I slowed it down. "I said shut. The. Fuck. Up."

He scowled. "How dare you!"

I scoffed. "How dare me? How dare you, asshole? Your daughter is amazing and a million times the person you are. She hasn't been whoring around, as if that's any good reason to cut your daughter off anyway, because it's not." I had a huge problem with the term "whoring," but I wasn't about to get into that now. "The point is she's been working on, let's call it, a secret mission, and because of her, she literally helped save lives. Her magic... You know, the magic you think is useless, well she's incredible at it, and she—" I paused. I couldn't actually give everything away. "Let's just say she's someone you want on your team when you're in a sticky spot."

He clicked his tongue. "Then why didn't she pass the test if she's *so* brilliant at it?"

"I'll bet it was because she was nervous, because of the pressure you put on her to be perfect, like you're anything close to it."

He waved his hand dismissively. "I don't need to hear this, especially from some witch from a lesser coven."

"You're hilarious if you think yours is any better than ours. We all have our uses, and without us, you'd be overrun with curses and dark objects. Alma called Edmund and Dora before she called you to go with her."

He crossed his arms over his scrawny chest. "You're on private property. You need to leave before I call the protectors."

"Happily," I spat. "But you should know you're making a huge mistake with your daughter."

He stepped out of the doorway and onto the porch step. "She's no daughter of mine."

Rage bubbled within me, spilling over. I held my breath, turned on my heel, and punched him hard in the side of his face. He staggered back, touching his cheek, slack-jawed. His wife screamed as if I'd murdered him or something. I rubbed my knuckles and hurried away, adrenaline carrying my jog all the way back.

***

Night came too fast. I wasn't ready for it, but the moon appeared anyway, kissing the sun into darkness. I waited for someone to come to the door, to arrest me or something for hitting the grandcaster, but to my surprise, the afternoon passed without so much as a magic quill to any of us about what had happened, so I figured it was best to keep quiet about the whole thing. I waited for regret to seep in, but it never came. That punch felt so damned good, and honestly, I had wanted to do it for a long time. Every time Naomi had cried over the years because of him, each belittlement and spiteful comment he'd have, my anger had built, but this was crossing the line.

Aziel walked into the kitchen, clattering pans as he turned. I swore his muscles had muscles. "Hello." He looked me down and peered around me. "I am here to see Raiden."

He must have been out hunting Freya, who, as goddess of the hunt, was good at evading it. "He's coming down now."

"Good."

Naomi walked in behind us. "Az." She smiled widely. At least her bad mood seemed mostly over. "You're back."

"Yes."

If stoic were a person, it would be him. Naomi looked at him, then gestured in my direction with wide eyes.

He scratched the back of his neck, clearing his throat. "Right. Uh, Elle, I apologize for blaming you for Thalia."

Naomi gave him a look.

He continued. "I was hurt, and it wasn't fair. It wasn't all your fault."

She clicked her tongue. "It wasn't her fault at all."

He exhaled slowly. "This has always been Freya, and a little Raiden."

I shook my head. "Well, he's suffering enough, so…"

"I know." His forehead wrinkled, eyes glossing slightly. "He's always been a romantic. It was expected."

I couldn't help but laugh. "Raiden? A romantic?"

He shrugged. "He's always fought with his heart and made mistakes because of it too. Freya, on the other hand, is unforgivable. I will make her pay."

"Raiden will make her pay," I said to correct him. "Because he's the one who's going to take your father's place."

"If he can kill him there." The muscle in Aziel's jaw ticked. "The underworld is Lucius's domain. It will be difficult, and that is why I will be going with him."

"What?" Naomi's voice lowered.

"I must," he said.

My heart raced. "Then we can go too. I mean, to help."

He shook his head, flicking his ponytail as he did. "Mortals cannot enter the underworld. Your immortal souls will separate from your mortal bodies, and you will not be able to return to them."

My heart sank. "So Raiden won't be able to return either."

"Perhaps occasionally," he explained. "It's not easy to get from the underworld to the mortal realm, and if he takes Lucius's place, he will need to rule it."

"Like a king?"

I heard footsteps approach, then Raiden's voice. "I've never imagined myself in a crown, but I think I could pull it off." He grinned as he stepped beside me, lightly touching the side of my waist. He looked at Aziel.

"Brother, we will leave in the morning. You know the plan."

"Yes."

I arched an eyebrow as I looked up at him. "You're not leaving now?"

He shook his head. "The underworld can wait one more night."

Naomi nudged me, smirking. "Yes, perhaps you should say your good-byes."

I turned back. Raiden's gaze burned into mine. "That's why I'm not leaving now."

***

Raiden's fingers traced along my knuckles. I lay back against my pillows, looking at the rain-splattered window. "What happened to your hand?"

I bit my lip. "I punched Naomi's dad."

An amused smile curled his lips. "What did he do to deserve such a thing?"

"He's just an ass."

"Say no more." He raised my hand, brushed his lips against it with a whisper of a kiss, and the bruises healed. "You're so strong, Elle. When I first got here, you couldn't see it. I hope you do now. When I'm gone from here, you should go to see your sister."

A lump formed in my throat. "I'm." I paused. "I'm afraid too."

"I know, but you'll always be putting it off if you don't. Don't wait until it's too late. Edmund will let you go. You know he will."

I closed my eyes. "I know."

He nodded slowly. "I have something for you." He stood, reached into his bag, and pulled the weapon out.

I stared at the glowing, gem-encrusted hilt, moving my gaze along the smooth blue blade. "Thalia's dagger."

"It's yours. This way you can protect yourself when I'm gone."

"I can't." I blinked back tears.

"You will." He placed it into my hands. "And you can. I never gave you enough credit for killing that hound. You protected Thalia, for me, and she protected you, for me." Pain swept through his gaze, pulling at my heartstrings.

"If Freya comes back, I'll make sure to stick it in her heart," I said with promise, gripping the hilt and pointing it outward.

He smirked, lowering the blade with his finger. "I'm going to finish Freya once I've killed my father. I'm coming back. Lucius's going to make sure of it. I won't be able to come back for long, not with taking his place, but long enough to take her head."

My chest heaved. "I'm sorry you're leaving." I wanted to beg him not to go, but I couldn't be selfish. Not with him. "I wish…"

"Me too, but just enjoy being here, being mortal. Remember what I told you once?"

"About feeling alive?" I nodded. "It's just crazy." I laughed through the sadness. "You'll be alive forever, always remembered as a god. There are literal books written about you, about Thalia, Aziel, Leda…"

He ran his finger along my cheek. "In the end, Elle, we're all stories. Mortal. Immortal. It doesn't matter. When we die, an entire library dies with us."

"Then what's the point? Everyone stops reading them eventually, or listening to them," I said, tired of the book metaphor. "I know nothing of my great-grandparents. I'll be forgotten one day."

He grazed his lips against my hand, sending tingles through my fingers. "I'm immortal."

"I know."

"Then you'll never be forgotten."

My heart skipped a beat.

He continued. "You make me feel alive, Elle. You make me want to live a thousand stories right here with you."

I could hardly breathe.

"Now it's my turn." He lowered his voice to a whisper. "To make you feel alive." He lifted me off the bed, holding me tightly in his arms. "Hold on."

The breath whooshed from my lungs as he sped me through the house and to the edge of town. I held onto him when we stopped, steadying myself from the momentary lack of balance.

"What in the underworld are you doing?"

He smirked, the darkness growling around us. I panicked, until I realized the dark shadow was in fact a panther.

"Oh, gods." I stumbled back, almost tripping, but I caught myself.

"Don't be afraid." He placed a hand on the panther's glossy midnight coat. "He won't attack you."

Shaking, I reached forward. The beast's orange eyes locked onto mine. He curled, moving slickly in the night as if he belonged to it. I reached out and stroked his back.

Raiden stepped back, breathing the cold air deep into his lungs and stretching out his arms. "I'll miss this, being out among the trees and creatures in it."

I carefully stepped back, and a twig snapped under my shoe. The panther let out a low growl, and Raiden snapped his fingers. The panther slunk away into the trees. I didn't even know we had them in this part of Istinia. I mean, I'd heard of them, but they were so rare.

"Well." I laughed, holding my stomach. "You certainly made me feel alive."

He chuckled. "I actually didn't expect to run into a panther."

"No?"

"Sometimes animals find me."

"Well, you are the god of beasts," I teased.

"God of creatures," he said.

I closed the distance between us. "I know. So why did you really bring me out here?"

"You love the woods," he said simply. "As do I. Freya's way to the east, according to Aziel, and we're no safer there than you are here, with me." He ran his hand through my hair. "I'm trusting you, Elle. It's not easy for me to do that, after Freya." He held his breath for a moment. "That dagger can kill any immortal."

My eyebrows knitted together. "It can kill you."

"As I said, I'm trusting you." His stare intensified. "I want you to be able to protect yourself against anything that comes your way. There are shifters, too, and demons. They're both immortal. It will work against them."

My heart pounded. I pressed my hand against his chest, splaying my fingers until I could feel the rhythm of his heart match mine.

He leaned down and kissed me softly at first, then harder. I held onto him, running my hands up his back and to the nape of his neck. He pressed his hand against my lower back, holding me against him as if I might disappear at any moment.

He pulled away, breathing fast, torture in his eyes. A low growl escaped his lips as he gripped my arms. "You're so beautiful. In every way."

He traced his fingers along my thigh, his lips against my neck. I pulled his chin upward and met his lips with mine. The first splashes of rain pattered around us, mixing the earthy aroma with his cologne. I nibbled his bottom lip, feeling silky wetness gather between my legs. He traced his fingers along my navel and into my pants. The light touch of his finger on my clit sent a shockwave through my legs. He found the spot, pooling my wetness into the dip, rubbing until my legs buckled.

His length pressed against my hip, pulsating as I moaned into his mouth. He lifted me, and I curled my legs around his waist. He pulled my pants down, then slammed me against a tree trunk, ripping my top off, and threw it into the night.

My nipples hardened at a cool gust. Rain slicked us, glossing his muscles, illuminated under the pale moonlight. My breasts bounced when he grabbed my ass, pushing me farther up the trunk.

A low growl escaped him as shrugged his own pants down to his ankles, baring us to the forest. I wrapped my fingers around his cock—throbbing, ready for me. I closed my eyes as I stroked it, delighting in the frenzied glint in his eyes when I peeled back my eyelids.

He pushed the tip in first, then his whole length, and want rippled through me. He rocked his hips against me, gripping me against him tightly. He fisted my hair as he bit on his bottom lip. I pushed my hips upward, forcing him deeper inside.

"Fuck!" he yelled. His dick pulsated, and his eyes rolled toward the back of his head. He came inside of me as I tipped into my own orgasm. I moaned loudly, making birds take flight from the treetops. He groaned and bit softly on my collarbone.

He kissed his way back up to my neck, whispering my name like a prayer against my skin.

I rested my head on his shoulder and listened to him pant as he held me like I weighed nothing. At that moment, it was just us and nothing else mattered, but with each passing minute, the knowledge of tomorrow weighed heavier than before. It was a reminder of what this was: good-bye.

Chapter Twenty-Nine

Bacon. Eggs. Were those waffles I could smell? Mmm syrup. I walked sheepishly into the kitchen, which had been scrubbed to an inch of its life, and eyed Dora who was frowning over a frying pan.

"Hey." I cleared my throat, and she forced out a smile. "You cooking the full works?"

She placed her hand on her hip, tapping a long fingernail against the front of her apron. "I won't have him leaving without a good meal in his stomach. It's quite a journey."

I hadn't noticed Maddox standing just outside of the open back door until he choke-laughed on his coffee. "He's not going on vacation."

She pointed a finger at him. "He and that brother of his need sustenance. They're going to fight evil."

I cocked my head. She'd been so good with the whole thing, considering how she felt about the otherworld and

Estia. We'd all been careful to only talk about Lucius and the underworld, leaving her precious deity out of the mix. Still, Estia didn't sound much better than Lucius. I was just glad Dora's thoughts about the high god, Lucius, had changed since we'd told her what happened.

She shook her head, sighing in disappointment. "He is supposed to be a god, and he was going to hurt you and Naomi, two innocent mortals." She shook her head. "Bringing demons to our world."

"I know, Dora." I kept a brave face, sitting at the table as she served me a plate of waffles. I was ravenous after the night I'd had.

Maddox winked at me when I looked at him. "Good night?"

"It was—You know, it was none of your business." I scowled, desperate to change the topic. "Where's Edmund? Naomi?" I scoffed down a bite of waffle, muffling, "Aziel?"

Maddox laughed. "Except you make it everyone's business when the whole house can hear you both."

"Maddox." I snapped my fingers. "Where is everyone?"

"Aziel spent the night talking with Naomi."

I arched an eyebrow. "Just talking?"

Dora clicked her tongue. "Of course they were only talking."

Maddox grinned. "They really did just talk. They left the door open and spent the night in the living room." He rolled his eyes. "They both like reading. Apparently, it's what Aziel did a lot in his prison realm."

I laughed. "I cannot envision him reading."

"Me too. I went in, poured myself a martini or two at the bar," Maddox said. I recalled the globe filled with bottles and drinks in the living area. "Then went upstairs. I sent a magic quill to Aaron. He came over. Just left actually."

"I thought you didn't go back to you exes?" I drummed my fingers on the table.

He shrugged. "I was bored."

"Sure," I replied, smirking into my coffee.

"I don't do commitment." He walked over to make himself what I assumed was a second or third black coffee. "I'm married to my job."

Dora made him a plate of bacon and a couple of slices of wholegrain toast with a poached egg on the side. "Here's your breakfast." She turned toward me. "Special requests from his majesty here. Apparently plain old waffles and bacon wasn't enough."

Maddox sipped his drink and sat at the table. "Ah." He tucked a napkin into his collar, covering the front of his shirt. "I can always count on my main lady."

She rolled her eyes but smiled all the same. "Edmund should be down soon."

"How would you know that?" Maddox asked.

"H-he told me." She stumbled. "When I went to wake him, in his own room." She waved a spatula at Maddox. "Not all of us are like you."

I whistled out a breath, then chuckled. "Ouch."

Maddox winced playfully. "Raiden's sleeping then?" he asked, turning his attention toward me.

"Yeah." I played with a piece of waffle at the end of my fork. "We went to bed late. We didn't talk all night though, not like Nai and Aziel."

He laughed. "Yep. Raiden's not the talking type."

I looked at the ceiling thoughtfully. "What he does say counts more then." I closed my eyes, losing myself in the way he'd said my name last night, how he'd called me beautiful.

Maddox's lips twisted in disgust. "I miss when everyone wasn't as lovesick in this house."

"I'm not lovesick."

He shook his head as he delicately ate a slice of bacon. "Denial, girl."

"What does it matter?" I leaned back in my chair, pushing my plate away. "He's leaving anyway."

"Speak of the god, and he shall come," Maddox said over my shoulder.

I whipped my head around. Raiden's hair was tousled, a reminder of our night in the sheets. "We're leaving." His tone had hardened.

Maddox looked at me, then at Raiden. "We'll come to see you off."

"No need. We've all said our good-byes." He didn't even look at me. "Thanks, Dora, but we need to go."

Her shoulders slumped. "You should at least eat something."

"We'll eat when we're there."

I didn't even want to know what that meant.

Raiden called to Aziel who, in a flash, stepped at his side. "Thank you for all your kindness," Raiden said, looking at Maddox, then Dora. He carried his gaze over me but did not pause. "Stay safe."

I stood, screeching my chair back.

Raiden turned with Aziel, and they both walked out.

"Raiden." My voice croaked.

He was gone. My lips parted as my good-bye remained silent on my tongue. *What just happened?*

***

Naomi stacked books that she and Aziel had looked through, I assumed, back onto their shelves, organizing them by color. "So he just left without saying anything?"

I nodded slowly.

Maddox chimed in from the sofa. "It was hard to watch."

She winced. "Maybe it was just too difficult for him to say good-bye."

My bottom lip shook. "It didn't seem that way. It was like he flipped a switch." I felt the dagger he'd gifted me sheathed to my thigh. It was all I had, a reminder he cared, that what we'd had was real. "It doesn't matter. He's gone."

"Now what?" she asked.

We all slumped onto the sofa. It was a good question. Silence hung over us. Our lives had become filled with so much adventure and pain that without it, everything felt a little empty. "I punched your dad," I admitted finally, needing to break the quiet.

Naomi leaned forward, looking at me incredulously. "You what?"

Maddox let out an *oooo*. "Makes sense now." He glanced at my hand. He must have noticed the bruises yesterday.

"He deserved it," I said simply. "He was an ass."

"When was this?"

"Yesterday. After you told me what he did."

Maddox nodded. "He really did deserve it. Good on you, Elle."

I stared at the bookshelf, my gaze trailing over a spine labeled Gods and Monsters. Things had been so insane, I'd barely had a moment to myself to think. Whenever I closed my eyes in silence, I saw Bryan's body in the woods or Thalia's head on the ground. "Wait. Maddox, when Thalia was killed, shouldn't someone have replaced her?"

His groomed brows furrowed. "Good point." He mulled a moment. "Lucius killed her, but he's already a god, so he can't take her place. He could have allocated someone to take her place, but he was killed—well, sent back to the underworld anyway."

A horrible feeling snuck over me, making my skin crawl. "Then who?"

"Whoever claimed her," he guessed aloud. "Or Lucius did. I don't know. Whoever it is, they need to be careful."

"Why?"

Maddox's eyes bulged. "Isn't it obvious?"

I gave him a look. "Humor me."

"Raiden is going to take over the underworld, where his sisters are. Do you think he's going to allow anyone to have their place? He will have the power to send them back."

"Are you sure?"

"I'm assuming so. They like being in our world. Why would they want to remain stuck in the underworld when their brother can let them out?"

"Raiden said he can't come back for a while," I said.

"Doesn't mean they can't."

Naomi looked from him to me. "Raiden can't just come and go when he pleases because he needs to rule the underworld. They don't."

Edmund's shaky shout reached us from the kitchen. "Elle. Maddox. Naomi. Run!"

I jumped to my feet. "Edmund!" I shouted back.

Naomi grabbed my hand. "It might be—"

I pulled my hand from hers. "I don't care."

I ran to the kitchen, my breaths shaking from my lungs with each lunge. When I reached the kitchen, Freya's eyes locked onto mine, along with a second pair of bright, glittering blues I thought I'd never see again.

My heart felt like it stopped. Numbness waved through me as I stared at them, slack-jawed.

Her bright blue eyes hadn't changed. Her frizzy red hair had grown out to reach her elbows, but her other features looked nothing like those of the sister I remembered. She was a woman now. Her auburn eyebrows pinched downward. "Is that you?"

I didn't know how to answer. I'd forgotten every word that had ever existed. "Yes." It was all I could manage. My gaze drifted to Freya's. "Whatever you're thinking of doing—"

Rage fueled Freya's expression. Every feature on her face seemed sharper since I'd last seen her. "Alexander was right. You do have a sister."

I held my hands up, approaching her slowly.

She wrapped one hand around Mona's throat and pressed the other against the side of her neck. "Take one more step and I break her neck, then yours." Tears welled in her eyes. "Where's Raiden? I'm not here to play games."

Edmund answered. "He's gone. You're too late."

She cackled, a madness in her stare that was intensified under the bright lights of the kitchen. "Seems I'm right on time."

I stared, slack-jawed, at my brilliant, taller-than-me, beautiful sister. Her eyes welled with tears. "Ellie." Only she ever called me that.

"How did you find her?" I asked, a tear falling down my cheek.

"It wasn't hard once I knew where to look."

I moved my gaze back to my sister. "Are you okay? Did she hurt you?"

Tears fell down Mona's cheeks. "Ellie, she... she..." She shook her head, looking down. "She killed my mentor and my friend."

Goose bumps covered my skin. "I'm sorry, Mona. I..."

Maddox panted, rushing to the doorway behind me. Naomi joined him, and I heard her gasp when she saw Freya.

Freya scowled. "Raiden thinks he can kill me, but he can't because I have something more precious to him than his mortality."

My stomach twisted. "I would rather die than go with you."

"Oh, lovey, no. You're not coming with me. You see, I have your sister, and you will do anything for her, according to Alexander." She smiled. "And we both know Raiden will do anything for you. That's how leverage works."

I wished I hadn't told Alexander about Mona, but I hadn't thought anything of it at the time. I had been trying to make him understand why they were hunting Freya— why family was so important. If I'd known it would lead to this, I would have kept my mouth shut. "Alexander was wrong."

"Alexander, darling. Come here," she called, and he stepped through the door. His ash-blond hair had been swept into a braid, his wide, dreamy eyes brighter than before.

"My love." He kissed her cheek.

I inhaled sharply. "Alexander took Thalia's place."

"He did. Did you really think I would leave him dead? He'd do anything for me. I waited in the shadows until you all left. You were stupid enough to leave her body without taking her essence with you, so I took it for my Alexander." She brushed her fingers along his.

"That doesn't sound like love," I snapped, praying he would see through her, but his far-off stare remained on her.

"Love only gets you killed. See what it did to Raiden?" She looked me up and down. "What it'll do to you?"

"Mona." I swallowed hard, trying to remove the lump in my throat. "I'm going to fix this."

"Like you promised to come back for me?" she asked, and my stomach dipped.

Freya laughed. "I love a good family drama."

I fumbled my fingers. "It wasn't as easy as that."

Freya's eyes brightened. "Yes, it was. She's a keeper. She has access to all manners of magical items that could have got her back to you."

Gods, I hated her. "I wasn't a keeper until recently."

Freya tapped Mona's shoulder. "She had access to them before that."

"I wasn't able to." I was seething. "Please, Mona, understand. I wanted to come back for you. I really couldn't." Another tear trickled out. "I was afraid you wouldn't want to see me."

Mona looked down for a few seconds, then brought her gaze back to meet mine, and for a heart-stopping moment, I was ten again. "I always wanted you to come back. You're my sister. I never stopped loving you."

Everything in me shattered. Every misbelief, every fear, was gone. She loved me. No matter what. I wanted to hug her, to hold her, and cry with her, but she was in the grip of a monster.

"Wasn't that a happy ending? Now we're all reunited." Freya tilted her head. "Eleanor, you will come with us or watch your sister die, along with your coven. Your choice."

My breath hitched. "Where are we going?"

"To see Lucius."

I ran cold. "He's back in the underworld."

She put a finger in the air. "Was, Eleanor. He *was* in the underworld. Don't worry, lovey. I made the deal in your favor—well, mine really."

I shuddered. "What deal?"

"Raiden is about to be given a very important choice: let you die or let you take his place as a god—well, goddess. You can take his immortality like I did Leda's. He'll do it. I'm certain."

I balled my fists at my side. "He needs to die for that to happen."

She looked at me incredulously. "Obviously. That's the whole point."

"If that happens," I spat through gritted teeth. "I will never stop hunting you."

She laughed. "Oh, Eleanor, why do you think I have your sister? Now, now. Mona, you'll be going with Alexander here. He will take you somewhere safe and cloak you. Eleanor, you will be coming with me."

Mona looked over her shoulder as she was pushed into Alexander's arms.

"Mona." My breath hitched. "I'll find you. I'll make this right. I promise." A cry stammered in my throat.

Mona's eyes didn't leave mine. "I'll be okay, Ellie," she stated, and she looked a lot braver than I did as she was dragged out of the door with the new god of the dead: Alexander.

Freya extended her hand toward me. I eyed it like it was a venomous snake.

Naomi pulled me back from behind. "She's not going with you."

Maddox stepped in front of me. "You'll need to go through us."

Edmund leaped at her from behind, and without a flinch, she flung him back into the shelves. They fell on top of him, sending pans and jars crashing to the floor.

She looked only at me. "Eleanor."

I nodded, then looked at Edmund across the kitchen, who was now covered in flour. "Don't. She'll have Mona killed. I've got this."

Naomi held onto my arm. "No."

I ripped my arm away from hers, then grabbed Freya's. A cold breeze swept my hair behind me as she whisked me away and out of the house. I felt the dagger's sheath push against my thigh. She held me close. I leaned down and pretended to itch my leg but almost toppled from her arms. I grabbed the hilt as the trees became blots inking out into the distance. I closed my eyes, not letting dizziness settle in. I needed her this close. We'd be there soon.

I steadied myself by holding her shoulder with one hand, then moved the hand holding my dagger to her waist. I braced myself for the inevitable crash. I reached higher, allowing every powerless, helpless moment she had placed me in slide into my mind, pushing anger-driven strength behind the dagger as I stabbed the blade into the back of her neck.

We tumbled through the air and slammed into the ground. The air was knocked from my lungs. Blood splattered my hands and arms. I held my head as the forest spun around me.

Sitting up, I examined the cuts and bruises on my arms and the tears in my pants. I let out a long, shaky exhale as I brushed my hand along one of the cuts from where I must've hit a rock.

Freya convulsed a few yards from me. She tried to speak, but blood pooled from her ruby-red lips.

I crawled to her side, grabbed a fistful of her hair, and pulled out the dagger. "Rot in the underworld, you vile excuse of a person."

Her wide eyes narrowed, her pupils growing tiny, as realization swept through us both. She was going to die. A part of me enjoyed it, to watch the light fade in her predator eyes as she had done to countless others. I pointed the knife against her neck again while she struggled for air. I imagined my family dying at her hands, how she would have killed any one of us without a second thought if it had suited her. "I stuck it in again, then again, never closing my eyes to her blood splatters and gurgling. I kept going, cutting through her windpipe, each rage-fueled cut pushed on by thoughts of Mona, Raiden, and everyone she had threatened.

I stepped back, coated in her blood. Her head was almost detached from her body. A white light left her body, floating up, then shot into my chest.

I covered my mouth and was taking in the scene when the realization hit me, freezing me numb; I would now be goddess of the hunt. I had unwittingly taken Raiden's sister's immortality, and now Leda would never be able to return unless I died.

Energy buzzed through my veins, feeling like flames licking my skin. I dizzied down, catching myself on a low branch before I hit the ground with a thud. The pressure in my brain crushed every thought, and the forest darkened, then faded to black.

Chapter Thirty

Pink pinched the indigo sky, and clouds rolled over the forest. The smell of rain hung fresh in the air. I lay upon the mossy mattress, surrounded by underbrush and fallen dewy leaves. The ground muddied under my fingers as I sat upright, gasping in precious breaths. Squirrels foraged nuts nearby, their chattering and scurrying filling my ears. The wind whistled through the trees, catching wisps of moss and cobwebs and drifting them to the ground. I closed my eyes as another sound babbled in my ears: a trickling of a stream. I whipped my head around, tilting my head, and stared at the long luscious blades of grass and how they seemed to whisper in their sway, catching thick droplets of rain, in tiny domes of light, and the splashes they caused. Everything beautiful was breathtaking, and every ugly thing, horrendous. Bugs crawled out of a log. My eyes narrowed as they feasted upon one of their own recent dead, their mouths and feelers desperate for the food of its own.

I shuddered, turning away. My eyesight had never been so sharp, my hearing never so acute, and suddenly it felt like I had been living my entire life muted, with the volume down and a film over my eyes until this moment.

Drizzled rain touched my skin like a thousand kisses, sending goose bumps along my skin. A branch creaked, followed by breaths. Yes, they were definitely heavy breaths. Each one had a slight whistle to it, and footsteps. Whoever was close crept through the trees, trying to be silent, but it sounded as if they were right in front of me.

"She has to be close." Naomi's voice drifted to me, echoing like a melody, a song in each word. I shook my head as if to scatter the sound, but it was followed by a distinct second voice.

"If someone hadn't stopped for food," Maddox said. His sassy tone low but light. "We'd have found her by now."

"I was hungry," Naomi snapped back. "What am I supposed to do? Starve? We're hiking. We needed the energy. I didn't see you complaining when you dug into those pancakes."

"Enough," Edmund ordered, and they fell silent, followed only by a small sigh from whom I presumed would be Maddox. "We need to whisper. Freya could hear us if she's close."

Whispering would do nothing. I could hear their hearts racing as clear as drumbeats. My nostrils flared. I smelled Maddox's cologne—rich, spicy, and deep, with a hint of cinnamon. I sniffed it out, following it into the trees. I went to run normally but sped too quickly and headed right for a tree trunk. I stopped myself before I hit it, with perfect balance, and steadied myself. I felt lighter than expected.

This was how it felt to be a goddess.

After readying myself, I moved and whisked through the trees. Expecting the blur I usually got when I was in the arms of Raiden or Aziel when they ran, I blinked twice. Everything was crystal clear: each time-chiseled tree, flake of bark, veins on the leaves, and droplets caught on webs. There was so much beauty in the world, and for a moment, I wanted to capture it, as Alexander had in his paintings. I wanted to take it and show it to my friends and my family, so they could see what I did, but it wasn't possible.

Within a few seconds, I reached them and stopped in front of Edmund. He dropped his compass, wide-eyed. Maddox jolted back, and Naomi gasped.

Maddox gulped. "Well, this is a lot to unpack."

"Elle?" Edmund hesitated, holding his hand out as if I could be an illusion. Did I look different?

Naomi's hand shot to cover her mouth. "You're immortal," she said between her fingers. "Or something close to it."

"I killed Freya." My voice sounded different to me, each note crisper, sharper than before. "I took her place."

Maddox smirked. "Jeez. To think we'd come to save you. Looks like we could have saved ourselves the journey." He tugged at his belt, which was snagged at the side. "This was expensive and now ruined. Stupid branch caught it."

I rolled my eyes, delighting in the normalcy for a second. Maddox was processing it better than the other two. Edmund looked as if he was going to pass out at any moment, and Naomi hadn't yet lowered her hand from her open mouth.

"I'm okay," I explained. "Well, sort of. Everything feels so different." I extended my arms and gasped at the dried blood coating my skin, soaked into my pores, and dried on the tiny blonde hairs. No wonder they were shocked. I looked horrific. Freya's blood smelled like rusted iron but with a cloying sweet tang. "It's Freya." I tried to pick the blood off, but there was too much. I needed a bath. I wondered how a bath would feel now. How water would feel on my skin...

Maddox snapped his fingers. "Even as a goddess, you're still just as distracted. Nice to know some things don't change."

I arched an eyebrow. "You know I can beat you now, right? At weapons training. With magic."

He smirked. "Finally, after all the years of mediocrity, a challenge."

Edmund tugged at his collar and cleared his throat, bringing our attention back to him. "All right. So this is a new development," he said slowly, looking up, then down—everywhere but at me. "We need to replan."

"Replan." Maddox scoffed. "We need to go home. Elle can find her sister herself. We're hardly any help."

Naomi punched his arm, having finally snapped out of the mini-trance she'd appeared to be in. "We're still her friends, and we're going to help her. She can't face Alexander alone. He's a god too now."

"Also." I bit the inside of my lip. "I imagine I might need some help with Raiden. He and Aziel are not going to be happy. He could have brought Leda back, but now that I'm goddess of the hunt, he can't unless he kills me." My stomach knotted. He wouldn't. He cared for me. I had felt it with each kiss. He had given me the dagger. But Leda was his favorite. He missed her and loved her. She was family. I was not. When it really came down to it, could I trust him not to kill me?

I didn't want to think about the answer.

Naomi slowly approached me, as if I were a wild predator. She touched my arm and breathed relief. "You're warm."

I side-eyed her. "What did you think I would be?"

She shrugged. "Cold, I guess. Like a dead person."

Maddox's eyebrows knitted together. "Way to be creepy, Naomi."

Edmund interrupted their squabble. "Would you like to go back first? To, well, bathe?"

"No," I replied. Mona's face swept back into my mind, bubbling rage under the surface. My emotions felt stronger. I felt like I could move mountains if I wanted. I wondered if I could. "I'm going to get my sister back, then kill Alexander." I paused, looking up at the lightening, pastel sky. I rubbed my fingers against my temples and cussed under my breath. "I can't. I need someone to take his place, and that someone needs to be Thalia. I can't replace both his sisters."

Maddox nodded along. "Yep, that would make you an asshole."

"What do I do?" I looked at Edmund.

He paused, glancing upward like he did when he was deep in thought. He tapped his fingers against his thigh, then nodded. "Raiden will be returning, albeit briefly, to kill Freya after he's gone to the underworld. Either you can wait for him and explain, then go with him to kill Alexander and have Thalia take his place because Raiden needs to be the ruler of the underworld first for that to happen, or…"

My stomach dipped. "I go to the underworld."

"Yes." He inhaled sharply. "I'd rather you didn't."

"I'm immortal now. I can go and I should. I can help him take Lucius down." Fear gripped me as I looked out through the trees. "If he doesn't kill me for this first."

Maddox clicked his tongue. "Girl, he is not going to kill you. Like I said before, he—"

"He doesn't," I snapped before he could say it again. "Besides, this is his sister, Maddox. His sister." I repeated myself with emphasis thick in my tone. "He loves her so much. He's known her for centuries. He's known me for weeks."

Maddox licked his lips. "Unless you plan on running from him, like Freya, then you don't really have a choice but to face him."

Naomi sighed. "I hate to say it, but the asshole's right."

Maddox smirked. "See? I'm right."

"Still an ass." Naomi scowled, clearly not over the creepy comment.

"I can't leave Mona," I said quickly.

Edmund chimed in. "He's not going to kill her. She's leverage. As long as Alexander believes Freya is still alive, he has no reason to believe otherwise. He thinks she's gone to summon Raiden and kill him, with you, so you have about a day, I reckon, before he starts looking."

"Then I need to leave now."

Edmund grabbed my hand before I could prepare myself to speed away. "Elle. We need to talk about this." He looked me up and down. "You're immortal now. We need to find out if there's a way to reverse it. If there is, I know Maddox and I can find it."

Maddox laughed. "If she even wants to reverse it. Imagine being a goddess. I wouldn't give it up."

Edmund's jaw clenched. "Elle is nothing like you. She doesn't want this."

Naomi tapped her foot against the ground. "Has anyone even asked her what she wants?" She turned toward me. "Elle?"

I swallowed thickly. "I can't stay like this. If there's a way out, it means Leda can come back." I looked at Edmund. "If you can find a way, I'll do it."

Ferocity burned in his bright eyes. "You can count on us. We will always have your back, Elle."

I smiled. "I know." I scratched the back of my neck. "Uh, so do I like carry you back, or... Well, could one of you go on my shoulders and..."

He shook his head, and Maddox rubbed the back of his neck. "Girl, I don't think any of us want that awkwardness today. You go. We're only an hour from home, and Alexander isn't coming after us, so we're good."

My eyes widened. "Wait here." I sped back to Freya's body, pulled the dagger out of the ground where bugs had covered it during the night, and wiped it on my dress. If Alexander saw this, as unlikely as it was, he'd kill Mona instantly.

I grabbed Freya's body, flung her over my shoulder, and dug an effortless hole next to a tree. After dumping her in there, I refilled the dirt and pressed my lips together.

Realization washed over me like a splash of cold water. I was a murderer. Even if it was the right thing to do, I'd still taken a life. My mind swarmed, and I pushed it back. I couldn't think about that right now.

Holding onto the dagger, I sped back to them and hugged them each in turn.

"Be safe. We love you," Naomi said.

Tears welled in my eyes. "I love you all too."

Naomi and Edmund softened, and even Maddox smiled.

I didn't know where to start. "How do I even get to the underworld?"

Edmund and Maddox tried to answer at once. Maddox fell silent and let Edmund explain. Of course they would know. They'd read everything in our library and more. "There's a gateway, a portal of sorts. It's in the mountains. I can get you a map."

"What does it look like?"

He licked his lips. "It's a cave, hidden well, and around it, there are symbols engraved in the walls. You must offer blood to pass. Immortal blood. You can cut yourself."

I couldn't waste any time. "I'll find it."

"It's to the east, about fifteen miles southeast, then—"

"I won't follow any of that," I admitted, and Maddox chuckled.

"This is Elle we're talking about. Just point."

I shot him a glare. "I'll find it. East, right?"

Maddox pointed in the direction, an amused smile playing on his lips. "That way."

"Thanks so much," I replied, my tone thick with sarcasm. I squeezed Edmund's hand and smiled at Naomi before running in the direction Maddox had pointed. I'd assumed east was in the opposite direction, so the pointing helped, but I wasn't going to tell him that.

"Try not to die," Maddox called as I raced between trees, spanning miles in a minute without needing to catch my breath.

Amid an opening in the forest, a large lake sparkled, glittering icy blue as the mountain's peaks came into view. I let out a misty breath and kneeled by the waterside. With cold droplets in my palms, I tipped water over my arms, washing the blood into the lake and turning the dried brown-red to liquid once more. I washed my face and got as much of it out of my hair as possible before deciding it was the best I was going to get. My clothes were still covered, but I didn't have time to stop and find more clothes.

The closer I got to the mountains, nausea crept over me, sending shivers along my skin. I had no idea how Raiden was going to react. If I had a moment to stop and think, I'd probably break down under the realization of my new reality. Overthinking was my specialty, and a flood of thoughts waited behind the dam of fear in my brain, ready to drown me. If I let them in, I wouldn't be able to do what I needed to. Every so often I felt myself disassociate and almost ran into something, but my sharp reflexes wouldn't let me.

After thirty minutes of searching, which had me scaling most of the mountains in the east, I found the crevice between two jagged, tall rocks. A bottomless black cave led downward. I wiped the snow covering the arched entrance with my hand and trailed my fingers along the ancient symbols of Lor.

Heed warning to thy who come, for essence is all to pass.

I assumed they meant blood or the soul was the only thing that would pass, unless I was an immortal. Either way, I decided to follow Edmund's instructions. I grabbed a nearby rock and snapped a piece off, then ran it against my hand and stared at the cut for a few seconds. I hardly felt it. I went to press my hand against it, but the cut had already healed.

"Seriously?" I sighed aloud.

I cut my hand again, shivering at the eeriness of the lack of pain, and quickly pressed my hand against the symbols before it could heal.

The symbols glowed white, and the blackness of the cave turned misty. A gray fog creeped out like hands reaching into this realm. Inhaling sharply, I extended my hand and moved slowly inside, not sure if I would be returning again.

CHAPTER THIRTY-

ONE

Mist followed me, snaking and hissing as I wandered through the other realm, down into the underworld. A howl reverberated along the rocky ground, taking me back to the night the demon hounds stalked us and wounded Thalia, weakening her and ultimately killing her.

Whispers crawled along my skin as I stepped off the rocky ground and climbed over a ledge and down, ankle-deep, into what appeared to be an endless creek. Scents of sulfur mixed with rotten eggs and seaweed invaded my nostrils. I scrunched my nose, wading through the creek as it deepened. Peering down, I gasped as floating heads stared back with accusing eyes. I carefully moved them out of the way, forcing back the bile that threatened to bite up my throat.

A shiver danced along my skin, spreading an ache through my muscles. I raised my tense shoulders and leaned back when I felt a breath on the side of my neck.

Nausea gripped me. A slimy hand stroked my arm, slick fingers curling around my elbow.

I whipped my head around, coming face-to-face with an eyeless demon of the water. His skin was tinged the color of the moss-stricken, stagnant water around us. His white lips were paler than the faces of the floating heads. "Get away." I dug my nails into his arm and forced him back with medium effort.

The demon's mouth hung open, too far, with a seemingly endless jaw. "You are a god," he hissed, his swirling black tongue slipped out like a serpent.

My gaze narrowed as I stepped back. "Yes."

I blinked twice as he melted—literally melted—and became one with the creek. Climbing out onto the cracked ground, I stared across a crop field with a stick for an absent scarecrow. The wind cooled even my skin. A blaring, crimson sunset lowered in the dark sky. My lips parted. Something rustled among the golden crops, rolling in my direction. My breath hitched as adrenaline coursed through my veins, forcing me to run. I turned quickly and watched another rustle in the crops come from the opposite direction.

The game prickled excitement along my skin. My pupils dilated, and my teeth bared. I shook my head. What the… I didn't want to hunt them. Did I?

Instinctively, I crouched and curled my fingers into the ground, listening acutely for each step and every rustle. Even the sound of the wind blocked in an area told me their exact locations. Their short, shallow breaths told me they were small in stature. Their quick footsteps showed me they were fast, but were they fast enough?

My lips curled at the corners as something animalistic in me took over. I showed my teeth, my fingers shaking at the excitement pulsating in my bones. They were close. I scratched the ground, alerting them to my position. Delight hiccupped their next breaths, and they darted in my direction. On all fours, I watched the crops around me with bulging eyes. Three seconds later, the crops opened, and I stared slack-jawed. Every instinct to hunt, to fight, dissolved. Two little girls, twins it seemed, stared at me with hollow eyes and sad expressions. Their long hair hung to around their waists, over off-white dresses. On their feet were white shoes with pink bows.

"Will you play with us?" they asked in echoed unison.

I stood and stepped back. The way they moved seemed... disjointed. Inhumanly. If they were in the underworld, then they weren't alive.

One of the girls held out her hand.

I shook my head. "No."

Her sad expression contorted, fury spilling through her soft features. I stepped back when she stepped forward. Her voice deepened too low for it to belong to a little girl. "You will play with us."

Their eyes hollowed to a deep matte black, void of emotion.

One rushed me at a speed half of mine. With a flick of my wrist, she twirled and flung through the air, then landed on her back. She stood and let out a low growl. They both ran at me. I extended my arms, lowering myself to their level, and held my fingers out to reach their tiny necks. I grabbed them both by their throats and flung them back through the crops with a skull-crunching thud.

I heard movement behind me. Turning, I looked out past the crop field and saw Raiden standing, hands in his pockets, on a slight hill.

I ran toward him, looking back over my shoulder at the crop field. "That was insane."

His hard tone sent goose bumps along my skin. "What the fuck, Elle?" He grabbed my arm, and my wrist turned under his strong grip. "You're indestructible. Did you even feel that?"

My eyebrows pinched downward. "Was it supposed to hurt?"

"Yes." He let out a low growl. "What did you do?"

I closed my eyes briefly. How could I tell him I'd taken his sister's place? That I'd pulled a Freya, in a way.

He took my hands in his, his gaze burning into mine. "What the fuck do you think you're doing here?" He ran his finger along my arm but stopped at my collar bone. "Lucius is still here. This is his domain."

My eyebrows furrowed. "Aren't you—wait, what?"

"Get out of here, Elle. This isn't the time to be a hero."

I swallowed thickly. "You're upset because I'm in the underworld?"

"Yes."

"Not that I'm a goddess?"

His jaw clenched. "I'm not happy about it, but I assume it means you killed Freya."

"I'm sorry."

He arched an eyebrow. "Why are you sorry?" His lips parted, knowing flashing in his eyes. "You think I'm upset because of Leda."

I looked to my left, then back at him. "Well, yes."

"If you managed to kill her, then it means you were in danger and took the chance. I'm not mad because of that. I'm upset you've been forced into immortality, but mostly I'm angry because you came down here when—" A thunderous boom halted his next words. "It's Lucius."

My brain faltered. "You're not going to kill me then?"

He grabbed my hands in his, intensity rippling through our touch. "Elle, I would never, ever hurt you. Did you really think I would?"

His pained gaze shot through my chest. "It's your sister," I explained. "I know you want her to come back to our world."

"I'm not thinking that far ahead." A muscle in his jaw ticked. "You need to get out of here. Go back to Istinia. Aziel is coming, and Lucius isn't far behind. If he sees you here, he'll try to kill you. He'll know you're a goddess."

My heart skipped a beat. I grabbed his hand before he could run away. "Not this time. I can catch you now."

A ghost of a smile curved his lips. "Leave."

"No." I pulled him back to me. "I've come to help you."

"I don't need your help." His gaze softened. "Please, Elle. Don't do this to me."

"I have to," I said slowly. "I can't leave you here. I need you."

He hesitated. "Elle."

"Alexander has my sister."

His jaw clenched. "What?"

"Yeah, and he took Thalia's place. If I kill him, I need someone to take over as god or goddess of the dead, and it should be Thalia."

He released his fingers from mine, his eyes widening. "You came here first, before saving your sister?"

I swallowed hard, trying to remove the lump in my throat. "I wouldn't kill him and leave your sister unable to come back. I already did it once, by accident." I pressed my lips together. "Because I care about you."

"This much? Enough to leave your sister?"

I held my next breath. I felt so stupid, standing there. I cared too much and in doing so had made a huge mistake. His eyebrow flickered, his expression set permanently to surprised. When he said it out loud, it was a lot. Too much for him. Did Edmund, Naomi, and Maddox realize what I was doing? My heart ballooned. My cheeks heated. Fuck. Stupid heart. "I shouldn't have come."

He looked over his shoulder, then back at me. "You shouldn't have."

The lump in my throat swelled. Tears lingered on the barriers of breaking, and my bottom lip trembled. He looked at me with the same stoic, cold stare he'd shown before he'd left. "I know you don't mean that."

A thunderous boom shook the underworld once more. He looked over his shoulder again, fear lacing his eyes. "You need to run back out of here."

My hands were shaking. "Did it all just mean more to me?"

He opened his mouth to say something, but a loud boom shook the ground. "Fuck, Elle. Yes, it did, okay? So get out of here." His eyes darkened. "I don't want you here."

"I don't believe you." A tear trickled, running down my cheek. "You said you would never hurt me."

He shuffled from one foot to the other, continuously checking over his shoulder. He grabbed my shoulder and moved me back toward the creek. "You're innocent," he said quietly. "I don't hurt innocents, remember?"

I inhaled deeply. "That's it then."

"Yes."

"Then I'll go. I'll kill Alexander."

"Do whatever the fuck you need to do," he growled and a third, closer boom sounded. "Now leave."

I swallowed hard. "Fine."

I sped away to the edge of the creek, not ready to cross it yet. Heaving back a deep sob, I rolled back my shoulders.

I was an idiot for thinking it was any more than sex or friendship. I cried for a minute when the cave trembled. Rocks fell from the ceiling. I shielded them with my hands and ducked under a crevice. The mist thickened. Even if he didn't want me there, it didn't matter. I wasn't just here for him; I was here because I was doing right by Thalia. She'd been good to me. She'd protected me even when she shouldn't, and I wasn't going to abandon her because he'd had enough of me. My sister had approximately twenty hours left before Alexander would start getting suspicious.

The ground shook, but this time I stood. I glanced back, watching Raiden stand upon a red, barren hill. Lightning struck from the skies, cracking the mud. Aziel appeared atop the hill, and a storm followed. I closed my eyes, steadying myself as the ground shook with more ferocity.

Lucius's low voice boomed throughout the underworld, reverberating through every piece of it. "Show yourselves."

Demons slithered in their direction, an army at Lucius's disposal. They sped out from their habitats and in the direction of Raiden and Aziel.

CHAPTER THIRTY-TWO

Raiden and Aziel fought demons sent to weaken them by Lucius. It was too late. They were already preparing to fight Lucius. Crowds of demons swarmed them. Lucius was nowhere to be seen, but it didn't mean he was far.

In the far distance, a tall obsidian castle towered into gray storm clouds. Around it was a moat of lava, and over it, a drawbridge made of green marble. There were no windows, but then why would they need them in the underworld?

A crash of thunder sounded overhead, the ground rumbling as cracks formed in stone and mud. Time was running out. I rubbed my hands against my eyes. Demons devoured everything in sight, always hungry, never fulfilled. Everything swarmed with darkness. It was a plague of a realm. Nausea swept through me. I couldn't help them here, but I could if I went back home. There was a way for me to save us all, but only if I was quick enough.

Fingers slimed against my ankles in featherlight touches as I sped through the creek, breaking water too quickly for the dead to grab me. I looked back one last time when I reached the misty cave.

Demons emerged, their black, soulless eyes scanning the creek and crop field that extended to the red hills and led toward rocky mountains and a never-ending crimson sunset. Crows screeched overhead, settling near vultures that sat on low branches around the cornfield, waiting for something to die so they could pick at it; but everything here was already dead in some way.

My heart skipped a beat when I saw them through a fluff of hair that had made its way around to my forehead. Tucking the lock behind my ear, I crinkled my nose, grimacing. Souls—new ones, I presumed, from the horror on their pale faces—with their misty bodies, a ghost of who they once were, shivered in an illusory dance. They fell from the sky and were quickly grabbed by demons who devoured them as they landed. Some escaped, heading for the cornfield or creek. I averted my gaze as things leaped out of the water, snatching the new souls from the air, and dragged them into their depths.

Before I changed my mind, I looked back at Raiden one last time, my heart in my stomach, then turned and sped for the portal out.

I fell out into the powdered snow, coughing as the portal closed. Darkness slithered over me as I turned. Two demons had come through when I did. Before I could reach them, they slipped into the shadows of the rocks, disappearing from sight.

Glancing at the northern mountains, where Mona was probably being kept, I sighed. I swore on my soul I would come for her, but I couldn't do it alone. For the first time, I felt strong, powerful even. I knew how to help the gods, Mona, and everyone else, but it would come at quite the risk. I wasn't stupid enough to try it alone. I had to rely on my family, my friends back home. I was stronger with them; it had just taken me a while to realize it. Inhaling deeply, I cast my eyes in the direction of home and took off into the forest.

＊

Everyone gathered in the kitchen except Dora, who was taking a nap. Maddox made a coffee, Naomi sat at the table, fumbling with a teaspoon, and Edmund leaned in the doorway, stroking Benji who was curled up on the countertop.

"We can do this," I urged as my plan unfolded to them. "Our coven has dark magic. It's why we were created. We are the keepers of all that is dark, and it's our job to keep Istinia safe from dark magic, and the underworld is that. Demons can get out. Some followed me through the portal. Lucius will keep coming back whenever he feels like it, and we're in danger when he does. Alexander is on the loose, and since Freya is now in the underworld, who knows if she'll ever break out? We need to seal it like our people did a century ago, when the prison realms were created."

Edmund pressed his lips into a hard line. "It's a good idea, brilliant even, but Raiden did break out of his realm and—"

"Yes." I put a finger up, pausing him for a moment. "But our people had to create three realms and seal them. This realm already exists, and we just need to make sure it remains that way. It would be the future keepers' jobs to do it. We were meant for this. It's why our coven even exists at all. Freya needed someone to guard the keys the blood witches created. We are the only blood witches, so no one else can do this but us."

"Might I add," Maddox said, "your boyfriend would be trapped ruling the underworld if we don't seal Lucius in there. But I'm sure that has nothing to do with your sudden idea."

I swallowed thickly. "He is not my boyfriend. Not even close. Trust me."

Maddox's eyebrows pinched when he saw tears in my eyes. "If we close it," he said, changing the subject, "no one can get in or out."

I fumbled my fingers. We all knew what that meant. Any demons left in this world would be able to stay here, for good, and any souls left inside would be trapped. "I know."

Naomi nodded. "Unless you die."

Edmund interjected. "I'm not sure if it would still work after that."

Maddox nodded. "Then I guess everyone's going to the otherworld." He rolled his eyes. "Talk about offsetting the balance."

"You weren't there." I shuddered at the memory. "It was terrible. Unless you're a truly horrible, evil person, then no one should end up there. That type of punishment is reserved for the darkest of the dark, and I can't believe all the new souls I saw were pure evil. So much darkness can't exist in the world at once."

Naomi agreed. "Let's close it. Let all the bad in there feast upon itself. It has no place in our world."

Maddox shook his head. "It's a bad idea. If dark souls can't get in, then where will they go?"

"Wouldn't they just stop existing?" I asked. "Or turn into ghosts or something? I don't know."

Maddox arched an eyebrow. "You don't know? You didn't get a telepathic encyclopedia of knowledge on the afterlife when you became a goddess?"

Edmund shot him a look. "This isn't Elle's fault. She's trying to help."

Maddox shrugged. "Do whatever you want. I think it'll backfire on us."

Naomi clicked her tongue, placing her hand on her hip. "You know what, genius? You're always telling everyone how brilliant you are? Well this is your time to shine. We'll go save the gods, and you can figure out the after part."

He choked on his coffee. "I know I'm good, but you're talking about figuring out another afterlife. No one is that amazing."

I rolled my eyes. "You know, Maddox, that sounded almost humble, by your standards anyway."

Edmund chuckled quietly. "Maddox can't do it alone, but together we can. Elle's right." He smiled at me, the corners of his eyes creasing. "We have dark magic in our veins. We have Naomi, a skilled magician."

She suppressed a coy smile.

"If Elle thinks we need to seal the underworld, then we will, and I will make sure no one is ever getting out."

"We need Alma," Naomi said.

Edmund shook his head. "They won't. They don't get involved with gods or other realms. It offsets the politics of their system. No, for this we will need to go behind their backs."

Maddox gasped, feigning a look of horror. "Good-guy, by-the-books Edmund wants to break the rules? I never thought I'd see the day."

I suppressed a smirk, but my expression hollowed the second I thought about the stakes. There were so many things that could go wrong. "We're going to Alexander first, and I'm going to need that dagger back."

Naomi's lip quivered. "I don't know, Elle. If he finds out about Freya and sees you without her, he'll kill your sister."

"He won't because I have a plan, so huddle in. We leave in an hour, and I need to make sure you all know what we're doing."

Naomi smiled widely. "I like this get-shit-done new-goddess Elle. I still can't believe you're a freaking goddess." She rested her head against mine. "You're such a badass now."

Maddox emerged holding two ancient spell books, one of them the skin-bound grimoire we had once needed to catch the murderer, who ended up being Freya. It felt like a lifetime ago.

Edmund gave Naomi the dagger. "Are you sure you can perform the spell, Nai?"

She nodded. "Everyone always forgets magicians can perform spells too. It's just a different style of magic."

"Oh, I never forgot." I smiled. "You've got this. Edmund, you got the dark objects?"

"Everything we need is in here." He lifted his large brown bag. "Including the empty key."

"Empty for now," Maddox said. "Dora's staying here to protect the mansion."

"Good." My stomach knotted. From the other side of the kitchen, Benji meowed. I liked to think it meant good luck. "Let's pray this works."

Maddox nudged me playfully as he passed, heading for the back door. "We don't need luck. We have you."

Naomi spluttered. "Was that an actual compliment?"

Maddox called as he headed out the door, "I'll deny it if you tell anyone."

My cheeks heated. "Edmund," I said as he squeezed my shoulder on the way out. "Do you think the transfer box will work?" The box we used to hold a curse before transferring it to another object was simple, but it was the only thing I could think of to hold a soul, temporarily even.

"It's the only option we have."

I grabbed Naomi first, holding her in my arms. "I guess we're doing the awkward carrying after all."

She locked her arms around the back of my neck as I gripped onto her tightly. "I'm kind of excited."

"Underworld. Death. Saving lives." Maddox snapped his fingers. "This isn't a carnival, girl."

"Ignore him." I shot him a look. "He's just bitter because he wasn't the one to figure this out."

Naomi shot him one last smirk before I sped her to the mountains. I'd head back for Edmund next, then Maddox.

When we landed, she vomited all over her shoes, then sat on the snow-blanketed ground.

I stepped back. "Lovely."

"That was just... way too fast." She blinked several times. "I'm dizzy."

"It's okay. I bet Maddox will be just as disoriented."

"Good." She sighed. "Make sure to go extra fast with him."

"I will," I smirked.

Her expression straightened. "Elle, for real, this is a brilliant plan. We're going to save everything because of you."

My legs felt like they'd turned to gelatin. Gods I hoped my plan worked. If not, then I'd have killed us all.

After whisking Edmund and Maddox to the cave opening, I leaned back against a snow-powdered rock. "Once I open this portal, things can get out," I explained. Although they already knew, Naomi didn't. "Time will be of the limit. The last time I got out, two demons came with me. If any realize this is open, they'll swarm."

Naomi leaned over her spell book. "Then we wait to open it until we're prepared. How long will the spell take?" She looked at Edmund.

"Thirty minutes maybe." He looked at me. "Do you think you can get your sister out before then and kill Alexander?"

I gazed up, into the oblivion of white. "I hope so."

"We need the soul of the goddess of the dead if you want this to work," Naomi said, as if I didn't already know. It was the only way I could repay Thalia for what had happened. I already needed to keep Leda trapped in the underworld, else I would die, and getting Raiden and Aziel was the right thing to do—even if he had broken my heart.

"Try not to miss!" Maddox shouted as I left, the dagger sheathed to my thigh.

Chapter Thirty-Three

The mountain disappeared in a flurry of white. My boot crunched against the ice as I scaled the jagged rocks, feeling invincible with the knowledge I couldn't die. Mona was somewhere close. I could hear the steady beat of her heart and the racing of Alexander's. Edmund, Maddox, and Naomi were far away now, even though I left them mere minutes ago. The distance I could travel in such a short time was invigorating. I could go anywhere, do anything. The cold was nothing as winds kissed my skin, spreading goose bumps along my arms.

I held my breath, letting my hunting senses overthrow the mortal version of Elle who'd never have crouched over a rock, listening for heartbeats, or smelled the air for a hint of blood or flesh. My lips curled, a snarl escaping them when I heard Alexander's voice reverberate down the mountains. The words, although intelligible, carried an unmistakable angry yet fearful tone.

Quieter than a whisper of a breeze, I climbed the side of the mountain, finding crevices to hold onto with ease. My sharp vision latched onto them, my hands instinctively reaching for them. The clumsiness attached to my mortal self had all but disappeared. My lips parted when I reached the small cabin, nestled into the ledge on the mountain as if it were a part of it. It was more like a house. It was made from stone, undoubtedly Freya's doing. Only she would have had the strength to build something like this up this far and the desire to do it somewhere so out of the way. The stone bricks jutted out, arching over a door of thick oak. Carefully I stepped forward, holding my breath as I reached the front door.

Hesitance paused me for a second. One mistake and he could snap my sister's neck just as fast as I could reach them. I closed my eyes, recalling our plan word-for-word, and opened the door. Tears welled my eyes when I saw Mona hunched over by a crackling fire. Alexander whipped around from the sofa. My bottom lip quivered, and a tear trickled out. I let every emotion spill through me, crashing into me like a waterfall. I used the memories of Mona and me as children to guide my anger toward Alexander. It helped make my story believable.

"Where's Freya?" I looked around, scanning for her even though I knew where she was. Fortunately, I'd had the sense to change out of my blood-soaked clothes before making the journey. "She said she was coming back here after hunting Aziel."

He looked from me to Mona, uncertainty frowning his lips. "She's not here."

"She did this." I balled my fist. "Raiden's dead." My breath hitched. I placed my hand against my chest. "He's gone, and she made me take his place."

"You're a goddess?"

"Yes! I'm here to kill her for it."

"No." He stood, shaking his head. "I won't let you hurt her."

"Where is she? She must've killed Aziel by now."

"She hasn't. She must be still hunting him because she hasn't returned yet."

Mona's shoulders slumped as she looked from Alexander to me. "Ellie, I'm sorry."

She was so close. In arms' reach. If I could just get close enough, maybe I wouldn't have to go through with the plan. Maybe I could...

He stood in front of her. "You can have her back once Freya says so."

"You've both taken enough from me," I cried, cupping my face in my hands. "At least let me have my sister. If you don't, I will hunt you. Both of you."

His bottom lip trembled as I watched him through the gaps between my fingers. "She'll return your sister once she returns."

"Aziel won't let her get away with this." I lowered my hands. "He'll kill her for it. He's stronger than her. She may have tricked Raiden, but Aziel doesn't care about me or Mona. None of us. You know it's true." I maneuvered my next words carefully. "But in a way, I'm glad you're being stupid and staying here, protecting leverage she doesn't even need anymore. It means Aziel will actually get the chance to kill her when she goes up against him in the forest—alone."

His eyes darted to the door. "Where did Aziel go?"

"They both fled to the east of the forest," I lied.

He stepped away from Mona, relief flooding me, but then paused his foot in midair. "I smell blood on you." He sniffed the air. "Yes, I'm sure that's blood."

I must have missed some. Crap. I hesitated, then gulped, pushing another tear over the edge. "It's Raiden's."

His expression dropped. "I-I am sorry, but understand." He moved toward the door. "I did this for love."

"I know." As soon as he was away from Mona, I unsheathed the dagger, looked at her and mouthed *run,* and jerked my head in the direction of another door.

She took off, and I lunged at Alexander, dagger in hand. He was too fast, spinning around and kicking my legs out from under me. I caught myself before tumbling to the ground and jolted upright, then lunged for his neck again. He sped out of the way before I could plunge the blade into his side. I rushed him again, but he hit my shoulder and knocked me back against the sofa, which splintered to pieces under my fall.

Alexander looked me over quickly and fled out the door. I ran out into the cold and raced through the wind-caught flurries, blinking as my eyes adjusted to the white as I traced his scent into the snow. He was stronger than I expected, even for a god. Alexander had always seemed so weak.

He'd left a trail in the snow when he raced around the ledge, and handprints along the ledges scaled down the side. I lowered myself, holding onto dips and rocks until I reached the bottom, and threw myself onto the snow-carpeted ground, the air whooshing from my lungs. I whipped my head around, sniffing the air and looking at the silent fir trees that welcomed me into the forest.

A twig snapped, and I followed it, then another. Separating snaps and cracks from the sound of a boot versus an animal was easier than I thought it would be. The way twigs sounded against rubber was hollower. I sped toward the sounds, picking up his scent again on a nearby tree, until his heartbeat pounded in my ears, his quick breaths a song to my senses. Baring my teeth and curling my lips up, I curled my fingers, then turned my head slowly. He was close. As I moved through two trees, bloodlust took over, guiding me to his warm body. I didn't recognize the beast that took over me. It was as if the goddess of the hunt were its own being and we were simply intertwined.

Looking up at the pale sky, I inhaled deeply, the cold-pinched air filling my lungs. A leaf crunched under a sole, and my eyes snapped open. I sped toward him, lunging through the air like a tiger to its prey. Slamming into his hard body sent a crack through the ground and toward aged trees.

"I don't want to kill you. I just want to find Freya," he said.

I gazed at his dreamy, far-off eyes, and for a moment, guilt shocked through my chest. He wasn't like Freya. He didn't truly deserve this, but he would kill us if he found the truth, and he would have killed us if she had asked.

Closing my conscience, I licked my lips and dropped my arm. "You're right. It's her I hate. Not you."

He stood, catching his breath. "Please understand, she's not a bad person. She only does what she needs to do."

I held onto his arm, leaning over to catch my breath, with the dagger in my other hand. "I know you believe that. We don't need to fight. You're not the one I'm mad at."

"I will always protect her."

I nodded. "Then we are unwilling enemies."

He gifted me with a small, soft smile, which only made it hurt more.

I went to stand but slipped. He was reaching down, as expected, extending his hand to help me up when I struck. I plunged the dagger into his chest, hearing the blade pierce his heart. Blood spilled in his chest. His eyes widened when he realized, gazing into mine.

Tears hazed my vision. I wanted to look away, to pull the dagger out and run, leaving him behind to die, but I couldn't. This wasn't like Freya. I watched him die, and I didn't blink as the light left his far-off stare.

"I'm sorry," I whispered when his heart stopped, and his body limped in my arms.

A lump formed in my throat as I placed him onto the snow-covered ground, his final resting place. I turned to walk away, but I couldn't bring myself to leave the clearing. "Really?" I cussed at my conscience, then turned back, picked his body up in my arms, and carried him toward where Freya was buried. I was a goddess-damned idiot for caring this much, but I couldn't not. Despite all he'd done, all the pain he'd caused, it had all been for love, and while the motive didn't justify his actions, it was one I could sympathize with more than Freya's or Lucius's.

I trudged through the forest until the snow melted and the ground became leaf-carpeted and underbrush-coated, where I found Freya's blood and her freshly dug grave.

After waiting for the pale orb as it left his body, which Edmund had said would be there like it had been with Thalia, if any of us had stuck around for it, I captured it in a small vial I'd brought with me. I buried him next to Freya, marked the tree where their bones lay, and looked back toward the mountain. The orb would allow me to make someone else a goddess, and I planned on giving it to Thalia if I could find her in the underworld.

I made my way back up the mountain and rushed into the open door of the house. "Mona," I said, croaking. Her panicked breaths sounded from the next room, but I didn't want to scare her. My being a goddess was a lot to process. My being here at all probably was too. She'd grown up in a world filled with humans. All of this would be a lot, and I hadn't got the proper reunion with her that I'd always daydreamed of.

"Ellie," she whispered, and I heard her knees cracking as she stood from wherever she was sitting. "You're alive." Relief flooded her tone, and my eyes welled again. My heart caught in my throat as she appeared in the doorway, her red, fiery hair a mess and her icy-blue eyes bloodshot from crying. She ran at me and flung her arms around me. I gasped at her touch and breathed back a sob. She smelled like lilies and vanilla, and I knew that from then on I would never forget her smell.

She prodded the logs with a poker, and the fire hissed in response. I sat cross-legged across from her on the rug. I couldn't stop staring. She was so beautiful, but her age served as a reminder of everything I had missed.

"I don't know what to say," I admitted.

"Were you ever going to come for me?"

"I was." My words dried up at the end. I cleared my throat. "I was so scared of seeing you again or finding out what happened to you. It prevented me from just going. I was going to send a letter, but I wasn't allowed."

She nodded slowly. "No communication is allowed between residents of the kingdoms."

Her Salviun twang made me smile. I hadn't heard it in a long time. "I told myself when I became keeper I would go to you, find a way to bring you here, but the truth was I could have all along. I chose not to because I was afraid you wouldn't want to see me." I looked at the fire. "That you hadn't forgiven me."

She arched an eyebrow. "Hadn't forgiven you? For what?"

"If I hadn't hurt Miss Thompson, revealing my powers, I would never have been forced to leave. If we hadn't snuck out to see the witch hanging..."

She reached across the rug, and her clammy fingers curled around mine. "None of that was your fault. You were trying to protect me."

"I left you alone there."

"Believe it or not…" She gave me a sad smile. "I did okay."

I looked her up and down. "I can see that."

"I wouldn't have wanted to come here, even if you did come."

My lips parted. I hadn't considered she'd actually enjoyed life in Salvius—or had one to leave—only that I could bring her here, away from there. To me, Salvius had always been a grizzly, horrid place. "Of course. I'm sorry."

Her lip curled at the corner. "I work with a doctor of the mind. We help people in asylums. I'm his apprentice. I travel all over." She twirled her fingers, and the flames danced taller. "I found out I had magic a few years ago. I never told anyone. I knew I could come to Istinia, and I'd get to see you, but everyone told stories about how evil it was here, and when you grow up hearing it, it's all you know, ya know?"

My brain faltered. "You're a witch."

"We're sisters." She tapped her fingers against her knee. "Of course I am. They tried to see if I was for years. Miss Thompson was especially awful, but my powers never surfaced, and when they did, I was scared. I didn't want to come here, especially when I didn't hear from you. I had no idea what they'd done to you. I thought the worst."

I covered my mouth with my hand. "I didn't mean to make you worry."

"I knew there was no contact between Istinia and Salvius, so I hoped you just couldn't let me know even if you were okay."

"I should have found a way."

She leaned back against the wall. "Maybe, but I could have done the same."

"So, a mind doctor, hmm?"

"Yep." She leaned forward, anticipation in her eyes. "Dad would have a field day. He did always hate all of that psychology stuff and talk of witches—well, anything that required being open-minded. I wonder if he knew Mom was a witch."

"You think it was Mom?" I asked.

She nodded. "It definitely wasn't Dad. We'd have known, and we didn't really know Mom."

"I guess she's the logical choice."

She blew out a tense breath. "Enough about me. Let's talk about how you're a goddess. I'm so sorry that guy had to die."

"Oh." I slapped my hand against my mouth. "No, I should have said. I just said that to get Alexander out of the house and away from you. I needed him to believe Freya was alive."

"The goddess who kidnapped me, correct?"

"Yes," I answered. "She's dead now."

"Did you?"

I nodded. "She was a bad person. She killed a lot of people."

"Alexander?"

"Also dead." I swallowed hard. "Less deserving… But he would have come after us, and he took the place of a friend of mine. She deserves to come back."

She whistled out a breath. "It's a lot to take in. So you took Freya's place?"

"Yeah, so it seems."

"How… How does it feel?"

I exhaled slowly. "Honestly? Amazing. Everything's sharper, clearer… like I'm really seeing the world for the first time."

She fumbled with her necklace. "Does it mean you can come to visit now? I'd like to have my sister back."

My heart ballooned. "Yes. Well, if I can. We have something else to take care of." Time suddenly existed again. My other family would be waiting for me. "I want to stay, to talk to you and hear everything about your life, but I have to go. It's the others."

"Your coven, right?"

"They're my family," I admitted. "Like you."

Pain flashed in her eyes, but she nodded. "I understand."

"We're going to save the other gods."

She laughed. "It's so weird to say. Gods. They actually exist." She looked me up and down. "You're one of them." She placed her hands against her ears, then brought them outward to imitate an explosion. "Mind blown. This is all insane."

"Insane only begins to explain my life."

"They said the guy… What's his name?"

"Raiden, you mean."

"Yes." She leaned forward. "They seemed to think he'd die for you. Is he your husband? Boyfriend?"

My stomach dipped. "Neither."

"Do you love him?"

I couldn't answer her. "He doesn't want me like that."

"Then why did they think he'd die for you?"

I looked down. "Because for a moment, I actually believed he would, so I'm not surprised they did. He's good at faking it, it seems."

"He told you he doesn't love you?"

"He made his feelings about me perfectly clear." I swallowed hard, trying to remove the lump in my throat. "But he doesn't matter. I have you now."

"Well." She smiled. "It's his loss."

I stood, brushing the leaves and pines from the forest off my pants. "I'm taking you back to Dora, then coming back here. I need to know you're safe."

I glanced at the window. A storm was brewing outside. Time was running out, and if I didn't get there in time, Lucius would kill them all.

CHAPTER THIRTY-FOUR

I white-knuckled Thalia's dagger as the winds picked up. They howled through the forest and up the side of the mountain. The portal opened as I pressed my bloodied cut against the symbols. I held my next breath, turning toward Edmund, Maddox, and Naomi as the eerie fog crept through the opening, its fingers grappling for a taste of our world. "If anything comes out—"

"We know." Edmund shivered against the cold, gripping the grimoire in his blue fingertips. "We have dark objects to capture any rogue demons. Don't worry about us. We have everything we need."

Maddox gazed at the portal, then turned his attention to me. "It's not like we're keepers who have years of experience and knowledge to—oh, wait."

I sighed. "I know, I know. I just need to know you'll be safe."

Edmund's expression softened. "I'm more worried about you. We're out here. The biggest thing we have to fear is frostbite and a potential demon. Promise me, Elle, if anything happens in there, you will get yourself out." He paused. "Even if you need to leave one of them behind. They've had lifetimes. You've not had one."

I swallowed thickly. Could I really leave them behind? Even after what Raiden had said? His words cut deep. I couldn't help how I felt. Truthfully, it wasn't just some moral compass guiding me back into the underworld to get them out before we sealed it; it was more than that. "I'll get out if things get bad."

Edmund's gaze darkened. "Because if you don't, I will go in there after you."

"You'll die."

His eyebrows raised. "I'm well aware."

My eyes widened. "Don't do that."

"Then don't get trapped in there."

Naomi found her voice. "Please, Elle. He's not worth dying for."

"I'm not just going in there for Raiden," I said.

Maddox side-eyed her, then looked at me. "Then why are you bothering going in there at all? We could just seal the underworld now, protect the world from Lucius and the demons inside."

I inhaled sharply. "I'm bringing Thalia back."

Naomi shook her head. "This isn't about her, and you know it. Just be careful."

I licked my dry, cold lips. "This is it. You have the transfer spell ready?"

Edmund shook his bag, which clattered objects, as an answer. "Let's hope it works."

Naomi chewed on her fingernail. "It's super-advanced magic."

"I have full faith in you all." I hugged Edmund first. He was the man who had taken me in, treated me like a daughter, showed me respect, and always did right by me, and he was the wisest person I knew. "Especially you," I whispered as I pulled away. "I'll see you all on the flip side. Oh." From my pocket, I pulled the vial with the orb from Alexander's body, containing the essence of the goddess of the dead. It shimmered like liquid silver. "Thalia should be the first through if this works."

Naomi glanced at Edmund's bag. "If this works."

"If it works." I exhaled shakily, then stepped into the portal.

A barren wasteland greeted me when I made it across the creek and into the burned crop field, now a pile of ash and embers upon the dry ground. I kicked a small rock into the crumbles that once were hills. Everything had been destroyed, and none of the gods were to be seen. Was I too late? I sped north and stumbled to a stop. The castle was still intact, but everything was too silent. Thalia had to be in there—and Raiden—if Lucius hadn't killed them. When things died inside the underworld, they stayed dead, wiped from existence. I shuddered and tightened my grip on the dagger.

I didn't have much time before Edmund would need to seal the underworld. With the portal open, demons could escape; they were neither mortal nor immortal but simply dark creatures stuck in between the living and dead, feeding off nothing but negative energy as fuel. Two had gotten out the last time I'd ventured into the underworld, more if they realized it was open. Things in our realm could get ugly really fast—and not just our realm but the human realm as well, because demons didn't need magical objects like us to pass through the barrier. I prayed the demons remained ignorant.

"You can do this," I whispered aloud to no one in particular. "Keep Lucius alive, trap him, get Thalia to the entrance, have Edmund transfer her back to the living, then get Raiden and Aziel out." I gulped, my breath shaky. "Should be easy."

I squeezed my eyes shut one last time, finding brief solace in the darkness, opened my eyes to the red-orange horizon, and fixed my stare on the obsidian castle. The hot air prickled my skin, and I sweated even as a goddess.

I took off, pockets of warm air hitting me as I sped over what felt like branches and dead twigs crackling under my boots. Stopping at the drawbridge, I looked over my shoulder. The hills were tiny in the distance, the portal miles away.

I trailed my gaze up and over the looming towers, the long bridge, and black doors to the castle. It was Lucius's home, I was sure.

In the mostly empty courtyard were two stallions, blacker than night, with fiery eyes appearing as if they were forged from the lava running in the moat under the drawbridge. Hesitantly, I stammered forward, finding my resolve weaken with each step. When I placed my hand on the silver handles of the double doors, they creaked open.

Shock stole my next breath. An emerald-green, grand staircase led up to the second floor, where a wraparound balcony ran around the entirety of the castle. To my left, endless rooms. To my right, a void of black.

"Impressive, is it not?" a cold snakelike voice hissed from behind me.

Shivering, I slowly turned my head. Lucius. He pushed his hands into the pockets of his robe.

"This is where mortal souls come through once they die." His calculating, cold smile forced bile into my throat. I waited for him to attack, anything, but he'd never seemed so relaxed. He pointed at the void. "Our high demons go to ensure the souls coming here never stop."

I stared into stark blackness. "Why?"

"My demons." He gestured around us. "They were created by your realm's sins, fed by darkness, but they make good guards in keeping the bad souls in line," he explained, too casually for my liking. "They require souls to keep, and I ensure more are brought here to satisfy them. Every action has a reaction. All we do is give people choices. If they choose to take the wrong path, then that was not me—or any demon."

"You make deals with them?" I asked. I'd heard the folklore of people supposedly finding demons, coming to them in moments of pain or weakness and offering them what they wanted in exchange for something bad in return. "So they end up here."

"We can't have the otherworld filling up."

I shook my head. "You're despicable."

"No." He paced around me in a circle. "I'm honest. Everyone makes a choice. I created the underworld to keep the evil things from your realm, from the otherworld, to protect. I am your savior, and yet you come here, seeking to kill me." He shook his head, making an indiscernible noise under his breath. "Do you believe Raiden will do better than I at containing this realm?"

I jutted my chin. "I think he wouldn't try to lure innocent mortals here."

"Any soul that ends up here is far from innocent. Let me assure you."

I eyed the void. "So demons can get out through this void?"

"No." He glanced at Thalia's dagger, the blue reflecting in his silver eyes. "Things can only come in, not leave."

"So your demons leave through the portal."

Suspicion crowned his eyes. "Perhaps."

"Where's Raiden?" I asked, changing the subject.

"He's been taken care of."

My lips parted as waves of numbness swept through my body. My heart twisted, sending nausea through my stomach. "He's dead?"

"He won't be a problem anymore," he said, evading answering directly. "Is that why you're here? Why you became a goddess? So you could kill me, then take your place at his side, as queen of the underworld?" He cackled. "The silly things you witches will do for love."

My jaw clenched. I felt like I was going to die. If Raiden was dead, then... Then all of this was for nothing… because Naomi was right. Everything I was doing was for him, even when he told me he didn't want me—because my stupid, stupid heart tugged to him every damn time. "You forget I'm no longer a witch," I spat through gritted teeth. If he had killed Raiden, then I was definitely going to kill him.

"Ah, empty threats. Forget not, Goddess, you are in my realm now."

"Is Raiden dead?" I asked again.

He tapped his fingers against the dip in his chin. "His existence is neither here nor there. Back to you, my new goddess. You chose to be goddess of the hunt, which comes with responsibilities. It is no secret I have longed to replace my children with those worthy of being deities." He arched a thin eyebrow. "Are you worthy?"

My eyebrows pinched. "How can you be so nonchalant toward your own children? How can you disregard them so easily, as if their souls mean nothing?"

His fingers curled. "They were given everything, born to serve the realms, to bring peace, unity, and love, and enforce the rules set by Estia and me for the good of your realm."

I couldn't help but let out a quiet laugh. "You have no idea what it means to be mortal or what's good for our realm."

His nostrils flared. "Perhaps you are more like my children than I hoped. We will see." He pulled a small green bottle from his pocket and squeezed the atomizer. A white, glistening powder puffed from the nozzle and into my face. I breathed it in before I realized what was happening, then crumpled to the marble floor.

SPELLBOUND

I sat upright, feeling velvet covers around me. My gaze moved to the only shadow in my peripheral vision. "Raiden." I couldn't keep the relief from my tone.

He sat on an empty chair, his elbows propped atop his knees, his head in his hands as he gazed down at the snake-green marble floor. "I told you to leave."

I scratched the back of my neck. "I did, but I came back. I found a way out of this, for all of you."

He slowly looked up, his blue-black eyes meeting mine. "What would that be?"

I looked around for the dagger, but Lucius had taken it. Of course he had. "Edmund, Maddox, and Nai are at the portal. They can seal it, Raiden. I killed Alexander. I can bring Thalia back. Edmund has the spell at the portal, and…" I looked around. "I wanted to stop you from killing Lucius and taking his place, but I see now I had nothing to worry about."

He let out a low growl and stood, then sped toward me before I could catch my breath. "All you've done is signed your fucking death warrant. Tell me the portal wasn't left open."

I stumbled over my words.

He turned and punched the wall, shaking the room. "Fuck, Elle. Before, it was harder for him to leave, and for his demons. It was rare when someone came through the portal, leaving it open. The last to open it before Aziel and me was Freya. She opened it and ran. An hour later, my father got out and came for us. She took a risk. She knew he might go for her, but she needed us gone more."

My eyebrows furrowed. "Lucius said his demons go to our world sometimes to make deals. How can he if the portal isn't open?"

"Yes." He balled his fists. "When the portal is opened by some stupid shifter wanting to make a deal—or a God—but it's rare. We closed it behind us when we came in." He rubbed his forehead, smoothing the wrinkles that had formed.

"How were you going to get out?"

He pulled a small emerald from his pocket. "We had one way out: this." He held it up, showing it under the dim lights. "It was spelled to allow one of us to step between realms. Once I killed Lucius, I was going to use it to come back, get Aziel out, then kill Freya, but you already took care of the last part."

"Use it now then. You don't need to kill him. As I said, we can seal it so it can never be opened, by anyone."

"He could still find a way out. I did from my prison realm."

"We'd just need to keep the spell reinforced," I explained, recalling Edmund's words. "Future keepers would be assigned with the job, like how we protect dark objects now. It was blood witches like me who created your prison realm. Our coven is strong enough."

"I don't doubt it," he said, seething. "The problem is now we can't get out."

"There has to be a way out of here. Where's Aziel?"

He didn't say anything.

"Raiden?"

My heart skipped a beat.

"What happened?"

He threw the emerald onto the bed, torture glittering in his irises. "He's dead. No-coming-back kind of dead."

My hand shot up to my mouth. "Did Lucius…"

He punched the wall again, sending a tremor through the castle. "He wiped him out of existence."

I gripped the blankets, holding my breath as I gazed at the black iron fireplace with a silver ornate mirror hanging over its mantle. Focusing my eyes on the burnt coal, I breathed deeply. "Who did he replace him with?"

"He didn't. He won't. The god of thunder will be no more. He wants the very existence of us erased."

"He can't do that," I said hastily, remembering how the gods needed replacing.

"He's the high god, Elle. Fuck, he can do whatever he wants here."

I felt like someone had stuck their hand in my chest and twisted my insides. "Your sisters."

"Leda's gone," he whispered, as if the words would be truer if they were said louder. "He wiped her out of existence a long time ago. I didn't know until we came." He pressed his arms against the wall, leaning his forehead against his fist. "Thalia's soul is still here, but he'll kill her soon. He's weighing us all!" he shouted, pure rage guiding his tone. "He deemed Aziel unworthy, as he had with Leda."

I swallowed thickly. "That was what he asked me."

His gaze snapped to mine. "What?"

"He asked if I'm worthy."

"What did you say?"

"Nothing." I ran cold. "Is he going to kill me? Wipe me from existence? He took Thalia's dagger."

"No, he's not."

"Why?"

He sped to the emerald on the bed and rubbed it between his fingers. "Because you're getting out of here. Once you're out, seal the underworld. Make sure it stays that way. Do what you said. Go back to your coven."

My heart hammered as I glared at the deep-green gem. "What about you?"

"There's no way out of this castle. Don't you think I've tried?" His shoulders dropped. I heard each of his pained breaths as he tried to stay standing against the wall.

"I'm not leaving, even if you don't want me here." My breath hitched. "Even if you don't want me. I'm not giving up hope. I came in to get you and Thalia out, and I'll be damned if I'm leaving without either of you."

He gestured toward the door. "Go, open it."

I sped to the green door, so deep it could have been black, and lifted a trembling hand to the handle. I gasped when it swung open into a black void filled only with the faint screams and echoes of my question. "I thought we were in his castle."

"We are. These are prisons, meant for the worst of the worst. There's no way out unless he lets us out."

"Why not just kill us? Why put us in here?"

He scoffed quietly. "He believes in giving everyone a fair trial." His jaw clenched. "As if he even knows what that is. He thinks himself above us all, the god of justice, the fair ruler," he spat, venom lacing his words. "The trial could be now or in a century. He'll keep us in here for as long as he feels is necessary. He went after Aziel first." His expression contorted. "He always hated him the most."

I walked slowly to his side, feeling calm in using my legs at a normal speed. "What do we do?"

"We do nothing." He moved away from me. "I'm sending you out of here and then you are sealing this place so he can never get out again."

"I can't just leave you here."

"Why?" He turned to face me. "Why would you possibly stay when I already told you I don't want you here."

A lump formed in my throat. I didn't know what to say. My heart dropped. Stupid thing. "You're hurting. You lost your brother and—"

He slammed his hand into the wall next to my head, jolting me. "Stop trying to save me. I don't want you to save me."

"I know you care, that a part of you does. It has to," I whispered, moving my fingers to his arm. "No one's that good an actor. This can't just be about protecting innocents. You wouldn't be trying to send me back if you didn't. You wouldn't give up your only way out of here for me if you didn't."

"I don't."

"Don't lie to me," I begged. "There was a moment, with Lucius, when I thought he'd killed you and me." I paused. "I felt like the world had been pulled from under my feet. I can't help how I feel. I—"

"Don't," he warned before I could say anything else. He pulled away, walking to the other end of the room, and paced. "What do you want me to say to you?" he shouted. "That I care? That I want you? That I'm capable of love?"

Tears brimmed in my eyes.

"Because even if I did, it doesn't mean anything anymore. Aziel's gone. Thalia's fuck knows where, and I'm trapped here. I can't be that man for you."

I wanted to go to him, to hold him, but something told me to stay back. "I'll find a way back here. I'll go to Edmund and—"

"No." He stormed toward me, closing the distance between us. "You'll go back. You'll close that portal, seal it, and forget I existed because, Elle, trust me, I'm not worth saving. Not anymore." He held the emerald. "I wouldn't have used this anyway, not knowing Thalia is trapped here. I couldn't leave her… Wherever her soul is."

"Raiden, please."

He pushed it into my hand, his penetrating eyes finding mine for the last time. "Don't come back."

"No!" I shouted as I was transported through realms. The air was pulled from my lungs, and my limbs pulled each and every way until I landed flat on my back in the snow, gasping for air.

Naomi came into view, swirling overhead as my vision reset. "What happened? Where's Thalia? Raiden? Aziel?"

Pain pinched through my head.

Edmund rushed to my side. "Are you hurt? What happened? Elle?"

I sat upright, and Edmund extended his hand, then helped me to my feet. Even Maddox's eyebrows were set downward. "You've been gone for hours. Three demons got out."

I couldn't let anything happen to them. They were all I had left. And three demons? I pressed my hands against my temples. My mind wasn't whole. I couldn't think straight, let alone form the right words to explain what had happened back there.

Edmund held me up, even though I was more than capable, but the touch, the closeness, I needed. Edmund sighed. "We can't hold off the demons. More will come. What happened? Is Thalia coming? Raiden and Aziel?"

The words left my mouth before I even realized I was saying them. "No." I gulped. "Close the portal."

CHAPTER THIRTY-FIVE

If Raiden thought I was going to leave him there, he had another thing coming. I wasn't going to abandon him. I passed the emerald from one hand to the other. Naomi had forged an illusion of sunshine, but it did little to shield them against the cold of the mountain. She snuggled into Maddox's fur coat. Only he'd been sensible enough to bring one.

He shuddered against the cold. He loved us way more than he'd ever let on, but moments like this warmed my heart.

I cut my hand and dripped blood into the little metal box Edmund had brought. I cut myself again and repeated it several times until it was brimming with immortal blood. "This should work." Edmund arched a light eyebrow. Snowflakes caught in his ash-blond hair and melted into the golden strands.

"It was your idea, so it probably will." I smiled and gestured him toward the opening of the cave.

He inhaled deeply, then dipped his fingers in my blood. He smoothed it against the symbols around the opening, and the foggy portal opened.

"You're a genius." I grinned at Edmund.

"Simple but effective," Maddox said. That was considered high praise when coming from him. "You don't have the dagger. It's not safe for you to go back in there."

"I'll be careful." I handed him the emerald. "This doesn't work anymore?"

He lifted it to the sky, examining it through pale light. "No. Whatever spell it held was strong though, a level six if we'd had it."

"Vault-worthy." I raised my eyebrows. "Then my only way in or out is through this portal, which means my life is literally in your hands."

Ferocity hardened Edmund's strong features. "We won't abandon you."

My heart swelled. "I know you won't."

Naomi placed her hand on mine as I stepped to the portal. "Elle, are you sure he's worth it?"

My heart was doing all the deciding. "He has to be."

Edmund cleared his throat. "Set your watches. We're going to go back to the forest and build a fire. I will climb back here and open this at ten ten."

I looked at the time on the watch Edmund had gifted me on my birthday. It was almost six minutes past seven. "If anyone can do this," Naomi said, "it's you. You're the strongest person I know."

I leaned down and hugged her. "Take care of them," I whispered in her ear. I didn't know how to break the news about Aziel. I knew she liked him. At least I thought she did, going by the few interactions I'd seen. "Um, Nai, I need to tell you something."

A screech sounded at the opening as a demon attempted to escape. It clawed through the fog, its snarling, black tongue and lips tasting the air.

"Later!" I lunged at the creature, falling back through the portal. "Close it!" I shouted out of the opening, and the cave sealed into a void.

The demon grabbed me, wrapping its slimy fingers around my arm as it tried to escape even though the portal had closed. Its matte-black eyes stared into mine, penetrating and soulless. "Goddess," he spat, sensing my immortality. He was a lesser demon. From what Lucius had said, this creature didn't strike me as a high demon or whatever. It reeked of desperation.

"I could wipe you from existence," I said threateningly, a snarl escaping through bare teeth.

It retreated, slimed back against the rugged wall, and slithered away. I smoothed my hair down and sucked in a deep breath.

I sped in the direction of the castle but stopped between two barren trees in the wasteland. Silencing my pace, I moved slower but quieter toward the moat. There was no way I could walk through the doors again without Lucius being alerted. In the distance on the horizon of the wasteland were demons, stalking and searching.

I glared down at the bubbling lava, cringing at what I needed to do. Slowly, with vomit ready to climb up my throat, I stepped into the molten rock. Pain seared through me, but it was tolerable enough to keep going. I waded knee-deep, my eyes wide as heat prickled through my melting skin. It healed, then burned, then healed again in a vicious cycle as I moved through the moat. I looked down and saw one of the bones in my leg, then threw up into the lava.

"Careful," Thalia's voice whispered near me.

I whipped my head left, then right, but I couldn't see her.

"Stay in there too long, you'll stop healing eventually. It's underworld lava, not normal lava."

I looked around again. Was I imagining things? I moved through and tried to speed toward the edge, but I couldn't run fast.

After wading as fast as I could, I made it to the stone ledge, feeling mortal again. I climbed out and vomited again, then looked back at the moat. I didn't want to see my legs until they were healed again.

Thalia's voice whispered again, "It slows your powers."

I looked at the moat of fiery red-and-orange liquid. "You think?" I whispered back and looked around. "Where are you?"

She slipped out from the shadow of a stone. Her moonstruck gaze landed on me, and kindness creased the corners of her eyes. "You're not the only one trying to save him, you know."

I sighed with relief. "You're okay."

"I know how to hide here. I was goddess of the dead."

"Aziel's dead."

Her expression dropped. "I know. I couldn't get to him in time." A tear hesitated on the edge of tipping from her eye. "Lucius will pay."

"I think an existence trapped in here is punishment enough."

"It is not." Her mouth twisted in disgust. "He will pay with his life."

"Then someone has to take his place here." My stomach knotted. "I can seal this place so no one can ever leave, so he can't leave."

"The underworld does not need to be sealed." She spoke with an heir of regality. "It needs better leadership."

My eyebrows furrowed. "You think Raiden can offer that?"

She evaluated my expression until a small smile tugged her lips upward. "Raiden loves your mortal realm too much." She looked me up and down. "Immortality suits you."

"I'm sorry you died," I admitted. From my pocket, I pulled out the vial with the essence of the goddess of the dead. "I got this for you. You can come back."

Her gaze flickered with uncertainty as she took it and placed it between her breasts, covered with white silk fabric flowing over her curves: a dress fit for an empress. "Thank you for this."

"You need to come to the portal so Edmund and Naomi can join you with it again, and you can come back."

She answered with a smile. "We must go help Raiden."

"The only problem is I lost your dagger."

"Lucius has it?"

I nodded.

"Then I'm going to need to trust you."

With no windows, the only way in without walking through the front doors was through a side door. Thalia kept to the shadows, and I used my sharp sight and hearing to hide from lurking demons. We climbed a spiral staircase to a second floor, then reached a row of doors that ran along a dark corridor, which seemed to go on forever. "Which one is Raiden in?"

She shook her head. "Space is not the same here." Her tone seemed to float somehow. "There are thousands of doors, with thousands of souls inside them. The castle is a prison for the evilest of souls, so they can never roam, never escape, unlike the mortal souls kept down in the pits in the wastelands, tormented by demons."

I shuddered. "Do we open each one to check?" I reached for a handle but she grabbed my wrist, her touch icy cold.

"They will be able to escape. We must find another way." She gazed down the corridor. "If we hear punching and swearing through one of them, it's probably his."

I couldn't help but smile, even though I was terrified. "Where is Lucius?"

Her smile fell into a frown. "We will be dealing with him after we find Raiden."

We walked the corridor, occasionally jolting at the sound of a screech or pummeling against one of the doors.

Thalia touched each one, but I had no idea what she was feeling for. "I'm sorry about Aziel," I said after we'd walked for several minutes.

"Thank you. My brother is lucky to have you."

"I don't think he thinks that."

"He does," she said simply. "When Leda died, he was heartbroken. Freya broke him, and I didn't think he would ever be able to be happy again. Then we were locked away in our prisons and that was it. I thought I'd lost him."

"Freya's dead," I explained, hoping it brought her some peace. Leda was her sister too.

She looked at me. "You are now goddess of the hunt, so I assume you're the one who killed her."

"I am."

"How do you feel about it?"

I swallowed thickly. "I'm sorry, I don't understand. I mean, she was a bad person."

"She was still a person. We must all work through something when taking a life, whether it is good or bad. There is a unique feeling that comes with taking a soul."

I fumbled my fingers, my lips parting. "It was Alexander, her lover, who got me," I admitted, finally letting it sink in. "He'd done bad things, but I don't know." I scratched the back of my neck. "He didn't feel bad. Does that make sense?"

"It makes perfect sense."

"He would have hurt my sister and hunted us," I said before she could judge me, though I got the sense she wasn't like that. "I had to kill him. Right? I also did it for you."

"If you want to hear you did the right thing, I can't tell you that. Only you can decide. You need to find peace with it yourself."

I nodded and slowed my pace. We'd passed a hundred more doors. "Wait." I halted, my eyes widening when the sound reached my sensitive ears. A low growl, a cuss word… I'm sure he'd hate to admit it, but Thalia was right. "He's here." I walked ahead, focusing on his breathing. "Is he… crying?" I swore I could hear it, but he didn't cry. He had never.

I opened the door, certainty guiding me as his heart rate picked up. As soon as I pushed it all the way open, he lunged at me, and we both rolled onto the floor.

Lifting his hand, his bloodshot eyes latched onto mine, his dark eyebrows furrowing. "Elle." He quickly moved from on top of me. "How?"

I looked around. "Tha—"

She was gone.

"Your sister was here."

"Thalia?"

She stepped out from a shadow. "Brother."

I placed my hand against my chest. "You scared me. I thought I'd hallucinated you for a second."

She hugged Raiden and stepped back. "Now that you're safe, I need your help, brother."

His shoulders tensed. "Anything."

"We're going to kill our father."

My stomach dipped. All of this, and he was going to rule the underworld anyway and take his place. "No," I said, interrupting. "We can seal this place, and all of us leave. Now."

"I'm sorry," she replied. "He killed our brother and sister. He must pay. He cannot be left to rule here."

I felt like I'd been punched in the stomach. "I came here to save you both."

Raiden grabbed me and pulled me back into the room. "A minute," he told Thalia, then half closed the door. He walked me to the edge of the bed, cupping my cheeks in his. "What I said before, I didn't mean it."

"Raiden."

"Wait." He brushed a lock of hair from my face. "I have to do this, Elle. He needs to die. I wish—"

"Then don't," I pleaded. "Let this go. Come back with me."

He took my hands in his. "Vengeance is the only thing I have left."

I closed my eyes. My heart raced to his touch. "That's not true. You have me."

"You can't want this." His breaths quickened. "I'm not good for you. Look at you—at everything you've sacrificed."

"I like who I am," I said. "Feeling this strong, seeing the world this way… It's not a sacrifice, and I would have given it all up for your sister to come back if she were still here, but she's not, and I'm happy like this."

A muscle twitched in his jaw. "You like the power."

"I'm not Freya." I scowled. "It's not like that. I'm here, aren't I? I never left you. I never hurt you. I won't."

"You deserved better than this."

"Don't do that." My gaze burned into his. "You make me feel alive. I feel like I can do anything. You made me see the best version of myself, and because of that, I became it. My sister's back. I saved her, and I killed Freya. So no, I regret nothing. I have sacrificed nothing. For the first time in my life, I'm not afraid of everything."

He lowered his lips, inching closer to mine, but pulled away. "I have to go with Thalia. I'm sorry. I am."

My arms dropped to my sides as he turned his back toward me, heading for the door. I couldn't believe I was thinking it, let alone going to say it, but I couldn't deny it anymore. When I looked at him, all I wanted was to be by his side, to take on every obstacle and enjoy the beauty in our world, together. "I love you, Raiden."

Everything stopped. Time. My heart. My breath. Him.

CHAPTER THIRTY-SIX

With my heart feeling like it was in my throat, I waited for him to say something or turn and look at me, but silence deafened the room.

"You shouldn't. I'm not good for you. You can't have a life with me here," he finally said and stepped out of the room.

I ran out behind him into a dark, empty corridor. Thalia moved out from a dark corner. If not for her cape swishing through the air, I wouldn't have known she was there. "He didn't mean that."

My cheeks heated. "You heard."

"You're not the only one with strong hearing." Her silver eyes took shape in the darkness as if tiny moons were reflecting back at me. "He's afraid of your love, of what it means, but it doesn't mean he doesn't want to, because he does." She smiled knowingly. "You didn't see his face when he left the room. He's used to being hurt, to being abandoned."

"I know how that feels. I'm not going to leave him, not when he needs me," I said. "Even if I have to show him a hundred times."

The corner of her lips lifted. "He's gone to kill Lucius."

"Yes."

"Are you going to stay here?"

My stomach swirled. I had my sister back, my family, my coven... "I-I don't know. I have people who need me too." My heart tugged me in two directions.

"I understand." She nodded and took a step back. "Down the staircase, four doors to the right is the main living area," she said, answering my unspoken question, then slid back into the shadows. "I will see you there." Her silky voice whispered, her echo caught in a thousand cries of the dead from behind the closed doors.

Lucius's stare darkened as Freya stepped out from behind him, her painted lips curved into a sadistic smile.

"Son." He gestured his arms out in welcome toward the marble room. It had couches of velvet green and a glass table with an ornamental snake upon it that coiled up in a shard of glittering white. The palace was the epitome of elegance, the type of place I could see Maddox owning in our realm. A music box played a sweet but eerie melody from the mantel over the fireplace, its fire with gray and green flames.

Freya traced a painted nail along her lips. "It seems you escaped yet another prison. Perhaps you're not entirely useless after all, not unlike your brother. How is Aziel?" Her laugh cackled.

Raiden's gaze fixated on Freya's. Blood was splattered over his face from the demon whose head he had taken off with his bare hands. A muscle in his jaw twitched, his fingers curling into fists.

Lucius's deep robes flicked out when he stepped forward. "Have you come to try to kill me again? You always were reckless, like your brother, never thinking with your head."

Raiden gritted his teeth, and the muscles in his back and arms tensed. "I'm glad you're both here. It'll make it easier to kill you both."

She rolled her eyes, letting his words roll off her as if they meant nothing. With a tilt of her head, she moved her attention to me. "I would say being a goddess suits you, but I definitely wore it better." She moved her gaze to Raiden's, a smirk on her mouth. "Isn't that right, Raiden? Although, you never did get to enjoy my immortality."

"Immortality you stole," he snapped.

She looked back at me, a flash of green crossing in the reflection in her eyes. "Has he told you he loves you yet? Has he whispered your name in his sleep like he did mine?"

My jaw clenched.

She grinned in response. "Oh it seems I hit a nerve then. You're not really his type. Raiden always did like women with more substance."

He stepped forward, fists clenched. "Don't fucking talk to her like that."

She laughed. "She killed me, honey. Do you think I would let her simply get away with it? Play nice?"

He scoffed. "Vengeance and hatred have twisted you into something I don't recognize."

"Whose fault is that?" she snapped, her smile falling into a hard line. "If you and your sisters hadn't come"— her nostrils flared—"I wouldn't be this person."

He laughed sardonically. "Give me a fucking break. You knew what you were doing. I never had control over those hounds, and you knew it. You used it as an excuse, so you wouldn't feel as guilty for killing my sister!" he shouted. "After everything I did for you."

Tears swam in her eyes, and a ghost of the girl she once was, before all of this, crossed her expression. "Everyone hurt me. I had no choice. I took my power back."

"I didn't hurt you. You never told me what happened to your son. I had no fucking idea. All I did was love you, and you broke me. You tore apart my family, and for that, I will never forgive you!" he shouted, his tone manic, speaking what I was sure he'd wanted to scream for the past century. "Your selfishness cost me all that's dear to me, so yes, I'm fucking glad Elle is nothing like you because she actually has a heart and that's why I love her and could never, ever love you."

My lips parted. Had I heard him right?

He stepped toward her again, closing the distance between them. His lips pulled back, baring his teeth. "You always were afraid of death."

Panic flitted in her eyes. "Raiden."

"Now you can face it." He grabbed her by her throat and lifted her off her feet. Lucius ran at him, but Raiden sped to the other side of the room with Freya and slammed her into the marble wall. I jolted as the entire wall crackled, trembling the fireplace and fracturing the mirror above it.

Lucius screamed at them as her eyes emptied, her head toppling from her shoulders and rolling on the floor. Raiden turned, dropping her body to the ground, and tilted his head at Lucius. Blood had swept over his features, and his eyes were wild with rage, his jaw tight as he sped at his father.

Their collision rocked the room, but rage guided Raiden as he wrapped his hands around his father's throat and whispered in his ear through gritted teeth. "This is for Aziel and Leda, mother fucker."

"You don't have the guts," Lucius taunted, cackling. "You're the same now as you were when you were a child: a coward, always with your sisters. Perhaps they rubbed off on you."

Raiden's laugh echoed right through me. "It seems it served me well."

I went to run to help him, but Thalia slipped out from a shadow behind them before I could move. She pulled a sword from her scabbard and moved it through the air with deadly precision, not even a slither of hesitation on her cold features. Raiden let go, moving back just as the sword sliced through Lucius's neck and sent his head rolling. Blood pooled along the glossy floor, trickling like a stream toward where I stood.

Thalia closed her eyes as the spirit of the underworld flowed into her. A crown of diamonds and bone formed on her head, entwining with her silky hair. She opened her silvery eyes and faced her brother.

"Sister."

"I wanted this," she said before he could continue. "I was always lost among the dead when I was alive. I can rule this place fairer than our father ever did."

His gaze searched hers. "I can stay."

She peered around him, glancing at me. "I don't think you want that. Besides, I'm perfectly content here. I have a million souls to keep me company, and many demons who are happy to satisfy any desires I may have."

My breath hitched, and my eyes bulged. I averted my eyes, looking instead at Freya's broken and crumpled body.

"Fuck, Thalia. Too much," he said, voicing what I was thinking.

"Go be with your girl."

I held my breath when he turned to face me. He was covered in blood, his hair disheveled, and a dark unsatisfied rage swam in his blue eyes. He took long strides, closing the distance between us. Thalia sped out of the room, a knowing smile on her face.

He pressed a bloodied finger against my chin and tilted my head upward to look at him. "I would never hurt you." He must've mistaken my expression for fear.

"I'm not scared of you."

"I enjoyed it," he admitted as if it would push me away.

I splayed my fingers against his chest. "So did I when I killed Freya. It wasn't like Alexander, when I was plagued with guilt. Freya deserved it. She was a monster." I'd confessed something I hadn't even admitted to myself, until now. I'd felt powerful when I pushed the dagger in her, delighting in the violence when her life was in my hands. She'd taken so much from everyone, from good people, so when I heard her last breath, I'd felt no guilt. "Maybe I'm not as good as you like to think."

He shook his head, an incredulous stare in his eyes as he lowered his lips to mine. I tasted Freya's blood on them, but I didn't care. "You're good, baby girl," he whispered against my lips. "With a taste for the dark. There's nothing wrong with that." He walked me backward and pushed me against a wall. His arm was next to my face, his hand against the marble pressing cold against my back. "It comes with being a goddess. You're stronger than anyone now. You can bring down entire buildings if you want. No one can make you do anything you don't want to again." His gaze burned into mine. "An immortality to match your fierce heart."

I ran my fingers around his neck, kissing him with an animalistic ferocity. I bit his bottom lip until I heard him moan against me, rocking his hips against mine. "I love you," I whispered when I pulled back an inch, feeling freedom in those three words. "Maybe too much."

"I don't believe in too much." He kissed me harder, ripping my pants down. "My Elle," he said, ripping my top off and baring my breast. "My love."

Sweat mixed with blood as it dripped down the muscles on his back. He lost himself inside me, gliding his dick against the silk of my wetness and going deeper until I bit my lip, screaming out. Digging my nails into his arms, I gasped when the wall cracked with his next pound. His wild eyes latched onto mine. "I love you!" he shouted and let out a low growl as the wall crumbled under us, shaking the entire building. I didn't care who heard or saw us. All that existed was us, tangled in a mess of desire and panting.

I screamed his name as my orgasm rolled through my body, tipping him over the edge. He erupted inside me, his hips rocking as his eyes rolled toward the back of his head. After one final rock, he rested his forehead against mine.

I looked around at the rubble and couldn't help but laugh while trying to catch my breath. "Thalia's going to kill us for destroying her living room," I said. After all, it was all hers now.

His eyes never left mine. "I don't care. Nothing matters but you."

My heart ballooned. "I'll never leave you."

He thumbed my lip. "I will never leave you either."

***

I watched as Raiden said his good-byes to Thalia and joined me at the portal. "Are you sure you can't come back?" I asked her again.

She shook her head. "I am happier here with the dead than I ever was alive. I spent enough time with them, this feels like home."

I nodded slowly. "Then I guess no one will replace you as goddess of the dead."

She pulled out the vial with the small glowing orb inside it—the vitality of the goddess of the dead—and handed it to me. "You can gift another with immortality. It's yours to do with what you wish."

Raiden clicked his tongue. "That's a lot of pressure, Tal."

"She's strong enough." Thalia winked at me and turned on her heel. "I'll ensure nothing gets out. Well, mostly."

I couldn't help but smile. I shoved the vial into my pocket and knotted my hand with his. "Are you ready to step back into my world?"

"Yes." He squeezed my hand, but I saw pain quiver his smile, his fixated glare on the portal lost for a second.

"Your brother would be proud of you."

His breath hitched, but he said nothing else, and the portal opened to Edmund, Naomi, and a shivering, furious-looking Maddox.

"Three hours," Maddox said, berating me. "It's been five. We must have opened the portal four times. We're almost out of blood."

Naomi slapped his arm, then looked at Raiden. "Where's Aziel?"

His expression dropped.

I inhaled deeply, my tone lowering as I looked at Naomi. "Not all of us made it back alive."

She blinked back a tear, moving her eyes to meet Raiden's. "I'm sorry."

"Freya and my father paid for it," he said stonily. "Don't seal it. Thalia rules the underworld now. She won't let anything get out."

Maddox and Edmund looked to me for confirmation.

I nodded, letting them know it was okay. "Let's go home." I squeezed his fingers as I looked out over the horizon. So much death, so much pain had happened, but out of it, we were each stronger and still had each other. In the distance, my sister waited for us at the mansion, along with Dora. "All of us."

EPILOGUE

One Month Later

Naomi ran her hands along my black lace sleeves. "Gods, or should I exclaim 'goddesses' you're so pretty, Elle."

I wiggled my fingers, admiring the glittering black polish on my nails. "You did the best job on my nails."

I looked around the large, white, adjoining corridor. It was lined with several smaller rooms and led to the main temple where people were gathered. I could hear their heightened, excited chatter through the walls. Blocking it out, I let out a long exhale. I wanted to do this in the gardens at the mansion, but Maddox and Naomi had insisted on a big affair, and Raiden never minded showing off.

"I suppose it is quite pretty here," I admitted, looking up at the flowers curling around the archway that led to the closed door.

"It is." She admired the room. "So, I was going to talk to you about it this morning, and I know it's your wedding day, but…"

I arched an eyebrow. "Spill."

"I'm opening my own store. Raiden got me the funds." Naomi scratched the back of her neck. "I didn't ask from where."

I rolled my eyes. "Probably best not to."

"I'm going to be selling portable illusions."

I placed my hand on my hip. "I'm so happy for you, but I've never heard of that before."

"It took a few times to replicate it, but to hold my spells, I used the transfer box you keepers use to move a curse over. So when I create an illusion, I can pocket it by replicating the box."

I tapped my fingers against my chin. "That's really impressive. I'm so proud of you." I pulled her into a tight hug. "I actually have something for you."

I'd mulled over who I'd offer the vitality of goddess of the dead to ever since we'd returned from the underworld. Edmund wouldn't take it—I already knew he'd refuse—and with Maddox, I was afraid the power would go to his head, but Naomi had always been so strong and humble that I couldn't pass up giving her the chance of immortality.

I pulled the vial from my pocket and placed it in her hands, closing her fingers around it. "If you want to be goddess of the dead, then it is yours."

She shot me a small smile but handed the vial back. "I'm grateful. Like, I think it's so amazing that my best friend is a goddess, but I'm okay being mortal. I do know someone else you can offer it to though."

My heart pounded. So did I, but I was afraid to offer it to Mona. I didn't want to mess her life up. She couldn't go back to Salvius if she was a goddess, and she loved her studies and work. "I don't know, Nai. She has her life."

She fixed the flower crown of black and white roses entwined with thorns where it sat on my head. "She's still here. You've offered to help her get back to Salvius, but I haven't seen her make a single move to go back home. You know, you two are way more alike than you'd think. She too has a problem saying what she feels."

"I don't. I told Raiden I loved him, didn't I?"

"Way after you realized it," she said. "Or you suppressed. You and he make a great couple. He did the same thing."

Naomi curled a few more strands of my loose hair, then pulled away. "Now for makeup."

"I want—"

"Black. Yeah, no shit."

I laughed. "I'm glad you're here with me."

"Me too." She pulled out a brush. "Now close your eyes. I'm adding silver too. I actually laced it with some of my magic. It'll look like it's shimmering to anyone who looks at you."

I smiled. "If you weren't selling illusions, I'd say you should sell this stuff. No one has made makeup as good as you have. You even created that black stuff that goes on eyelashes."

She shrugged. "It's just stuff I mixed up in my room."

"It works. Seriously, you should sell it too."

She bit the inside of her cheek, looked up, and smiled. "Maybe I will."

She finished with my eyes, applied a deep-purple lipstick, and stepped back, clasping her hands together.

"You're ready. I'll send a magic quill to the others to come."

"No need." I could hear their breathing through the door. "You can come in now."

Maddox pulled down the handle, grinning. "Well you shine up nicely, I guess, and your hair doesn't look terrible, so good job."

I chuckled. "Thanks for the dress. You chose well."

He arched an eyebrow. "Girl, of course I did. It flatters your figure, and I love lace."

"Who'd have thought the new elder in the council would be picking out dresses for me?" I exclaimed, but we were all so proud of him. After Alma and the rest of the council had learned about everything, they offered him and Edmund positions on the council. Edmund had refused, choosing to stay as grandkeeper, but Maddox had taken the position without hesitation, promising Edmund he'd still help him if something urgent came up.

He flashed a pearly white smile. "You've been through a lot. You deserve to look drop-dead gorgeous on your wedding day. Besides, half the town has shown up, now that you're a goddess and all."

I hadn't even thought about that. "Will they be expecting anything from me?"

He laughed. "Girl, I think they're just hoping you don't eat their babies or sacrifice them in the night."

Naomi shot him a glare. "No one thinks that. All the lies about the gods have been cleared up."

He shrugged. "It takes more than the council's word to pull a lifetime of stories from people's minds, but no one is saying anything bad out loud to our faces, which is what matters."

"Great." My stomach ached. "I feel tons better."

"You'll be fine. You actually care about other people, so I'm sure they'll all see in time you're not too bad."

"Right."

"Plus." He whistled out a breath. "You should see Raiden in his tux." Maddox looked upward, lost in a thought I probably didn't want to imagine. "He is something else."

Naomi packed her makeup into a bag. "You *would* say that." She pushed past him, whispering to me as she passed, "He is right though."

I smirked. "Where's Edmund?"

"Coming soon."

My stomach dipped. "Mona?"

"On her way now."

"Good." I sat on a white, stone bench. "Is Raiden okay?"

Maddox grinned. "He's not about to run, if that's what you're worried about."

I looked down. "I didn't mean that. He's been lost since Aziel died. He thinks I don't notice, but I see it when he thinks I'm not looking. He looks so... broken."

The makeshift funeral we had held after we got back lingered in my mind. We'd engraved two headstones, one for Aziel and one for Leda, and we left the portal unsealed so Raiden could go to the underworld whenever he missed his only remaining sibling.

Naomi squeezed my shoulder. "You can't help that. I know you don't like feeling helpless, but it's something he has to do on his own."

"I know." I fumbled my fingers. "I just hate seeing him in pain. I wish I could take it away. You know."

Maddox sat next to me. "You really love him, huh?"

"So much, it feels like it could kill me."

His eyebrows raised. "Jeez, well if I meet someone who loves me half as much as you do him, I'll count myself lucky."

My spirits brightened. "Wait, did you say something nice?"

"Think of it as a wedding gift."

"You did actually get me a real gift, right?"

He lifted his hands nonchalantly. "Wait until you hear my speech."

I tilted my head. "Edmund's doing my speech."

He pulled a few pieces of paper from his pocket. "Then what's this?"

Naomi clicked her tongue. "You are not doing the speech. Don't worry, Elle. I'll keep an eye on him today. We're going to get ready anyway. It'll be starting in fifteen minutes, and my hair isn't done."

I smiled as I watched them bicker out the door. I loved my family. I picked at my nails but stopped. Naomi had just done them.

I heard her before I saw her. Mona pressed open the cracked door, a small black bag hanging from her fingers. Her fiery-auburn curls were smoothed into a high bun, with occasional loose curls hanging down. Her deep-purple dress brought out the blue in her eyes. "Ellie, you're so beautiful." She rushed to me and curled her arms around me. "I got you something." She pulled out a two-finger ring of silver, with branches and leaves curling outward, and a thick bracelet to match. "I saw it and thought it would suit you."

"I love them."

She placed them on me. They matched my dress perfectly.

"Thank you."

"I know we haven't had much time together." She picked at her freshly painted nails but stopped, just like I had. "It's why I've decided to stay here for a while. I love my work, but I've missed all these years with you... and my magic." She wiggled her fingers. "It's been stronger here. I figure, what's a few years in the grand scheme of things? I can join a coven or something."

I felt the pulse of the vial in my pocket. I loved Maddox so much for finding me a dress with pockets. "I have something for you if you want it." I pulled out the vial. "You can be a goddess, like me, if you want."

She parted her lips, her eyes widening.

I pushed it into her hands. "Don't decide now. Take your time, years if you want, but know it is yours if you ever do want it."

She tucked it into her bag. "This is incredible. I want to try out a little more magic, but I have to admit, it's definitely tempting." She leaned over and kissed my cheek. "I'm proud you're my sister. Everyone's talking about you in town, how you killed Freya and protected them from her murderous instincts."

"It's probably the first time they've talked about me in a good light," I said. "Maybe they won't put down human-born witches in the future."

"No." She giggled, mirroring my own. "I don't think they will." She looked up and down my dress. The cleavage slit ran down to just above my navel. "If Miss Thompson could see you now."

I laughed. "She'd probably keel over."

She snorted. "Good riddance."

I whipped my head around when I heard footsteps. Edmund and Dora appeared, holding hands. "Finally," I whispered to Mona. "I'll meet you out there."

She squeezed my hand. "Good luck."

She left, smiling at Edmund as she passed. He was already doting on her. He turned his pale eyes to meet mine. "Are you sure you want to do this?" he asked for the hundredth time since Raiden had proposed.

Dora tut-tutted quietly. "Edmund, stop."

I smiled at them both. "I'm certain. I love him."

His shoulders slumped. "If he hurts you."

"I know."

"God or not," he said with promise. "I'll find a way to kick his ass."

Dora rolled her eyes. "He wouldn't hurt Elle."

Edmund smirked. "You always did have a soft spot for him."

"He's a good boy," she said, conviction in her tone. "He did right by all of us."

"She's right," I said.

Edmund nodded begrudgingly. "Maybe I'm not ready to let you go yet. You'll always be my little girl."

"You'll always be my favorite man. Just don't tell Raiden," I joked. Bells sounded from the temple. Cold prickled my hands and feet. "It's time."

Edmund held his arm out for me to take. "We'll go together."

Dora moved for the door. "I'll see you both out there."

The aisle felt miles long as hundreds of stares followed me, but when he looked at me, everyone else melted away. I reached the front, and he took his hands in mine. Maddox stood by his side as his best man, and Naomi at mine. Edmund handed me off.

"Holy fuck." Raiden looked me up and down, a burning in his stare.

Maddox rolled his eyes from the stand. "Only you'd say that on your wedding day."

Alma cleared her throat to beginn the marriage vows. I couldn't take my eyes off him as our immortal promises were exchanged.

He slipped the white-gold ring, glistening with an emerald skull surrounded by tiny black roses, onto my finger.

"Do you take Eleanor Moore, Goddess of the Hunt, to be your wife until the end of your worldly time?"

"Forever," he said almost instantly.

I placed a black skull ring on his finger. "I do too."

His lips were gentle when he kissed me, his nose bumping against mine. "I love you so much."

I breathed heavily, my chest heaving as I looked up at Raiden. He'd been through so much hurt that I only wanted to heal his heart, to show him every day how he was loved and deserved love. Together, we were going to change things, feel alive in a mortal world, and bring some real good to Istinia by showing them a god and goddess who cared.

"Always," I promised, then kissed my husband.

The End

Heart of a Witch

Rebecca L. Garcia

Coming December 14th, A vengeful fantasy standalone romance perfect for fans of The Bridge Kingdom and A Touch of Darkness.
An Embracing Darkness Collection Novel

I'd never particularly liked humans, but I'd never wanted to kill one. Until now.

Hidden in a kingdom that hates witches, I'm forced to hide what I am. With my sister working in a secret dark magic club, and our family's shop gaining unwanted attention, things couldn't be worse when the notorious witch hunter, Damian Shaw, comes to town.

When my sister shows up dead, and my family's name is called into question, we're forced to adopt new aliases and leave the home we cherished. As I watch my life fall apart, I vow to destroy the hunter responsible, but his punishment would not be swift. Death was too easy.

Redforest is a quaint town, with a church, pretty shops, and like any good town, a dark past. When me and my family move in, I set my sights on the Shaw family, quickly learning everything I can about them.

Damian's son, Elijah, is the hunter's greatest pride. His heir. His confidante. The only family he trusts.

I came up with a plan. I was going to shatter every good thing in Damian's life, ending with his son.

My goal: make Elijah Shaw fall in love with me, twist him into the very thing his father hates, then kill him.

But when secrets about his family surface and strange things begin happening, I realize the monster hiding in the shadows might be closer to home than I first thought.

With my heart challenged, the attraction growing, I find myself trapped in a deadly game. In a twist of fate, Elijah might just end up being the death of me.

Preorder now
mybook.to/HeartofaWitch

ACKNOWLEDGMENTS

I want to begin by saying thank you to my awesome beta reader team, so thank you so much Kelly Kortright, Rebecca Waggner, Linda Hamonou, Belle Manuel and Lauren Churchwell. You ladies are the best and help me polish and navigate the story. I appreciate your enthusiasm, notes, comments and everything you all have done. You watched as Spellbound grew from an idea to a full-length novel. Next up, a huge thank you to my editor, Angie Wade, who is the coolest, funniest editor I've met, a grammar nerd, well all-round nerd but I love you for it, and incredible editor. You help me polish my book babies and I trust you inexplicably. Also, a big thank you Janna for your perfect proofreading skills. You guys are the dream team.

To my husband who designed the map of this world, and in doing so, had to listen to me talk about it for weeks and read the spicy scenes aloud, thank you. I'm so lucky to have you and your loving support and faith in my books.

Finally, Spellbound wouldn't be anywhere without marketing, so thank you to Kiki and the whole team at The Next Step PR for all you do, and for putting up with me forgetting to tell you important things, and to my PA

Gladys Gonzales for arranging the takeovers, events, coordinating with other authors, and just our late-night spooky chats, and Amanda at BOMM tours who holds the highest quality tours and is such a lovely lady to boot. You're all inspiring and amazing, and I'm lucky to work with each of you on my books.

GLOSSARY

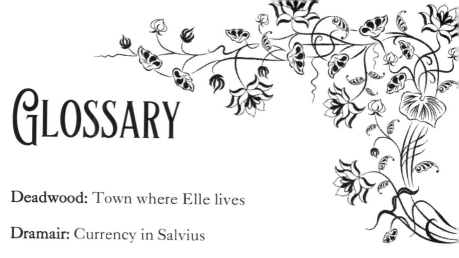

Deadwood: Town where Elle lives

Dramair: Currency in Salvius

Fairwik: Province where Elle lives

Istinia: Territory of witches and magic

Navarin: Main city in Istinia

Otherworld: Ruled by Estia, goddess of love

Prison realms: Realms made to imprison Thalia, Raiden, and Aziel

Purple Adins: Common plant used in potions

Regedam: Province in Istinia where Freya grew up

Salvius: Kingdom of humans

Skal: Currency in Istinia

Underworld: Ruled by Lucius, god of justice

Also By Rebecca L. Garcia

REBECCA L. GARCIA

Rebecca lives in San Antonio, Texas, with her husband and son. Originally from England, you can find her drinking tea, writing new worlds, and designing covers. She writes YA & NA fantasy. She devoured every book she was given and fell in love with magical worlds, and when she got older, her imagination grew with her.

When she's not writing or spending time with her family, you can find her traveling and hosting book signings with Spellbinding Events.
You can find more information, updates, social media, and more on her website:
www.rebeccalgarciabooks.com